Summer On Seeker's Island

Jana DeLeon
Tina Folsom
Colleen Gleason
Jane Graves
Denise Grover Swank
Liliana Hart
Debra Holland
Dorien Kelly
Theresa Ragan
Jasinda Wilder

ISBN: 149049376X
ISBN-13: 978-1490493763

DEDICATION

To all those seeking answers, may you find your heart's desire.

CONTENTS

The Alligator Incident

Jana DeLeon

CHAPTER ONE

Megan Riley closed the door to the lifeguard stand and grabbed her backpack, ready for a shower and a drink. Summer tourists on Seeker's Island were the reason she had a job, but often, they were exhausting and pushy. Like today, when strong waves had forced her to red-flag the beach and shut it down. Some had booed. Even more impolite sentiments had emitted from others' mouths, but Megan knew what she was doing. That surf would have eaten amateurs alive. Even in her prime, Megan wouldn't have risked swimming in it.

And in her prime, Megan was one of the best female swimmers in the world. She had the trophies to prove it.

She heard the ATV racing up behind her and turned around just in time to throw up her arm and block her face from the spray of sand thrown from the tires as the boy on the four-wheeler slid to a stop in front of her. It was one of the few gasoline-powered vehicles on the island, but it was assigned to the sheriff, not his constantly taxing son.

Megan held in cursing even though the boy was thirteen and had likely heard everything she was thinking before, and probably a bunch of things she didn't know.

"Miss Megan!" Johnny Wells shouted from the ATV. "You gotta come quick. There's a problem at the spring."

Megan shook her head, already aware of what the problem likely consisted of. "People seeing Amos's naked butt isn't my problem."

Johnny's friend Dale – another troublemaker – clung to the deer rack on the back of the ATV and decided to jump into the conversation. "Everybody already saw Amos's butt when he streaked right down the middle of Seeker's Trail past a tourist group. Ran all the way home and refuses to come out of his cabin."

A tickle of worry formed in Megan's belly. Amos naked was nothing new and the tourists would get over it—all the ones before them had. What concerned her more was the circumstance that would have caused the ancient caretaker to run several miles. Hell, she didn't even think he was capable of running.

"Where's your dad?" Megan asked, thinking this sounded more like a problem for the sheriff than for a lifeguard.

"Some tourists got drunk and one hit his wife right there in the lobby of the hotel. He can't leave yet so he said to get you and see if you had any ideas."

Sighing, she pulled her cell phone out of her backpack and called the island emergency hotline. "Send a paramedic over to Amos's cabin," she said when dispatch answered. "And let me know if there's a problem."

She shoved the cell phone back in her pack and climbed onto the deer rack next to Dale. "Let's go," she said, not even bothering to ask what the problem was. It would take too much energy to care, and besides, in a few short minutes, she'd be able to see for herself.

***

Nick Domingo stared at Seeker's Spring, completely at a loss for only the second time in his life. After a slow day, he'd dropped off his helper on the other side of the island, then turned his fishing boat back to the dock when he saw Amos streak across the bank to his cabin. Everyone on the island had seen Amos naked at some point in time, so that wasn't particularly disturbing, but the fact that Amos was running gave him a moment of pause.

As Amos was usually only naked in Seeker's Spring, Nick pointed his boat toward the beach directly behind it and anchored in the shallow water before hiking up the bank to the spring, where the cause of Amos's streaking was readily apparent. Nick was just about to go back to his boat and rig up something—he had no idea what—when he heard the ATV screech to a halt on the other side of the thick ring of trees surrounding the spring.

The sheriff. Good.

A second later, the sheriff's son and his buddy came bursting through the brush, but the woman behind them was the last person Nick expected to see at the spring, and the one person he'd been avoiding since she'd returned to the island a week ago. His chest constricted as if being squeezed by the hand of God. His pulse pounded in his temples as he took in every perfect inch of her. She'd changed since she left. He noticed that immediately.

She's gotten even more beautiful.

Megan drew up short when she caught sight of him, and he saw her chest heave as she sucked in a breath. Clearly, she hadn't expected to see him either, and she didn't appear any more comfortable with it than he was. But at the moment, ancient history was the last thing either of them needed to dwell on.

"We got a bit of a problem," Nick said and pointed across the spring to the twelve-foot alligator, which had half his massive body across a flat rock, basking in the sunlight that shone down the center of the foliage.

Megan's eyes widened. "Holy crap! They usually don't migrate over from the mainland. What in the world is he doing in the spring?"

Nick shrugged, the motivation of alligators less interesting to him than the problem of how to get him out of the spring and even more importantly, how to avoid dwelling on the perfection of Megan Riley. "Build a preserve and they'll come? Or maybe he wants his heart's desire?"

"Yeah, well, as there's a caravan of tourists on their way here right now, that's a rather alarming thought."

Nick nodded. "I've got a shark cage on my boat. I was thinking if we could get him in there, the mainland game warden could relocate him somewhere more appropriate."

Megan raised her eyebrows. "A shark cage?"

"I was thinking about expanding my business. Fishing dies off some in summer."

"Okay. Can you get the cage up here?"

"I can with the ATV."

Megan motioned to Johnny. "Give him the keys."

"Ah, man," Johnny complained. "Why can't I drive?"

"Because you're not supposed to be driving the ATV at all. Do you want to compound the trouble you're already in by having me tell your dad you wouldn't cooperate?"

Johnny sighed, the long dramatic sigh of a teen, and handed Nick the key.

"See if you can figure out a place to set the cage," Nick said to Megan. "I'll bring the bait with me."

He jumped on the ATV and circled around the path to the spring before crossing the small stretch of preserve to the beach. He could feel his heart thumping in his chest and knew it had nothing to do with the alligator and everything to do with Megan Riley. He wasn't much for sitting in a chair and basking in the sun—long days fishing took care of that—so he didn't need an excuse for avoiding the beach. But if he was being honest with himself, he hadn't been to Seeker's Paradise, the tiki bar at the beach, since the night he'd heard Megan was back in town.

Not that Megan was a party girl. In fact, exactly the opposite was true. Megan was an athlete in top physical condition and determined to remain that way. The most he'd ever seen her drink was a sip of champagne the night she found out she'd been accepted to Stanford University on a swimming scholarship. When he realized that Megan's dream meant leaving the island—and him—he'd finished the rest of the bottle, figuring full-on drunkenness and a nasty hangover were better alternatives to telling her the truth.

Now he was afraid if he saw her, all the words he hadn't said five years ago would spill out, drowning him in the process. He needed time to plan…time to prepare, which is why he'd been avoiding the places she might be, like the bar where her old friends would be gathered. At least, that's what he'd been telling himself.

Then when he'd least expected it, he'd walked right into her.

And he still had no idea what to say.

***

Megan watched as Nick drove away, her heart and head priming for an emotional battle. All this time she'd dreaded running into Nick…no idea what her reaction would be to seeing him in physical form, even though he'd haunted her dreams for the last five years.

It was worse than she'd imagined.

She took a deep breath and clamped down her warring emotions, transferring her focus to the situation in front of her.

"Dale," she said, "head out to the end of the trail and don't let anyone back here. Too many people might spook the gator into charging."

Dale's eyes widened and he hurried off down the trail to stop the tourists from entering the spring.

"What do you want me to do?" Johnny asked.

Megan studied the rocks along the edge of the spring. "I'm going to skirt the edge of the spring to find the best place for the trap. You stay here and watch the gator. If he so much as blinks, you let me know."

Johnny nodded and Megan was pleased to see that, although the teen was flushed with excitement, it wasn't enough to mask an appropriate amount of fear. Maybe the boy wasn't as foolish as his actions usually reflected. She picked her way around the edge of the spring, careful to avoid the slick mossy areas. If she tripped and fell into the spring, she'd probably have a heart attack before she ever hit the water.

"Careful, Miss Megan. You step in the water, and you'll get a husband like all the other women on the island."

Megan could hear the nervousness in Johnny's voice and knew the teen was teasing her to attempt to lighten the situation, but his words sliced through her like a knife. Island legend said the waters of Seeker's Spring brought people their heart's desire. For a lot of women, that had been the husband of their choosing.

But not for Megan.

Megan had known her heart's desire since she was in elementary school, and it had nothing to do with a man. She'd sat in the spring, swam in it, used drops of spring water in her tanning lotion, moisturizer, and bathwater for over a decade. She'd even kept a vial of it and put a single drop of water into every beverage she'd consumed her senior year of high school.

None of it had mattered.

A drunk driver had cut Megan's dreams off at her shattered knee. Fifteen years of work, training, and praying gone in a matter of seconds. Now Megan's heart was hardened. Her only desire was to make it through one more day without feeling sorry for herself. Without crying.

The spring is the biggest lie of all.

"The spring doesn't bring you a man," she said, trying to keep her voice steady, "or I guess you'd be dating Dale." She pointed to Johnny's tennis shoes, which were an inch deep in the spring water.

"Gross," Johnny said and chuckled. "I didn't know you were funny, Miss Megan."

I used to be.

She shook her head and focused on the gator, who was facing her…a good thing in this situation. If he'd been facing the back of the spring, they would have needed to turn him around, which would have been harder. About ten feet in front of the gator was a fairly flat spot on the bank. The trees were spaced far enough apart to place the cage. The challenge would be getting the cage out with the seven-hundred-pound beast inside, but she'd leave that problem up to the mainland game warden.

As far as she was concerned, her somewhat sketchy obligation in the matter ended with ensuring that the gator couldn't hurt anyone. Then she'd hightail it away from the spring and Nick and try to pretend it hadn't crushed her to see both.

CHAPTER TWO

Nick pulled on a pair of jeans and a T-shirt and ran his fingers through his wet hair. If she were still alive, his mother would yell at him that he needed a cut, but Nick liked the unkempt wavy locks. He thought it looked natural and more fitting of his carefree lifestyle than the short, professional-looking cuts he saw on the suit-and-tie men who left the island by ferry every day and returned in the evening, ties gone and looking harried.

He pulled a beer out of the refrigerator and looked out the kitchen window. It was a beautiful view. The house had been in his family for over sixty years. It was tiny, but the location was worth a million dollars. The beach lay right outside his front door, and palm trees and hibiscus bushes littered the white sands on the sides of the cabin, leaving a clear view of the ocean from the front of the house.

Tonight, a full moon hung on the horizon, shining down on the pristine sand like a spotlight. They called to him—the moon, the tide, the rhythmic sound of the waves crashing over the sandbar, then gently flowing up the beach toward his cabin. He opened the front door and stepped outside, relishing the feel of the cool sand on his bare feet. It was the kind of night made for no shoes, a cold beer, and a midnight stroll, so he pulled the door shut behind him and headed toward the ocean.

It had been a long day, starting with a frustrating bout of fishing that had yielded barely enough catch to cover the cost of fuel, and had stretched into eternity, working with Megan to get the alligator caged, then waiting on the mainland game warden to take over. Even sadder, the alligator had been the easy part. The giant beast had been unable to refuse the offer of fresh fish and had strolled into the cage without a bit of fuss.

Sitting in silence with Megan for the hour and a half it took the game warden to arrive was far more painful. The teens, who had kept them distracted for a bit, finally had to head home at suppertime or risk the wrath of Dale's mother. As soon as they were gone, it was painfully obvious where all previous conversation had originated.

Nick had started a million different conversations in his mind, but none of them had seemed appropriate. Finally, he'd made a banal comment about the high tide and its effect on fishing. Megan had agreed and said she'd shut down the beach early.

And then they'd lapsed into uncomfortable silence once more.

He'd never been more relieved than when the game warden walked into the spring clearing and took over. Megan had thanked the man, given him a wave, and headed down the trail toward town. He'd hiked around the back of the spring to his boat, pulled up anchor, and headed for the dock.

The shower had released some of the tension from his back and neck, but the ocean was what truly relaxed him…what centered him. He couldn't imagine a life inland. It would be like slowly suffocating. And that's the very thing that had gotten him into trouble—he'd assumed Megan felt the same.

Sure, he'd known she applied to colleges on the mainland, and she'd always said she wanted to be an Olympic swimmer, but he'd never really thought it would materialize. Not because she lacked the talent. Megan was the most talented swimmer he'd ever seen. But because he thought when push came to shove, she wouldn't leave the island.

And him.

Five years ago, he'd watched her open that envelope from Stanford. Saw her face as she read the acceptance letter, and in that instant, grief, longing, and an intense anger at himself slammed into him like a tidal wave. He'd been a fool. This was the opportunity that she'd worked for her entire life. The opportunity that only a handful of people were extended. Of course she would take it.

Unless he gave her a reason not to.

But Nick loved Megan more than he loved himself. No way would he stand in the way of her dreams. That night, he slipped the tiny diamond ring he'd been so nervous about deep into his pants pocket, then he'd stuffed it into the back corner of his dresser, where it had remained ever since.

Part of him always wondered what would have happened if he'd asked her to marry him that night, as he'd planned. Sometimes he thought she would have said no, and the past would have played out exactly as it had. Sometimes he thought she would have said yes and given up everything to remain on the island with him. But how long would she have been happy? How long would it have taken before she resented him for being the one barrier to the thing she'd always wanted?

He couldn't risk it. Having Megan momentarily upset and angry with him, then ultimately happy with her life, was a much better option than having her slowly descend into resenting him and always wondering what might have been. So he did the only thing he felt he could do—he broke up with her. Set her free so that she would do the one thing he was certain she was meant for.

Three months later she was gone, and his heart went with her.

His feet brushed against something in the sand and he looked down at the towel that had wrapped around his ankle. It was the first time he'd noticed the terrain since he left his house, and he was surprised to see how far he'd walked. Even more surprised to see the location he'd walked to.

A splash in the ocean caught his attention and he turned, already knowing that he'd see her—Megan—swimming in the surf in the moonlight. This spot was a good distance from the town, and the way the beach curved created a secluded area that was perfect for nighttime swimming.

It had been perfect for a lot of things.

Nick watched her spin and roll, then dive beneath the surface, as he'd done a hundred times before, but it never got old. Megan was enchanting in water—like a ballerina with a stage. Every movement blended with the tide, as if she were born to be in the water. And maybe it was that simple. Maybe she was.

He sat on the flat rock where he'd spent so many nights before and lost himself in her all over again.

***

Megan leaped up as a large swell rushed toward her and dove over it, cutting into the glossy ocean surface behind the wall of water. She did a somersault as soon as she broke the surface and sprang back up just in time to clear the next wave. Her pulse spiked. Her entire body tingled.

It was the most exhilarating thing in the world.

She loved swimming. Loved the water. But nothing in the world compared to frolicking in the ocean surf under a full moon. It was simply magical. Another set of waves approached and she bobbed over them, letting her body move with the ebb and flow of the tide, allowing the natural rhythm of the water to take her over. She closed her eyes for a moment and the entire world drifted away.

A twinge in her right knee brought her crashing back into reality, and she grieved the moment as it slipped away into the past that was and the future that would never be. She turned around and allowed the tide to sweep her into shallow water, then left the comfort of the sea for the cool touch of the sand.

"You're still magnificent."

She knew it was him before she ever lowered her towel to look. His voice stirred something in her...an acute longing, and something far more primal.

He sat on their rock, basked in the moonlight, and it was as if five years melted away. All of the uncomfortable silence this afternoon suddenly seemed so silly, so wrong. They'd been friends their entire lives. Lovers for a good part. Should they have to forget what they were in order to become who they would be?

"I'm not where I can be," she said. She moved toward the rock and slipped onto the cold surface next to him, tucking her arms around her legs, as she'd done so many times before. "But I'm getting there."

His dark eyes studied her, seeming to look behind her words and straight into her heart. "I heard about the accident. I'm sorry doesn't seem good enough, but I *am* sorry. I know how much it meant to you."

"You probably know better than anyone."

"Maybe. I'm glad you came home."

She laughed. "Some accused me of running away."

He shook his head. "You've never run from something in your life. You run toward things, but the people left behind probably don't see it that way."

Her chest tightened and her heart clenched. Was he referring to her friends in California, or had he felt that way when she left? Did she really hear longing and regret in his voice, or was that just wishful thinking on her part?

Five years ago, Nick had insisted their relationship had run its course, and that it made more sense for them to split given that they'd be living separate lives thousands of miles apart. Logically, she knew he'd been right, but emotionally, his decision had devastated her. She'd always assumed their relationship would continue, even after she left the island, but looking back now, she saw clearly that was the pipe dream of a young girl. The realities of maintaining a relationship with someone you saw a handful of times a year weren't pretty, and those relationships were rarely successful.

"I don't know that I'm running toward anything anymore," she said finally. "I came here because it was a place I thought I could heal. A place where I would be able to meet expectations, rather than disappointing those around me."

"Home."

"Yes. I suppose it's that simple."

"And once you've healed?"

She looked out over the ocean and shook her head. "I don't know."

He touched the side of her face and turned it toward him. Her heart began to pound in her chest, because she knew he was going to kiss her. She also knew she should jump off the rock and run back to her parents' house, but her heart and body pushed logic aside.

He leaned over and brushed his lips across hers, soft as the night breeze. But that slight touch was all it took to send her heart and body into overdrive. Five years fell away, leaving only the eighteen-year-old girl sitting on a rock in the moonlight, being swept away by the only man she'd ever loved.

She leaned into him, her mouth seeking his, her heart yearning for simpler times when at least this one thing seemed so certain. It would be so easy to lose herself in him again. To bury her failure in the overwhelming feelings he unlocked in her.

Suddenly, a giant wave from the incoming tide crashed into the rock, sending a spray of water over them. Reality crashed into her just as the wave had into the rock, and she jumped up.

"I can't," she said and hurried down the shore.

She'd had too much loss already. Nick had cut her loose once before. She couldn't take it again.

CHAPTER THREE

Stupid! What were you thinking, kissing her like that?

Nick hauled the fishing nets onboard his boat and cursed himself once more, knowing full well what he'd been thinking—that he'd never thought he'd get the opportunity to kiss Megan at their special place again and when it was in front of him, he took it. He'd been crazy, hoping that one kiss could heal five years of hurt and disappointment…that they could start over as if she'd never left. As if he'd never told her to go.

You're a fool.

He slammed his hand against the steering wheel and started his boat, directing it to the dock. His aggravation stemmed from the fact that he wasn't normally a fool. In fact, everyone who knew him considered him to be one of the shrewdest people they knew. Except when it came to Megan, where all common sense seemed to fly right out the window.

"You gonna keep brooding, or you gonna tell me what's eating you?" Nick's fishing hand, Paulie, pulled a beer out of the cooler and tossed one to him.

"Nothing's eating at me but the lack of fish."

Paulie raised one eyebrow. "Really? 'Cause you started muttering under your breath before we even left the dock. So unless you got a crystal ball in your pocket, I don't know how the lack of fish was responsible for your foul mood this morning."

Nick took a drink of the beer and sighed. Paulie was a good guy, but he was far too observant for Nick's taste, at least at the moment. "I took a walk on the beach last night…ran into Megan."

Paulie whistled. "At the cove? Man, I bet that stung."

Nick stared. "How do you know about the cove?"

"Dude, I may be younger than you, but I'm not stupid. Some of us used to sneak up there at night and watch Megan swim."

"You what?" Nick struggled between wanting to clock the younger man and not being able to blame him.

"Don't worry," Paulie said. "We always cleared out after the swim show was over. We weren't pervs or anything. It's just that in the ocean, she looked like something that wasn't real—like a water goddess."

"Water goddess? She would have liked that description, but not the peeping."

Paulie shrugged. "Best-looking girl on the island, half-naked and in the water. Four thirteen-year-old boys. Would have been weirder if we'd known about it and kept playing *Mario Bros.* instead."

Despite his initial irritation, Nick chuckled. "I guess I can't argue with that."

Paulie grinned, then the grin faded away and he studied Nick for a moment. "Look, man, I've never been in love with anybody. Hell, after watching my mom and dad go at it all these years, I'm not even sure I ever want to be. But even though I was a kid, I could see there was something different about the two of you."

Nick frowned. "Different how?"

Paulie shrugged. "Like you fit, you know? Same way you do with this boat. Wouldn't seem right seeing you any other place."

Nick stared out over the bow of the boat at the tip of the island that seemed to peek out of the vast ocean. Paulie was right. He hadn't exactly been a monk for the last five years, but none of the women had been right.

Bottom line—none of the women had been Megan.

***

She dreamed of him that night.

An intense, vivid dream like the ones she'd had in high school. They'd haunted her when she first left the island, making rest all but impossible, but eventually, they'd tapered off. She'd told herself that it was because she'd finally accepted that Nick was her past and swimming was her future, but deep down, she knew it was a lie. The truth was, her physically and emotionally exhausted mind and body had carefully constructed a wall around the past in order to protect her future.

She'd planted roses on it in her mind—the kind that climbed the uneven stone surface and made you concentrate on their beauty, rather than what hid behind the wall. But she knew what was there, lurking just beyond the twisted vines and vibrant flowers, waiting for a crack in the surface. Waiting to remind her what she'd sacrificed for her dream.

"Megan?" Her mom poked her head into the lifeguard station and smiled. "I wasn't sure you were in here."

"Just locking up," she said and secured the windows on the front of the station.

"Your dad and I spent all day painting the living room so we're taking a break from cooking duty. We're having a bite at Seeker's Paradise. Do you want to join us?"

"You have to paint the living room to get out of cooking? Sounds harsh."

Her mother laughed. "Well, if I'm being honest, I've cooked more since you've been home than I have since your brother went off to school. It seems like a lot of work for only two people."

Megan smiled as she stepped out of the lifeguard shack and padlocked the door. "You won't get an argument from me. If there was such thing as a black thumb for cooking, I'd have two."

Her mother nodded as they started walking across the beach. "Do you remember when you were sixteen and your dad thought I should teach you to cook?"

Megan laughed. "And I told him that I was going to college so I could afford to eat out. I've lived up to that, by the way."

"Well, you eat like a bird, so that's no huge accomplishment. Seeker's has a great burger. I bet your dad a week of lawn maintenance that I could get you to eat one, and since I carried you for nine months, you owe me a win on this."

"Does it count if I know about the bet?"

Her mother grinned. "It does if you don't tell."

"I guess I owe you silence as well?"

"You got it."

Her mother slung her arm around Megan's shoulder and gave her a squeeze. "It's wonderful having you back home. I miss your brother, too, but having another woman around is a different kind of nice."

"If all these compliments are to butter me up so I eat a hamburger, it's working."

"Good." Her mother waved to a man on the deck of the bar. "I asked your dad to get us a table on the deck. After spending all day cooped up inside, I feel like a bit of sunshine, but we can move inside if you'd prefer."

"No. It was a gorgeous day. It's going to be a great outdoor evening."

They made their way up the stairs to the deck of the bar, where Megan's dad had secured them a prime table in the corner.

But he wasn't alone.

The man who sat across from her dad wasn't a stranger, but Megan wouldn't call him a friend, either. Brett Thompson, the son of her dad's best childhood buddy, was the quintessential golden boy. His father was a state senator and Brett was following in his footsteps, first Harvard for law school and now working in the Florida State Prosecutor's office.

He was tall, broad-shouldered, good-looking, tanned, and privileged...everything Megan's dad had wanted for her, which he'd made painfully obvious all the times he'd practically shoved the man in Megan's face. Brett hadn't helped matters, as he'd made his interest in Megan clear.

Her father never understood her resistance. On paper, Brett was perfect.

Megan saw her mother's smile falter as Brett waved and smiled at them with his perfect white teeth, then she pasted on the fake smile that she usually reserved for her mother-in-law.

"I didn't know he was on the island," her mother whispered, her fake smile never wavering.

Megan nodded. She knew her mother would never try to arrange a man for her, and if the thought even crossed her mind, Brett wouldn't be on the list. Her mother found him as dull and pompous as Megan did. But Megan knew her dad wished she'd fall in love with the "good catch," settle down in a mansion in nearby Florida, and provide him some grandchildren while preparing her husband for a position in Congress. Megan couldn't think of anything she was less interested in doing.

Her father had liked Nick well enough and respected his work ethic, but it had always been clear to her that he wanted more for his daughter than to become a fisherman's wife. He was probably the only person who'd been thrilled when she left the island for college. Megan was certain he believed that distance and time would eliminate her childhood infatuation with Nick.

He'd been wrong—about the elimination and the infatuation. She'd loved Nick.

"Honey," her dad beamed at her as they approached the table. "Look who I ran into at the bar. I hope you don't mind that I invited him for dinner."

Megan plastered on a smile at what she was sure was an out-and-out lie by her father. "Not at all. It's good to see you again, Brett."

Brett jumped up to pull out her chair and gave her a kiss on the cheek. "The pleasure is all mine. You look fantastic."

She looked like a woman with no makeup, hair in a ponytail, who'd just spent eight hours standing in ninety-degree heat, but she managed a "thanks" that sounded reasonably genuine before taking her seat.

"Are you visiting your grandmother?" Megan's mom asked Brett.

Brett nodded. "Just for the weekend. I don't get back here as often as I'd like."

"You have a demanding career," Megan's dad said. "I'm sure your grandmother understands, especially as you're following in your father's footsteps."

"I can only hope to have the career my father has," Brett said, but Megan didn't buy it for a second. She'd met more than one guy like Brett in her lifetime and knew his aspirations wouldn't stop at his father's accomplishments.

"I'm sure you'll do fine," her dad said. "You're near the University of Florida, right? I hear they've got a good law program."

Megan bristled and struggled not to scowl.

"Yes, it's excellent." Brett smiled across the table at Megan. "If you're interested, I have some contacts at the university. Application deadlines for fall have passed, but I'm sure I could call in a favor."

"No, thank you. The interest in law school is my father's, not mine. I just can't seem to convince him of that fact." She cut her eyes at her father, who chose that time to inspect the menu, as if he didn't already know it by heart.

Brett glanced at her father, then back at her, apparently catching on to the undercurrents. "Well, I'm sure no matter what you decide on, you'll do well. Let me know if I can help."

"Thanks," she said, forcing a smile. Brett already had the politician thing down pat.

"So your dad tells me you had a bit of excitement at the spring yesterday," Brett said, clearly trying to change the subject.

She nodded. "It was a bit of a surprise. I'm just glad no one got hurt. Amos was overexerted after streaking home, but he's the only one who suffered any consequences."

"You're forgetting everyone who saw him streaking," her mother said dryly. "That man is a constant trial to this island. Why can't he reserve being naked for his own home?"

"That's one of the island's greatest mysteries," Megan said.

A waiter stepped up to the table to take their order. Megan had already agreed to help her mother win the hamburger bet, but after the stunt her dad had pulled with Brett, she felt no guilt and was actually pleased.

Now she just had to get through the meal then shed them all. Her people meter was beyond maxed out. She needed some peace and quiet. No suggestions about how to live her life, no pressure to be anyone she wasn't.

Nothing but her and the sea.

***

He saw her on the balcony with her parents and the other one and scowled. Brett Thompson already had everything but Megan. If he managed to snag her, he would have his perfect façade, the public face he needed to move himself all the way to DC.

When they were kids, the two men had been friendly enough. Brett lived on the mainland with his parents during the school year, but he usually spent summers with his grandmother. At first, he'd been the typical spoiled rich kid, but eventually, he'd figured out that his father's money and influence didn't extend to the island boys and had settled somewhat into an island boy personality. But Nick knew he'd always considered himself better than the rest of them.

And maybe he was.

He was smart, came from money, had a great job now, and his future looked excellent. The woman he married would never have to worry about money. Would never have to worry about working for a living or finding someone else to care for her children. She'd have the best of everything—houses, cars, jewelry, vacations—and all for simply being beautiful in front of politically connected important people.

None of that had stopped Nick's hand from clenching when he saw them getting ready to have dinner, as if they were already family. Not wanting Megan to see him, he'd forced himself to move past the bar, but not before he'd seen her smile at Brett, or him kiss her possessively on the cheek.

The farther away from the bar he walked, the angrier he became, then resolute. No way would he stand back and watch Brett move in on Megan without a fight. Nick had never been a superstitious person, but he was about to open his hopes to include things that he couldn't see and touch.

Mind made up, he headed for Seeker's Spring. He had no doubt what his heart's desire was, and even if it meant sitting naked in that spring like Amos, by God, he was going to get it.

CHAPTER FOUR

This time, she saw him as he walked into the cove. She'd been watching as she swam…hoping he'd return. As soon as the disastrous dinner had ended, she'd mumbled polite goodbyes and fled the bar before her dad could even formulate a protest. She'd walked through the preserve for what seemed like forever, deliberately avoiding the coastline where happy families and couples might be enjoying an evening picnic.

Her father didn't know it yet, but he'd done her a favor with his little stunt that evening. It had totally backfired on him and would launch him into certain dismay and provide her mother with years of ammunition, but she'd save that bit of news for tomorrow. In his attempt to push onto her the life he thought she should have, it had become so clear what life she wanted.

With every step through the preserve, her doubts fell away, and she was left with one single-minded purpose—to see if a future with Nick was possible. Sure, he'd tried to kiss her, but what if that was habit as old memories surfaced? What if Nick had gotten over her, even though she hadn't gotten over him?

She knew of only one way to be certain.

She waited in the ocean until he sat on the rock, then swam a couple more minutes. Nick had always loved watching her swim, and she was not above taking every advantage she could. If this wasn't her future, then she had no other answers for why things had happened the way they had. Why her heart had softened the second Nick had reappeared in her life.

As the moon emerged from behind clouds, she walked out of the ocean, following the moon's trail as if it were a spotlight. She'd shed everything this time…had wanted to completely bare herself, to discard everything and emerge from the ocean reborn. She'd told herself that if he came, it was a sign. That all this time, she'd been wrong about her heart's desire. That everything she'd ever needed was right here on the island.

He slid off the rock as she approached, his eyes taking in every square inch of her. She stepped directly in front of him, so close she could feel the heat coming off his shirtless chest.

"I wasn't sure you'd come," she whispered.

"I couldn't stay away."

He drew her into him, her bare chest pressed against his own. She could feel him straining through his jeans, and knew the denim was the only thing separating her from certain ecstasy. He lowered his head to kiss her, first softly, then deeper, as his hands moved down her back and forward to cup her breasts, as he had so many times before.

She tugged at his jeans and he pulled away for a moment. "Are you sure?" he asked.

"This is the only thing I'm sure of."

He shed his jeans and tossed her towel on the ground before gathering her in his arms and gently laying her down. The cool sand penetrated the beach towel, and she shivered—maybe because of the chill, maybe because of anticipation—but she knew that in a matter of seconds, she'd be warmed through and through.

He positioned himself over her and leaned down to kiss her again. She kissed him lightly first, then pulled him down to her, into her, and everything but this moment fell away.

***

"Megan." Her mother poked her head into her bedroom, holding the house phone. "There's someone on the phone for you. Says he's the head swim coach at Stanford?"

Despite the fact that she'd barely been in bed a couple of hours, Megan popped up, her mind already whirling with a million questions. She'd graduated a year ago, and the coach she'd trained under was long gone. No good reason existed for the new coach to contact her.

Save one.

She jumped out of bed and took the phone from her mother. "Hello, this is Megan Riley."

The man began to speak and her heart started to pound. Her vision slightly blurred and she sat on the edge of the bed, clenching the phone, aware that her mother hovered nervously in the doorway.

"I'm flattered by the offer," Megan said, finally finding her voice. "Can I have some time to think it over?"

She waited for his reply, then dropped the phone on the bed.

"Well?" Her mother's voice sounded from the doorway.

"He offered me the assistant coach position for the women's swim team."

Her mother's hand flew up to cover her mouth. "Oh, Megan. That's wonderful!" Her mother hurried to the bed and sat beside her, giving her a squeeze.

Megan nodded but couldn't find the words to reply. A week ago, it would have been wonderful. Perhaps even a day ago. But after last night with Nick, the offer was an unnecessary complication…a temptation that she wished she'd never been given.

She glanced at the clock and hopped up. "I can't believe I overslept. I have to take a shower. Nick is picking me up in twenty minutes to go sailing."

Her mother's eyebrows shot up, but Megan hurried into the bathroom, closing the door behind her to effectively avoid the slew of questions she wasn't ready to answer. They'd still be waiting for her when she got home that evening, but she'd worry about that then.

***

Nick couldn't hold in his smile as he walked up the beach path to Megan's parents' house. Last night had been incredible. He and Megan were so in sync it was as if the last five years had never happened. As if she'd never left the island. Never left him.

They'd talked at length about her injury and the huge bout of depression she'd gone through when she'd gotten word that her knee would never heal properly, and how the Olympic career she'd worked her entire life to achieve had been stolen from her by a man who'd already had his license taken away for drunk driving.

His heart broke for her…for the lost dream that was within her grasp. He couldn't imagine the devastation she'd felt, knowing that everything she'd so desperately desired had been stripped away in a matter of seconds.

They'd talked about how he'd taken over his dad's fishing boat after he passed away. How his mother never recovered from the loss of her husband and slowly faded away, despite all of Nick's efforts to pull her back into life. Nick told her of the grief and guilt he'd felt over his mother's death because he hadn't been able to save her, something he'd never told another person.

The comfort and security he'd only ever felt with Megan was still firmly intact, and he could tell she felt the same way. They talked, and laughed, and made love again before he walked her home before daylight.

Today was already planned. He hadn't even bothered with sleep, electing instead to head to the dock and prepare the sailboat for their day. The small black velvet box in his cargo shorts fell against his leg as he walked, making him nervous for the second time in his life...the first being when he'd carried that ring in his pocket the time before.

The ocean breeze carried Megan and her mother's voices out the open bedroom window and down the walk. He smiled at Megan's voice, anxious to get their day under way, then he heard her words and froze.

This can't be happening again.

But it was. The offer was the next best thing to being the Olympic athlete Megan had wanted so desperately to be. Done well, Nick knew the job could eventually lead to a position coaching an Olympic team. Her mother's excitement was clear. It registered in every word she spoke. She must be reflecting what Megan also felt.

He spun around and hurried back down the path before either of them glanced out the window and saw him approach. It would hurt her for a moment, but Nick knew he should do what he'd always done—step away so that Megan could live her dream.

CHAPTER FIVE

Megan looked out the kitchen window and checked her watch for at least the twentieth time in the last thirty minutes. Nick had never strictly adhered to schedules, but he was rarely more than a couple of minutes late. She grabbed her cell phone off the counter and checked it again. No messages. She dialed his number, but it went straight to voice mail, as it had the previous five times.

Had something happened at the dock? She shook her head. If he'd been in an accident, word would have spread around the island before the paramedics got there. Maybe he'd overslept. That had to be it.

She grabbed her beach bag and called out to her mom. "I'll be back this evening."

Her mother poked her head out of the laundry room and gave her a wave before she headed out. She drew up short when she got to the beach path. Someone had already passed this way this morning. Large footprints were impressed in the sand on the path, which had been wiped clean the night before by the tide. She frowned. Her dad had left early for the mainland, so they weren't his prints, and the path connected only to her parents' house, so it wasn't like just anyone would utilize it.

Her stomach clenched as she hurried down the path, a ball of anxiety began to form. Something was off—she was certain. She forced herself to breathe and stop the rash of awful thoughts that ran through her mind. Nick's cabin wasn't terribly far, but every step seemed like a mile.

The cabin was quiet when she arrived, reaffirming her previous thought that he'd simply overslept. She knocked on the door, lightly at first, but when no one answered, she knocked harder. On the last rap, the door opened a bit. She frowned. Crime was fairly low on the island, but people still locked their doors.

She pushed the door open wider and stuck her head inside, calling out. When no answer was forthcoming, she stepped inside. Nick's bedroom was off the back of the kitchen, so she headed that way, but as she passed the breakfast table, she drew up short. In the center of the table was a black velvet box.

Her hands shook as she lifted it up and opened it, but she already knew what was inside. The ring was a simple solitaire, but it glittered beautifully in its case. She pulled it out to get a better look, so tempted to slip it on her finger but knowing that she should wait. That the first time she wore that ring should be when Nick placed it there.

That had to be his intention, right?

As she went to place the ring back in the box, she noticed a slip of paper peeking out from below the ring cushion. She lifted the cushion and pulled out the paper—a registration card for the ring. As she slipped it back in place, her eyes locked on the date.

Five years ago.

Instantly, she chided herself for not clueing in sooner. She'd only reconnected with Nick last night and had barely gotten home before sunrise. He'd hardly had time to rush to the mainland and buy a diamond ring. She placed the card and the ring back in the box and closed it, setting it back on the table where she'd found it.

Why hadn't he asked her? Five years ago, they'd been so in love…or at least that's what she'd believed. Nick had convinced her then that their relationship had run its course, but the ring said something else entirely.

She walked to the bedroom and peeked inside, but it was empty and the bed didn't look as if it had been slept in. Confused, she turned around and then it hit her—like one of those mystery movies where all the elements run together at the end—and everything suddenly made sense.

Nick's complete change in personality the night she'd been accepted to Stanford. The ring that had been in that box for five years. The footsteps on the path to her parents' house this morning. Her open bedroom window. The ring sitting on his kitchen table now.

He'd lied to her all those years ago. He hadn't stopped loving her. He just didn't want to stand in the way of her dreams. The full weight of all of it hit her like a freight train. Nick had sacrificed his own happiness for the future he'd wanted for her.

For her.

A wave of guilt washed over her as she remembered all the times she'd raged at him, cursed him for hurting her the way he had. He'd been just as hurt but unable to rage…unable to even admit the truth.

This morning, he must have overheard her conversation with her mother about the coaching offer. For Nick, it was five years ago all over again, and he was doing what he'd always done—trying to give Megan what she wanted. He was giving her her freedom, refusing, again, to get in the way of her dream.

Except this time, he was wrong.

The job wasn't her dream. She had a new dream. One that she was determined not to to let slip away.

She rushed out of the cabin and hurried to the dock. When Nick was troubled, he always headed for his boat. No doubt, she would find him there now. As she hurried across the sand, she pushed her knee a little too hard in the sand, and it started aching. Stopping a minute to collect herself, she scanned the pier and caught a glimpse of Nick, adjusting the lines on his sailboat.

Her heart leaped at the sight of him—so strong and sexy, and with the biggest heart in the world. How could he not be enough? She ignored the twinge in her knee and hopped up on the pier, not even bothering to go around to the steps, and hurried down the dock before he pulled away.

"I hope you're not going to claim you were sick," she said as she stepped in front of his sailboat.

He turned around, almost unable to meet her eyes. "I figured you needed to rest longer, as late as you got in."

"So that's how you're going to play it?" She shook her head and stepped onto the boat. He froze as she approached him, his uncertainty so clear.

"You heard me and my mom talk about the coaching job this morning," she said. "I saw the ring on the table. I don't have to be a genius to put things together."

He sighed. "I don't want to get in your way now and have you resent me later. Can't you appreciate that?"

"More than you'll ever know. But I don't need you to protect me from loving you. You couldn't even if you tried."

His eyes widened. "But coaching is the next best thing—"

"No, it's not. All these years, I thought I knew exactly what I wanted, but I was wrong. The truth is, the Olympics were the next best thing to you. And I'm not letting you walk away again."

"You're sure?"

She nodded. "I know now, it's the only thing I've ever been sure of."

"But the job offer?"

"Isn't what I want. I want a master's in marine biology. I may be gone a couple days a week for classes on the mainland, but I want to live on the island. With you."

The uncertainty disappeared from his face and he smiled as he reached for her. As he wrapped his arms around her, he lowered his lips to hers. Megan leaned into him, her arms circling his chest. Her heart pounded and every inch of her skin tingled, just as it did when she frolicked in the ocean under the moonlight.

If she'd had even an ounce of doubt, it disappeared in that moment. Nick's love caressed her like the ocean's waves. Her heart's desire had been right in front of her all this time—at home on Seeker's Island.

A Mortal Wish

Tina Folsom

CHAPTER ONE

Eric watched the man as he tied the ferry to the boat dock, then proceeded to move the gangplank over the gap between dock and ferry and secure it tightly, before he hollered to the captain, "She's tied up."

The captain waved back, then shifted his gaze to Eric. "Have a pleasant stay."

Eric walked over the gangplank and onto the dock. He'd been the only passenger on the evening ferry. He assumed that most visitors descending upon this tiny island of barely over two thousand inhabitants did so with an earlier ferry, but he hadn't had a choice. Traveling during daylight hours was impossible for him.

"Mr. Sanders?"

At a voice calling his name, he turned his head and noticed a gangly kid who couldn't be more than twenty years old waving at him from next to the harbormaster's hut. His red hair was like a beacon in the night, as was the scent that came from him: fresh, young blood. Luckily, Eric had fed plenty before his departure from the mainland, not wanting to be caught hunting on the island. With such a small population and an area of not more than five-by-ten miles—he guessed—he didn't want to take the risk of being discovered. Small town people looked out for each other and would interfere when they saw something odd happening, whereas in the large cities, anonymity was his friend.

"I'm Eric Sanders," he called out to the kid and approached.

When Eric stopped before him, holding his overnight bag in one hand, the youngster gave him a wide smile. "I'm Carl. Welcome to Seeker's Island. Mrs. Adams sent me. I'll take you to the Sunseekers' Inn."

Carl made a motion for the bag, but Eric didn't relinquish it. "Lead the way."

The kid gestured to the street that ran alongside the small harbor. "I'm parked right here."

Eric arched an eyebrow. He hadn't expected this island to allow cars. "Where?"

Carl pointed his finger toward a white object that stood at the curb.

"A golf cart," Eric murmured.

The kid nodded enthusiastically. "We don't have cars on the island. And I get to use one of the golf carts to drive tourists around. I mean, it's practically mine."

Eric forced a smile and followed him. Great, Carl was a chatterbox. That was just what he needed. If he'd had a choice, he wouldn't have come to a small island like this where everybody knew everybody else's business, but he hadn't had a choice. This was his last resort.

As Eric slunk into the passenger seat and set his bag between his feet, Carl started the electric engine and pulled into the street that ran alongside the coast. Houses and shops lined the quaint road and made Eric feel like he'd entered Disneyland. And maybe this island was just like Disneyland, full of make-believes and wishes for things he couldn't have.

"Are you here for the…you know?" Carl continued.

Knowing that the kid was referring to the hot spring, Eric gave no direct answer and instead let his eyes wander toward the ocean and the impenetrable darkness beyond the shore. "The…. you know what…doesn't really work, does it?"

He felt Carl sit up taller as if wanting to display more authority. "Of course it does!" Then he lowered his voice and leaned closer, whispering now. "Everything you've heard is true. If you drink from it, you'll get your heart's desire."

Eric felt a smile tug around his lips. The youngster sounded just a little bit too enthusiastic. "Sure, whatever you say." And maybe Eric was just cynical—what three-hundred-forty-seven-year-old vampire wouldn't be?

"You'll see!" Carl prophesized and brought the cart to a stop. He pointed to the large Victorian house that stood behind a white picket fence. "We're here."

Eric pulled a five-dollar bill from his pocket and handed it to the kid. "Thanks, Carl."

The youngster grinned as he pocketed the money. "And if you need any transportation on the island, I'll be happy to drive you around."

Eric had no doubt about that. He was sure that opportunities for making money on the island were few and far between. "I'll let you know." He got out of the cart and walked up the entranceway to the house, bag in hand.

The electric engine made barely any sound when Carl left.

Eric opened the front door and entered. The foyer was cozy and well lit. A large wooden staircase led to the upper floors. To his left was a reception area that looked like a booth with a high counter in front and shelves at the back. He approached it and set his bag on the floor. Seeing nobody, he hit the little bell on the counter.

As the soft ping chimed through the foyer, he heard a sound, and an instant later, a woman rose from behind the counter, righting the sleeve of her colorful summer dress, while giving him an apologetic smile.

"Oh, dear, you've caught me now!" She chuckled and blushed furiously. "Those darn straps, they never stay in place."

Eric could only imagine that she was talking about her bra straps and tried not to focus on her ample chest. Instead, he looked at her face. She was still attractive even though she seemed to be in her early sixties. Had he met her twenty or thirty years ago, he would have seduced her.

"Mrs. Adams?"

"Yes, and you must be Mr. Sanders." She let her eyes roam over his face and body, not hiding the fact that she found him attractive.

He was used to those looks. He got them from women of all ages. But all they saw was his perfect shell: the dark hair, the chiseled chin, the classical nose, the piercing blue eyes, and the sculpted body. What they didn't see was the man inside, the man who yearned for a real life, for a mortal life.

"I have a wonderful room for you. On the top floor. It's got a gorgeous view of the bay on the other side of the island." She reached for the board of keys behind her and took one of them down, placing it on the counter.

"Perfect." He smiled and grabbed the key.

"Breakfast is included." She pointed toward a door next to the stairs. "The breakfast room is through there. We serve breakfast from seven till nine-thirty."

"That won't be necessary. I'm not much of a morning person. In fact, would you mind if I declined housekeeping? I'm quite a night owl actually and sleep really late." Late as in *until sunset.*

"Oh?" She cast him a surprised glance. "I hope you won't be too disappointed about the nightlife here, but there is practically none. A lot of our visitors are here for the hot spring." She leaned forward, her boobs resting on the counter as she did so. "I assume you came for the same thing?"

Eric sighed. He'd been here for less than half an hour and already two people had managed to ask him the same question. But being the intensely private man he was, he had no intention of getting dragged into a conversation about his very personal desires.

"I hear fishing is good out here."

A disappointed frown spread over Mrs. Adams' face as she straightened. "Yes, yes, it is."

"Top floor, you said?" He pointed toward the stairs and picked up his bag, not waiting for her answer.

"Turn left at the top of the stairs."

The stairs creaked as he walked up the first flight. Runners covered the worn floors on the landing. Eric let his eyes wander over the old paintings on the walls and the antique sideboard that adorned the second-floor hallway. His eyes lingered on the fine workmanship for a moment longer, while he already continued around the banister.

He ran into something soft. His head jerked around, and his hand released the grip on his bag in the same moment as he instinctively reached for the person he'd run into. His eyes perceived a woman, her arms flailing, releasing the handbag she'd carried. As its contents spilled onto the floor, Eric caught the woman, preventing her from falling.

"Ooops!" he called out. "Gotcha!"

"Uhh!"

She breathed heavily, and his superior senses picked up her elevated heartbeat.

"I'm so sorry, I didn't see you," he apologized.

"That's quite all right," she answered breathlessly. "It's my own fault. I was running around the corner without looking." She eased from his grip and stepped back.

Eric's eyes fell on her face. Her eyes were just as blue as his and her long hair as black as the night. Her skin was flawless, but pale, almost like porcelain, and it made her lips look as red as fresh blood. Hunger surged within him instantly, despite the fact that he was sated. He pushed it back. Instead he looked to the items that had fallen to the floor and bent down.

"Let me help you with this," he offered and handed her the handbag.

She took it and crouched down opposite him, quickly picking up some of the fallen items: a lipstick, keys, a cell phone.

Eric handed her a handkerchief and a pen, then searched the rug for anything else that might have fallen out, but found nothing.

"I think I've got everything," she said and rose.

He got up from his hunched position and offered his hand in greeting. "I'm Eric, by the way."

She hesitated, before she shook his hand very briefly. "Claire." Then she motioned to the stairs. "I've gotta go."

He watched as she hurried down the stairs. Her footsteps echoed in the foyer as she rushed out the entrance door. Only when it fell shut with a loud thud, did he pick up his own bag and proceed to his room.

CHAPTER TWO

After a refreshing shower, Eric left his room. It was time to do what he'd come here for. No need to drag out the inevitable. He walked down the first flight of stairs, reaching the spot where he'd run into the very enticing Claire. For a moment, he stopped there. She'd stirred something in him, awakening a sense of wanting to protect her, even though he'd never felt that way toward a human. He'd always been the predator, taking what he wanted, not caring whom he hurt. But it was all different now.

He was done being the monster they feared. He was done with this life. Too many kills lay in his past, too many bad deeds lined his path. The senselessness of it all had come full circle. His life had no meaning; he understood that now after having lived as a vampire for two hundred twelve years. And he couldn't do it any longer; he couldn't hurt people any longer. Because he'd developed a conscience. A fucking conscience!

He stared at his shoes and cursed silently. Who'd ever heard of a vampire with scruples? But no, he had to suddenly want a meaningful life, a purpose. And he knew there was only one way to have a meaningful life: he had to become human again.

His discontent with his life as a vampire had come gradually. Every time he'd watched humans celebrate another milestone in their lives, a new love, a wedding, or a birth, he'd felt himself grow more envious. And he'd started comparing his miserable life to theirs and found it lacking. There were no joyful events in his life: he slept, he hunted, he fed. And he was always hiding. But most of all, he had nobody who cared for him or whom he cared about. Tender emotions were foreign to him. Yet he recognized them in others, in humans, and he wanted to feel the same. And if he couldn't achieve that, then he'd rather not feel anything at all.

That's why he'd come to the island: to drink the water of the hot spring and wish for his heart's desire. And if the legendary spring failed him, then there was only one other thing to do. If he had the courage to do it.

He let out a bitter laugh when he noticed an object beneath the sideboard he'd admired earlier. Out of curiosity, he bent down and reached for it. His fingers closed around a transparent orange colored prescription bottle. He read the label on it and froze.

It belonged to a Claire Culver—the woman he'd bumped into. The pill bottle must have fallen out of her bag and rolled under the sideboard, and they had both overlooked it. He read the name of the medication. As a vampire he wasn't susceptible to any diseases, therefore he wasn't familiar with the name, even though he remembered having heard this name on a TV program. What had it been for? He searched his brain, but couldn't recall it.

Chastising himself for his inappropriate curiosity, he continued down the stairs. It was none of his business what medication Claire took and what it was for. She was a stranger to him and would remain a stranger.

When he reached the foyer, Mrs. Adams was pulling the curtains shut in the hallway. She turned to him.

"Out for a nightcap?" she asked.

"Yeah, I figured I'd explore that nightlife you were talking about earlier." He winked at her and enjoyed the fact that she blushed once more.

"Luke runs a tiki bar not far from here. You might want to try that," she suggested.

"Sounds right up my alley." He rolled the pill bottle between his fingers. "Oh, and Mrs. Adams, I found this on the floor upstairs. It belongs to Miss Culver. She must have dropped it." He handed it to her and decided not to tell her that he was the reason it had fallen out of her handbag. "Would you please give it to her when you see her?"

"Oh, dear." She sighed heavily, making him pause for a moment.

"Something wrong?"

"Well," she started, "such a shame. And she's so young and pretty too. Has her whole life ahead of her, except she doesn't."

A cold shiver crept up his spine. "Excuse me?"

She motioned to the medication in her hand. "Miss Culver." She took a step closer and lowered her voice. "I shouldn't tell you this, but since you found her medication, you'd probably be able to figure it out yourself anyway. I only know because she had a seizure the other day, and I had to call the doctor, and he's my cousin's husband. And you know, she told me. My cousin, that is. Because her husband told her."

Eric took a deep breath, hesitating for a second. Should he stay and allow her to divulge private medical information about Claire? Wouldn't it be better if he simply walked away and didn't get involved? But Mrs. Adams had mentioned seizures, and that word had peaked his interest.

"Yes?"

She leaned in. "Brain cancer. Apparently she got diagnosed six months ago. It's inoperable. The doctors have given her another few weeks or months." She pointed to the pills. "She takes those to keep the pain at bay. But the seizures continue. The doctors have given up. That's why she's here. You know, for the hot spring."

He nodded, shocked at the revelation. No wonder Claire had looked so pale. Had he sensed her illness? Was that why he'd had the feeling that she needed protection? "She's come to wish for a cure."

A sad smile played around Mrs. Adams' lips. "Several times a day, she goes there. She's there now. And on the way back, she stops at the bar and drowns her sorrow. And tomorrow she'll do the same thing again. It's so sad to watch."

"So the hot spring doesn't have any real power, does it?"

"Oh, it does, but sometimes we're not wishing for the right thing. Sometimes we don't know what our heart's true desire is. And the spring only grants those desires that are pure and true."

"What could be purer than wanting a cure for her cancer?" he wondered.

"I'm not saying that her desires are not pure. Sometimes the spring just needs a sacrifice to work," she answered cryptically.

Visions of slaughtered animals popped into his head. But he was sure that Mrs. Adams was talking about other kinds of sacrifices.

"Maybe you just want to tell Miss Culver that you found the pill bottle yourself. There's no need for her to think that I know what's going on. I'm sure she values her privacy."

Without waiting for her response, he left the house and turned toward the main road on his search for the tiki bar. After the information Mrs. Adams had shared with him, he wasn't in the right frame of mind to visit the spring right now.

CHAPTER THREE

Claire cast one last look back at the hot spring. When she'd arrived over an hour earlier, she'd found the caretaker, Amos, sitting in it. Naked! She'd heard other people on the island talk about him, but this was the first time she'd encountered him. She'd quickly hidden in the shrubs and waited patiently until he'd finally left—dressed in only overalls. It appeared that Amos was not into clothes.

Once alone at the spring, she'd captured some fresh water from where it poured out of the rocks with her cupped palms and swallowed it. At the same time, she'd prayed for a miracle. Just like she'd done for the past five days since she'd come to the island. So far, nothing had changed. Her headaches were as painful as ever and were only subdued by the strong painkillers her oncologist had prescribed. But even those didn't dull the pain for long. So she'd started drinking in the evenings to drown out the pounding in her head.

With each day that passed, hope faded further into the background as reality pushed to the forefront. Science had given up on her long ago, and the miracle she was hoping for by making the same wish at the spring over and over again wasn't happening. In a few days the pain would be so excruciating and the seizures so severe, she would most likely fall into a coma from which she would never wake. Her time was up.

As she walked back on the dirt path that led into the village, she reflected on her life. But looking back on it made what lay ahead of her even harder to bear. She wasn't ready to die. There was so much she hadn't done, hadn't seen, hadn't experienced. It just wasn't fair. She'd been a good person, honest, reliable, decent through and through. She'd never hurt anybody.

Like the other nights before, she headed for the tiki bar. Some alcohol would numb her mind and stop her from speculating whether things would have turned out differently if only she'd gone to the doctor earlier when her headaches had started. She didn't want to think about things she couldn't change.

As she approached, she saw that it was half full like the night before. A bar stood in the middle of a hut without walls, its shutters, which protected the liquor from theft during the day, were lifted and secured to the ceiling during opening hours. Soft music came from the speakers. One couple, embracing, danced slowly on the tiny makeshift dance floor. Others sat at the tables or at the bar, drinking and talking. Laughing. She steered for the bar and took the only vacant bar stool next to a tall dark-haired man whose back was turned to her as he watched a basketball game on the muted TV that hung from the ceiling.

Claire motioned to the owner. He'd introduced himself the first night. "Evening, Luke."

"Hi, Claire. The usual?"

She nodded and watched how he prepared her Whiskey Sour the way she liked it. Might as well go out in style, she figured. When he put it in front of her, she lifted her glass to her lips and took the first sip.

The man next to her turned. "Cheers."

She almost choked and quickly set the glass back on the counter. The man next to her was Eric, who she'd crashed into as she was running down the stairs at the bed and breakfast.

"Oh!" Just like earlier, she was unable to form a coherent sentence.

This time she couldn't blame her monosyllabic response on the fact that they'd bumped into each other. No, she had to admit that she was tongue-tied because Eric exuded such pure maleness that her entire body was bursting into flames. She'd had her share of boyfriends, of course, good-looking ones too, but she'd never been with a man like the one who now gazed at her with such intensity that she wanted to rip her clothes from her body and offer herself to him.

Good God! What was she thinking? She was clearly going mad. Yes, she was finally slipping into insanity, unable to control her mind.

"Hi," she said quickly before the silence between them stretched any longer. "Guess it's the only bar in town." She sounded silly in her own ears, but Eric smiled at her nevertheless.

"Not much of a nightlife here on the island, I gather. But I suppose that's not why people come here." He gave her an expectant look.

"Have you been to the hot spring?" she asked him and took another sip from her drink so that her hands had something to do and he wouldn't notice that they trembled.

"Not yet. I'm not in a rush. It'll be there when I'm ready."

She stared at the bottles that were lined up on the shelves suspended over the bar, nodding in agreement. "Still figuring out what you want?"

He shook his head. "I know what I want."

Claire was surprised at herself. She wasn't one to start a candid conversation with a stranger, but oddly enough, his openness was inviting her to talk as if they'd known each other for a while. Maybe it was because they were two lonely strangers in a bar, both with a wish they wanted fulfilled. Even though she couldn't imagine what Eric could possibly wish for: didn't a man like him have everything? Looks, strength, power? Women throwing themselves at his feet?

"Do you believe in it?" she heard herself ask.

"The hot spring?"

She nodded.

"I don't know what to believe."

"Is that why you're waiting?" She turned her head to look at him.

His blue eyes locked with hers. "Is that why you're going every day? Because you don't know whether to believe in it or not?"

Her breath hitched. "You seem to know an awful lot." If she were in a large city, she would be worried about him being a stalker. However, she knew how things on this island worked: nothing stayed a secret for longer than five minutes.

He shrugged, then took a sip from his red wine. "The islanders seem to keep a close eye on who's visiting the hot spring."

"They're very protective of it," she agreed and downed the rest of her drink in one big gulp. She made a gesture to get down from her bar stool, when she suddenly felt his hand on her forearm.

"Don't leave," he said quietly. "I didn't mean to scare you off."

She hesitated, staring at his hand, then lifted her gaze to his face. His eyes were warm. She allowed herself to get drawn into their blue depths.

"Dance with me," Eric whispered.

"I . . . uh," she started.

"What have you got to lose? It's just a dance between two strangers. I'll be gone in a couple of days, and you'll never have to see me again."

He was right. She had nothing to lose. And why shouldn't she allow herself to sway with the rhythm of the music, a stranger's arms holding her for a few minutes, making her forget her sorrows?

"One dance," Claire agreed.

"One dance," he repeated and with ease lifted her from her barstool.

A moment later, she found herself on the dance floor, his arms holding her close to him, his thighs brushing hers, his hand on the small of her back pressing her closer to his torso, so she could feel his body heat engulf her. She closed her eyes and let herself fall into the dream that her life could only just be beginning. That it wouldn't end.

CHAPTER FOUR

Eric pulled her closer and moved to the rhythm of the music. He hadn't danced in a long time, but the steps were ingrained in him nevertheless. He'd always loved dancing, always loved the feel of a woman in his arms.

Pressing his cheek to hers, he spoke softly. "I heard that sometimes the hot spring needs a sacrifice to grant a wish."

Claire pulled her face back to look at him. "Who told you that?"

"Mrs. Adams."

She leaned back into him. "She never mentioned anything to me about that."

"Maybe you're not the one to offer a sacrifice." Maybe Mrs. Adams had meant this only for him—without knowing what his wish was—, because he was the one asking for the impossible, and his wish demanded a sacrifice.

"What if it's all a lie?" she mused. "What if the spring does nothing? What will you do then?"

"What will *I* do?"

"Yes, you. If you found out tonight that the spring doesn't work, what would you do tomorrow?"

He'd thought about it ever since he'd decided to come to the island. "I would go to the beach and wait there until the sun rose." He wouldn't seek shelter from it, but allow the sun to turn him into dust and the ocean surf to sweep his remains away as if he'd never existed.

"Yes, your life would just go on. I wish it were the same for me."

Eric didn't correct her assumption. He heard the rising tears in Claire's voice, but he wouldn't allow her to cry. Not as long as she was with him. At least for tonight, he wanted her to feel joy and pleasure.

"Come to the beach with me, now. And I'll make you forget the things you want to forget. Just for tonight. Just you and me. The world around us doesn't exist. The spring doesn't exist."

She didn't pull away from him despite his outrageous offer. Instead he felt her nod. "Yes, make me forget, just for a little while." Then she lifted her head and looked at him. "You must think me easy."

He moved his head from side to side. "Do you think *me* easy?"

Clearly surprised at his question, she shook her head. "No."

"Then why would I find *you* easy? Just because you allow yourself to say yes to something you want? I don't judge people who follow their desires."

Eric lowered his head until his lips hovered over hers. "You still have a chance to change your mind, but once I kiss you—"

He didn't get an opportunity to finish his sentence, because Claire leaned in and kissed him. Stunned and elated at the same time, he savored her soft lips for an altogether too-brief moment, before she pulled back again.

"I won't change my mind." Her whispered words blew against his face.

Without waiting for the song to end, he led her toward the bar, tossed a twenty on it and left. It didn't matter what the bartender thought of them. Finding his bearings, he turned into the next side street and headed northwest.

The beach was deserted. And just like he'd thought he'd seen from his bedroom window, there was a small shed. He approached it and read the sign on it: *Beach Rentals*. A small padlock denied access to the contents of the shed. He reached for the lock.

"What are you doing? You're not going to break in, are you?"

He winked at her. "Let's live on the wild side for tonight." Then he moved so she couldn't see how he was opening the lock: with pure vampire strength.

The shed contained what he was looking for: cushions for the lounge chairs that were neatly stacked up next to the shed. He pulled two of them out and spread them in the sand.

When he caught her still-stunned look, he put his arm around her waist and drew her against his body. "Trust me, we'll both be more comfortable that way."

"I'm not looking for comfortable." Her lids swung open, her lashes almost crashing into her eyebrows.

God, she was beautiful. It hit him right there—that this beauty would be gone from this world very soon. That knowledge squeezed his heart like an iron fist clamping around it. The pain was palpable even though he shouldn't feel any physical pain.

Eric brought his lips to hers, almost touching them, but not quite. "What are you looking for?"

"To feel alive."

"Just alive? I can do better than that, baby."

Her lips were soft and yielding when he slid his mouth over them and captured them gently. There was no hurry. The sun wouldn't rise for another seven hours. He had time to make leisurely love to her. To give her everything she needed, just so she would feel cherished once more.

Claire wore a summer dress, and pressed against his short-sleeved cotton shirt and his linen pants, he could feel every curve of her body. She wasn't voluptuous by any stretch of the imagination, but she was well-proportioned. Pulling her closer, he slipped his hand onto her backside, palming the alluring swell.

A soft moan issued from her throat. He swallowed it just as her lips opened, allowing him to sweep her tongue inside to explore her. Tasting her sweet essence, his body hardened, one appendage more so than the rest of his body: his cock, while already semi-erect when he'd danced with her, now surged to its fully erect state.

He couldn't resist and pressed his hips more firmly into her soft center, letting her feel what she'd done to him. In response, she lowered her hands down to his backside. He could feel her fingernails digging themselves hard into his flesh, a feeling he welcomed more than she could know.

He'd always loved it when his vampire lovers had dug their claws into him, drawing blood while he drove his cock into them. He wished for the same thing now, for some fierce lovemaking, a no-holds-barred experience.

His fangs began to itch at the very thought of it, and he could feel them lengthen. Desperate to keep his vampire side from emerging, he ripped his mouth from hers and lifted her off her feet. Then he lowered her to lie on the lounge cushions he'd spread out, and joined her.

His hands searched for the zipper of her dress and lowered it. Like a shy virgin, she looked away, but he wouldn't have any of it.

"Claire," he prompted her, drawing her gaze back onto him. "I want you to watch me undress."

He noticed her swallow hard. But she said nothing. Slowly, he opened the buttons of his shirt, then shed the garment. Her eyes danced to his chest. She pulled her lower lip between her teeth, showing him her appreciation. When her gaze dropped to his pants, his heart suddenly beat faster. Claire was looking at the bulge that had formed behind the zipper, all shyness gone now.

When she licked her lips, he groaned involuntarily.

Eric lifted himself up, opening his pants at the same time. Then he stepped out of them, leaving him only with his boxer briefs. They stretched tightly over his ever-growing erection. When he looked down at himself, he noticed that a drop of moisture had oozed from him and was showing through the fabric.

He was sure she saw it too, the moonlight providing sufficient light even for a human's eyes to see. Standing above her, he hooked his thumbs into the waistband of his boxer briefs then shoved them lower until he'd freed his cock. Cool night air blew against his hard-on, but it did nothing to quell the raging organ.

Claire was still staring at him, her eyes wide, her lips parted, when he rid himself of the garment. Her chest heaved, and he could see her hard nipples press through the fabric of her dress.

"Now you. Undress for me."

He lowered himself onto his knees, close enough so nothing would escape his watchful eye.

With hesitant movements she pushed one strap off her shoulders, revealing creamy skin, then she dropped the second one and pulled on the fabric, exposing more of her skin. The top of her breasts came into view, then a second later, the perfectly round mounds topped with hard rosy nipples lay bare.

Eric sucked in a gulp of air. "You're beautiful. So perfect."

Encouraged by his words, she pushed the fabric lower. When she reached her hips, she paused.

"Show me more," he demanded.

Claire pushed the dress below her hips and freed herself from it. She wore the tiniest slip he'd seen in a long time, the triangle of fabric barely covering her dark nest of hair, the strings holding it up so thin, he knew if he touched them, he would rip the thing to shreds. And that was exactly what he wanted to do.

When her hand went to her panties, he stopped her. "Wait."

She gave him a startled look. "I thought you wanted me to undress."

"I've changed my mind." He went onto his hands and knees and crawled closer. "I want to do the rest myself, unless you object."

She leaned back with a smile. "I don't object."

For a long moment, he simply looked at her, drinking in the sight. "I could look at you forever and not get tired of it."

Claire chuckled softly and blushed. "You don't have to say that."

He leaned over her. "It's true." Then he lowered his head to her breasts and licked his tongue over one nipple.

A strangled moan came from her lips, and her body arched toward him.

"Just like I guessed," he whispered against her warm flesh. "Perfect."

Then he captured the nipple between his lips and sucked on it, while his hand palmed her other breast and kneaded it until she was writhing underneath him, her arousal now permeating the air around him. She tasted young and pure, so unspoiled he almost forgot what life had in store for her. But he didn't want to think of it, not now, not when he wanted to give her more pleasure than she'd had in her entire life.

This night was for Claire, even though he knew he would get his fair share of pleasure too. Just watching the way her body moved and her heart beat against her ribcage filled his heart with pride. And his cock with more blood, making him as hard as the rocks the surf was crashing against.

The moonlight bathed her in a warm light, the way sunlight could never achieve. It lent her face an almost mystical glow as if she wasn't real and only a figment of his imagination. And maybe she was; maybe he was dreaming in order to try to escape the monotony of his long life. It didn't matter, because what he sensed underneath his roaming hands felt real: warm flesh, smooth skin, hot blood. She was the personification of perfection.

As he continued to lavish her breasts with kisses and caresses, his hand moved lower, stroking along her torso until he reached her panties. He slid his fingers between fabric and skin, exploring the coarse hair that guarded her sex.

A hitched breath escaped from Claire's lips as he moved lower, but at the same time her hips tilted toward him in invitation.

"Yes, baby, I'm here," he encouraged her and slipped lower, encountering warm and moist flesh that felt as smooth as silk. He bathed his fingers in her arousal, coating them with it before he moved back north.

"Oh, God!" she called out.

His experienced fingers found the tiny swollen organ that lay protected by a hood. He pulled the hood up, exposing her clit fully and slid one moist finger over it. Claire nearly leapt off the ground, her heartbeat accelerating in the same instant.

His own body heated when the scent of her arousal grew stronger. His cock pressed against her thigh, impatiently waiting to get its turn. But it would have to wait a little while longer.

With slow and steady movements, he circled the swollen bundle of nerves underneath his fingers. He kept his touch light, savoring the moment. She was at his mercy now. With his touch, he could command her body and give her pleasure. There would be no escape for her now. No turning back.

"For tonight you'll be mine," he murmured against her breasts. And he would take everything she was willing to give him—and more, he realized that too now. Because she had awakened not just the desire for sex in him, but a darker desire. One she would not freely agree to.

Suddenly impatient, he pulled his hand from her sex and gripped her panties. With one rapid movement, he ripped them off her.

"Fuck it, baby," he cursed and lowered himself between her legs, spreading them wider before lowering his head to her glistening pussy. He slung her legs over his shoulders, one to each side of his head and sunk his mouth onto her.

Surprised gasps echoed through the night. "Eric, oh my god!" she cried out. "You don't have to . . . "

But her voice died when his tongue lapped over her slit, gathering her arousal. Her taste was intoxicating and invigorating at the same time. He sucked, nibbled, and licked, leaving no spot unexplored. She was beautiful in every way. Her body welcomed him, and opened up to his caresses, to his tender ministrations as he now stroked his tongue over her clit and lavished it with gentle touches.

He loved the way she responded to him, the way she lay in front of him, spread out for him to do with as he pleased. Him, a stranger. His own excitement rose when he felt her body tense and press against him with more urgency. The sounds of pleasure coming from her intensified and spurred him on to give her more. Without removing his lips and tongue from her clit, he brought his hand to her sex and stroked against her soft folds. He extended his middle finger and probed, easing it into her with one continuous slow thrust.

Her muscles clamped around him tightly—more tightly than he would have expected. How long had it been since a man had touched her there? Since a man had driven his cock into her? The thought that nobody had done so in a long time, made him even more impatient to seat himself in her clenching pussy.

"Yes," she moaned. "Oh please, yes."

Claire begging for it nearly made him spill. Fuck! He couldn't hold back much longer if she continued like that.

Driving his finger harder into her, he sucked her clit deeper into his mouth and pressed his lips together. Her body erupted, the waves of her orgasm ripping through her and crashing against his lips. Her interior muscles spasmed around his finger, gripping him so firmly that he thought she'd never release him. Not that he would have cared. He loved being inside her.

It took minutes for her body to still and for Eric to remove his lips from her sweet sex. When he did so and looked at her, her eyes were closed. But from her breathing he could tell that she wasn't sleeping.

"I've gotta be inside you now," he told her and positioned himself between her legs, bringing his cock to her center.

Claire's eyes opened slowly and a soft smile played around her lips. "Yes," she whispered breathlessly. "Let me feel you."

"You've made me so hard," he pressed out between clenched teeth, barely able to prevent his fangs from descending. His hunger was pushing to the forefront now.

Unable to slow himself down, he thrust inside her with one powerful move, robbing her of the air in her lungs. As she took a breath, her eyes widened.

"Oh my god, you're big. Even bigger than earlier."

Most vampires were. Sex was part and parcel of who they were, and once turned, their vampire blood ensured their cocks were hard and big to pleasure their female partners and give them what they needed. And they had another feature too: once inside a woman's sex, small bumps would appear on a vampire's cock. With every stroke, they added to the friction and stimulated a woman's G-spot, ensuring a woman's orgasm even without clitoral stimulation.

Eric could feel his cock transforming now as it was coated in her juices and submerged in her body. When he pulled out of her but for the very tip of it, he could already feel the difference. Then he pushed back inside her and watched her reaction.

Her eyes rolled back and her mouth dropped open, her nipples turning into hard points once more. "Oh God!" she mumbled.

"I told you. You'll feel more than just alive." He smiled down at her and continued to drive in and out of her, increasing his speed. His body found its own rhythm, fucking her hard and fast. He pulled her legs up, spreading her wider in the process, plunging deeper. Her pussy gripped him even tighter now that his cock was wider due to the bumps. *Love swells* the vampires called them. He hadn't yet met a woman who didn't appreciate them, and Claire seemed to enjoy their effects now without even knowing what was giving her such pleasure.

He wished he could have gone on forever, but her pussy was gripping him too tightly, and the scent of her arousal almost drove him insane with lust. Knowing she was as close as he, he increased his rhythm and let himself go.

He felt the rush of his semen through his cock just as her interior muscles clenched around him as her orgasm broke. He joined her, thrusting into oblivion with one last stoke, spilling inside her as he did so.

Breathing heavily, he dropped his head to the crook of her neck. "You're perfect," he repeated once more and kissed her neck only to realize that his fangs had descended.

He knew what his vampire side demanded from him now. And he couldn't deny himself what he'd craved ever since he'd first touched her.

"Claire," he said softly, whispering into her ear. "Sleep now." His suggestive powers, skills every vampire possessed, lulled her into sleep.

He licked over the plump vein in her neck and peeled his lips back from his teeth. When his fangs touched her smooth skin, he shivered. Then he sank his fangs into her neck and pierced her vein. Rich blood ran over his tongue and down his throat, revitalizing his body. His cock moved of its own volition, delivering gentle thrusts, and his hands caressed Claire's sleeping body. She moaned softly.

"Yes. Take me," she murmured in her sleep.

Did she know what he was doing? Could she feel him? It couldn't be—his suggestive powers had put her to sleep. Or had he subconsciously only put her into a light slumber so she could still experience what he did to her? Because he wanted her to know what was happening?

He sent a question into her mind. *Claire, do you like what I'm doing?* He sucked harder on her vein while he thrust in and out of her sex.

"More . . ."

Yes, baby, I'll give you more.

Because he wanted more too. More of Claire.

CHAPTER FIVE

Claire had woken in her own bed, alone, her body still humming from a night of lovemaking with Eric. To her surprise, she wore her nightgown. For a moment she lay there, daydreaming. She felt no regret having given herself to a stranger she'd met only hours earlier. In fact, it had been liberating to be with a man who knew nothing about her. She could just pretend to be who she wanted to be: a young woman who had her life ahead of her.

She couldn't remember how she'd gotten back to her room. And she'd had strange dreams: of Eric biting her neck while he made love to her. She'd enjoyed it, loved the way it had made her feel. She shook her head at the strange notion and got out of bed.

Instantly she swayed, her head suddenly pounding. A sharp stab of pain radiated through her. "Oh God, no!" she whimpered. Another attack was imminent. She searched her room for her handbag and found it sitting on a chair. She rushed to it and opened it, rummaging through it, trying to find her pills. But she couldn't see them. Frantically she spilled the contents of her bag onto the bed, but her pill bottle was not among them.

Another stab of pain assaulted her. She gripped the bed frame for support, waiting for the wave to pass. Then she ran to the door. She had to get Mrs. Adams to call the doctor, the one she'd seen a few days earlier.

As she grabbed the doorknob, her eyes fell onto the dresser next to it. On it stood her pill bottle, a neatly written note underneath it.

I found it in the hallway, it said on stationary belonging to Sunseekers' Inn.

Relieved, she snatched the bottle, twisted its top off and popped two pills into her mouth. She swallowed them down with the last swig of the water from the bottle that stood on her nightstand.

Her heart beat frantically now, and none of the bliss she'd felt last night was left. Her illness was encroaching further and further into her life, trying to wipe out any joy she had.

She didn't want to wither away and have the last image of her life be that of excruciating pain. No, the thing she wanted to remember was the pleasure she'd felt when making love to Eric. She wouldn't allow her illness to overshadow that. That's why she had to take charge of her life now—or rather, her death.

She'd never truly believed in the power of the hot spring. She'd lied to herself, not wanting to confront the inevitable. But now she was strong enough. She'd felt something beautiful the night before, and she wanted to leave this world while this memory was still strong in her mind. For a few hours she'd been happy. It was all she could have hoped for.

Ignoring the pain in her head, she set her bag on the bed and started packing, even though she couldn't take anything with her where she was going.

***

Eric woke from an uneasy sleep. During the entire day, he'd drifted in and out of sleep, which was unusual for him. But the events of the previous night had shaken him. His mind couldn't rest, because it was working overtime. It wasn't fair that Claire should die so young, when he was contemplating taking his own life. How ironic was that? She wanted to live but would soon die, while he wanted to die instead of living forever. Life was cruel.

Last night he'd felt needed for the first time in his life. Needed by another person. He'd been able to give Claire pleasure and make her feel desired because he desired her. More than he'd desired any other woman before. Was it because he wanted to save her? Or was it more? Had he finally met a woman who could give him the purpose in his life that he so desperately craved? Had he found somebody to take care of, somebody to give his soul to?

And what about the reason that had brought him to the island? If the hot spring really had any powers, then why wasn't it granting Claire's wish? Or did it indeed need a sacrifice, one that *he* could make?

He had to speak to Claire. After last night he felt close to her, and he hoped she felt the same. If she did, there was something he could offer her. But it had to be her choice.

Impatient for the sun to set, Eric took a shower and got dressed. As soon as the sun dipped below the horizon, he tore out of his room and headed for Claire's. He knocked at the door, but there was no answer. He tried the doorknob and it turned. When he looked inside the room, he jerked back involuntarily: the bed was made and the room was empty. All of Claire's personal effects were gone.

Panicked, he rushed downstairs and found Mrs. Adams behind the reception counter.

"Miss Culver? Where is she?" he asked without as much as a greeting.

Mrs. Adams raised her eyebrows and gave him a curious look. "She checked out."

His heart stopped. "Where did she go?"

"I don't know."

"What did she say to you? She must have said something." He didn't care that he sounded desperate.

Mrs. Adams frowned. "Now that you're asking. Well, hmm, she said she was ready to leave now. When I asked her where she was heading, she just said *where there is no pain*."

His heart clenched. "And you didn't stop her?" But he didn't wait for her answer and instead charged out of the house.

Eric stared into the night. Where would she go to end it all? Where would he go? For a moment he let his mind travel, then he could see the place where he would go to end his life: the last place where he'd been happy.

He ran as fast as he could, not caring if anybody saw him and wondered how a man could run as fast as a car. He had to get to Claire. His legs carried him to the beach where they'd made love the night before. He passed the shed, his eyes scanning the shore, when he perceived a movement to his right.

He whipped around and saw Claire standing there, staring at the surf. Relief swept through him.

"I'm a coward. I couldn't do it." She turned to him, tears in her eyes. "I'm dying, Eric. I have brain cancer." She pointed her arm toward the ocean. "I tried to kill myself before the pain gets too much, but I…"

He captured her in his arms, holding her closely, and stroked his palm over her hair. "I know, baby."

She pulled back slightly to look at him. "You knew?"

"I found your pill bottle. Mrs. Adams told me the rest."

A sob tore from her chest. "Is that why you slept with me? Because you pitied me?"

He felt her pull away, but he didn't loosen his grip. "No! I made love to you because I desire you. I want you more than anything else in this life."

More tears streamed over her cheeks. With his thumb he wiped them away.

"Claire, what I tell you now might seem fantastic, but it's the truth. Do you think you can keep an open mind?"

"About what?"

"You want to live, don't you?"

A sob bigger than the previous one disturbed the night.

"Then I have a solution for you. The spring worked, Claire. Because it brought us together. You've wished for a cure. I can give you one."

Her big blue eyes stared at him, half in hope, half in doubt. "How?"

"I'm a vampire, Claire, I'm immortal, and I can give you immortality."

He watched her eyes as her expression changed to disbelief. "No." She shook her head and pulled back. He dropped his arms to release her. "No."

"It's true. And you know it. Deep down you know, don't you?" He focused his gaze on the spot on her neck where he'd bitten her the night before.

Her hand came up to touch that some spot.

"You know it because you felt it last night. You sensed my bite when I was making love to you for the second time."

Her lips parted as if she wanted to say something, but nothing came out. Then she stroked over her neck. "I dreamed it."

"It wasn't a dream."

Slowly, realization seemed to settle in. "It was too real for a dream."

He nodded and put his hand on her neck, brushing over the bite mark. Only he and other vampires could see it. To humans, the mark was invisible.

"How?" she whispered and looked straight at him.

"I can turn you into a vampire. It will wipe out any illness or disease you have. You'll be immortal and without pain."

"Immortal? And how would I live? In the dark? Drinking blood?" Her lips trembled.

"The dark can be beautiful." He pointed to the canopy of stars in the night sky. "Even in the dark there's light, there's beauty."

"And the blood?" she whispered.

"There are ways. You wouldn't have to feed from humans. There are blood banks. Or you could feed from me."

Her eyes widened. "From another vampire?"

"As long as one of us drinks human blood, it would be sufficient to nourish us both."

She looked at him for a long while, clearly contemplating his words. "I'm scared."

Eric reached for her, stroking his knuckles over her cheek. "I know. But I'll be here for you."

Slowly she stepped closer, until their bodies touched. "Why would you do that for me? Didn't you come here with a wish too?"

He smiled. "Do you know what I wished for?"

She shook her head.

"To be mortal again." He sighed. "But I understand now that it wasn't my heart's true desire. It wasn't my mortality I wanted."

"How do you know that?"

"I know because I'm holding my heart's true desire in my arms right now. I know now that I was drawn to this island so I could meet you and fulfill *your* wish."

"So the spring really does work?"

He kissed her lips. "Yes. But only for those who are prepared to open their eyes and trust in the impossible. So, Claire, do you trust me to give you a second life?"

Slowly, she nodded. "I trust you. I don't know why, but I do."

Gently, he pulled her down into the sand and placed her on his lap, cradling her in his arms.

"It won't hurt," he promised. "I'll drain you of your human blood, and at your last heartbeat, I'll feed you mine. When you wake, you'll be like me, a creature of the night."

"What if it doesn't work?"

"I promise you, it will work."

She swallowed and her voice trembled when she spoke her next words. "When I wake, will you still be here?" Her eyes glimmered with hope.

"Claire, I want a life with you. If you want that too, I'll be with you through eternity as your lover. If you don't, I'll be by your side as your friend. The choice is yours."

There was no hesitation in her voice when she responded to him. "Bite me, my lover."

She closed her eyes and whispered again, "My lover for eternity."

His heart jumping with joy, he lowered his lips to her neck and pierced her skin with his fangs.

THRILL SEEKER

COLLEEN GLEASON

CHAPTER ONE

Seeker's Island

Population 2,310

Home of the Legendary Hot Springs

"Where you find your heart's desire"

My heart's desire? Teddy Mack grimaced. *My only heart's desire is to figure out the bloody ending to my damn book.*

She tossed the pamphlet onto the foyer table at Grantworth Cottage and swept past it, dragging her rolling suitcase and computer bag toward the bedroom.

"I'll finish it by the end of the month," she'd promised her agent Harriet—who'd gone on to guarantee her editor that, yes, the next T. J. Mack book would be turned in on time.

Or nearly on time.

Well, six months late wasn't really on time. But publishing was a slow business at best, and it wasn't as if Teddy hadn't turned in her other five manuscripts—all of which went on to be bestselling thrillers—when they were due.

"This book is kicking my ass," she told Harriet two weeks ago. "I don't know why."

"You need to get away. Somewhere where no one will bother you. Where you won't be tempted to post pictures of your office on Facebook instead of writing, or go out to lunch every day instead of writing, or watch Netflix instead of—"

"That's research. Netflix is," Teddy defended herself. "I have to stay up on pop culture, or how will I know what to write about? And Facebook is social media, and I have to have a presence there, and on Twitter, and—"

"You have to write a good book. That's what you have to do. Forget Facebook and Twitter, and watching a whole season of *Friday Night Lights* in one week—"

"Five seasons. Kyle Chandler is impossible to resist."

"*Five seasons? In one week?* No wonder your book isn't done!" Harriet's voice rose, then tapered off into a more modulated tone. "You need to go somewhere without Internet or Wi-Fi. Somewhere where you won't be distracted."

And that was how Teddy had come to be settling in at the smallest, most remote rental cottage on Seeker's Island. The ten-mile-wide tourist destination was just a thirty-minute ferry ride from the west coast of Florida. But it might as well be the middle of nowhere, for Harriet had ensured that Grantworth Cottage was too far from the small business district to have Wi-Fi. No e-mail, no Facebook, no Wikipedia. No Netflix or Hulu.

She'd even left her smartphone at home so she wouldn't be tempted to try out the 3G connectivity on Seeker's Island, temporarily transferring her number to a cheap cell phone.

The bungalow was more than four miles from the array of quaint shops. As there were no motor vehicles on the island, Teddy had been transported to her temporary home in a jouncing golf cart. The young man who brought her, Carl, dropped her bags on the porch and returned to town without delay—presumably under orders from her mercenary agent. There were supposed to be food deliveries every other day, so at least she wouldn't starve.

The place was small and efficient, with a kitchen area that merged into the living room, two tiny bedrooms, and a smaller bathroom. No television either.

"I can take some time to unpack," Teddy said aloud, as if Harriet might be lurking about, judging her for hanging up her sundresses and finding a place for her underthings, three pairs of sandals, and two swimming suits.

Of course she'd overpacked. That had been part of the procrastination, and the indecision that paralyzed her for the last nine months. It wasn't as if she'd be wearing anything besides shorts or yoga pants and a tank top for the next few weeks.

She felt sick to her stomach. Weeks. *I've only got two weeks. I* have *to finish this.*

"Maybe I should go check out the damned hot springs," she muttered, setting her laptop on the table next to the bedroom armchair. "Drown myself in it for a while. It couldn't hurt."

CHAPTER TWO

"What do you mean, you made a mistake?" Oscar London swiped a forearm across his forehead to catch the trickle of sweat, and the heavy bag of equipment he was holding clunked into his shoulder.

"Uh…well, Dr. London, I'm so sorry, but there was a last-minute booking that came in, and someone *else* approved it, not realizing you'd already leased Grantworth Cottage for the month, and…well…there's someone else staying here already."

Oscar looked at the three man-sized equipment bags he'd just lugged onto the porch, then back at the golf cart where a fourth one, as well as his backpack, sat. Then he looked at the gangly, red-haired college kid named Carl who'd just arrived in his own golf cart to deliver the bad news. "I'm not leaving. You people made the mistake, I paid for the rental, you can just move your other client to another location."

"Uhm…but, like, there's…not any other location available. You see, there's a wedding happening on the island, and—"

"Look." Oscar set down the heavy bag he was still holding and put his hands on his hips. "I'm not trying to be unreasonable, but I need to stay here. I rented this place because of its location and because I won't be disturbed, plus it has the space I need to set up my lab. So I'm not giving it up."

"Well. Uh. You brought your own *refrigerator?*" The kid looked at the compact unit next to the rest of the equipment, then at Oscar, who just nodded wearily. "Well, uh…there are two bedrooms. You could, like…both of you could stay." Carl rushed out this suggestion. His cheeks matched his flaming hair.

"Fine. I don't care. As long as they don't get in my way. Wait. How many of them are there?" With his luck, he'd end up sharing the damned place with a couple on their honeymoon. *No fucking way.* He thrust away visions of Marcie and Lew.

"Just one person. A, uh, writer named Teddy Mack."

"Great. Now let me finish unloading my stuff so I can get to work." He looked around, picturing the map of the island in his head. The hot springs were on the westernmost part of the island, just about where the terrain rose in a low, rolling hill.

"Do you...uh...want me to tell Teddy?" ventured the kid.

"Huh?" He turned from scanning the horizon. Carl was already edging off the porch, clearly ready to flee, so Oscar took pity on him. "No. I'll take care of it. But if there are any problems, I'm sending him to you."

Carl didn't delay, speeding off in his golf cart as Oscar lugged the rest of his supplies inside. *Thirty minutes to set up the basics, then I'm off to the so-called Legendary Hot Springs.*

It was a ridiculous way to spend his summer, analyzing a supposed magical pool of water. Oscar was fully aware of this. But it beat staying in Baltimore. He didn't want to be anywhere near the city when Marcie married Lew, because with his luck, he'd run into them, or her parents, or their mutual colleagues who'd been invited. Since he wasn't teaching any summer classes, he got the hell out.

So he was here. In a small white cottage with cobalt blue trim and shutters, a covered porch, and a gray roof. With a one-room kitchen/dining/living space that didn't appear to have air conditioning, but was equipped with very large ceiling fans. A space he was going to have to share with a writer. Oscar grumbled a curse.

At least writers were supposed to be anti-social. Maybe the guy would be locked up in his bedroom all day, working on whatever he was working on.

One thing was sure. The writer wasn't going to be using the living room or kitchen, because that was where Oscar was setting up his lab.

Forty minutes later, he had the basics in place: the small fridge for samples, the enclave for sanitizing, plus the pressure cooker, incubator, and two microscopes. Good thing he brought his own power strips, because the bungalow—which was probably built in the fifties—was severely lacking in outlets. It'd be a miracle if he didn't blow a fuse when he had everything up and running.

Oscar pulled on his work vest and tucked gloves and syringes into their slots. The rest of his equipment (cubitainers, glass bottles, and biohazard bags) he packed in a small cooler. Then, slinging it like a messenger bag, he set off on foot with a bottle of water in hand.

The walk took him along a clearly marked, narrow trail. The path was overhung with palms and studded with bright, tropical flowers, winding through unkempt terrain. Not as thick and lush as a rainforest, but certainly not like a common, scrubby Floridian landscape. As it was well into the afternoon, the sun was hot and high, but there was enough shade to make the hike comfortable.

He could hear the rumbling of the springs before he reached them. The air seemed to become more humid and heavy, and the birds and what light breeze there was had quieted.

A sign read: *Hot Springs.* There was a metal garbage can, a park bench, and even a few dirt parking spaces right next to the notice.

He came around a sharp corner to find himself in a small clearing. Thc rumble he'd heard earlier was probably more from the small waterfall than the actual springs themselves, but either way, the pool was a gently roiling mass of steaming water. Sitting in the water, messing up his plan and contaminating everything, was a woman.

Well, at least it wasn't a whole schoolroom of kids with their pretty blue-eyed teacher. Or a bachelorette party. *Stop thinking about Marcie, dammit.*

The woman looked over at him as Oscar approached.

"I see you ignored the signs too."

Though her hair was dry, her face was rosy and moist from the steam. It was a pretty face, no denying it, with fine, arching brows and full lips. And from what he could see above the surging water, the rest of her bathing-suited self wasn't too bad either. She had brown hair pulled back in a clip or something, and even from here, he could see her eyes were filled with humor.

Oscar looked around. She seemed to be by herself. "Yep."

"I bet pretty much everyone does." She shifted and he caught sight of more cleavage than was healthy for a guy who was avoiding women like the plague right now. But whoever she was had a nice rack and smooth, toned arms.

"You here by yourself?"

"Yes. Is there something wrong with a woman being in a hot spring by herself instead of with some guy?"

"No. Just wondered." He unslung his tool bag, considering whether there was a polite way to ask her to leave. Probably not.

"If I were a nervous sort of woman—which I'm not—with a great imagination—which I do, in fact, have—I'd be wondering what's in that bag. And why you want to make sure I'm here all alone." She narrowed a look at his things. "For all I know you could have rope in there. Or duct tape. Maybe a gun or a knife, even. A camera, to take pictures of the scene?"

"Or syringes and plastic baggies and gloves." He produced them with a flourish. "You do have an imagination."

"Yeah. Sometimes." She slumped down in the water so it bubbled up around her shoulders, suddenly looking miserable. "*Only* sometimes." She tipped her head up, closing her eyes as she rested her head against the stone rim behind her.

Oscar ignored her as he pulled on a pair of gloves. He could still take a sample, but he'd much rather have one not freshly contaminated with sunblock, perfume, deodorant, and whatever else she might have clinging to her body. Shampoo. Body lotion.

"Gloves? Hm. Maybe I *should* be worried." She was sitting up again, watching him with interest.

If you don't stop talking to me, maybe you should. He dug out a cubitainer and syringe, closing the top of the cooler to keep it cold.

"What are you doing?" She sat back up and was watching with bright eyes. "What's all that for?"

"I'm sampling for E. coli in the water," he said, slanting a sideways look at her. Maybe that would get her out. "Among other nasty things."

"Really." She didn't sound concerned. "I thought this was a magical hot spring. You know, where you get your heart's desire if you sit in it." Her expression dimmed and she slid back into the roiling pool, a wash of desperation on her face. "I wouldn't think that sort of stuff would grow in a magic pool. You know?"

"This isn't Harry Potter," he growled. "There's no such thing as magic."

"So why are you testing the water then? Is there really a chance there might be E. coli in it?" She did look a little concerned now.

"I don't know what's in it. That's why I'm testing it." He moved over to the edge of the pool. The heat rose in waves, dampening his skin. Droplets of water splashed up from the churning water, spraying him in the face.

He hesitated, scoping out the situation. To get a good sample, he should be in the center of the pool, not near the edge, where it was shallow. Although the water was so enthusiastic, there was no danger of his sample being stagnant. Still, the sample needed to come from the center, where the grit and dirt from the floor wouldn't be mixed in.

"What's wrong?" The woman was still watching him. Still asking questions.

He was close enough now to see strands of dark hair clinging to her cheek and the damp skin of her neck. She had a smattering of freckles across her nose, and another dash of them over her bare shoulders. He put her age at around thirty or so. "Nothing. Just trying to figure out the best way to reach the center."

"If you don't want to get in, I can do it for you," she offered.

Oscar looked at her, ready to refuse—then decided that wasn't a bad idea after all. That way he wouldn't have to zip off his switchbacks and remove his shoes and socks—which would entail taking off the sterile gloves he'd just donned. Which he'd have been thinking about previously if he hadn't been distracted by her. "You'd have to wear gloves."

"I think I can handle that." She scooted across the pool toward him and he gave her a pair.

"Don't touch the inside of the container," he instructed when she was ready. "And put it below the surface about six to eight inches, like so." He demonstrated by turning the cubitainer upside-down and bringing it straight down. "Fill it all the way up, then empty it out. Do that three times, and the last time, keep it filled. I'll give you the cap when you're finished."

"Why do I have to fill it—and empty it?—three times?"

"To make sure every area of the surface is touched by the sample before you actually fill it up."

"Are you sure you trust me to do this?" She gave him a sassy grin, holding out her gloved hand for the container.

"I'm beginning to wonder," he muttered, but let his mouth soften into a little smile. She seemed harmless—relatively intelligent and able to follow directions.

"Well, you could climb in yourself. But then you might get your heart's desire…or *worse*," she teased, "the spring might not be magical at all, and you might *not* get your heart's desire. And that would be a big bummer." Her grin faded a little, and she exhaled deeply. "For more than one of us."

Apparently, she was hoping for *her* heart's desire.

And as for his…well, Oscar knew what he wanted more than anything in the world. And it wasn't going to happen unless—in about twenty-four hours—Marcie left Lew standing at the altar.

He handed her the container a little more abruptly than he intended, but she didn't drop it. As she turned to swim to the center, he caught a glimpse of her rear end, tight and curvy, covered in a bright blue swimming suit.

He couldn't wait to get out of here.

CHAPTER THREE

Teddy ate dinner in town.

Her excuse for doing so, should Harriet happen to ask, was that she wasn't sure whether any food had been delivered to the cottage yet. And it was nearly evening by the time she left the hot springs, after helping the adorably nerdy microbiologist—at least, she assumed he was a microbiologist, but she'd never gotten around to asking—and Teddy was getting hungry.

She could use the exercise and fresh air the walk to town would bring. Maybe it would kick her creativity into gear.

Plus…it was too late in the day to actually set up her computer and start working. She figured a good night's sleep, acclimating her to her new, quiet, Wi-Fi-less surroundings, would put her in the right frame of mind to get to work first thing in the morning.

And that would also give the hot springs' ju-ju a chance to work. Just in case they really *were* magical.

At this point, Teddy figured, nothing could hurt.

So, she put the sundress back on over her swimming suit and left the geeky scientist packing up his equipment. The well-marked path to town was about four miles; when she returned to the cottage later, she would complete the last side of a triangular journey from cottage to hot springs to town and then home.

Teddy ate a leisurely dinner of blackened grouper, wondering if she'd run into the microbiologist again. Despite the fact that he didn't say much and was bordering on *Big Bang Theory* nerdliness, he was pretty cute. His white button-down shirt had looked crisp and cool, contrasting with his freckled forearms and their rich, gold tan. He had a great head of thick, reddish-brown hair and large hands that should have been clumsy, but had handled his tools and accoutrements with ease. He was wearing zip-off cargo pants with lots of pockets, so she hadn't been able to see his legs, but the bag he carried with ease appeared damn heavy.

Unfortunately, the interesting microbiologist didn't appear and dinner was over all too soon. But Teddy wasn't ready to return to the cottage and her lurking deadline. Instead, she wandered in and out of shops on Main Street. And when she heard live music streaming out of a place called The Tiki Bar, she went in to listen.

By the time she was ready to go, it was after midnight. (No procrastination here.) Fortunately, Carl was in the bar too, and she offered him twenty bucks to give her a ride back to the cottage (she'd have to plan better next time she stayed so late in town).

Tired, and a little—just a little—tipsy from one too many pineapply umbrella drinks, Teddy let herself in the front door of the cottage. She fumbled around for a light switch, didn't immediately find one, and gave up looking, choosing to use the moonlight to find her way to the bedroom.

But she wasn't so out of it that she didn't notice the boxes on the kitchen and living room tables. *The food's been delivered. Jeepers. That looks like enough to feed an army. I'll check it out in the morning. Hope they put the perishable stuff away.*

Five minutes later, she was tucked beneath her covers and slipping into sleep.

***

A loud noise had her bolting upright. Sun blazed through the window and a squinty-eyed look at the bedside clock (her cell phone was too far away to reach) told her it was just after seven. Groggy and shocked out of a sound sleep, Teddy stumbled out of bed. Whatever had awakened her sounded like a heavy thud—very nearby.

Like, in her living room.

She of the very active imagination looked around for a weapon—although why someone would break in in the morning rather than in the dead of night was beyond her—and her eyes lit on a pair of water skis propped in the corner.

Another loud noise from beyond, followed by a muffled human exclamation, had Teddy grabbing one of the skis (it was either that or the hairdryer). Hefting the unwieldy weapon, she hurried to the bedroom door and peeked around into the living room.

There was a man there.

Teddy ducked back inside. Her heart pounded, her palms slick, she drew in a deep breath, calming herself. *What the hell?*

She peered back out and took a better look. All she could see was an arm and a shoulder, plus the hint of a leg and hip as he moved around. Whoever he was, he had stuff—equipment—all over the place. All the boxes and things she saw last night and assumed was food belonged to him.

"Who the hell are you?" She stalked out, ski in hand. Unfortunately, the damn thing was too long and the pointy end snagged in the shag carpet from the seventies, causing it to catch and her to stumble, bumping her head against the ski. *Nice going, Mack.*

The man turned and they both froze, gaping at each other. "It's you?" he said.

"*You!* What the hell are you doing here? Did you *follow* me?" Teddy couldn't have written a better story herself: the man who'd set up some sort of scientific lab *in her summer rental* was the nerdly scientist from the hot spring.

But maybe he wasn't a nerdly scientist after all. Maybe he *was* a serial killer. He had enough of a lab set up to torture her if he pleased. And they were too far away from civilization for anyone to hear her scream… (Great tagline for her next book.)

"*You're* the writer?" he said, snapping off a plastic glove. And he didn't sound at all pleased about it.

"*I'm* the writer," she snarled, and realized her head was pounding, right above her nose. Maybe she shouldn't have had that extra drink last night after all. "And this is my cottage—where I'm supposed to have privacy and solitude so I can finish my damn book—and what in the hell is all *this*?"

"Carl—did you meet Carl?"

"Yes, I met Carl. And I'm going to be having words with him about—"

But he was already shaking his head. "It won't help. They screwed up and rented the place to both of us, and there aren't any other rooms available on the island. So we're stuck sharing the place." He looked at her, his eyes tracing the ski and then skimming over her tank top—under which she was braless, of course, then down over her legs (bared by a pair of loose shorts). "When he said there was a writer, I didn't know it was you—I mean, that you were a woman. He said your name was Teddy."

"Teddy Mack. Wish I could say it was a pleasure to meet you, but I can't." She set the ski to lean against the wall and crossed her arms over her breasts. "Are you serious—there's nowhere else you can go? I have to finish a book! I'm already late, and I can't write with all this going on!"

Panic rose in her chest. She'd planned to wake up this morning, bright and early, have a cup of tea on the wrap-around porch and absorb the fresh air and sunshine...and then pull out her laptop and dive right in to the story.

But now everything was off. Mucked up. And her thoughts couldn't be further from the edgy, cliff-hanging thrillers about Sargent Blue, who saved the world at least once in every single book.

What the hell am I going to do? Teddy felt the sting of frustrated tears gathering at the corners of her eyes. *I'm so damn behind, so uninspired, so freaking burned-out and scared...I just don't think I can do this.*

And now this.

My career is over.

She realized with a start the man—whose name she still didn't know—had said something. "What? Sorry...I...was thinking." She blinked and refocused. *Get it together, Mack. You're not giving up yet.*

"I guess that's natural for a writer—daydreaming. I offered you coffee."

"No thanks. I have some tea. But it sure would be great to know your name." *So when I call Harriet to chew her butt over this, I have a name for my problem. No,* her *problem. She booked the place.*

"Oscar London."

"Seriously?"

He grimaced and opened a small fridge (he'd brought his own

fridge?). "My parents had no idea."

"No, really—it's a *great* name. I know names, believe me. It took me three weeks to come up with my main character's name, but once I did, I knew it was perfect. And Oscar London…it's great. It suits you."

"I'm delighted you approve." There was a little more snarkiness in his voice than she'd expected. "I have work to do, and so, apparently, do you. So…" He made a little waving gesture, as if to say, *Off with you, you pesky creature.*

"I can't write with you making all sorts of racket out here. And I can't concentrate with you *in my space*." The panic escaped and clawed her chest again, its talons sharper than ever. "This isn't going to work. One of us is going to have to leave. And it isn't going to be me." Teddy knew her voice had gone high and thready, and she despised herself for it. But her career was on the line.

Oscar London ignored her. He'd turned back to his project—whatever it was—and was putting a glass container in a machine that looked like a small front-loading washer.

"What's that? And what are you doing, anyway? Are you really testing for E. coli?"

"It's an autoclave. Used for sterilizing equipment with steam." He closed the door and turned to a computer. Ignoring her, he began tapping on the keyboard, using the hunt-and-peck method. Just watching him pick at the keys with two fingers made her twitchy.

"You never learned to type?" She edged closer, looking at the screen, and conveniently ignoring how much she hated it when someone looked over *her* shoulder while she was working.

"No."

The screen was filled with a form he was completing: numbers, date, time, location, etc. Nothing worth being distracted over. "So the autoclave sterilizes equipment before you put the samples in it?"

He turned. "You sure are talkative for someone who has a book to write."

Teddy exhaled a long breath. "Yeah. Well, I've been having a little writer's block." She watched as he measured out a sample of water from the container she'd filled yesterday, pouring it carefully into a smaller vessel that had, presumably, been sterilized. "Microbiologists don't get writer's block. You just know what you have to do, and you do it. You follow the procedures and *voila!* Done."

"Yep. It's that easy. So if you're going to stand there instead of work, how about getting me another cup of coffee? Black."

"Might as well." When she came back, he'd stripped off the gloves he was wearing. His reddish-brown hair was standing nearly on end, obviously rumpled from a hand jamming through it, presumably post-glove-removal.

"So you've got writer's block." He took the cup and sipped. "What kind of story are you working on?"

Teddy wandered over, looking in the boxes of equipment. Tubes, small bottles, larger bottles, petri dishes, labels, and syringes of all sizes. "You brought your own refrigerator?"

"Yes." His voice sounded *very* patient. "I have to make sure the samples are kept at a precise temperature, and the only way to do that is to use my own equipment. I check the temp first thing in the morning and several times through the day."

"Have fridge, will travel. Huh. That's one dangerous-looking microscope you have there." She walked over to the complicated instrument branded Horix and peered through the eyepieces. She saw nothing but black.

"It's a digital microscope. The image appears on that computer monitor. But of course, the light has to be turned on, and there has to be something on a slide." He snapped on another pair of gloves. "And it's worth over two-K, so please be careful."

"Fascinating." He gave her a jaundiced look, and she said, "No, seriously. This is the kind of thing I find utterly interesting. You never know when I'll learn something that will show up in a book—hey. *Wait.*" A spike of excitement rushed through her. "Maybe you can help me!"

He muttered something that sounded like "Oh, joy," but she wasn't certain. Either way, Teddy didn't care. If there was one thing she'd learned about being a writer was that ideas—and plot solutions—could come from anyone at any time. She just had to be open to them.

"So I have my character in a real fix. I need to have him—"

"Let me guess. Save the world." Even though he was facing the other direction, dropping something on a glass slide, she swore he rolled his eyes.

"Hey. It *sells*."

"Why doesn't someone ever write a book about the world *not* getting saved? Just to see what happens—you know, the aftermath and all? What would it be like fifty years after the earth was destroyed?"

"Wow. You sure are an optimistic kind of guy." Teddy edged closer.

"My former fiancée is getting married today. Sorry I'm not in a great mood."

"Well, that's a bummer. I'm really sorry. Is that the wedding that's here on the island?"

"No. Hell no. Do you think I'd stick around if it were? I left Baltimore yesterday morning—I teach at Maryland—and came directly here."

"Equipment and all. To test the hot springs water." He grunted an ambiguous reply and she said, "So, can I help?"

"I thought you were supposed to be writing." But he gestured to a box of latex gloves. "I could use an assistant. Just don't touch anything with your bare skin, don't sneeze or cough or otherwise spread germs."

CHAPTER FOUR

Oscar didn't really need an assistant, but it was obvious the writer wasn't going to leave him alone. And at least her incessant questions and poking around kept him distracted from what was happening back in Baltimore.

Whenever Teddy pressed him about why he was testing the hot springs water, he launched into a long-winded explanation about major cations and anions, and how the turbidity could be problematic if it was too high, and whether the total iron level complied with the expected presence of tardigrades and phages in the body of water, among other things, until her eyes glazed over.

"I get the impression you don't read very many action-adventure novels," she said, neatly handing him a petri dish he'd requested. "Oh, there's an idea." Her blue eyes sparkled with interest. "The villains could be growing some random bad stuff—"

"Random bad stuff?" He lifted a brow. She was quite entertaining, he had to give her that, with a conversation that bounced around from topic to topic. And with those nice, perky breasts shifting beneath her snug tank top and her pretty feet with pale blue nail polish and a smattering of freckles on top, he found himself finding her presence less and less intrusive.

"Well, we'll have to figure out what it exactly *is*."

"We?"

"But it's something bad…and they've been growing it in a slew of petri dishes. They're going to release it into the New York City water system—no, wait, they're going to put it in the water pitchers at the United Nations! You know how they always have water for all the attendees at a meeting like that—you see those pitchers at their seats?"

"Right. Someone's going to grow some…what did you call it? Oh, right, 'random bad stuff' in a bunch of petri dishes…and poison the water at the United Nations…and why are they doing this?"

She drew in a long, deep breath, then expelled it forcefully. "I don't know. I haven't the foggiest idea. That's why I'm stuck. I've got my hero in New York City, and he's got to save a bunch of people—"

"Besides, I hate to tell you this—even if they grew a variety of specimens of the RBS—"

"RBS? Oh, I get it." She grinned and her eyes lit up. Her face changed and she went from being irritatingly cute to a woman who totally pushed his hormone buttons. *Whoa.* "Random bad stuff."

He found his voice. "Right. So. Even if they were growing a variety of these specimens, first, there's no way to transport them safely—"

"Sure there is. We'd figure it out."

He couldn't quite get with the "we" stuff, but Oscar let her continue. It was fun and stimulating to have a brainstorming session with someone who wasn't restricted by science, but only by her own creativity. Which seemed bountiful.

"They could transport the petri dishes in a cooler, for example. And bring it in with the caterers for the UN. It'll be a big meeting, with all the important world leaders there."

"That could work, if it could get past security—which is a big if—but the bigger problem is the minute the RBS is released from the petri dishes, it'll be exposed and most likely die. You can't grow microbes in a carefully controlled environment like petri dishes and then release it to the wild, so to speak. The chances of it surviving are very low."

Teddy grumbled. "Right. Well, there is a *chance*, isn't there?"

"A very slim one. Can you grab me that pencil?"

She reached for it too quickly, bumping a beaker, which knocked the pencil into rolling off the table. She, of course, had to bend over and pick it up…which gave him an uninterrupted view directly down the front of her tank top. Nipples and all.

"So it must be tough being a scientist and watching action adventure movies or reading those kinds of books," she said, having no idea what a sight she'd just displayed. "You know too much, and the suspension of disbelief is even more difficult for someone like you."

"I can only get through the ones where the author has actually done research," he said, turning away before he found himself trying to find something else for her to pick up. "And when the story makes sense, even from a scientific point of view."

She looked as if she were about to say something when the James Bond theme began to play from one of the bedrooms. Teddy's entire demeanor changed to sharp tension. "Oh, crap," she wailed. "That's my agent. And I haven't even opened my laptop." Nevertheless, she stripped off her gloves and tossed them on the table, then hurried to the bedroom.

Oscar couldn't hear the ensuing conversation, although the rise and fall of her tones came through the cottage walls. It didn't sound like a happy conversation, but it wasn't any of his business. With a glance at the clock—just pushing eleven—he turned his attention back to the distraction of work.

He had to focus on something, or his mind would head back to Baltimore where, at four o'clock, Marcie was going to walk down the aisle in a white dress and veil to marry Lew Benson.

Finally, he had a good, sterile sample ready and put it in place on the microscope dash. Turned on the lights, made a few adjustments—magnification, light—and took a look. Normal water molecular structure. Tardigrades, ostracods, phages, and a variety of other, harmless microbial specimens.

"Hm." Oscar frowned. He dialed back on the magnification to see the full image. A little jump of interest spiked inside him. *Never seen anything like that before.* He adjusted the magnification and looked closer.

Instead of the soft, organic shapes he was used to seeing, Oscar was examining something that appeared crystalline and spiky. Shiny and silvery, even under the microscope. That little jump of interest turned into something more like a leap, and he moved the slide around to see if there were other examples of this unfamiliar microbe. There were...randomly, but more than one example. He quickly pulled out samples from a different cubitainer—maybe that first one had somehow been contaminated.

But no. There they were, the unrecognizable crystals, noticeable only at one hundred magnification. His flare of interest had blown into full excitement and disbelief.

Was it possible? *Was* there something special about the hot springs?

He'd never seen anything like this spiky crystal organism before. It didn't look like anything else.

Impossible. But....

A wave of hope suffused him, and he abruptly pushed it away. He was a scientist. Not a New Ager, not a spiritualist. He didn't believe in magic or mysticism or angels or any of that paranormal-supernatural stuff. So even if there *was* something unusual...unique...floating in the water, it could easily be attributed to some undiscovered species of microscopic crustacean or some rare microorganism native only to this small island.

It couldn't mean anything else.

But he looked at the clock. It was almost noon. Four hours till Marcie walked down the aisle. His palms were clammy, his insides churning. But what if...? Legends normally had to be rooted in something.

Don't be an idiot. You know better than to believe in that stuff.

"I should go get another sample," he said aloud. Just to make sure it was uncontaminated. He'd get it himself this time. He'd climb into the pool, gather three samples himself, making sure it was done correctly...and then he'd take another look.

"Another sample of what?"

He turned. Teddy was now attired in a sundress, which was probably a good thing. She looked determined, for her hair was pulled back into a knot at the back of her head and she carried a slim silver laptop that looked as if it weighed hardly more than a magazine.

"How did your phone call go?"

She made a face. "I don't want to talk about it. What are you getting a sample of?"

"The hot springs."

"Great. I'll come with you." She put down the laptop as if it were a hot potato. "Wait till I change."

CHAPTER FIVE

Teddy knew she should stay at the cottage, sit her ass in a chair, and pull out the laptop. What better time to work than when her distracting housemate was gone?

But here she was, traipsing through a near-jungle with the kind of grumpy, almost-redheaded scientist who'd taken over her space. Maybe if she helped him do what he needed to do, he'd finish up and leave and then she'd have the cottage to herself. *That* was a plan she could justify even to Harriet.

Maybe.

And besides, no one should have to be alone on the day his ex-fiancée married someone else. Teddy was going with him because it was the right thing to do.

Plus, she figured, it couldn't hurt for her to get into those hot springs again. Just in case the legend was true.

"For a famous hot spring, it's surprising there's no one here," Teddy said as they entered the clearing where the springs were. "Two days in a row."

"Fine by me. Less chance of contamination or disruption of my work." Oscar set down the heavy pack he'd been carrying and began to take off his hiking boots.

"It's pretty far from town, and there's no easy way to get here besides hiking. Plus they sell the water in little vials at some of the shops, so I guess if someone really wanted the effects of the pool, they could get it that way without traipsing all the way out here."

"Yep," he grunted, yanking off the second shoe. "You don't really believe in that legend stuff, do you?" Oscar looked up, shielding his eyes from the sun.

She shrugged. "I have an open mind. Who knows. And besides, you wouldn't really know if it worked or not, would you?"

"Doesn't the legend claim the hot springs give you your heart's desire? Seems like you'd know it when that happened."

"True. But what if you only *think* you know your heart's desire? Like, mine right now is to figure out how to finish this damn book. That's all I want. But what if deep down inside, my heart's desire is really to find another career? Or to write something different? Then I wouldn't finish the book, my career would be over—or at least it would change—and then I'd move on."

He shook his head. "I'm pretty sure most people know what they really want."

"So what's your heart's desire? What do you really want? After all, you're going to be sitting in the hot springs in about two minutes." She looked at him. "Oh. You want your fiancée back."

He didn't respond. But he didn't need to; it was written all over his face. Suddenly sober, Teddy walked over to the other side of the pool and slipped off her Dansko sandals, which worked just fine over any terrain *and* kept her feet from getting too hot. She pulled off her sundress, under which was her bright blue one-piece bathing suit, and climbed over the rocks to slide into the pool.

"Ohhh," she groaned as she settled into the heat of the water. It felt good, but it was *hot*. She swam over to where the waterfall poured into the pool and let the cool spill wash over her.

When she opened her eyes, her hair slicked back from her face, she saw that Oscar had zipped off the bottoms of his cargo pants, turning them into shorts, and taken off his shirt. And…he looked pretty damned good for a nerdly scientist who was mourning the loss of his fiancée.

Good enough that Teddy took her time checking him out when he wasn't looking. He wasn't bulky or hugely muscular, but wiry and toned and well-proportioned. Though he wasn't tanned, his shoulders and arms were covered with freckles that gave him a naturally bronzed appearance. His calves were muscular and he didn't have knobby knees, which was a major bonus in her book.

When he came over to the pool, Teddy looked away, suddenly acutely aware of the fact that, not only were they were alone here and now, but later tonight, they'd both be sleeping under the same roof. Separated by a thin wall. All of a sudden, the pool seemed even hotter, and she smoothed a hand over her wet hair and moved under the cooler waterfall again.

Get a grip, Teddy. You have a book to focus on.

But getting laid might lube things up…so to speak.

As if! I don't even know the guy.

You could get *to know him.*

"Pretty warm, huh?" Oscar said as she came out from under the waterfall. "Your face is really flushed." He eased into the pool with his own sigh of pleasure.

I'll bet it is. "So is yours."

"Even though it's damned hot today, it feels good in the water." He leaned against the side of the pool and the water surged and bubbled against the rocky rim. The waterfall splashed down between them, sending little sprays of cool droplets against her skin.

"So you don't like my RBS idea, huh?" Teddy asked, pulling her attention from his freckled shoulders.

"No."

She sighed and sank deeper into the water, despite the heat. Rivulets of sweat and water ran down her cheeks and throat. But maybe if the pool was going to do its work, she had to soak in it for a while. "Well, I've got to get my hero out of a difficult situation regardless."

"That's right. He's got to save the world." Oscar eased lower in the water too. His hair, now damp from the humidity, had begun to curl up into attractive little waves around his temples and neck. "You know what always gets me about books and movies like that is how complicated they get. Why does villainy have to be so complicated? Why can't it be a more simple situation than a plot to infect the entire city of New York with a virus or mechanized robots that are going to pilot a bunch of planes and crash them into the ocean with important people on them?"

Teddy sat up and the water surged away from her. "Hey, that's not a bad idea. Mechanized pilots…they could be flying Air Force One, maybe."

"No, no, no," he said. "Too complicated. Couldn't you just write a computer hacker who sends out a false news report—sort of like *War of the Worlds*, but done purposely—that causes the stock market to crash or even the Internet to go down because of too much traffic and not enough bandwidth? Then he could take over communication and cause all sorts of chaos."

She stared at him. "*Yes.* I like it. Hmm. That might work. Let me think on that..." She settled back and stared at the waterfall, working through the details.

"Like I said...too complicated. What about a trap door? Or what about a skylight? Put in a trap door or a sky—"

"*Yes!*" Teddy shouted, erupting from the pool. Her brain exploded with ideas and images and *answers*. "That's it! That's it! That's perfect!" Exhilaration and relief burst over her, and she was filled with joy. *That was it.*

Before she realized what she was doing, she surged toward Oscar and threw herself into his arms. She hugged him, then pulled back and smacked a kiss onto his warm, damp lips. "Thank you! You're amazing! You're—"

He pulled her back to him and kissed her again...this time much more thoroughly. His lips were warm and full and he tasted faintly of salt and sulphur. When she pulled away, she saw droplets of water clinging to his eyelashes and that his pupils had widened.

But her brain...it was on fire. It was furious—unleashed, undammed, and finally, after *months*, the ideas were flowing and spilling free. The energy pulsed through her like the roar of pool churning around her.

She had to go.

She had to *write.*

CHAPTER SIX

One minute, Oscar was easing into a long, deep, wholly unexpected kiss…and the next, he was sitting in the hot springs pool alone. The water surged and splashed even more violently than before.

"Thanks again!" Teddy was saying as she shoved her feet in a pair of thick-soled sandals. She looked as if she'd just been awarded a million dollars: her eyes bright, droplets of water spraying from her hair, movements quick and energetic. "You're absolutely brilliant, Oscar! I'm going to dedicate this book to you!"

And with that, she charged off into the bushes in the direction of the cottage.

Oscar stared after her, figuring he owed himself at least a good long look at her rear end. Which, as it happened, was barely covered by the blue swimming suit. And it was, in fact, quite a fine rear end.

He spewed out a long breath and slid under the water to his shoulders. That had been an unexpected but extremely pleasant moment, a fact which his long-neglected hormones were still reminding him. He wasn't certain what he'd done or said to induce such a reaction from her, but he wasn't complaining.

And now that Teddy and her distracting conversation were gone, Oscar had the opportunity to get back to work uninterrupted. He heaved out of the pool and got his equipment, then methodical as always, went to work.

***

Ninety minutes later, he returned to the cottage with new samples. The hot Gulf sun had nearly dried his clothes, and he was hungry for lunch. He wondered if Teddy had, by chance, made anything. Maybe she'd left something for him to nibble on. It would be the polite thing to do. After all, he'd made the coffee this morning.

But when he got inside, the place was quiet. He set his samples on the table and unslung his pack, then tiptoed down the hall to the bedroom commandeered by the writer.

All of a sudden, he heard a thump, like someone smacking a fist onto a table. He tensed, but then "Brilliant! My God, am I *brilliant!*" crowed a voice from behind the closed door. After that, silence.

Oscar scratched the back of his neck, chuckled to himself, then went to the kitchen for lunch. At least now he could work uninterrupted. He ate, and within sixty minutes had another fresh, uncontaminated sample on his slides.

"It's the same thing," he muttered. They were there—those microscopic, spiky crystalline shapes that had no business being in the hot springs. They didn't even resemble anything from nature. That niggle of excitement tickled his brain and he looked again, admiring how beautiful the shapes were. Like spiky snowflakes, all shades of blue and gray.

Surely it didn't mean the hot springs had magical powers. That would be ridiculous.

He tried another sample on another slide. And took a different sample from one of the three cubitainers he'd filled up himself. He continued to find the same results. He pulled out his laptop, which had satellite connectivity, and began researching, sending off images of what he'd found to friends and colleagues. He did some more research, looked up a few unrelated things, and then checked his e-mail. All the while, Oscar felt a strange sort of comfort knowing that Teddy was just down the hall, doing her own work…and not bothering him.

The next thing he knew, he had to turn on a lamp—and he was hungry. Oscar looked at the time on his computer. Nine-thirty?

Where had the time gone?

And where was Teddy? Surely he would have noticed if she'd come out of her room.

He crept down the hall again. Silence. Maybe she was sleeping. When he got to her door, he carefully opened it a crack. But he didn't even need to look inside, for he heard the busy clicking of a keyboard. Damn, she typed *fast.*

"You bastard!" she said. At first he thought she was talking to him, but then she added, "I've got you right where I want you." Then she actually gave a maniacal chuckle, and the keyboard clacked faster.

Oscar peered inside and saw her sitting at a desk. He wasn't certain whether to bother her or not, but he did take a minute to admire the way her clipped-up hair exposed a long, delicate neck. All at once, he had the urge to plant a kiss…right there. At the base.

And then he remembered the handful of warm, soft, curvy woman who'd thrown herself at him earlier today. He swallowed.

And then with a start, he realized…it was nearly ten o'clock at night. The day of Marcie's wedding.

She was either married, or…she wasn't.

Oscar's heart plunged into his belly. He looked back at Teddy, then closed the door. *She'd* found her heart's desire in the hot springs today.

He closed his fingers into fists, then opened them. Silly. *Ridiculous.* There was no way those spiky, crystalline things in the water were related to any paranormal or magical effects of the hot springs. Absolutely an outrageous theory.

Yet, he found himself back at the computer, searching through his e-mails. Two of his colleagues had already responded to the digital images he'd sent. Neither of them had seen anything like those microbes, and one even asked if he'd done it in Photoshop.

There is something peculiar in that water.

Oscar drew in a deep breath. His empty belly felt more than merely hungry, and hope gnawed there. He flexed his fingers again.

Then he logged in to Facebook.

And there it was, all over his feed: Marcie and Lew. Married, glowing, and happy, surrounded by friends and family, pictures, well-wishes, and even a few wedding-themed memes.

Oscar expelled a long breath.

He closed his laptop.

Well. There went that theory.

***

The next morning, Oscar made coffee again. And then he boiled water for tea. He hadn't slept well at all, and it wasn't due to the rhythmic clicking of the keyboard. No, under normal circumstances, he thought that might have been quite a soothing way to slip into slumber.

He showered, then wandered down the hall to the bedrooms once more. Hesitating at Teddy's door, he paused, then knocked.

No answer. More clicking.

He knocked again, a little louder.

No answer. More clicking. A muttered curse.

He opened the door and peered in. "Teddy?"

No answer. More clicking. A louder curse followed by an emphatic return on the keyboard.

He hesitated again, but, damn, as far as he knew, she hadn't been out of the room for more than twenty hours. Surely she needed to eat. Or…something. So he went in and said her name again, rather loudly and near her ear.

She jolted and shrieked, spinning in her chair. "Oh my God, you scared the hell out of me. Don't sneak up on me like that!"

"Sorry. I thought you might be hungry. You haven't eaten since yesterday."

Teddy blinked. "I had a few granola bars and a couple of apples."

Oscar noticed the papers on the floor. And two brown cores. Some empty water bottles. "Oh. Good. Well, I won't bother you then."

"Okay. Thanks." She turned back to her computer and was clicking away before he even shut the door.

Well *hell.*

Yesterday he'd been "brilliant" enough to warrant an enthusiastic hug and a sleek, sexy kiss…and now he was nothing more than a pesky gnat, buzzing around her head.

Oscar went back out to the dining/living room where all his equipment was spread out. He ignored it—what was the point?—and went into the kitchen to scrounge for something to eat in the well-stocked refrigerator.

Apples and a couple granola bars? He shook his head and made an extra omelet. He had no idea if Teddy had any food issues, but unless she was vegan, the tomato and spinach dish should give her a little more boost than some honey-soaked oats.

When Oscar brought it into her makeshift office, he merely slipped it onto the table next to her and left the room. He didn't like to be bothered when he was in the throes of his work. The delicious smell would eventually penetrate her fog and she'd eat when she was ready.

At least, that was how he worked.

Oscar busied himself cleaning up the kitchen and then took another look at his temporary lab. He could put it away and head home, or he could find something else to do. He had, after all, paid for a week at the cottage.

Hours later, he brought Teddy a sandwich. She grunted, glanced at him with glassy eyes, and said, "Almost there." And went back to clicking.

And so it went. He hiked around the island and found a stream where he pulled four samples of water. It would be interesting if the spiky crystalline microbes were present there as well…but Oscar found he was no longer as concerned about it as he had been before. Marcie was married and that was the end of it.

Later that evening, he grilled some chicken and made a salad and brought a portion to Teddy, who actually thanked him this time.

About two hours later, he was sitting on the screened-in deck of the cottage, nursing a Blue Moon and contemplating life when he heard a loud shriek.

Bolting to his feet, Oscar slammed into the house and ran to Teddy's room. He flung open the door to find her dancing around, whooping and shrieking.

Either she'd been bitten by something or she'd finished her book.

Teddy saw him and, with another whoop, flung herself into his arms. She smacked a kiss on his cheek, then pulled away and announced, "I'm finished! I'm finished, I'm finished, I'm *finished*!"

He was laughing by now, and he found he didn't want to let her go, even though she was still wriggling excitedly in his arms. "Congratulations, T.J. Mack! I'm sure the world will be delighted to read your sixth book."

She looked up at him in surprise. "You know who I am?"

"I'm a scientist. I know how to do research."

Teddy hadn't stopped dancing around, so he let her go. "Thank you so much for everything—for the food, for letting me alone to work, and most of all, for the trap door idea."

"So that worked, did it?" Oscar thought it would be fun to tell his dad—who was a *big* T.J. Mack fan—that he'd helped the author out of her writer's block and had given her the ending of what was surely going to be her latest blockbuster.

"Well, not really. I didn't end up using a trap door at all. But you got me to thinking, and that's how I ended up with a remote-controlled trolley car that helps Sargent Blue save the day."

"Oh." And here he thought he was brilliant. "But at least you got your heart's desire."

"I certainly did." By now, her giddiness had eased into mere delight. "And what about you? Did sitting in the hot springs help you find your heart's desire, Oscar?"

He felt a pang, but not as sharp as he'd expected. "No. Marcie got married yesterday, as planned. It was all over Facebook. She looked really happy."

Teddy just looked at him, tilted her head, and smiled. "Well, maybe Marcie wasn't really your heart's desire after all."

Something bumped deep inside Oscar's chest as their eyes met and held. He remembered that sleek kiss, that bundle of warm curves, the saucy, stimulating conversation, the comfort of hearing her work while he went about his own business.

"Maybe she wasn't."

Flipping For Francie

Jane Graves

CHAPTER ONE

Francesca Callaway stood in the bathroom of the house she was renovating, admiring the marble floor she'd just installed. The rich sepia stone with veins of chestnut brown looked spectacular with the bronze sink fixtures, creating an atmosphere so luxurious that upscale buyers would descend on the house in droves. Then she caught sight of herself in the mahogany-framed mirror and sighed with dismay.

The bathroom might be stunning, but she wasn't.

Umpteen strands of hair had fallen out of her ponytail and hung in her eyes, and her T-shirt was drenched in sweat. If only the parts for the broken air conditioning unit had arrived when they were supposed to, one of her crew could have repaired it so the second floor of the house wouldn't feel like a sauna. For the past hour, all she'd thought about was that nice, cold Jack Daniels on the rocks she would be sipping at Seeker's Paradise tonight.

All at once she heard footsteps on the stairs and a deep, masculine voice. "Francie? Are you up there?"

She froze. *No! Not him! Not when I'm such a mess!*

She turned slowly, swiping her hair out of her face just about the time Dylan Bradford poked his head around the doorway. "Ah," he said brightly. "There you are."

He came into the bathroom looking as he always did, tall and smooth and confident, with sandy brown hair streaked with gold and clear blue eyes so stunning it was nearly impossible for her to look away. A two-day growth of beard shadowed his cheeks and chin, making him look wildly handsome and carelessly sexy all at once. Today he wore slacks, a dress shirt, and a tie, looking so pressed and polished it made her feel even messier than she usually did.

Three months ago Dylan moved to Seeker's Island to take over Bradford Realty from his uncle. The company ruled the housing market on the island and for miles across the mainland, with annual sales in the millions, making everyone in the Bradford family very wealthy. A big part of Dylan's business included finding distressed properties and making the deals for out-of-town investors. Then he'd find a contractor to do the renovations, overseeing the jobs until the houses were finished and ready to flip. Most of the time, Francie was that contractor.

George Bradford was in his fifties, balding, and as wide as he was tall. His nephew...wasn't. The first time Dylan showed up at one of Francie's job sites, she'd taken one look at him and damned near melted into a puddle of goo right there in the middle of the deck she'd been working on. Women loved him because he truly was one of God's more stunning creations. Men loved him because he was a man's man without lording it over them. She'd watched Dylan adjust his handshake for more timid clients, or go all out with a shake and a shoulder slap for his more overtly masculine ones. He could talk wine, woodworking, or women, whatever the occasion called for. In other words, he was the quintessential salesman, a great quality to have when moving real estate, but it made Francie leery about trusting anything he said.

"A dress shirt?" she said, looking him up and down. "A tie? What's up with that?"

"I have a meeting later with a high-end client. Very conservative. He only does business with people who look uncomfortable." Dylan set his briefcase on the counter and then examined the marble floor, letting out a low whistle. "Nice work. I take it the boss handled this project?"

"This tile was twenty-five bucks a square foot. If somebody was going to screw it up, I wanted it to be me."

"My investor choked on the price, you know."

"This floor was necessary. This is a high-end property. Didn't you explain that to him?"

"Sure I did. That's why he eventually agreed. I've got your back on this stuff, Francie. If you say the walls need to be purple, then paint the walls purple. I'll clear it with the client."

Francie didn't get it. If whatever she did was fine with him, then why was he constantly showing up at her job sites?

She bent over to grab marble tile scraps, gathering them onto a canvas tarp. And the whole time, she had the distinct feeling Dylan was staring at her ass. When several seconds passed and he continued to watch her in silence, she stood up and faced him.

"Dylan? What are you looking at?"

He gave her a smooth, congenial smile. "Marble scraps. I was looking at marble scraps."

"Yeah? Where are they? In my hip pockets?"

His smile never wavered, and Francie suppressed the urge to hide her face. Or, more accurately, her ass. But the moment she acted the least bit flustered, she'd lose all credibility with him. And she refused to let that happen.

"Your uncle left me alone to get the job done," she said. "He didn't micromanage. Ever think about following in his footsteps?"

"Is that what you think I'm doing? Micromanaging?"

"Yes. You're around all the time."

"Do I ever tell you what to do? What materials to use? How to schedule your crew?"

"No."

"Then what's the problem?"

The *problem* was that he was there. That was all. He was just *there*, joking, teasing, and smiling in that relaxed, confident way that only rich, handsome, entitled men could. Just being around him reminded her of the time she'd spent on this island as the poor, homely girl from the wrong side of the tracks, and she never wanted to think about that again.

"I just don't like people hanging over my shoulder while I'm working. Or," she said pointedly, "doing things that would get them in trouble with the average human resources department."

Dylan had the nerve to smile at that. "Well, then. I guess I'd better get right down to business." He reached for his briefcase. "I have the purchase offer for that beach house you want to buy."

"You have it with you? I told you I'd come by your office in the morning."

"I was in the neighborhood."

"This late in the day?"

"Why don't you just say, 'Thank you, Dylan, for saving me a trip?'"

"Fine," Francie muttered. "Let's see it."

He pulled out a few legal-sized sheets. "You know I'm not on board with this."

"You've made that clear already."

"A full price offer? That's crazy."

No. It wasn't crazy. Nobody was going to buy that house out from under her. If it took a ridiculous offer to make sure that didn't happen, so be it.

She flipped through the purchase offer, signed it, and handed the papers back to Dylan.

"I suppose it was only a matter of time before you invested in a house yourself," he said. "But this one is a lousy flip at this price. If you can get it cheaper, you'll have some room to work."

"Just present the offer."

"What do you know about that property the rest of us don't?"

She just stared at him.

"You're killing me, Francie. Full price offers give me hives."

"If you won't present the offer, I'll find an agent who will."

Dylan slid the contract back into his briefcase, shaking his head sadly. "Just when I thought I was dealing with a smart businesswoman, you go and do something like this."

"Just let me know when we have a deal."

"Won't take long. Wave this kind of money under Brittney Sanders's nose, and she'll snap at it."

Good. That was exactly what Francie wanted. To offer Brittney so much money for the property she couldn't possibly say no. Brittney's parents had bought the house ten years ago, eventually passing it down to their daughter. In the ensuing years, Francie had watched renters come and go with little done to maintain the place. It had gradually deteriorated as many rental properties did when the landlords were just biding their time until the real estate market turned around. But now the house was for sale, and Francie intended to buy it no matter what she had to offer.

Dylan grabbed his briefcase and strode to the door, only to turn back. "I'll see you tonight at Seeker's Paradise."

Francie's heart fluttered. "What?"

"You'll be there, won't you?"

"How did you know that?"

"I had a closing this morning at the title company. Laura told me you're meeting her there. After paying full price for that beach house, you're going to be broke. I, on the other hand, will be collecting six percent. So the drinks are on me tonight."

With yet another luminous smile, he left the bathroom, and Francie took her first deep breath since he'd arrived. Slowly she turned to look at herself in the mirror again. Even now she had to resist the urge to wipe her sweaty forehead on the sleeve of her T-shirt. But why? Why should she care what Dylan Bradford thought when he looked at her?

Then again, hadn't she felt this way in the past anytime one of the privileged, popular boys looked her way? In high school, she'd wished for highlighted hair and department store makeup and fingernails with bright, trendy polish. Big dreams for a girl who felt the sizzling summer sidewalk through the holes in the soles of her shoes and crossed the bay on the ferry to buy her clothes at Pennywise Thrift Store.

But in that same reflection in the mirror was the woman she'd become. One she was proud of. She'd learned the renovation business from the ground up as a worker on somebody else's crew, gaining all the knowledge she could until she was able to manage a crew of her own. She'd always known that success for someone with no capital to invest came only from her own sweat and tears.

Dylan might act friendly, but it was nothing more than his salesman shtick designed to make sure every woman within the sound of his voice wanted him. Undoubtedly a few of those women would be at Seeker's Paradise tonight, but she was *not* going to be one of them.

***

Dylan tossed his briefcase into the only conveyance allowed on the island—a golf cart—and hopped into the driver's seat. As he returned to his office, he remembered when he'd first moved to the island three months ago and went to one of Francie's work sites to check on the renovation. He'd opened the back door of the house and stepped onto the deck she was building with her crew. She was on her knees, nail gun in hand, wearing goggles and popping nails into the wood planks. He still remembered the moment she stood up and turned around.

His mouth had gone dry as sawdust.

She was a beautiful woman. Not in the classic way that most men went for, but he could honestly say he'd never met a woman who grabbed his attention the way she did. Her coffee-colored hair had been pulled up into a ponytail, with strands falling along her cheeks. As soon as she saw him, she removed her goggles, revealing brown eyes so deep and dark her pupils disappeared. As his gaze made its way down her body, he knew he was staring in a way he shouldn't, but he couldn't seem to stop himself. Her sweaty T-shirt clung to her full breasts, and her low-slung jeans hit all the right notes from her hips to her thighs.

Finally he'd jerked his gaze back up to her face to find her eyes narrowed and her lips pursed with irritation. He'd turned on the charm, but she was all business, throwing up so many walls a man would need a cannon to blast his way through.

At first he told himself he wanted her only because she didn't want *him*, and therefore she was a challenge. But it was more than that. She was a strong, competent, uncompromising woman who didn't cry over a broken nail or spend every dime she earned shopping for needless crap. Let other men chase after blonde Barbie dolls or rich heiresses. For him, a woman who could rewire an electrical socket or build a cabinet made his blood run so hot he got the sweats. And as frustrating as it could be, he loved the fact that no matter how hard he tried, he couldn't get under her skin. That was a new one for him. He was used to women who lined up for the opportunity to whisper in his ear the nasty-hot things they wanted to do to him. Not Francie. And that intrigued him more than anything.

But right now what he couldn't figure out was her single-minded insistence on buying that beach house for a price nobody in his right mind would pay. Evidently she knew something about that property nobody else did, which was why she was willing to pay a premium price. Was the house sitting on a gold mine? A portal to another dimension? It had to be *something*.

When he got back to his office, curiosity drove him to pull up the county tax records on the house in question. The Sanders family had bought it from a woman named Beverly Callaway ten years before, and she had inherited it only a month before that from a woman named Edith

Callaway.

Okay. So Francie was related to the house's former owners. That told him just enough to make him want to know more. But getting Francie to tell him anything would be a tough thing to do. She was hardly an open book. In fact, he'd bet she had more secrets than the CIA.

Tonight he'd be seeing her at Seeker's Paradise. With luck, he'd find out what a few of those secrets were.

CHAPTER TWO

Seeker's Paradise was a hangout for tourists and locals alike, full of tropical ambience, specialty drinks, and the kind of casual atmosphere that invited people to sit down and relax. The open-air establishment allowed the sea breeze to flow among the tables and carry away the memory of the day's intense summer heat.

By the time Francie arrived, the sun was hovering over the horizon, casting an orange glow across the nearby beach. She sat down at a table with Laura, who was already half-finished with her usual piña colada and checking out the place for any new men who might have shown up. Francie had gotten to know her because the real estate community on the island was a small one and Laura worked at the only title company. Most of the time their conversation centered around two things—real estate if Francie started it, and if Laura did, the subject was men.

A minute later, the waitress brought Francie her Jack on the rocks. She downed that one and asked for another. By the time she was a few sips into number two, she finally began to relax.

Laura's attention turned to a spot on the far side of the big, square bar in the middle of the room. "My *God,* that man is beautiful," she said, a dreamy tone in her voice. "Every time he comes into the title company to close a deal, I just about faint dead away."

Francie knew Laura could be referring to only one man, and suddenly all the relaxation she felt vanished. She turned to see Dylan sitting on a bar stool, his hand wrapped around a Corona. For some reason, Mr. Perfect was still dressed in the same shirt, slacks and tie he'd worn earlier. And he was sitting with Brittney Sanders.

Francie frowned. Just the sight of Brittney was enough to irritate her, and tonight was no exception. She wore a floral wraparound dress with a neckline that practically hit her belly button, highlighting the boob job she'd gotten the summer after their senior year in high school. She sat with her entire body turned toward Dylan, her fake breasts shoved so far forward Francie was surprised she didn't topple right off her stool. Brittney had always been one to scoop up all the hot guys within the sound of her voice, then throw back the ones she didn't want for other less fortunate women to fight over. But judging from the way she was zeroed in on Dylan, if she ever caught him, tossing him back would be the last thing on her mind.

"Though I must say I didn't expect to see him with *her*," Laura said.

"Why not?" Francie said. "They're both pretty people. Don't pretty people always hang out together?"

"Brittney may be pretty, but she's a horrible bitch. It'd be too bad if they hooked up."

Was that what Laura thought? They were hooking up? Just the thought annoyed Francie, though she didn't know why. Who Dylan associated with was none of her business. But tonight it was clear Brittney was making it *her* business.

Then Francie thought, *My purchase offer. What about my purchase offer?*

The music kicked up a notch, and a guy across the room who'd had his eye on Laura dropped by their table and asked her to dance. A minute later, Dylan left Brittney sitting at the bar, grabbed his beer and strolled to Francie's table. As he slid onto the stool Laura had vacated, Francie tried to act nonchalant, but her heart wasn't getting the message. Why was he leaving Brittney to talk to her?

Deep breath. Stop acting so dumb. It's just Dylan. You don't like him, remember?

"You're still wearing that tie," she said. "You are aware this is a tiki bar, right?"

"Meeting ran late."

"So go home and change."

"Beer first, comfort later." Dylan slipped a little orange umbrella into Francie's highball glass, where watery Jack Daniels swam around in what was left of a handful of ice cubes.

She made a face of disgust. "What's that?"

"You're a girl. Aren't girls supposed to have little orange umbrellas in their drinks?"

"If you believe that, you've been hanging out with the wrong women." She nodded across the bar. "Brittney, for instance. Good God, I thought she was going to give you a lap dance right there at the bar."

"Seriously? Wow. Maybe I should have hung around. Don't see that at Seeker's Paradise every day."

"She's hot for you. Better take her up on it."

"Nope. Tonight it was business. Her agent called me an hour ago about your purchase offer."

Francie stopped breathing. "And?"

"Brittney said no. Wait—not just no. *Hell*, no."

"*What?*"

"She turned down your offer."

"How could she do that? It was for full price!"

"Which I strongly advised you against, if you'll remember. But she still turned it down."

"Then take out my request for closing costs. I'll pick those up."

"It won't matter."

"Do you want your commission, or don't you?" Francie said. "Make the deal!"

"Look. I did everything I could. That was why I was over there talking to Brittney. I sidestepped her agent to see if I could get her to see things our way. Not the most ethical move, I'll admit, but it was a full-price offer and I figured her agent wouldn't object if I could get the deal done. But it's a no-go." Dylan took a sip of his beer. "Now. Suppose you tell me why there's bad blood between you and Brittney Sanders."

"Bad blood?"

"Don't play dumb. Nobody turns down a full-price offer unless they have a reason."

Oh, there was a reason. But a *good* reason? Hell, no. "Maybe you'd better ask Brittney."

"I did. She told me the last person on earth she'd sell the house to is 'that crazy-ass bitch Francie Callaway.' Now, where would she ever get that kind of opinion about a sweet little thing like you?"

Francie didn't want to go there. She just didn't. Her history with Brittney was the last thing she wanted to discuss with Dylan. "Offer her ten thousand more."

"Ten thousand *above* asking price?"

"That's right."

"Have you lost your freakin' mind?"

"I told you I want that house."

"Come on, Francie. You're smarter than that. Why does it have to be *that* house?"

She just stared at him.

"There at least half a dozen other properties on this island to invest in. I can hook you up with plenty on the mainland, too. Don't get hung up on that one."

"If you won't present the offer—"

"I know, I know. You'll find an agent who will. Well, maybe that's a good idea, because as much as I like my six percent, I have no desire to watch my clients make huge financial mistakes."

Francie hated this. She had the horrible feeling Brittney was going to carry her age-old grudge all the way to the grave, and then somebody else would be buying the house that should have been Francie's.

"Now, are you going to tell me why Brittney despises you?" Dylan asked.

Francie was silent.

"If you'll tell me what's going on, I just might be able to smooth things over and make a deal."

He looked genuinely sincere, but Francie was still afraid he was just like those guys who'd looked right through her all those years ago, the ones who dated girls like Brittney. Girls who went to movies and slumber parties while she sat in a crappy hellhole of an apartment wishing her drug-addicted mother would wake up one day and realize she had a daughter.

"If you must know," Francie said, "I once spilled something on her."

"It must have been battery acid to keep her from selling you that house."

"It was punch."

Dylan looked dumbfounded. "Punch?"

"Yes."

"When?"

"High school."

Dylan's eyes narrowed. "Let me get this straight. You're saying you spilled punch on her, so ten years later she won't sell you a two hundred and fifty thousand dollar property on a full price offer?"

"That's what I'm saying."

"How about you tell me the whole story?"

Francie finished her drink and then set the glass down. "That is the whole story. What can I say? She's vindictive."

"She doesn't seem to be the world's most caring and compassionate human being, so I'll buy that. But there has to be more to it."

She grabbed her purse. "I have to go."

"Hold on there," Dylan said. "I told you the drinks are on me tonight."

She tossed down a twenty and rose from the table.

"Francie! Will you *wait*?"

He followed her out of the bar into the parking lot, where he grabbed her arm and turned her back around.

"If you want that house, I can help you," he said. "But you have to tell me what I'm dealing with."

Francie cursed the alcohol she'd drank. Her head was swimming, making the music from the bar sound distant and muted until she heard little more than the underlying beat. The night breeze off the ocean swirled around them, and with Dylan's hand still against her arm and those blue eyes drawing her in, suddenly she heard the words tumble out.

"When we were in high school," she said, "we didn't like each other."

"Okay. And why was that?"

"The usual story," she said dismissively, easing her arm from his grasp. "People like her have to pick on somebody."

"Define *pick on*."

Francie shrugged. "The usual. Taunting. Teasing. Bullying. Knocking stuff out of my hands. Tearing up things in my locker. Making fun of me in class."

"That's the *usual*?"

"Oh, for God's sake, stop being naïve. That kind of stuff happens all the time."

"It didn't where I went to school."

"Of course it didn't. Because you didn't go to school with poor kids who had freaky mothers who never met a drug they didn't like. Kids who went to school in clothes that embarrassed the hell out of them. Kids who knew social workers on a first-name basis. So who was there to pick on? Everybody was just like you."

Dylan looked at her a long time, then spoke softly. "Sounds like you had it rough back then."

"No rougher than a lot of kids."

"Still."

For some reason, he wasn't wearing his usual teasing expression. His eyes seemed warm. Sympathetic. She had the feeling he could see right inside her, and suddenly she wished she hadn't said anything. She hated people feeling sorry for her, because that was what sympathy always felt like—pity.

"Tell me about Brittney and the spilled punch," he said.

She didn't want to talk about that, either. But alone with Dylan in the dusky light with him looking so sincere, she found herself talking whether she wanted to or not.

"It wasn't so much that I spilled it," she told him. "It was *where* I spilled it."

"Which was?"

"On her dress."

"Okay…?"

"At a school dance."

Dylan's eyebrows rose. "That's a little different than spilling punch on her jeans in the school cafeteria. I'm guessing this wasn't an accident?"

Hell, no, it wasn't an accident.

Francie had gone to the dance with a boy who was almost as much of an outcast as she was, but he'd smiled and told her how beautiful she looked in the short, sparkly dress and high heels she'd found at a thrift store, clothes that made her feel pretty for just about the first time in her life. But within fifteen minutes of their arrival, Brittney ruined it all by tossing off a snotty remark about her dress, telling her how nice it was that her pimp had let her off for the evening so she could go to her school dance.

In that moment, every insult, every physical altercation, every haughty, condescending glare Brittney had ever thrown at Francie became a swirling vortex in her mind. Before she knew it, she'd hurled a glass of cherry-red punch onto the lacy white bodice of Brittney's gazillion-dollar dress. The only thing that drowned out the crowd's collective gasp of shock was Brittney's howl of horror.

And now the grudge lived on.

"Let's just say she finally pushed me too far," Francie said.

"Actually, it sounds as if you showed a lot of restraint to make it that long without doing something worse."

"My 'something worse' would have gotten me five or ten years in prison."

"You know teenagers have shit for brains," Dylan said. "In Brittney's case, she turned twenty and forgot to flush."

"It was years ago. I don't give a damn anymore."

"Then why didn't you tell me about it in the first place?"

She didn't know. Maybe because the story made her sound so pitiful. Like a victim, and that was the last thing she ever wanted to be again. And it only made it worse to talk about those things with a guy who seemed as if he'd never struggled a day in his life.

"I'm sorry you had to go through all that," he said.

"I said I don't give a damn. I have to go."

He grabbed her arm again. "Francie?"

"What?"

Dylan tilted his head, and when he spoke again, the sincerity she'd seen in his eyes spilled out in his voice. "Why do you bite my head off every time I try to talk to you?"

She started to deny doing that, but she couldn't. But she didn't have an answer for him, either. She only knew his calm composure and his self-confidence rattled her when she had to work her ass off to feel those qualities herself.

"Better question," she said. "Why do care one way or the other?"

"We work together, don't we?"

"This isn't business."

"So I can't talk to you unless it's about paint colors or granite countertops?"

"I'm betting you had everything as a kid. Am I right?"

His brows pulled together with confusion. "Well, I'm not sure what *that* has to do with anything, but..." He shrugged. "Yeah. It was a nice life."

"More than anything I ever had."

"So?"

"We're just really different. Came from different places. That's all."

"So you treat me like crap because of an accident of birth?"

Francie felt a shot of frustration, knowing just how wrong that sounded. "No. Of course not. I just mean…God, Dylan! It's just that you're always…"

"What?"

"You're always so damned *perfect*!"

"Huh?"

"I mean, look at you!"

"What's wrong with the way I look?"

"Nothing! That's the problem. Absolutely *nothing*. Do you know how close I came once to turning a paint sprayer on you just to see you messed up a little?"

He grinned. "Yeah? What color was the paint?"

"Does it *matter*?"

"So you'd like to mess me up a little?"

"God, yes," she said longingly. "Just once."

"So do it. Go ahead. Mess me up."

Her heart skipped a beat. "I didn't mean *I* wanted to do it."

"But that's what you just said." He tipped his head down. "Start with the hair."

If she hadn't downed a couple of drinks, she might not have even considered doing it. But looking at him now, suddenly all her frustration came to a head and it seemed like a really good idea.

She put her hands on his head and smooshed his hair around. Then she grabbed his tie. Loosened it. Knocked it out of whack. Unbuttoned the top button of his shirt. Squished the collar to one side. Then she stepped back, her fist on her hip, and surveyed the results.

Oh, screw it. This was going nowhere. Now he just looked rumpled and careless and hotter than ever, as if he'd just had sex on a board room table on his lunch hour.

"Oh, forget it," she muttered. "You're unmessupable."

"That's not a word."

"It is now."

He inched closer to her and spoke softly. "Maybe you should unfasten another button or two."

Just the sound of his deep, hot, masculine voice tied her stomach in knots, not to mention the words he was speaking. Suddenly she had a mental image of him naked from the waist up. Then from the waist down.

Then she was naked with him.

Even with the cool sea breeze swirling around them, her skin felt prickly hot. All at once she realized how *tall* he was, so tall she had to tilt her head back to look up at him. How he could still smell so good so late in the day astonished her. That she was close enough to know how he smelled astonished her even more. They stood on one side of the parking lot, nearly obscured by a pair of palm trees, which meant nobody else could see them, making her more than a little nervous. After all, Jack Daniels was her other man of the moment, and he was screwing up her judgment big time.

Dylan rested his hand on her shoulder, then slid his palm down and tightened his hand around her forearm. She wanted to pull away, but his touch felt better than she ever could have imagined. But why was he doing this? *Why?*

"Do you want to know the real reason I'm still dressed like this?" he murmured.

"Why?"

"My meeting ran late. I was afraid if I went home to change, by the time I got here you'd be gone."

The most amazing feeling unfurled inside her, like a brightly colored ribbon fluttering in the breeze. But she didn't trust most people in general, and slick, shrewd men in particular, so how could she trust Dylan?

He came closer still, so close she swore she could feel the heat from his body filling the space between them. Then he dipped his head, his lips hovering over hers.

She couldn't believe it. He was going to kiss her.

Kiss her?

He brushed his lips against hers in the softest of kisses, and for a moment she forgot all her skepticism and gave in to the sensations just that tiny touch of his lips created, loving the faint taste of beer mingling with desire.

Her desire.

His other hand skimmed her cheek, then closed around the back of her neck. He deepened the kiss, slipping his tongue into her mouth and teasing it against hers. Oh, *God*, it felt so heavenly she wanted it to go on forever, even though she knew she had to stop. Dylan had to have some kind of ulterior motive, because men like him didn't go after women like her. She had to call a halt to this right *now*.

She put her hand on him to push him away, but when she felt the hard planes of his chest beneath his crisp cotton shirt, her hand lingered instead. She flexed her fingers, wishing the damned fabric wasn't in the way so she could feel his naked skin beneath her—

No! Enough!

It took every bit of willpower she had, but she finally managed to slide her lips away from his. Dylan leaned away, looking frustrated. "What's the matter?"

"Why are you doing this?"

"Doing what? Kissing a beautiful woman?"

"You can stop with the bullshit. I'm not beautiful."

Dylan took hold of her upper arms and stared down at her. "And you can stop with all the negative self-image crap. You *are* beautiful. I don't care what happened in high school. Just forget all that. You're a strong, bright, beautiful woman—"

"Just *forget* it?" She eased out of his grip. "Let me tell you something. When you've been through what I have, when you've been told all your life you're not as good as other people, forgetting is a hard thing to do. I don't expect somebody like you to understand that."

"So we come from different places. Does it really matter as long as we meet in the middle?"

For how long? Just until you get laid? Then what?

Then any interest he had in her would die.

Dylan was the ultimate salesman, so when he said nice things and heaped compliments on her out of nowhere, she had no way of knowing how much was genuine and how much was him using his super powers for evil. And that meant she had to stay on her toes and take everything he said with a grain of salt.

She eased away from him. Slowly and deliberately, she reached up and buttoned his shirt, then straightened his tie. He looked at her quizzically.

"Offer Brittney ten thousand dollars over her asking price," she told him. "Make the deal, Dylan. When I hear from you again, I want you to tell me I've bought myself a house."

CHAPTER THREE

After leaving Seeker's Paradise, Francie tried to put Dylan out of her mind, but it was impossible. She fell asleep thinking about him. Woke up thinking about him. Spent the morning thinking about him as she and her crew built bookshelves in the den of their latest renovation. At one point she was so distracted, she came within a millimeter of smacking her own thumb with a hammer.

She really wanted to lump Dylan in with people like Brittney, because Francie's experience had taught her that men like him went after women like her, and she wanted nothing to do with either of them. Because of that, last night when he'd acted as if *she* was the woman he wanted, it had felt all wrong.

But now she was thinking about the flattering things he'd said to her, and she decided maybe she'd overreacted and she should take him at his word. Apologize, even. Then she thought about his salesman's talent at getting exactly what he wanted, and she grew suspicious all over again.

With all that swimming around in her head, when she heard her text message tone just before noon and saw his name, her heart did a funny little dance. She had to take a few deep breaths to bring it under control before she touched her phone to reveal the message. *Problem,* his text said. *Call me.*

Her purchase offer? Was that what this was about? She punched his number.

"Dylan?" she said when he answered. "What's up? Does this have to do with the beach house?"

"No. Brittney's agent hasn't been able to get in touch with her yet. I left a message for him to call me."

"Then what's the problem?"

"I have a broken tile in the entry of my condo, and it needs to be replaced."

Francie slumped with irritation. A broken tile? *That* was why he was calling? "What happened?"

"I dropped a hammer on it."

"What kind of tile?"

"Reclaimed Tuscan."

"Do you have spares from the same lot?"

"The former owner left one. But only one."

"So what's the problem?"

"I need your opinion. I was told I should have it all replaced because getting the damaged tile out without tearing up the others would be impossible."

"Impossible? It's not impossible. Any pro can do it. And that's reclaimed tile. You do whatever you can to save it."

"So that doesn't sound right to you?"

"Hell, no, it doesn't sound right."

"And even if Frank can get the damaged tile out, he said that matching the grout—"

"Frank? Frank Havershank?"

"Yes."

"You hired *Frank Havershank*?"

"Well, yeah."

"Never hire Frank to do anything! He drinks on the job. His work sucks. The second you pay him, he disappears. *Never hire Frank Havershank*. Why didn't you call me first?"

"Hey! Your crew has been putting in overtime trying to get your current project done. When the A Team is tied up, what am I supposed to do?

She couldn't stand this. She just couldn't. Frank Havershank gave contractors a bad name. He screwed up as much as he fixed. The very idea that he was suggesting that Dylan replace all the tile in his entry hall just because of a single damaged one made her blood boil. Of course a shady guy like him would suggest that. Replacing a hundred tiles paid way more.

"I'll take care of it," she said.

"But your crew—"

"I said *I* would take care of it."

"You? No. I couldn't ask you to do that."

"Hey, if it's between me and Frank Havershank, if I were you, I'd take me up on my offer."

She heard him sigh. "Well, all right. If you insist. How about tonight? Maybe seven o'clock?"

"Isn't that a little late?"

"I have appointments until then."

"Fine. I'll be there at seven. And don't you even *think* of hiring Frank to do anything again, do you hear me?"

"Yes, ma'am. I hear you loud and clear."

Francie hung up. Frank Havershank? What was *wrong* with Dylan?

Wait. What was wrong with *her*? She was going to Dylan's condo tonight?

Then she told herself it was no problem. She was going in a professional capacity. He'd given her a lot of work over the past three months, so really, she owed him. She'd get in, do the job, and get out.

And that would be that.

***

Dylan realized he'd gone too far with Francie the night before at Seeker's Paradise. Pushed her too hard. Asked for too much. But knowing a little about where she came from explained a lot. And when her tough-girl crap had melted away and she'd dissolved in his arms...*damn*. Those few memorable moments made him want to get even closer to her no matter how much she tried to push him away. He hadn't been able to get her out of his mind all morning, and with every moment that passed, he'd grown just a little bit more obsessed with seeing her again. But now she was gun shy, and he'd wondered how in the world he was going to make that happen.

Then he remembered just how much she *loved* Frank Havershank.

He stuck his phone back into his pocket and looked down at the stone tile in the entry hall of his condo. That tile, imported from Italy, was a big reason he'd bought the place. He really liked the color and the warmth, and it blended beautifully with his furnishings. He had no doubt just the shipping to get it to the island had cost more than the tile itself, so of course he did everything he could to keep it in perfect condition.

He picked up the hammer. Squatting down, he reared back and brought it down on one of the tiles. A crack appeared its center, radiating out in a starburst pattern.

There. He'd dropped a hammer on it.

Okay. That had been painful. But it certainly helped to know he had a contractor who was the best in the business coming over to make the repair. And once she was there…

Maybe they could pick up where they'd left off last night.

***

A few minutes before seven, Francie stood on Dylan's front porch in one of the most exclusive condo complexes on the island. Each unit had a wall of windows spanning its length that revealed an ocean view to die for, and the first-floor units had winding decks leading from their back doors straight down to the beach. Francie had never seen one of the condos on the inside, but she'd always imagined how spectacular they must be.

She knocked, and a few seconds later, Dylan came to the door. He was dressed down in cargo shorts, a T-shirt, and flip-flops. She would have sworn such casual clothes would have made him look less polished.

Wrong.

She stepped inside, carrying a tool bag containing everything she needed—a drill, a hammer and chisel, a notched trowel, and enough mortar to do the job. After Dylan closed the door behind her, she took a quick look around. Yep. Spectacular. The entry hall had ten-foot ceilings with intricate crown molding, an iron chandelier, and a vintage Italian floor tile that was clearly very expensive. And he'd hired *Frank Havershank* to repair it?

The man had clearly lost his mind.

"Where's the broken tile?" she asked.

"Over here." He led her to a tile in the center of the entry hall with a large starburst crack. Francie knelt down, plugged in her drill and drilled a hole through the center of the tile. Through that opening, she used a hammer and chisel to chip away the broken square and the old grout to prepare the surface. She applied the mortar to the new tile and slid it into place, setting the appropriate spacers.

"That mortar needs twenty-four hours to set up, so I'll have to drop back by tomorrow to grout it." She rose from the floor.

"Hold on," Dylan said. "Don't go yet. I want to show you something."

"What?"

"Just come with me."

He led her from the entry hall into his living room, yet another spectacular space with a vaulted ceiling, leather furniture, and high-end wood flooring. Adjoining the living room was an open-concept kitchen with every upscale fixture she could possibly imagine.

"Nice," she said.

"Thank you."

He nodded toward the refrigerator. "I've been marinating steaks for the past couple of hours." Then he pointed to a bottle of wine on the kitchen island. "And that Cabernet should be perfect with them. I opened it about twenty minutes ago to let it breathe."

"Uh...okay." *Why are you showing me this?*

He nodded to glass doors leading to a multilevel redwood deck with a matching table and chairs. The sun was beginning its descent to the horizon, and yellow-orange waves lapped at the shore.

"Like the view?" he asked.

Did she like it? Was there anyone on earth who *wouldn't*? "It's beautiful."

Then she realized the table on the deck was set for dinner. Placemats. Plates. Silverware and glasses.

For two.

It took a few seconds for her brain to make the connection. Marinating steaks, a bottle of wine, a table set for two...

She couldn't believe it. Dylan had a date tonight? A *date*?

Anger welled up inside her. Now she knew for a fact she'd done the right thing by walking away from him at Seeker's Paradise. If he could kiss her last night and then have a date with another woman twenty-four hours later, did she really want anything to do with him?

"It looks as if you have a hot date tonight," she said. "I think I'll get out of here before she shows up."

"There's no need for that."

"What do you mean?"

"She's already here."

Francie glanced over her shoulder. "Well, then. I really do need to get going, don't I?"

He laughed. "Francie, *you're* my date. I want you to stay and have dinner with me."

She looked at him with suspicion. "Wait a minute. You invited me here to work, not to have dinner. So what's the deal? Did your real date stand you up?"

His smile slipped away. "My *real* date?"

"Yeah. No sense letting all this go to waste, right?"

He looked at her incredulously. "Are you *kidding* me?"

She drew back. "Huh?"

"Do you really not get this?" He walked away a few paces, then spun back around, throwing his hands in the air. "For God's sake, Francie! What more do I have to do?"

"What are you talking about?"

"I come to your work sites, and you're all business. I try to talk to you, and you blow me off. I show up at Seeker's Paradise when I know you're going to be there, but you won't so much as let me buy you a drink." He took a breath and kept talking, his voice escalating. "I try to compliment you, but you don't take compliments. I joke around with you, but all you do is treat me as if I have anthrax. I kiss you, and you just walk away as if nothing at all happened between us. So, what then?"

She just stared at him.

"I'll tell you what then," he said, pointing to his entry hall. "Then I smash my own fucking tile. *That's* what I do!"

"You *what*?"

"You heard me. I took a hammer and smashed a reclaimed Tuscan tile that somebody with more money than God shipped over here from fucking *Italy* just so I could get you into my condo to fix it. Then I thought maybe you might sit down and have dinner with me. How pitiful is *that*?"

Francie blinked. "You did all that just to have dinner with *me*?"

"My God. Are you seriously that blind? I like you, Francie. I want to see more of you. How much clearer can I possibly make it?"

"Why didn't you just ask?"

"Oh, right. After everything I've already done, how far would I have gotten with just *asking*?"

Francie was positively speechless.

"So here," he said, pouring a glass of wine and holding it out to her. Francie just stared at it.

"I have a bottle of Jack, too," Dylan said. "Shall I crack that instead?"

"Uh…no."

"Then take this. Say 'Thank you, Dylan, for inviting me to dinner.' And then drink it."

She took the glass. "Thank you, Dylan, for inviting me to dinner."

"Drink!"

She took a sip. *God*, it was good. "I can't believe you did all this," she said, looking around the kitchen and then outside to the beautifully set table on the deck. "Wine, steaks..."

"Dinner was nothing. The hard part was wadding up my shorts and T-shirt before I put them on and not combing my hair. Proud of me?"

She couldn't help smiling. Just a little. "Yes. You look really crappy tonight, Dylan."

"Damn right, I do."

All at once it finally struck her. Both barrels. Head-on. He'd done all this for her. All of it. He'd even messed himself up for her.

For *her*.

He took two steps forward to stand in front of her. "Now," he said, "are you staying or not? And if you say *not*, you'd better have a damn good reason *why* not."

"No. I'm staying."

"Good."

"As long as you promise me one thing."

"What's that?"

"That you won't ever break a tile again. Full price offers give you hives. Broken tiles give *me* hives."

"Fair enough."

"I'm not really dressed for dinner," she said. "Every time you see me, I'm a mess."

He shook his head slowly, a tiny smile crossing his lips. "When are you going to get it, Francie? That's what I *like* about you."

She couldn't fathom that, but something about his smile when he looked at her made her think he just might be telling her the truth. She decided that at least for tonight she'd take him at his word.

"Now, let me get those steaks on the grill," he said. "I don't know about you, but I'm starving."

***

Thirty minutes later they were sitting on the deck enjoying dinner and wine and watching the sun slip into the ocean. They chatted about nothing in particular, and for the first time, Dylan felt as if Francie was letting down her guard and talking to him as two friends might. After they finished dinner, she picked up her wine glass and looked out over the bay, wearing the kind of relaxed, contented smile he'd never seen on her face before.

Then all at once she focused on something in the distance. "There it is," she said, her voice hushed.

"What?" Dylan asked.

"The house."

Dylan turned to look across the bay, where he saw a white clapboard house, positioned in such a way that the evening sun reflected off of it. He'd never noticed it before, but she was right. That was the house. The one she wanted so badly.

"I didn't know you could see it from here," Francie said.

"I didn't, either."

For several seconds, Francie stared at the house as if she couldn't take her eyes off it.

"Who is Edith Callaway?" Dylan asked.

Francie whipped around. "How do you know that name?"

"It's a matter of public record. She used to own the house." Dylan held up his palm. "Never mind. I shouldn't have brought up the subject."

Francie set her wine glass down. "No. It's all right." She glanced at him, then looked away again. "I know what you're thinking. You're wondering why that house is so important to me."

"Only if you want to talk about it."

She closed her eyes with a ragged sigh, and when she opened them again, he saw just how emotional this was for her.

"I already told you a little about my mother," she said. "She was an addict. Drugs, alcohol, anything she could get her hands on. She dragged us from one place to another, one job to another, one man to another. Then when I was in high school, my grandmother contacted us. I'd never even met her before, but she'd been looking for us for years. When she found us, my mother had hit rock bottom. So she asked us to come live with her on the island."

"The house was hers?"

"Yes. And it was the only real home I'd ever had. And my grandmother…" Francie exhaled, closing her eyes for a moment. "My grandmother was wonderful. Whenever I came home from school, no matter how much of a mess my mother was, my grandmother was always there. She was in poor health and on Social Security, but she tried her best to give me whatever she could. Nothing big. Just decent meals. Somebody to talk to. Somebody to give a damn, you know?"

Dylan slid his hand across the table and placed it over Francie's. She turned her hand over, and he laced his fingers through hers.

"The night of that dance I told you about, she bought a bottle of nail polish and painted my nails. She told me it was about time I had a date, and that I was going to be the prettiest girl there." She paused. "I guess we both know how that turned out, right?"

A smile flickered on her face, but Dylan knew the memory still hurt. Then her smile faded into sadness.

"During my senior year, my grandmother died," Francie said. "My mother inherited everything, including that house. The funeral was barely over before she put it on the market. She moved us into a crappy apartment and used the rest of the money to feed her drug habit."

Dylan could only imagine how hard that must have been for Francie. First her grandmother died, and then the only real home she'd ever known had been jerked out from under her. How had she ever gotten through that?

"And Brittney's family bought it?" he said.

"Yes. And now she owns it. When she put it up for sale, I couldn't believe I was going to be able to buy it. I had no idea she wouldn't sell it to me."

Dylan couldn't believe this. Fortunately for Brittney, she wasn't standing in front of him right now. No telling what he might have done to her.

"I remember once when my mother did jail time and I got stuck in foster care," Francie said. "The people were nice enough, but..."

"It wasn't a home?"

Francie glanced across the bay again, a faraway look in her eyes. "Do you know my grandmother used to wait on the porch of that house every day for me to come home from school? Then she took me into the kitchen and gave me milk and cookies. Such a dumb thing. Milk and cookies. But it made that house feel so much like a home. I probably shouldn't say this because it sounds really pitiful, but..."

She looked away, and Dylan could tell she was trying to blink away tears.

"What?" he asked.

"She was the first person who ever loved me."

Her words just about broke his heart. Now he understood. He understood why she was wary of everyone, distrustful of everything, and why, no matter what the cost, she wanted to go back to that one place in her life where she'd finally felt loved.

"Where is your mother now?"

"Dead. People can only abuse themselves for so long the way she did before their bodies can't take it anymore."

"I'm sorry."

Francie lifted her shoulder in a tiny shrug. As he sat there holding her hand, the most amazing feeling came over him, an insatiable drive to give her the things she needed so much. It was too soon. He knew that. He hadn't known her long enough to feel the way he did, but those feelings were there just the same. And if he felt this way about her now, he couldn't even imagine what tomorrow might bring.

***

They sat on the deck, Francie's hand nestled inside Dylan's, until darkness fell and they could no longer see the house in the distance. Then they rose from the table and she helped him clear it.

"Thank you so much," she told him, as they brought the last of the dishes to the kitchen. "This has been a wonderful night."

"It has." He took the wine glass she held and set it down on the kitchen counter. "But it doesn't have to be over."

"Dylan—"

"No. Don't talk. Not yet."

He rested his hands on her forearms, then slid them down to take her hands in his. He pulled one of them to his lips and kissed it. Her heart shifted to a hard, thudding rhythm, but most of that was fear—fear that this couldn't possibly be real, that somehow she'd regret getting too close to him. But then he leaned in, slowly, so slowly, and touched his lips to hers. He closed his hand on the back of her neck and deepened the kiss, his tongue against hers, teasing, exploring, making every nerve in her body tighten with desire, and soon the fear coalesced into a small, insignificant cloud in the back of her mind.

"Now you can talk," he murmured.

Talk? When she was having a hard time even *breathing*? "Don't stop."

She barely got the words out before he was kissing her again. Kissing her until she barely knew where she was, until she lost track of time, until every reason she'd ever had for *not* kissing him vanished from her mind. Then he dropped his other hand to her hip, slid it down to her thigh, squeezing, releasing, pressing the length of his body against hers until she felt the ridge of his arousal along her lower belly. Then he traced his lips along her cheek until she felt his hot breath against her ear.

"I want you, Francie," he murmured. "I have from the moment I met you."

She listened closely to his words and his tone—anything to tell he might be lying—but she heard nothing at all like that in his voice.

He took her face in his hands, staring down at her with an intensity that made her shiver with desire. "Will you stay with me tonight?"

CHAPTER FOUR

Francie didn't have to ask herself if she wanted Dylan. Of course she *wanted* him. But would the aftermath be awkward? Upsetting?

Or would she be sitting on cloud nine?

"Come to bed with me," he murmured. "It's all I want. Just to make love to you until neither one of us can stand up."

And then he kissed her again, and she looped her arms around his neck, bunching his shirt in her fist and pulling him hard against her. She wanted him to keep that promise—to make love to her until she was breathing so hard she passed out.

"If you don't want this," he told her, "you need to say so now. But if you don't say so…"

"I'm not saying so," she said.

He stopped short. "Wait a minute. I got lost there. What does that mean?"

"It means yes."

"Yes you want to stay, or yes you don't?"

She looked at him with confusion.

"Sorry," he said. "It's taken a lot for me to get this far. I don't want to screw it up now."

She gave him a tiny smile. "You're not screwing anything up. Yes, I want to stay."

"Oh, thank God," he said, dropping his forehead against hers. Then he lifted his head again. "But I gotta warn you. It may mean I lock you in my bedroom and never let you go." His brows drew together. "Wait a minute. That makes me sound like a stalker. Cross that part out."

Francie had always imagined Dylan having his way with a woman, calling all the shots because he could, and then shrugging with indifference once it was over and moving on to his next conquest. But that wasn't what he was like at all. He'd been so kind to her when she told him about her the house, her mother, her grandmother, that she felt bad for all the times she'd assumed his motives to be less than pure.

He took her hand and led her through the living room into his bedroom, where she saw more floor-to-ceiling windows looking out on the beach. Dusk had fallen, and when he touched a switch on the wall to extinguish the lights, the darkness was almost complete. In the distance, she heard the surf hitting the shore, then falling back into the ocean.

He slid his hand along the curve of her spine to the small of her back, then further down to her ass. "I lied to you when we were in that bathroom," he said. "I wasn't looking at marble scraps."

"You weren't?"

"Oh, hell no. If you'd lived four hundred years ago and denim had been invented, there would have been sonnets written about your ass in these jeans."

Just the sound of his voice in the dark—deep, masculine, enticing—set off a hot, heavy pulsing between her legs, making those jeans so uncomfortable she damned near ripped them off.

"Good thing you didn't say that when we were in that bathroom," she told him.

"I know. You'd have tossed me out the second-story window."

He stepped back, took off his T-shirt, then came forward again. He grabbed the hem of her top and pulled it over her head, and as her arms came back down again, he reached around and pulled the elastic out of her hair that held up her ponytail. Her hair fell to her shoulders, and he burrowed his fingers into it, clasping the sides of her head and pulling her in for another kiss.

"I love your hair," he said between kisses. "You should wear it down more often."

"It gets in the way."

"Not in this bedroom, it doesn't. In here, I want you to wear it down. *Always*."

As she stood there in her bra, she had a terrible thought. She was wearing white underwear. Frumpy white underwear. Suddenly she wished for little scraps of hot pink satin covering just the critical parts of her body and nothing more, not yards of cotton and Lycra obscuring her from head to toe.

"Sorry," she said, feeling embarrassed. "I'd like to say I know Victoria's Secret, but I'm not much of a girly girl."

"I don't give a damn about that," Dylan said, flicking open her bra. "A woman with tools...*that's* what makes me hot." He leaned in to kiss her neck, his breath scorching hot. "And you work with your hands. You have no idea where my brain goes when I think about *that.*"

He peeled her bra off and tossed it aside. Then he lifted her breasts and teased her nipples with his thumbs until they tightened beneath his touch. She tipped her head backward and closed her eyes, relishing the feeling, wishing he would touch her forever.

Soon he eased her over to his king-sized bed and lay her on it, unzipping her jeans and taking them off along with her non-Victoria's Secret underwear. He froze, staring down at her.

"My God."

"What?"

"You are *so* beautiful."

When she turned away, he pointed at her admonishingly. "And no more of that crap about how you're not. From now on, I'll be the judge of that."

He stepped back and took off the rest of his clothes, and Francie could honestly say she'd never seen a man more beautiful than Dylan Bradford. He was tall and lean but muscled in just the right places, and when she saw his raging hard-on, she had to admit that all his talk of her turning him on just might be true after all.

He stretched out beside her, kissing and touching, teasing and tormenting, until she had to beg him to take her. He grabbed a condom and had it on in record time. He rose above her. Plunged inside her. She clasped his shoulders, rising to meet every stroke, loving how he seemed to lose all control, how all his smooth, polished behavior took a backseat to the kind raw sexuality she never would have imagined him showing her.

In no time she felt a spark, one that escalated into a roaring blaze so fast it took her breath away, culminating in a climax so deep and satisfying it seemed to go on forever. And when he came, he whispered her name in that deep, sexy voice she loved so much.

Dylan fell to the mattress beside Francie, breathing hard, his hand on his chest, looking totally spent but totally satisfied. Watching him now gave her the most wonderful feeling. *I did that. He feels that way because of me.*

Finally he took a deep, calming breath and exhaled slowly. When he turned to look at her, he was smiling. He pulled her into his arms and she rested her head against his chest, listening to the sound of the surf on the beach nearby and the strong, steady beat of his heart.

Francie had never known her father, but she remembered telling her grandmother she hated him anyway because he hadn't loved her enough to stay. Her grandmother told her to forget about him, to think instead about the man she would eventually marry. That man, she said, would love her forever. Francie had always wondered whether that was true or not. But lying in Dylan's arms right now, she felt like a desirable woman in a way she never had before. And for the first time in her life, she felt as if her grandmother's prediction was a dream that could actually come true.

***

Dylan was on the edge of sleep when his phone rang. He got out of bed and checked the caller ID, and his heart skipped with apprehension. He looked at Francie. "Brittney's agent."

Francie sat up, pulling the covers to her chest and waiting anxiously. Dylan hit the button and answered the call. He hoped Brittney had put away her grudge and accepted Francie's offer, but a few minutes later, he was forced to hang up and shake his head no. He tossed his phone aside and climbed back into bed, feeling as if he'd failed her in a major way.

"My God," Francie said, as she curled up next to him. "How much higher am I going to have to go to get her to sell me that house?"

"You can't go any higher. It'll only appraise for so much. So unless you can come up with a cash offer, you've hit the limit on what a bank will loan you."

"Cash offer?" she said. "I don't have that kind of money."

"I wish there was something I could do," he murmured. "Some way to get her to make the deal."

"This is Brittney we're talking about. She's not going to let go of that grudge."

Dylan knew that was true, but he still felt like crap.

"The house will sell quickly, won't it?" she asked.

"It's a good property with beach access, and the price is right." He hated every word coming out of his mouth, but it was the truth.

"Will you do me a favor?" Francie said.

"Anything."

"It's a multi-listed property, so you have the lockbox code. Will you take me there tomorrow? Before somebody else buys it? I'd like to see it one last time."

Dylan nodded, even as he knew there was nothing he wouldn't do to get Brittney to sell Francie that house. He just had no idea how he could possibly make that happen.

***

The next afternoon, Francie drove down the road toward her grandmother's house to meet Dylan, weaving past the mangroves and red cedars and the occasional hibiscus shrub with bright pink flowers. Then the tree-shaded road opened up to a spectacular view of the beach and her grandmother's house.

Dylan was already there, sitting in one of the Adirondack chairs on the front porch. Even at a distance, just looking at him reminded her of the night they'd spent together, and her heart pounded with the memory. Then she noticed something had changed about the *For Sale* sign in the yard, and she felt a stab of disappointment. A smaller sign was hanging beneath it.

Sold.

Her heart fell to the ground. Dylan had been right. The house had sold fast. She just hadn't expected it to sell *that* fast. So there it was. Somebody else bought the house she wanted more than anything. She walked up the steps to the porch and sat down beside him.

"So it sold," she said. "Do you know the details?"

"Yeah. The agent made the deal this afternoon."

"When is the closing?"

"The offer was for cash with no financing involved, so the deal is closing in three days."

Three days. Francie felt sick. "That's fast."

"Yeah. This guy knew he had to jump in before any other buyers did, and cash talks."

She swallowed hard, determined not to cry. It was just a house. That was all. But…oh, God. She'd wanted it so much.

"So who bought it?" she asked.

"Well, that's where things get a little crazy."

"Crazy? What do you mean?"

Dylan paused. "I bought it."

"You?"

"Yes."

Francie was stunned. He'd bought this house? The house she wanted? The house she loved? After watching her cry over the fact that she couldn't buy it, *he* had?

"I don't understand," she said. "Why would you do that?"

"So I can sell it to you."

Francie just sat there dumbly, waiting for his words to sink in.

"I got to thinking about it this morning," Dylan said. "I knew Brittney wouldn't sell the house to you, but she'd sell it to me. And once I'm the owner…" He took Francie's hand. "Whether she likes it or not, pretty soon it's going to be yours."

Francie could barely fathom what he was saying. "You're going to sell it to me?"

"You do still want it, don't you?"

"Want it? Are you *kidding* me?"

"Now, wait a minute. There's a catch. You have to give me exactly what I paid for it."

"Oh, I will! Whatever it takes! I was ready to give Brittney the full asking price. So of course I'd be willing to give it to you. Or ten thousand more. I don't care."

Dylan looked at her admonishingly. "Francie. Please. I told you full price offers give me hives."

"What?"

"I offered her twenty thousand less than her asking price."

"Twenty *thousand*? Surely she didn't—"

"Surely she did. Turns out she had a few debts to pay off. She'll take her grudge against you to the grave. But the minute I offered her something close to the sales price, she took it."

"But she could have gotten so much more!"

"I never said she was smart."

"I don't believe this," Francie said. "I'm getting the house, *and* I'm paying twenty thousand less?" Tears filled her eyes. She blinked, and a few spilled down her cheeks. She brushed them away, but more came. Then, in spite of everything, a tiny laugh escaped her lips. "Oh, my God. Brittney is going to be furious."

"Oh, yeah. So maybe we'd better keep things quiet until I have the property in my name."

Francie nodded. "I can't believe you're doing this for me."

He reached out and put his hand over hers. "Sweetheart, I'd have done anything in my power to make sure you got this house."

Francie had never felt so overwhelmed in her life. She took Dylan's face in her hands and kissed him. Then she kissed him again. And again. Then she decided maybe she'd just sit on this porch and kiss him from now on.

"So," Dylan said, when they finally came up for air, "what are you going to do with the place?"

Francie looked around. "Restore it. I want the house to look just like it did when my grandmother lived here. It was beautiful, Dylan. Seriously. Somebody has painted all the woodwork. Renters, probably, because it's a mess. But I can strip all that and refinish it. And the kitchen is a wreck, but give me a few weeks and I'll have it looking like a million bucks. And the grounds. I know with a little bit of attention, the landscaping will be beautiful again."

"Sure you can handle all that?" he said with a smile.

"It's what I do, buster. Just sit back and watch me."

Over the next few weeks, after working on other properties during the day, Francie headed to the beach house in the evenings. She painted and reworked and refinished the place, leaving the vintage charm to shine through. Dylan worked alongside her, helping her make the house come alive. And when he showed up one evening looking just a little too perfect, it was definitely worth cleaning up the mess for the fun of nailing him with the paint sprayer.

As the days passed, Dylan wrapped her in the kind of love and affection she'd never known before. Her wariness and suspicion fell away until she finally believed him when he said she was beautiful and trusted that he'd always look out for her. She relaxed in his arms, letting all her doubts and worries about life and love seep out of her to be washed away with the tide.

Dylan spent so much time at the house that he finally quit going back to his condo altogether. It was on the market now, and the market was hot. He'd have a buyer in no time. The place was beautiful, he told her, but it wasn't a home like the home they'd made together.

Then early one morning, with the sea breeze swirling through the bedroom window, he leaned in close and whispered that he loved her. And she told him she loved him, too. In that moment, her grandmother's prediction that someday she'd find the man of her dreams who would love her forever had finally come true.

Coming Home

Denise Grover Swank

CHAPTER ONE

Jane squeezed her eyes shut at the sounds coming from the bathroom. The guy had three beers in the span of a few hours, and he had a hangover, retching in the toilet as proof.

But that wasn't fair. Raymond didn't usually drink and was reluctant when Jane and Raymond's cousin Steve encouraged him to keep up with them. Poor Raymond hadn't stood a chance and was paying for it now.

Nasty sounds filtered through the bathroom door. Jane threw back the covers and padded across the hardwood floor to the window, throwing open the shutters to face the morning.

She was getting married in two days.

Funny how months ago, marrying Raymond had seemed like the sensible thing to do, but the closer she got to the date, and the closer she'd gotten to Seeker's Island, the more unsure she was about her decision.

The first part she blamed on pre-wedding jitters. The second part she blamed on J.B. Hunt.

J.B. Hunt had been blamed for many things over the last eleven years, and truth be told, he only deserved about half the blame.

But in this instance, he deserved all of it.

With a heavy sigh, Jane leaned out the second story window and breathed in the smell of gardenias and moss. Jane hadn't realized how much she missed the smell. She hadn't been home in years, eleven to be exact, and she wouldn't be here now if it weren't for her lifelong best friend, Isabella. After Jane's grandmother died her freshman year in college, Isabella was the closest thing she had to family.

Raymond began a new round of vomiting in the other room. Jane knew she should go check on him, but she wasn't ready to face him yet. For the last fifteen hours, every time she saw him, her heart raced, and her skin grew clammy. After the numerous drinks Jane had at the Seeker's Paradise tiki bar last night, the voice in her head still needled her. *This is a mistake.* Was it? Raymond was dependable and levelheaded. He was everything J.B. Hunt was not. That alone was reason enough to marry him.

Her cell phone rang, and she dug it out of her purse, frustrated she'd forgotten to charge it before she'd fallen into bed the night before. She answered on the third ring, smiling as she sat on the end of the bed. "Bella, how was Liam's game last night?"

Isabella sighed. "The boy has two left feet, but he loves baseball. He's lucky he gets to play. Most coaches of eight-year-olds are too competitive."

"I really wish I'd come to watch him last night. I'm dying to see you both." Raymond had agreed to go, but Jane knew by the way his lip pulled higher on his left side that he'd only agreed to appease her. He hated crowds, and she was fairly certain he would have been on edge listening to moms and dads cheering on their kids. But if they'd gone, he might not be hugging the toilet right now.

"What's on the agenda today?"

"Raymond had his heart set on taking a boat out on the ocean."

"Raymond doesn't seem like a boating type of guy."

Jane laughed. "Oh, he's definitely not. He hired a charter boat to take us out for several hours this morning and afternoon. Something about a tour and gourmet lunch."

Isabella paused for a second before answering in a strained voice, "Who's the tour with?"

Jane reached over to the nightstand and picked up a piece of paper that Raymond had scribbled the name and number on. "Paradise Boat Tours." Turning toward the bathroom, Jane puckered her mouth in disapproval. "Not that we're going now. Raymond had three beers last night, and he's throwing up his breakfast from two days ago."

"He's hung over from three beers?"

"You know he can't drink." Isabella and Liam visited Jane in Charlotte a couple of years ago when Jane and Raymond had just begun dating. They'd gone out to dinner, and Raymond hadn't realized the lemonade he was drinking had been spiked. He drank three and spent the entire next day in bed.

"So Raymond can't go?"

"I don't see how. I told him he'd probably get sea sick anyway, now he's sure to puke his guts up." Jane knew she should be more sympathetic, but she couldn't be anywhere near someone throwing up without losing it herself. "It's okay. I didn't really want to go anyway. I was just going for Raymond."

"I'm going to ask you something, Jane, and it's only because you know I love you." Isabella paused. "Are you really, really sure you love Raymond?"

"How can you ask me that?" But there was no indignation in Jane's voice. She'd asked herself that same question the last few weeks. She couldn't say yes, but she couldn't say no either. "I have to admit that I've wondered."

She looked back at the door to the bathroom. While it was true she'd never experienced the full on lust she'd had with J.B., she couldn't help wondering if that wasn't a good thing. Especially after how *that* had turned out. "It's just cold feet, Bella. That's all. I'm sure it's normal to be nervous before making a big commitment like this. I always get anxious before a big presentation at work, wondering if I've taken the right angle, pursued the right strategy. It's the same thing. There's no one hundred percent guarantee with anything."

"Are you really comparing a marketing presentation to getting married?"

"You know what I mean."

"So you're admitting that you're not head-over-heels in love with Raymond."

"Bella, that kind of love doesn't exist."

"It does, Jane. I've had it."

Jane sighed. "But you're still alone."

"I'm not alone. I have Liam."

Jane leaned her head into her hand. "I love that little guy, and you're so lucky to have him. But I have no one except for Raymond."

"You had that kind of love yourself once."

"Yeah, and J.B broke my heart."

"But you loved him, right? Once upon a time?"

"You know I did." When Jane could look past the way J.B. betrayed her, she had to admit that what they'd had was almost perfect. But J.B. taught her that there was no such thing as perfect. The kind of love she had with J.B. didn't last. Jane needed reality. Jane needed someone dependable like Raymond.

"Jane, I think you should go on the boat tour by yourself." Isabella's voice was soft and hesitant.

"By myself? No. If I can't cancel, I'll see if Raymond's cousin wants to go instead."

"No!" Isabella took a breath and lowered her voice. "No. You've been working so hard and getting ready for the wedding. You should go by yourself and relax in the sun. You love the ocean. When was the last time you went out on it?"

"Yesterday on the ferry," Jane said dryly. "It's the only way on the island."

"You know what I mean. Do this for me. Please? You know I never ask anything from you."

"That is so not true. You asked me to have the wedding here on the island at Paradise Wedding Chapel."

"That's because it will be so perfect. But seriously, go on this tour and lie in the sun and think about whether marrying Raymond is what you really want. And if you do, we'll finish up all the wedding preparations tomorrow, and you'll have the most beautiful wedding Seeker's Island has ever seen."

Jane sighed. She would love to get away from everyone and everything and spend some time alone out on the sea. Isabella had always helped put things in perspective. "Okay. But only if Raymond is okay. I can't leave him if he's really sick."

"Of course, but if he's okay, you should go, and I hope you thank me later. And just one more thing."

Jane shook her head with a laugh. "Yes?"

"Visit the hot springs."

Jane groaned. "That is where I draw the line. You're the

superstitious one who believes in that nonsense. *You* go."

"I did a couple of days ago." She pauses. "What can it hurt? Besides you haven't been on the island in forever. You should walk around and see what's changed."

"I suspect not much." Jane closed her eyes. Isabella was right. What could it hurt? "Fine. If Raymond is okay, I'll get him settled and rent a golf cart to go up to the hot springs before I go to the marina. I'll have plenty of time."

"Just relax and have fun."

"Sure." Easy for Isabella to say. She wasn't the one getting married on Saturday, in front of three hundred guests. Two hundred and seventy of them were invited by Raymond's family.

Deep breath. She could do this.

Jane cracked the door to the bathroom and peeked in on Raymond. He sat on the tile floor, his legs extended, leaning his head on the arm he draped around the toilet seat. His pale complexion was whiter than usual and made his auburn hair even redder. The poor guy looked miserable.

"How are you?"

He gave her a weak grin. "Terrible. Sorry if I woke you."

"You didn't wake me." It was a lie, but he felt bad enough already.

"We were supposed to go on that cruise…"

Seeing Raymond like this cemented the fact that she couldn't leave him. "I'll call and cancel."

"You can't." He closed his eyes. "It's nonrefundable."

"Maybe Steve wants to—"

"He already has other plans." He groaned and leaned his face closer to the bowl. "You should go. You're always talking about how much you miss the sea. I booked the trip for you."

Tears filled Jane's eyes as she rested her temple on the doorframe. He'd done this for her. "I can't leave you like this, and what about your parents?"

He shook his head with a grim smile. "Honestly, I hope to sleep most of the day, and we'd planned to go on this thing anyway. And my parents won't be in until tonight." His eyes opened, full of love. "Go and have fun. I'll be here waiting for you when you come back."

The look in his eyes sent a shard of guilt into her heart. How could she doubt their relationship? Raymond would do anything for her. She was lucky to have him.

"Please, Jane. I want you to go. This was a gift for you."

She nodded, unable to speak through the lump in her throat. She didn't deserve him.

"I made the reservations under my name with a guy named Brandon. We were supposed to have a romantic lunch at sea." He groaned and leaned over the toilet. "It wouldn't be so romantic if I went. I love you, Jane. Go and have fun."

A half hour later, Jane felt like the worst fiancée in the world. She was sure Raymond wasn't hung over and instead had food poisoning from the potato salad he had yesterday afternoon, before they got on the island. But he'd still insisted she go, especially since the worst of his bathroom experience seemed to be over. She tucked him into bed and made sure he had some crackers and water before she left.

Mrs. Adams, the owner of Sunseekers' Inn, was in the dining room with several others of the bed and breakfast guests when Jane came downstairs. Jane guessed her to be in her sixties, but she was still very attractive. One of the elderly men couldn't take his eyes off of her ample breasts.

Jane pulled her to the side. "My fiancé isn't feeling well, but he insists that I go on this boat tour." Jane still wasn't sure this was a good idea.

The gray-haired woman patted Jane's arm. "Not to worry, dear. I'll check on him later and make sure he's okay."

Jane smiled, relief easing her guilt. "Thank you."

"Are your future in-laws still coming in early this evening?"

A ball formed in the pit of Jane's stomach. Their arrival made the wedding all too real. "Last I heard."

The innkeeper nodded with a friendly smile as she turned back to her guests. "Not to worry, Jane. Their room will be ready."

The day was already hot and humid, and she was grateful she'd chosen to wear a sundress. Unsure what to expect with the cruise, she packed a swimming suit and a towel in a bag, but she stopped by one of the tourist shops for sunscreen. With any luck at all, she'd be able to lie out during the cruise. If she and Raymond were supposed to have a romantic lunch, maybe she'd be alone and wouldn't be self-conscious about it.

The shop was on the main tourist strip, close to the bed and breakfast she and Raymond stayed in. She'd been right about not much changing, although she couldn't remember a Paradise Boat Tours back when she'd lived on the island over a decade before.

After she grabbed an iced coffee and a scone from the bakery, she rented a golf cart. She and Bella had often walked or ridden their bikes on the eight-mile round trip when they were younger, and Jane was tempted now, but she'd never make it up and back in time for the boat tour. She turned down a side street toward the hot springs to avoid the main route taken by tourists. The only options for motorized transportation on the island were golf carts and riding lawn mowers. It was one of Seeker's Island's appeal to tourists. Most people couldn't imagine living without cars. Jane had thought it odd to find so many on the road when she left the island for college.

In any case, Jane couldn't believe she'd agreed to Isabella's ridiculous request. The legend may be ingrained in island folklore, but it was a myth, no matter if Isabella believed in it or not. Nothing could give you your heart's desire, especially a hot spring at the edge of a small island off the Florida Keys. Not that it stopped the tourists from traipsing up there seven days a week, rain or shine. But today was a beautiful morning—no rain in sight—and it was nice to be back somewhere familiar. No matter how far Jane ran from Seeker's Island, it always felt like home. Almost.

When she reached the spring, the tourist crowd was smaller than she expected, but Amos, the self-appointed caretaker, shuffled at the edge of the trees surrounding the pool. He used to spend a lot more time in the spring than out back when Jane was younger. It was a wonder he hadn't turned into a prune, although his face was wrinkled enough. Amos had to be in his eighties by now.

The legend stated that you had to touch the water to find your heart's desire. How many times had Isabella and Jane sneaked up here as kids? Daydreaming about the men they'd eventually fall in love with and marry. One hot summer afternoon between their seventh and eighth-grade years, they made their wish, and on the way home, Jane's bike had gotten a flat tire, throwing Jane off her bike and skinning up her hands and knees. J.B. Hunt had stumbled upon them and sat on the side of the road with her until she stopped crying then pushed her bike home to her grandmother's house.

Jane had known J.B. practically her whole life, but that was the first time she'd thought of him as anything more than an annoying boy.

That was the day Jane fell in love.

Six years later she found J.B. on his dad's fishing boat with Sheila Sewell, both of them naked and in a compromising situation.

There was no such thing as true love and your heart's desire. The spring was a joke. But a promise was a promise, and Isabella always knew when Jane was lying. She'd touch the stupid water, make her request, then drive down to the pier so she could catch the boat tour.

The water was just as warm as she remembered, which was surprising, given the cold waterfall that dumped into the opposite end. Jane closed her eyes, reached out to the pool with her fingertips, and whispered, "I want my heart's desire."

Tears burned her eyes when she opened them. This trip was a wasted effort. Any hope of her heart's desire died eleven years ago on J.B.'s father's boat.

CHAPTER TWO

The sun shone bright and hot overhead when Jane reached the marina. The ocean cruiser was tied to the dock behind a sign that read *Paradise Boat Tours*. Jane guessed the yacht to be over forty feet long, and it looked fairly new and shiny. Raymond must have paid a fortune for this excursion, making her feel even guiltier about her doubts and her irritation with him this morning. He'd gone out of his way to do something nice for her, and she questioned if she loved him.

Goodness, she was a bitch.

A teenage boy emerged from the cabin, wearing a grin. "You must be Mrs. Brinkley."

Tilting her head, she gave a tiny shake. "Not yet."

Confusion flickered in the boy's eyes.

"I'll be Mrs. Brinkley in two days."

His mouth formed an *O* as his face lit with understanding. "So *your* wedding is causing all of the excitement on the island."

Jane held up her hand. "Guilty as charged. Are you Brandon?" He seemed too young to own a boat this nice, but maybe his daddy bought it for him so he could run the cruises as a hobby.

The boy laughed. "No. I wish." He moved toward her. "I'm Austin. Brandon got tied up running an errand. I'll be serving your lunch today. Brandon said to greet you and Mr. Brinkley when you got here and get you settled." Austin looked over her shoulder toward the marina. "Is Mr. Brinkley coming?"

She offered him a grim smile. "No, Raymond is feeling a bit under the weather. It'll be just me." Her eyes widened. "Will that be a problem?"

"A problem? Shoot no. I'll get the leftovers, and today's lunch is really good. But don't tell Brandon that I told you that." He winked. "I'd tell you what the lunch is, but it's supposed to be a surprise."

"Raymond didn't share much information about the cruise. Is there anyone else joining us?" Jane tried to peer around him to see if anyone else was on board.

"No, the excursions are private." He waved to her bag. "Did you bring a swimming suit?"

"Yeah."

"You can change in the cabin below, and after you get out to sea a bit, you can lay out on the deck. Are you ready to climb aboard?"

Jane glanced over her shoulder toward the shore. "Should I wait for the captain?"

"Oh, no. He'll be here in a minute or two."

She grabbed his outstretched hand, stepping onto the yacht.

When she found her footing, Austin dropped her hand. "You're welcome to explore the boat. And if you want to go down to the cabin below and change, feel free."

She glanced into the cabin and saw a gorgeous interior with a cloth-covered table. The seats were upholstered in leather and the furnishings were impeccably clean. This was a far cry from Brandon's dad's fishing boat, where she'd spent a lot of time dodging fishing nets. "Maybe I should wait to change until after lunch."

He laughed. "It looks fancy, but you can wear a cover up, and you'll be fine. Or since it's just you, you might rather eat a picnic on the deck."

She hesitated.

"Future Mrs. Brinkley—"

Jane laughed. "Jane. Jane Morgan."

Austin paused for several seconds, the smile frozen on his face before he gave his head a tiny shake. "After you look around, go ahead and change down below, Ms. Morgan. Brandon should be here any minute, and we'll head out to sea."

***

Brandon Hunt was frustrated as hell. Yesterday, he'd heard through the island gossip-vine that Jane Morgan was back on the island. After a long, sleepless night, Brandon knew he had to see her. Especially if the rumors were true.

Jane was getting married.

He wasn't sure why it surprised him. Whenever he allowed himself to think about her, he always pictured her married, with kids, living in a sprawling house and driving a minivan. Her parents died when she was in grade school and she'd moved in with her grandmother. After that, Jane had been obsessed with having a family of her own. If anything, he was surprised she was thirty years old and just now getting married. But when he thought of her married, and with someone else, it strangled his heart. Jane was the first girl he'd ever loved. She'd probably be the only girl he'd ever love. After his idiotic stunt eleven years ago, he'd tried to move on, dating other women, but no one could measure up.

For Jonathon Brandon Hunt, there was only Jane.

When he woke up that morning, Brandon knew he had to see her. He had to know she was happy. He might not know where she was staying, but he knew the first place to look. Isabella Kelsey's daycare.

He caught her while the kids were outside with the other workers. She walked through the common play area picking up toys, refusing to look at him. "What are you doing here, J.B.?"

"You know I go by Brandon now."

"Sorry, but you'll always be J.B. to me."

No one had understood his need to change his name once he'd finally grown into a man, but most had relented and accepted it. All but Isabella. "I need to see her."

She stood up and put a hand on her hip. "Seems like you made sure she saw plenty of you years ago, when she found you with Sheila, didn't you?"

"That was eleven years ago, and you know I was an idiot. *Everyone* knows I was an idiot."

Her eyes pierced his. "I don't know what you intended with that stunt, but you didn't just break her heart, J.B., you destroyed her. She's not the girl you once loved. You took care of that."

His breath caught in his chest. Brandon had often considered asking Isabella how Jane was doing, but for several years, she'd refused to acknowledge his presence, let alone talk to him. She'd finally had to concede to civility when Liam had started Little League and Brandon helped with his six-year-old team. But even then, they never discussed life before he sent Jane away.

"I didn't mean to hurt her."

Her narrowed eyes pierced his. "That's a lie, and we both know it. You knew she was coming to your boat that night. You could hardly stand Sheila Sewell. You meant to destroy Jane."

He shook his head. The crazy thing was he thought he was doing her a favor all those years ago. "No, Isabella. I only wanted what was best for her, and I wasn't it."

"Wasn't that for her to decide?"

Brandon didn't have an answer.

Isabella dumped her load of toys into a toy box. "Do you still love her?"

"I…it's been—"

"Cut the crap, J.B. You know I've always been able to see through all of it. Do you love her? Yes or no?"

He hadn't seen Jane in eleven years, but not one day went by that he didn't think of her. How he wished he'd done things differently. "Yes."

Isabella sucked in her bottom lip while she watched him. The back door opened, and the sound of boisterous children filled the room as they poured inside. She picked up a stack of napkins and began to set them on the short tables.

"I can't tell you where she is."

"But—"

"Go back to your boat, J.B. Don't you have an excursion to run today?"

He did, and if it wasn't already too late, he would have cancelled it. He wasn't in the mood to deal with clients. Any other day he loved his job, but today he couldn't pretend he was happy and cordial. He'd stay at the helm and let Austin take care of everything and cancel tonight and tomorrow's trips.

By the time he got back to the marina, Brandon was in a foul mood. Austin emerged from the back of the cockpit, antsy with excitement.

"Brandon—"

"Let's get this boat out on the water," Brandon growled.

"Brandon, listen—"

Brandon began the checklist he always ran before taking the yacht out to sea. "I need you to run—"

"Brandon!"

Exasperated, he turned around to face the teen. "What?"

"She's here." Austin whispered. "On the boat."

Brandon's heart seized. "Who?"

"Her. Your Jane."

Brandon's eyes widened. He'd told Austin his sad tale several times, mostly as a warning not to be a fool like Brandon had been. "How? Where?"

"She's your charter today."

Shaking his head, Brandon's eyes narrowed. "No, the reservation was for two. Raymond Brinkley and guest."

"His guest is Jane."

Brandon stepped backward, the window pressing into his back. "She's here with her fiancé?" He had to cancel and refund their money. There was no way he could take them out for four hours and watch another man touch her.

"No, she's alone."

The blood rushed from his head. "*What*?"

"Her fiancé's sick. She's here alone."

"Does she know—?"

"That you're the captain? No."

Brandon looked around the small salon. "Where is she?"

"Down in the cabin changing into her swimsuit."

In a split-second decision, Brandon pushed Austin toward the dock. "You're not going today."

Austin broke into a huge smile. "What if she doesn't want to spend the day with you?"

"If we're out to sea when she finds out, she won't be able to do anything about it."

Austin leapt over the side, onto the deck, and began to untie the boat. "You better get going. She's been down there for a bit. She'll be out any minute."

Brandon practically vaulted up the stairs to the helm and started the motors. Technically, what he was doing couldn't be considered kidnapping. Her trip was prepaid.

Austin untied the last rope and shouted, “Good luck!”

Brandon waved and pulled the boat away from the dock. He was definitely going to need it.

CHAPTER THREE

Brandon hadn't been this nervous in years. His heart hammered against his ribs and his sweaty palms slipped on the steering wheel. Once he was far enough away from the dock to deter Jane from jumping overboard and swimming back to shore, a small bit of tension eased. But he was still anxious about her reaction when she realized she was alone with him on the yacht. Hopefully, he'd be farther out before she realized. The more distance between them and land, the better chance he stood.

What he hoped to achieve, he wasn't sure. He didn't dare hope to win her back. Too much time had passed. He'd hurt her too badly. Maybe he needed to hear from her that she was happy. Or maybe he needed to tell her how sorry he was and what a fool he'd been.

One thing was certain. She was going to kill him.

***

The sound of the engines caught Jane by surprise. She'd spent more time dawdling downstairs and investigating the cabin than she intended. The yacht was by far the nicest she'd ever been on, and growing up on an island, she'd spent a lot of time on boats. She changed into her bikini, then put her sundress on over it. She suddenly felt self-conscious being the only woman on the boat. For now, she'd leave her dress on. She could remove it later if she felt comfortable.

After she covered herself with sunscreen, she pulled her sunglasses out of her bag and found a fluffy towel that Austin must have left for her. She wished she'd thought to bring a book to read, but she hadn't even brought one on the trip, which was totally unlike her. But one didn't typically bring a book to their wedding.

The yacht swayed, but Jane easily found her footing, an ingrained habit. When she climbed the steps to the salon, she looked around and saw that they were already a good distance from the marina and out on the water. Jane glanced around for Austin, but he was nowhere to be found. Unsure what to do, she sat on one of the pristine white leather cushions in the open-aired section at the back of the boat.

The captain stood up in the helm above, his back to her as he gazed out onto the water. He had the engines open full throttle, racing away from the island, which seemed strange. Weren't these things supposed to be leisurely cruises? She thought about calling up to him, but the wind would drown out any attempt at conversation.

Instead, she stretched her legs out on the long bench, leaning back on her elbows and lifting her face to the sun. The wind whipped Jane's long hair behind her, and she tried to tuck her hair behind her ear, before the wind grabbed hold and blew it around her face. She left her hair band in her bag, and considered getting it, but enjoyed the sunshine and the water too much to move. Isabella was right. The sea had always helped her put things in perspective. Maybe she'd feel surer about her decision to marry Raymond before she stepped back onto land in a few hours.

***

Brandon's breath froze in his chest when he saw Jane emerge from below.

After all this time, she was so close yet so far away.

She peered around then looked up at him over her shoulder.

His hands gripped the steering wheel until his palms burned. But she sat on the cushion, oblivious to his identity.

He blew out a breath of relief, but the truth was he was postponing the inevitable. Still, he was grateful to get this extra time—to bask in her presence—even if she was twelve feet away and unaware of his identity.

She stretched her legs out on the cushions and leaned back on her elbows, her long, thick chestnut hair blowing in the wind. Sometimes, late at night when he felt sentimental, he thought about her hair. How it draped over her shoulders, down her chest so the ends brushed her breasts.

They were each other's first love. They lost their virginity together the summer between their junior and senior year of high school, the night of Jane's seventeenth birthday. Brandon had tried to make the night special for her, a blanket on the beach with a picnic dinner. He brought his guitar and played a song he'd written for her. Afterward, her gave her the gift he'd saved his money for almost year—a ring—bigger than a promise ring, but not quite an engagement ring. He'd slipped it on her left ring finger, and the tears in her eyes had been his undoing. Brandon was too young to realize the significance of what they had. Too inexperienced to realize it was once in a lifetime.

Their first time was awkward as they fumbled in the dark, learning each other's bodies. But by the time Jane left the island for college a year later, they were well in tune with one another. They were creative with places to be together, but his father's boat was the most frequent. It shamed him now that he realized what he'd so casually thrown away. Jane deserved so much more.

But that was a lie. He hadn't casually thrown her away. He'd done it because he loved her, and she was considering dropping out of college to be with him. Brandon had always known he belonged on Seeker's Island, but Jane had wanted more. He couldn't bear the thought of her giving up her dream for him.

So he'd slept with the girl who'd been a thorn in Jane's side since middle school. Just to make sure he drove the stake through her heart deep enough to send her away.

It nauseated him now, when he thought of being with Sheila. He'd only ever been with Jane before her, and sleeping with Sheila tainted him, poisoned him somehow. Even now, it made him itch for a shower.

He glanced over his shoulder at Jane. Her dress had blown up nearly to her crotch and his groin tightened. *She's wearing a swimsuit, pervert.* But the thought didn't settle his hormones, only spiked them higher when he let himself imagine her naked.

His mind wandered to dangerous territory, dangerous because he couldn't act on his impulse. Jane was engaged. And even if she wasn't, she hated him. Justifiably. Brandon would be lucky if she didn't shove him overboard.

***

Jane had begun to doze off when the engines slowed. She'd forgotten how relaxing it was on the water. But any remembrance of the water brought J.B. close on its heels.

Would she always mourn the loss of J.B. Hunt?

She looked around, amazed that they were completely out to sea with no land in site. But then again, Seeker's Island was on the edge of the Florida coast, and it didn't take long to be out in the ocean.

The engines turned completely off, and she sat up. Where was Austin? She hadn't seen him since before she went down to the cabin to change.

The captain stood on the helm, facing forward.

"Are we having engine trouble?" she called up to him.

"No." He answered, still facing the sea.

Something about him seemed familiar.

A slight unease slid over her skin, soaking in her pores, and filling her with dread.

He leaned over and turned backward to climb down the stairs, his face hidden. When he reached the bottom, he slowly turned around to face her.

Jane's breath stuck in her chest, her diaphragm refusing to move. Tears burned her eyes, and some deep-seated instinct told her to flee, but her body froze.

J.B.

He'd changed, of course. He looked older, a little harder. His lanky frame had filled out, and his hair was shorter, but he was still her J.B.

No. He was no longer hers.

He watched her, his brow furrowed, but the rest of his face remained expressionless.

She had to say something, *do something,* but all she could do was let the tears fall down her cheeks.

"Jane." His voice broke as he reached a hand toward her.

His movement spurred her into action, and she jerked backward, the small of her back bumping into the side of the boat.

J.B. lifted his hands in surrender and took a step away. "I'm sorry. I didn't mean to startle you."

He's sorry.

How many years had she waited to hear him say that?

She choked on a sob, and her anger finally found a foothold, clamoring to the surface. She looked around. "Where's Austin?"

He swallowed, fear in his eyes. "He stayed on the island."

Jane brushed her hair out of her eyes. "I don't understand how you got on this boat."

"It's mine."

She shook her head slowly. "No. The boat belongs to a guy named Brandon." But even as she said it, she remembered. Jonathon Brandon Hunt.

His eyes pleaded with her. "I didn't know, Jane. I didn't know it was you until I got on board."

"And you still took it out?" She stood, clenching her fists. "Is this some kind of sick joke?"

J.B.'s mouth dropped. "No." His voice softened. "God, no. I just had to talk to you. I had to see you one more time."

"So you kidnapped me!"

"No." His jaw clenched and his eyes turned glassy. "I just had to talk to you."

She lifted her chin, glaring at him. "There's nothing you have to say that I want to hear." It was a bitter lie. How many nights had she cried herself to sleep, a one-word mantra in her head.

Why?

But she'd made a big enough fool of herself already, losing control and crying—crying for God's sake—at the sight of him. That must feed his ego, but even that was a lie. J.B. didn't have an ego. In the entire time they'd been together he'd done nothing but love and protect her. Cherish her. That's why his betrayal made no sense. Why it destroyed her. If she couldn't trust J.B., was there anyone she could trust?

***

Hearing the pain in her voice sent a knife through his gut, her tears twisting it deeper. Seeing her cry had always killed him, ever since the day he fell in love with her. The day he found her crying on the side of the road. He'd known her his entire life, but that day had imprinted her onto his heart. He vowed he'd do everything in his power to make sure she never cried again, even if she'd never known of his vow.

He'd betrayed her, and he wasn't sure he'd ever forgive himself.

Brandon kept his back to the wall, watching confusion wash over her face.

"You go by Brandon now?"

He nodded.

"Why?"

What could he tell her? That he'd died the day he sent her away. He wasn't the boy she'd known, and he'd changed his name to reflect it. "I grew up, so I changed my name."

She worried the right side of her lip between her teeth, a habit she'd had as long as he remembered. Nostalgia washed through him, hot and sweet, and part of him ached to kiss the spot, to feel her in his arms again.

But she was no longer his.

"You're getting married on Saturday?"

She nodded, her chin trembling.

"Does he deserve you?"

Pain flickered in her eyes and she inhaled sharply before she turned away from him and sat on the cushion. "I don't deserve him."

He moved next to her, easing himself on the seat beside her. "How can you say that?"

She looked up at him when she heard his voice break, fresh tears streaming down her face. "You ruined me, J.B. I'm not sure I love him. I'm not sure I can ever love anyone after what you did to me."

Panic and grief blindsided him. He thought she'd move on. Find a guy in college and get the family she always wanted. He knew he'd hurt her, but he never realized how permanent the damage would be. "I'm sorry." The words were heavy on his tongue and came out slurred. "I didn't mean to hurt you."

Jane shook her head and snorted, a bitter laugh that sounded unnatural coming from her. "I can't believe you just said that."

He wanted to ask her if she was happy, but how could she be when she confessed she was marrying a man she wasn't sure she loved?

What the hell had he done?

He stood and began pacing.

"Why am I here, J.B.?" Her voice broke as she turned to face him. "What the hell do you want from me?"

"I wanted to know if you were okay."

Her bottom lip quivered. "Why? Why do you care?"

"Because I still love you." The words were out before he could stop them. "In all these years, I've never stopped loving you."

She bolted off the bench. "How can you say that? What gives you the right to say that after you did what you did?" Her voice rose. "I loved you, J.B. I loved you with everything in me and you threw me away. Why?" Her fury fell away. "Why?" she whispered, searching his face.

Without her anger, she looked fragile and shattered. He'd done this. He'd broken her and he'd never forgive himself. "Because I loved you."

A sob escaped with a laugh, and she pressed her knuckles to her lips.

He took a step forward and stopped when she shrunk away from him. "You were talking about quitting school because you were afraid I wouldn't wait for you." He swallowed, forcing himself to continue. "I couldn't let you do that, Janie. I loved you too much to let you give up your dream."

"You were my dream, J.B." A new sob escaped. "*You* were."

"I'm so sorry." He reached for her and pulled her into his arms. She resisted, but he held firm, pressing her head to his chest as sobs wracked her body.

They stood there for several minutes, with Jane in his arms as the boat bobbed on the ocean waves. He berated himself for causing her this fresh misery, but he couldn't be sorry for the chance to hold her one last time.

When she settled down, he still held her close, grateful she hadn't pulled away yet. "I was young and stupid, Jane. I thought letting you go was the honorable thing to do."

She gripped his shirt in tight fists, squeezing them tighter at his words. "How could hurting me be honorable?"

"I told you I was stupid, Jane. I thought I was doing you a favor. I know it sounds naive, but we were kids. I wanted you to have the life you deserved. A career, kids…"

Tilting her head back, she looked into his face. "You were the life I deserved, J.B. I was lost without you."

"I'm sorry," he whispered, staring into her dark gray eyes before his gaze drifted to her lips. Her eyes were swollen, her nose red, and her face tear-streaked, but she was the most beautiful thing he'd ever seen.

He couldn't believe she was still here, her body pressed against his. He'd only wanted to talk to her one last time, get the closure he needed. Brandon planned to get her out of his system, but she was as much a part of him as the blood that flowed through his veins. He'd never get over her.

He definitely hadn't planned to kiss her, but stopping himself was like telling his heart not to beat.

CHAPTER FOUR

Jane lifted her face, every part of her wanting him to kiss her. When his lips touched hers, comfort and peace surrounded her. Kissing J.B. was like coming home.

She dropped her hold on his shirt and slid her hands up his chest, curling her fingers over his shoulders and pressing closer to him.

Her willingness made him bolder. His arm tightened around her waist, and his mouth became insistent, his tongue finding an opening and searching for hers. Jane's body responded, igniting with a fire that scorched her senses. Her hands moved to his face, capturing his cheeks, for fear he'd disappear if she let him go.

Her reaction set J.B. loose, his hands roaming her back, her hair, her face. He seemed just as desperate as she.

He pulled her toward the bench, sitting on the cushion, and bringing her down to straddle his lap.

"Janie, I never thought I'd see you again, let alone hope to touch you." His hands were at her waist, pulling up her dress in fistfuls of cloth. His fingers splayed against the bare skin of her back, sending shivers down her spine.

She wanted this man more than she'd ever wanted anything.

He lifted one hand to her face, cradling her cheek as he leaned his head back to look at her. "God, I've missed you."

His other hand slid up her back, cupping the underside of her breast as his thumb brushed her nipple over her bikini top.

Jane moaned, and his mouth captured hers again while his hand drove her to the brink of insanity.

Still kissing her, he pushed her down on the cushioned bench, stretching out next to her as his hand lowered between her legs. She arched up, desperate for J.B. to fill the void in her heart. Her hands fumbled with the button on his shorts.

"I don't have a condom." He murmured against her ear. "Is it safe?"

His words were like a cold shower.

There had only been two men other than J.B., but how many women had there been for him?

She pushed his hands away and sat up, horror rushing through her head. "What are we doing?"

J.B. sat up, looking shell-shocked. His mouth opened and closed, no words coming out.

"I'm *engaged*! I'm getting married in two days!" God, what had she done? She jumped up, feeling dirty and vile. She'd betrayed Raymond. She'd done the very thing J.B. had done to her years ago.

J.B. still didn't say anything, only watched her with wary eyes.

"How could you?" she asked, tears springing to her eyes again.

"How could I what?" he asked, his face and voice expressionless.

"How could you kiss me, and touch me…"

"I didn't force you, Jane. You were a very willing participant." There was no malice or accusation in his voice.

Yes, she'd been all too willing and much too eager. Even looking at him right now, with his lips full from kissing her, the desire in his eyes, she wanted to fall into his arms and make love to him.

And that was dangerous.

J.B. broke her heart eleven years ago. She'd be a fool to give him the opportunity to do so again. "I know who you are now," she said.

His eyebrows rose. "*Really*? How could you, when you didn't even know I was going by my middle name?"

Her eyes narrowed. "I don't need to know what name you give to your multiple women to know you're looking for one thing, *Brandon*." She spat his name with a sneer.

He had the decency to cringe. "There's a lot in the last eleven years I'm not proud of, and my biggest regret was sending you away." He swallowed and looked out onto the water before turning back to her. "And maybe I should be more ashamed of all those women, but every single one drove home the fact that there is only you, Jane." He stood and took her hand. "Forever and always, it will only be you."

His declaration scared her. She could handle it if this had only been a tryst for him. A chance to relive his youth. But he'd declared forever-love to her before, and look how that ended.

She lifted her shoulders and jerked her hand from his grasp. "Take me back."

J.B. blinked. "What?"

"Take me back to the island. *Now.*" She sucked in a breath at the pain that shot through his eyes. "You're eleven years too late."

"Jane."

"No. I'm getting *married,* J.B. Married in two days. You had eleven years to come find me. Where were you five years ago? Or two? What about last week? Why didn't you come find me then?"

Tears filled his eyes, but he remained silent.

"How convenient for you to wait until I come *here*, back to Seeker's Island." She shook her head and swallowed her disgust. "You've made no effort at all, J.B. You didn't search me out. Hell, the only reason we're talking now is because I had the bad luck to stumble onto your boat."

His chest rose and fell, grief covering his face.

"If what you did was such a mistake, why are you just now telling me?"

His jaw worked, and he finally said, "I don't know."

She ordered the tears rushing to fill her eyes to dry. He didn't deserve her tears. He didn't deserve any part of her. "I know why." Her shoulders tensed. "You don't want me, but you can't stand the fact that someone else does. You're like a toddler, and I'm your discarded toy." She paused to catch her breath. "I deserve better, J.B. I gave you everything and you threw me away." To her irritation, her voice broke. "Now take me back to my fiancé, the man who will stay by my side, no matter how tempted he is by some other woman."

J.B. didn't say a word. He climbed the steps to the helm, turning the motors back on, and steering the boat back to Seeker's Island.

Jane went down to the cabin and changed out of her swimming suit, vowing to throw the damn thing away as soon as she got off of the boat. She didn't want any reminders of her betrayal—to herself and to Raymond.

She stayed below until the engines slowed, signaling their approach to the pier.

When the boat was docked, she emerged from the cabin and stepped onto the pier, leaving J.B. and her heart behind.

CHAPTER FIVE

Brandon canceled his evening excursion, claiming illness. It wasn't a lie. Brandon was heartsick. He didn't think it was possible, but he hurt worse now than he did eleven years ago. Perhaps it was because he was older now and realized what he'd lost.

No, what he'd thrown away.

Seeker's Paradise was the only bar on the island, and Brandon usually avoided it during the summer months when it was overrun with tourists. But tonight he didn't give a shit. All he knew was that he didn't want to be alone, and he needed to forget everything. Forget that he'd royally fucked up his life. That he'd broken Jane. Forget what it was like to hold Jane in his arms again.

He sat at the bar and Luke, the owner, blurted out, "You look like shit."

Brandon smirked and shook his head. "Yeah, thanks."

"The usual?"

"No, give me a Jameson. Make it a double."

Luke raised an eyebrow as he got Brandon's drink, but didn't comment, until he set the glass in front of him. "I take it this is about Jane."

Brandon picked up the drink and drained the glass, setting it down with a thud. "What was your first guess?" He wasn't surprised Luke knew Jane was on the island. Luke knew everything that happened here.

"The fact that you never drink whiskey."

"Perceptive, give me another."

Luke poured the whiskey into Brandon's glass. "So is your solution to get shit-faced drunk?"

Brandon lifted his glass to his lips. "Got a better idea?"

"Yeah, about ten, actually."

Brandon drained half the glass. "It's too fucking late. I blew it."

"It's never too late."

"Yeah, well someone forgot to tell Jane. She pretty much told me to fuck off forever this afternoon."

Luke leaned his forearms on the bar. "So you saw her?"

Brandon's hand clenched the glass so tightly, he wondered how it didn't shatter. Thoughts of Jane flooded his head. Jane lying on the cushions. Her body against his. The taste of her lips… He drained the rest of the glass and set it on the bar. "Another."

Luke hesitated before he poured a smaller amount.

Picking up the glass, Brandon waved it toward Luke, the alcohol already throwing off his coordination. "She's right, too."

"Is she, now?"

Brandon leaned forward. "She asked me why, in all these eleven years, why I never came to find her."

Luke's face remained stoic. "And…?"

"I didn't answer."

"Why not?"

"Because I don't know."

Luke shook his head with a disgusted look. "That's a bullshit answer, and you and I both know it. And so does Jane, which is why she told you to fuck off."

A customer wandered up to the counter, and Luke walked over and made her drink.

Brandon looked out onto the ocean, his thoughts consumed with the past and the present, but all included Jane.

Why hadn't he gone after her years ago? While he'd considered it, he'd always convinced himself Jane was better off without him.

But if he were truthful, he had to admit part of him thought he might be better off without her, too.

They'd been so young when they fell in love. By the time Brandon slept with Sheila, he'd spent a third of his life with Jane. He had to confess, he wondered what he'd missed, committing to one girl. Shouldn't he sow some wild oats? But the saying that the grass was always greener on the other side of the fence turned out to be shockingly true.

No one had ever come close to Jane.

By the time Brandon had figured it out, six years had passed. How could he go back to her then? He'd let too much time slip, and he'd presumed she'd found someone else by then. He didn't want to steal her happiness for the sake of his own. He'd done that already.

But when he found out she was on the island. He had to see her, regardless. She was getting married. Jane was getting the family she always wanted. He couldn't take that from her. He only wanted to verify that she was happy.

Except she was marrying someone she didn't love.

Brandon jumped off the stool and stumbled, nearly falling on his ass.

Luke's head jerked up. "Brandon, where the hell are you going?"

"To get back the woman I love," he mumbled, trying to untangle himself from the stool.

"The hell you are. You're drunk. You're not going anywhere."

Brandon shook his head and nearly fell. "You don't understand."

"I understand better than you think. You'll never win Jane back if you go to her drunk." Luke set a coffee cup in front of him. "Set your ass on a stool and drink some coffee."

"I've wasted too much time already. I have to prove that I love her."

"She's not going anywhere. She's not getting married until Saturday. Get sobered up and you can go see her later. Besides, it sounds like you need a plan, if this afternoon went as badly as you say it did."

Brandon nodded and picked up his coffee cup. Luke was right. He needed a plan.

***

Jane was exhausted. The day started horribly and had gotten progressively worse. All she wanted was to go to bed, wake up tomorrow, and hope it was all a bad dream.

After she finished washing her face and brushing her teeth, she padded across the hardwood floor toward the bed, when she heard the first strains of a guitar.

Live music wasn't uncommon on the island, especially in the summer months, and the Sunseekers' Inn was on the main strip. But something about the notes of the acoustic guitar caught her attention, and against her better judgment, she opened the shutters to investigate.

It took her eyes several seconds to adjust to the dark to find the man in the gardens below her window. He stood next to a small fountain, a guitar hanging from his shoulder. His fingers strummed a familiar tune she couldn't place.

The light from her window spilled below, and he looked up toward her. Her breath caught in her chest.

It was J.B. and he was playing *her* song. The song he wrote for her eons ago for her birthday. The night be professed his love and claimed he wanted to spend the rest of his life with her.

She took a step back, and panic flooded his face. His fingers stopped, the music dying in the night air.

"Jane, I need to talk to you. I need to explain."

Jane shook her head. He'd had his chance earlier, and he'd had no explanation.

J.B. rushed forward, stopping underneath her second story window and leaning his head back to look up at her. "Jane, I'm an ignorant ass. I didn't go after you because I thought I needed some time and space to figure out what I wanted. But by the time I realized it was you, I figured it was too late." He took her silence as encouragement and set his guitar down on the ground. "I didn't want to upset you today. I didn't even dare to hope I had a chance with you. I only wanted to know that you were happy." His voice broke. "One of us deserves to be and that's you."

Tears burned her eyes, but she refused to let them fall. She'd cried enough tears over Jonathon Brandon Hunt.

"Jane, please. Listen." He paused. "Forget about me. Just ignore that I love you. Just listen to this: Whatever you do, please don't marry him. You said you didn't love him, but you deserve love. Incredible love that fills your heart until it overflows and you're drowning it."

Her tears ignored her order and slid down her cheeks.

"Don't cry." He shook his head as his face contorted in agony. "I can't stand to see you cry. I'll go and never bother you again, but promise me you'll go break it off. Promise me you'll tell him you won't marry him."

She shook her head, the tears burning her throat. "I can't."

Panic filled his eyes. "You can, Janie. *Please*. Don't settle for ordinary when you deserve extraordinary."

"You don't understand." She choked out. "I already did."

He froze, his eyes widening. "You already did what?"

"I already broke it off."

It took several seconds to sink in. "*You did*?"

She nodded. "When I came back, I knew I couldn't marry Raymond. I've only really loved one person and that was you." She gave him a weak smile. "There's only you."

He took several steps backward. "I'm coming up. What room are you in?"

Embarrassment swept through her. She didn't have on any makeup and she was wearing a tattered T-shirt. "You can't come up. I look terrible."

"Jane, you're the most beautiful sight I've ever seen. What room are you in?"

"Two-ten."

He grabbed his guitar and ran to the front of the building.

Jane paced the room, suddenly worried this was a bad idea. When she heard the knock on the door, her hand shook as she reached for the doorknob. But peace flooded her when J.B. filled the doorway, the love in his eyes settling her nerves.

"We can't start off where we left off, J.B."

He took her hand and nodded. "I know. We're different people now."

"But I'm willing to start over. Try us out and see if we still fit."

He brought her hand to his lips and kissed her fingers. "We will."

His certainty made her breathless. "How can you be so sure?"

"Because being with you is like coming home."

His words didn't make any sense. "But I was the one to leave."

His mouth lifted into a sad smile. "You took my heart with you, Jane. Home is where you are. Now that you're here with me, everything feels right."

When J.B. took her in his arms and lowered his mouth to hers, she knew that he was right.

Everything else would fall into place.

SEEKER'S HEAT

LILIANA HART

CHAPTER ONE

"This is stupid."

Luke Mallory pinched the bridge of his nose and closed his eyes before sucking in a deep breath.

"I've lost my mind. I'm just full-out, batshit crazy."

He directed the flashlight up the sandy path. The overarching palms cast nefarious shadows, and the scurry of lizards and God knows what else could be heard as he interrupted their slumber.

Perspiration slicked his skin and his shaggy hair curled damply at his temples and at the base of his neck. A haircut was on his to-do list—*way* down on the list. He had other, more important, matters to deal with—the first being to have his sanity checked. Only a crazy person believed myths could become reality. And he didn't believe. Not really. But desperate times called for desperate measures.

The Florida heat and humidity pressed in on him, making the trek up the side of the hill that led to Seeker's Spring as close to the path to hell as one could get without actually going there. He swatted at the palms with one hand while the flashlight held steady with the other. The waterfall gurgled in the distance and the temperature rose the closer he got to the springs.

He was a native to the island and loved everything about the place generations of his family had called home—from the wickedly hot summers to the hurricanes that blew through every few years. The Mallory's *were* Seeker's Island. It was in his blood, and he'd be buried right alongside his ancestors in the Seeker's Island Cemetery, whose graves sunk with haphazard uncertainty every time it rained.

Once he reached the top of the hill, Luke tossed the high-powered flashlight to the ground so it shone eerily over the moss-covered boulders and onto the blackness of the water. The waterfall splashed loudly against the rocks at its base—competing with the crashing waves of the ocean barely a hundred steps through the trees to the west—and sent ripples across the surface.

"Idiot," he muttered again, scrubbing his hands over his face and rolling his shoulders back to loosen the tightness.

At least no one was present to witness his stupidity. The sun hadn't yet come up, and theoretically, the springs were closed. Not that it mattered. The sheriff was his best friend—though Jed Wells, perverse bastard that he was, might enjoy throwing him behind bars just for the hell of it.

Before Luke could talk himself out of it he pulled his shirt over his head and tossed it on one of the boulders. His cargo shorts went next along with his boxers. Hell, he hadn't gone skinny dipping in the hot springs since he'd been eighteen and angry at the world. It was unfortunate that both times were because of the same woman—not that his wish had been granted the first time—but maybe he hadn't asked for the right thing at the right time. Fate was a bitch like that.

Jessie James had brought him nothing but heartache in his thirty-three years. She'd been his best friend growing up, though he knew Jessie had kept secrets from him. The shadows in her eyes were never hidden as well as she thought they were. And who could blame her, growing up with a bastard like old Jesse James? The old man had been harsh on her, and Jessie spent more time being confined to indoors as punishment than she had running wild and free around the island.

They'd loved each other like friends should, even though she'd never trusted Luke with her secrets. And then came the time when they started noticing each other a little differently. Hormones and bodies changed, and they both took notice. They'd been sixteen the first time the innocent kisses they'd shared previously had turned into something more—both of them fumbling and inexperienced as they gave each other their innocence. They loved each other like crazy, as only the young knew how to do—without reservations or bitterness from life in general stealing away pieces of that happiness.

At least that's what he'd thought. Looking back, he wondered if he'd ever been anything more to her than a distraction—a way to forget whatever was plaguing her. He'd never had her trust, and he wasn't sure he'd ever had her love either. Not really. Because one day their senior year she hadn't been on the ferry to the mainland that took them to school. And when he'd gotten back home that afternoon to check on her, old Jesse had looked at him with no expression whatsoever as he'd told Luke his only daughter had packed her things and stolen off with their boat in the middle of the night.

And she'd never come back. Not once. Because he'd waited for her. And he'd tried to look for her, even though her own father didn't lift a finger to try and find her. So Luke had done his damndest to move on but still keep the hole she'd left in his heart open and bleeding, because it was the best kind of reminder that the only person you could really trust was yourself.

Before he could talk himself out of it, he climbed over the boulders and sat at the edge of the spring, dipping his feet into the water. He hissed as the heat touched his skin, and sweat broke out in beads on his face, dripping down his neck and onto his chest. He knew it would be cooler by the waterfall since the water that flowed from there came from a different spring.

That's what made Seekers Spring so unusual and magical, at least according to the legends. And why tourists traveled from all over the world to this one spot, overrunning the island with ridiculous hats and rental golf carts, buying plastic bottles filled with spring water to take back home with them just in case they needed another dose to fulfill their wishes.

Whatever your heart desires...

A stupid scheme created by someone who cared more about money than the privacy and seclusion the island provided. And here he was, acting no better than a damn tourist out of desperation.

He treaded across the shallow edges of the pool and then hit the drop off in the center so his full body was submerged. There was no telling what the hell was at the bottom of the pool below him. He wasn't curious enough to find out like several of the other locals who believed in the legend.

He swam the rest of the way to the waterfall until the cold spray splashed his face, and he tried to maneuver his way around a few of the jagged rocks at the base of the falls—rocks sharp enough to slice a body to ribbons if care wasn't taken. The sun was trying to come up—the sky lightening briefly to a hazy gray—but the black storm clouds rolling in from the distance assured he wouldn't have to worry about being seen by any overzealous tourists wanting to see the springs before they officially opened.

Luke had spent years listening to those who'd claimed to have found their hearts desires from Seekers Spring. He still thought it was complete crap, but if there was even a sliver of a chance that it was real, he couldn't let it slip through his fingers. The stakes were too high this time.

He knew what he'd done wrong the last time he'd come to the springs. He'd swam to the deepest part of the pool and made his request there, his chest filled with panic as angry tears coursed down his cheeks. He'd begged for Jessie to come back until his voice grew hoarse. He'd held out hope for weeks until old Jesse had told him he'd gotten a letter from his daughter that said she was staying with a relative up north to finish school and that she wanted no contact with anyone from Seeker's Island—or what she'd called "her old life." Not even Luke.

He knew with clarity that was the turning point in his life—when the anger began brewing and bubbling beneath the surface so the people he'd known his whole life started giving him a wide berth whenever they saw him—when they started whispering behind their hands when he'd started drinking and getting into brawls. But that was the past. He no longer carried that violent anger—just a simmering brew he'd learned how to control.

And now Jessie was coming back and he could feel the old anger trying to push through. But his wishes for his heart's desire were vastly different this time. This was his island—his peace—and she no longer belonged here.

According to the information he'd gathered from the other fools that had made the trek to the springs, a person's wish was only granted if they stood in the place where the cold and hot water merged. Good thing he hadn't done it right the first time he'd made his wish.

Luke navigated his way across the rocks and wedged his feet securely as he stood to his full height. The wind picked up, almost as if it were a sign from God that he was, in fact, an idiot, and he smiled as the wind blew harder and the water from the falls slapped him across the face. A low growl of thunder rumbled in the distance. With his luck, the pool would answer his request by sending a hurricane and wiping out the whole island.

A sliver of panic worked its way up his spine when the flashlight flickered several times before going out completely and leaving him almost in complete darkness. Fortunately, he knew every part of the island and could walk it in his sleep, though he'd never done it in a raging thunderstorm and had no desire to try.

"All right, Mallory. Time to put up or shut up. Even if you are a complete idiot."

The mix of hot and cold from the pool and the waterfall made him shiver and pebbled his skin with chills. The water stung like needles as the wind pelted it like tiny daggers at his face.

"I'm just warning you," he yelled to be heard over the coming storm. "I'm not going to say it all out loud. You're supposed to know all this shit ahead of time. So I'll just ask for my heart's desire and leave it at that."

Saying it aloud didn't make him feel any less stupid, but at least it was done and he could head back to the bar. *His* bar. No matter what the letter from the lawyer said. He had inventory to do and orders to have filled. Old Jesse James was a bastard even from the grave.

The storm would be bad for business, and if the waves were too high it would delay the ferry from delivering the fresh fish that was supposed to be arriving for the dinner crowd.

Just as he was about to step out of the spray of the waterfall, a huge crack of lightning rent the air. The hairs on his arms stood up and the smell of ozone was sharp and bitter.

"Jesus." He dove into the water and swam like hell for the opposite edge where his clothes sat. That's all he needed was to be struck by lightning and found buck ass naked, floating in the middle of the hot springs.

The rain hadn't started yet, and by the look of the sky he figured he could just make it back to the bar by the time it hit. He didn't bother drying off, but just pulled his clothes on quickly and shook his hair out like a dog before sliding on his flip-flops and grabbing the flashlight. His golf cart was a quarter of a mile down the path where the road ended and he jogged down the steep incline swatting palms from his face as he went.

Another rumble of thunder sounded, this one much closer. He got into the golf cart and backed out a ways before he had room to turn around. The wind was vicious as he sped out from the cover of trees to the coastal road that led back to Seeker's Paradise, the bar and grill he'd slaved and bled over for the last twelve years. He wouldn't have been able to buy it to begin with if it hadn't been for old Jesse.

Jesse had been a silent partner, putting down the other fifty percent of the money with the promise if anything ever happened to him that Jesse's shares would go to Luke. But then old Jesse had died and Luke had found out very quickly that Jesse didn't ever plan on keeping his promise, because he'd given the other half of Seeker's Paradise to the daughter who'd deserted him all those years ago.

The thought of the betrayal had Luke's mood darkening as black as the sky, and he pressed harder on the pedal, wishing for reckless speed and the rush of adrenaline he'd constantly craved after she'd left.

Waves crashed violently against the shore and he tried to distract himself, mentally going through his checklist for when he got to the bar. The rain was an inconvenience and a hassle. The place would still be packed come dinnertime, only he'd have to worry about his waitresses slipping on the wet floors or the generators not kicking in if the electricity went out.

People enjoyed their drinks and conversation, no matter what the weather. He personally didn't understand the need for the latter, though he more than understood the need for the first. There wasn't a day that went by that he wasn't tempted to pour his own glass and take a stool at the counter like a couple of the other regulars. The need was there with every drink he served, but he relished the pain his hard fought self-control brought. He'd found other outlets to keep his mind off the temptation.

The sky opened up just as he pulled the golf cart beneath the covered patio near the kitchen, and fat drops of rain came down in a deluge followed by another flash of lightning. It didn't matter how fast he ran, he was soaked by the time he unlocked the kitchen door and pushed inside.

He kicked off his flip-flops and pulled off his shirt as he slammed the door behind him, muttering curses under his breath. His first priority was pulling down the screens on the side of the bar the storm was blowing from so the entire inside wasn't soaked, and there was no point putting on dry clothes until that task was done.

It took precious seconds to unlock the kitchen door that led into the bar area itself. Seeker's Paradise had been built to resemble a large, square tiki hut—fat bamboo posts sat at each corner and the roof was thatched to resemble straw. The bar was a square directly in the middle so people could sit at the long expanse of polished wood on all sides. The cabinets where the alcohol was kept were locked up every night as well as the kitchen where food was kept, but the restaurant itself was open at all times since there were no walls.

Luke pushed through the kitchen door and into the restaurant, grabbing the long hook he kept by the wall so he could pull down the protective screens. The overhang of the roof was enough to keep the rain out most of the time, but not with it blowing horizontal as it was now.

He'd just slipped the hook through the little hole at the edge of the ceiling when he felt the tingle at the base of his spine. He wasn't alone. Luke's shoulders tensed, but he continued on with his task. The island was a safe place to live, but that didn't mean there wasn't trouble from time to time. If someone wanted to rob him they were in for a huge disappointment. He deposited the cash every night and the liquor was the only thing of worth on the premises.

He pulled down the screen and it rattled and clanked noisily as it hit the floor. He bent over to fasten it down, waiting for whomever it was to make their move, but there wasn't a rush of air or a sound indicating someone was coming toward him.

His hand clamped in a white-knuckled grip around the hook in his hand and he rose back up slowly before turning to see who waited for him.

The sight of her made him wish for the robber instead. His heart stopped in his chest and his lungs burned with the air he couldn't remember to breathe.

City girl.

She'd changed in the fifteen years since he'd last seen her. The girl had grown into a woman, but gone was the softness he remembered. A short crop of black hair fringed around her face, making her green eyes look impossibly large and her cheekbones sharper.

There had never been much to her—she'd always been thin as a reed and willowy—her legs long like a dancer and her breasts small, though enough to fill his hands. He'd felt clumsy when he'd touched her—rough—but she'd wanted him anyway. At least for a time.

The sundress she wore was the same vibrant green as the moss around the springs that had just betrayed him and came just to the top of her knees. Her long, narrow feet were strapped into white sandals that crisscrossed all the way up to her ankles. He'd never known feet could look quite so sexy.

"Hello, Luke." Her voice still held the sultriness of the south and the sound of it sent pleasure straight to his groin as it had so many times before. Her voice had haunted his dreams for fifteen years—tortured his body as it begged for release in his sleep.

"Jessie," he managed to get past his frozen vocal cords. "I wasn't expecting to see you."

The corner of her mouth tilted in a sardonic smile. "More than likely you just hoped I wouldn't show up."

"Maybe," he shrugged. "Though maybe it's better this way. You can sign the papers and sell your half of the bar to me, and then you can go back from wherever it was you came from."

The challenging glint in her eyes made him go rock hard and he moved so he stood behind the bar like he was going to go on about his daily business.

"My father's dead," she said.

"I remember. I was at his funeral. Where were you?" Luke didn't find satisfaction in the way the color drained from her cheeks and a haunted look came into her eyes—a look he'd last seen during their childhood.

"I'm here now." Her voice dripped with ice and her shoulders stiffened. "And I'm not going anywhere."

"Don't waste your lies on me," he said, wondering if today would be a good time to pour the drink he'd only thought about until now. "You couldn't wait to get off this island fast enough. Why would you want to tie yourself to it now? Just sell me your half of the bar and you can go on with your life."

"My reasons for coming back are none of your business. Just know that I'm here now, and I'm claiming what's mine."

Fucking legends and stupid wishes. His teeth gritted so hard his jaw hurt and he pulled out a white apron from beneath the bar. He tossed it at her feet, and shame crawled across his skin as she reached forward to catch it and missed. But he couldn't back down now. She'd taken everything he'd ever had to give. He'd be damned if she took his livelihood as well.

"Welcome home, partner," he said, not bothering to disguise the anger in his voice. "I guess we'll find out how determined you are to stay when you're serving drinks and slopping up messes twelve hours a day."

CHAPTER TWO

Jessie didn't bend the rest of the way to pick the apron off the floor, but instead straightened back up so her spine was stiff with pride and her gaze steady on his. Aunt June had taught her better than to show weakness ever again, though the coldness in Luke's gaze made her want to turn around and start running.

This wasn't the same boy she'd loved. There was a hardness to him—a bitterness in his eyes that made her want to flinch with guilt because she knew without a doubt she was the cause of the changes she saw in him.

He was still as handsome as ever—dark blond hair streaked with the sun and long enough that an unruly curl hung rakishly across his forehead. A day's worth of beard stubbled his face and a white scar slashed diagonally across one eyebrow making him look dangerous. The scar was new, but the rest of him was so familiar it made her ache with the memories.

His chest and shoulders were broader, and a light smattering of pale blond hairs covered his chest. It was hard not to stare at the picture he made—his bare chest damp with tiny droplets of water and his cargo shorts sitting low on his hips, just below the muscular indents that made her mouth water. Luke hadn't been her only lover, but he'd been the only one who'd made her want with such burning intensity.

Jessie licked her lips and watched as his gaze dropped to her lips. There were explanations to give and apologies to make, but God, she'd missed the sizzle that happened between a man and a woman when their chemistry was off the charts. She missed the slow dance of innocent flirtations and gentle caresses, and later, the heat of hands and bodies as they grappled in the darkness. She'd missed it—yearned for it—for fifteen years. But not enough to stay if it meant dealing with her father.

"I'll do whatever I need to do," she finally said, her voice husky. "This is my bar now as much as yours."

His gaze snapped back to hers and he practically growled as he pulled out a notepad and started doing inventory of supplies behind the counter.

"Convenient," he said. "Especially since you didn't have to lift a finger or put blood and sweat into the building of the place."

"I can't imagine old Jesse did much in the way of that either." She'd never called him father. Not since the first time he'd taken a belt to her.

"No, but he was a silent partner. He put up the initial stake and then sat back and enjoyed the profits once we started making them. The intention for anyone else to stick their nose into my business was never up for discussion. This bar is mine, whether your name is on the deed now or not."

"I guess it's a good thing my name *is* on the deed then."

Jessie had plenty she needed to confess, but Luke had a few explanations to give as well. When she'd left Seeker's Island that night she'd left him a note, explaining why she couldn't stay. All he'd had to do was meet her where she'd asked and they could've been together. But he hadn't come and he hadn't bothered to get in touch to say goodbye. It seemed old Jesse had been right about one thing at least.

"A boy like Luke Mallory only wants one thing from a girl like you," old Jesse had spat. The belt had whistled through the air and caught her on the ribs when she turned to dodge the blow. "And from the eyeful I got down at the docks this morning it looks like you're already giving it to him. You think the high and mighty Mallorys are going to let their son marry a whore like you?"

"He loves me!" she'd shouted. Jessie didn't know where she'd gotten the courage to talk back to him, but it had only made things worse. You couldn't reason with a drunk. "And he'll kill you for this. I'm an adult, and I'm through being your punching bag."

"Is that right, *little girl*?"

The only thing she remembered from that night with complete clarity was his smile. How it sent ice down her spine and turned her bowels to liquid. She never saw his fist coming until she was already on the floor choking on her own blood. He grabbed her hair and pulled her head up so she could hear him better.

"You think your lover is going to protect you? That he'll have the balls to face me? Why don't I tell you what I'm going to do? How about I slip up to that fancy house of his and crawl right through the window." Wild animal sounds gurgled in her throat as she tried to pull away, but he was too strong. "I bet you've gone in that window lots of times, haven't you, whore? I'll slip right in and slice my knife right across his throat. No one would ever suspect me. And where does that leave your grand plan of telling on me? It leaves your boyfriend dead, me playing poker with Sheriff Biggs, and you confined to your room until my belt needs to be exercised again. There's no way out for you. Your mama made sure of that."

She didn't remember what happened after that. Only that when she'd finally regained consciousness, he'd taken the bottle of Jim Beam with him and locked himself in his room. Her left eye had been swollen shut and her wrist broken, but she'd packed as many of her things as she could in a small bag. She'd penned a quick letter to Luke and left it wedged between his bedroom window and the screen. How she managed to get the boat untied and herself to the mainland and redocked was still hazy, and she'd taken refuge on another boat, going in and out of consciousness, just waiting for the authorities to find her before Luke came to her.

The authorities never found her and Luke never came. So she called her Aunt June and begged her to not try and have old Jesse thrown in jail. Jessie had seen the sincerity in his eyes the night he'd threatened to cut Luke's throat, and knew with every breath in her body he'd do it in a heartbeat. June had reluctantly agreed, but she'd made Jessie swear that she'd have no contact with anyone from Seeker's Island. It was better for everyone if old Jesse didn't know where she was.

But Luke had loved her. She would have sworn to the depths of her soul that he'd meant the words when he'd spoken them. Only Luke had never bothered to come for her. Not even a phone call or an email.

Jessie stepped over the apron he'd tossed in her direction and made her way over to the bar, slipping beneath the pass-through. Her heart thudded wildly in her chest as she leaned against the counter so she faced him, her arm so close to his she could feel the heat sizzling between them.

He froze and his knuckles tightened around the pen he held until she was surprised it didn't snap in two, but he didn't look up from the list he was making. Her throat tightened, but she was determined to say what was on her mind.

"Don't presume to know anything about me, Luke. Just know that this is my home and it's going to take something more than Jesse James to make me leave again."

"It's your life," he shrugged. "The rest of us will go on like we always have the next time you get a wild hair." His blue gaze was direct and he sneered as he looked her over from head to toe. "Look at you. You won't last the summer in your designer dresses. Whoever you became when you left, it's not someone who belongs on Seeker's Island."

"I guess you know as well as I do what they say about people who assume things."

"What am I supposed to think?"

He moved in closer, so his arms caged her in on both sides, and his chest barely brushed against the front of her. She gasped at the touch and pressed back against the counter, but there was nowhere to go for escape.

His head lowered so his lips barely glanced against her jaw, and his words whispered like silk into her ear. "Is this what you're here for? To scratch an itch before you move on again? To see if it's as good as you remember? As good as you dream about?"

Her hands came up and flattened against his chest, and she would've pushed him away if she'd had the strength. She heard the underlying anger in every word he spoke, but she was caught in his trap. It felt so good to be in his arms, even indirectly.

"Luke, I—"

His lips touched the underside of her ear and heat speared straight to her core. Whatever she'd planned to say was lost at his touch. Her fingers clenched against his chest and a whimper escaped her lips as his tongue traced a path down her neck.

"Is that why you're here, Jess?"

Answering became an impossibility as his lips came down on hers. No one had ever fit her as perfectly as he did, and time and distance hadn't changed that. She expected to feel his anger in the kiss, but it was soft—gentle—as his lips caressed and tasted hers. A quickening of breaths and small sighs as memories flooded her system.

Her hands slid up his chest and around the back of his neck, and a whimper of pleasure escaped when he pressed against her—her breasts aching as his flesh seemed to scorch through the thin fabric of her dress.

Tears pricked her eyes as she opened herself to him, accepted whatever he had to give her. She melted against him and the long, slow burn of arousal took hold as his tongue slipped inside her mouth and slid sinuously against hers.

When he finally pulled away, both of their breathing was labored. He dropped his hands and took a step back as if she was poisonous, and his face twisted in a painful grimace before the anger came back.

"Go home, Jess. Scratch your itch somewhere else."

Her head was spinning and she still wasn't sure what had just happened, only that she wanted it again. But his words hit her like a bucket of cold water.

"I'm home," she finally managed to say. "You're going to have to deal with it. And you know nothing about my wants or desires."

"All I know is fact." Luke ran his fingers through his hair. "I know that nothing on this island mattered to you enough that you wanted to stay. And I know you're back now for whatever reason, wanting to take the only thing I'll ever love again. So excuse me if I don't feel like throwing you a welcome home party."

Jessie felt the hot spark of anger sizzle deep in her belly. "There's love and then there's *love*. I guess I'm glad you finally found something that mattered enough to fight for."

"What the hell is that supposed to mean?" Luke's arms crossed over his chest and his scowl was harsh enough to etch glass.

"It means mind your own damn business."

She pushed away from the counter and slipped back under the pass-through, heading toward the lone suitcase she'd brought with her. Her other belongings had been delayed on the mainland because of the storm.

Maybe she was wasting her time hoping for forgiveness or that he might understand the hell she'd gone through when she'd finally made the decision to leave once and for all. She could have just told him the truth and what had happened, but a part of her was still ashamed that she'd experienced it at all. No one had known, not her teachers going through school or her friends. Not Luke when he'd become her lover.

They hadn't noticed and she'd been too afraid of her father to tell. Maybe some part of her still held that fear, even though old Jesse was buried six-feet under in the cemetery.

The tears that threatened to fall were blinked away by the time she turned back to face him. Luke wasn't the same as he'd been when she'd know him before, and gone was any trace of the gentleness or caring that had once been as natural as breathing.

"I've got some things to work out this morning." Like figuring out where the hell she was going to sleep. She'd be damned if she stepped foot back inside the house that brought her nothing but bad memories. "I'll be back before the dinner shift and you can go over anything I need to know."

"I'll be here." His smile was harsh. "Just like I always am. The question is, will you have the courage to show up and face everyone again?"

***

Luke made himself look down at the list in front of him so he wouldn't have to watch her walk away. He was too afraid he'd beg her to come back.

He never should have kissed her. He could still taste her on his lips, feel her pressed against him. It was a taste that he'd never be able to shake from his system. Not even if he bedded a hundred women—a thousand.

A rumble of thunder boomed loud enough to shake the floor and he cursed as he remembered he hadn't seen another golf cart when he'd pulled up. Which meant she'd made the walk from the ferry to the bar, and was now forced to trudge the half-mile hike to old Jesse's place in the pouring rain. Not even he was a big enough asshole to let her walk through the rain and wind carrying a suitcase.

"Dammit."

He rubbed his hand through his hair again and hopped over the bar. She wouldn't be very far down the road, so he'd be able to catch her in his own golf cart. Only when he left through the kitchen door and stared at the empty spot he'd parked in, he realized that wouldn't be possible after all.

"Son of a bitch." She'd stolen his golf cart. His eyes narrowed and his mouth tugged in a reluctant smile.

"Game on, Jess. We'll just see who's left standing."

Now he only had to figure out a way to go after her and take what was his. It was a good thing he was already wet.

CHAPTER THREE

Jessie's laughter—as she imagined the look on Luke's face once he realized she'd taken his golf cart—was short lived. The closer she got to the cabin on the northeast end of the island, the more the fear she'd never hoped to feel again clawed at the pit of her belly.

She didn't know why she'd come this direction. She should've driven straight to the inn to see if there were any rooms available, but something had pulled her to take the opposite path and drive the cart down the rutted road that led to her childhood home.

The rain was unforgiving and she might as well have walked for all the protection the golf cart offered against the wet. Her dress plastered against her skin and droplets of water trickled from her hair down to the base of her neck. And though the temperature was already hot and muggy, she shivered at the sight of the two-bedroom clapboard house as it came into view.

Paint peeled in long strips along the boards and one of the blue shutters hung crookedly from the front window. The porch sagged and the screen enclosing the area had a jagged tear. It was a small square of a house and it sat on stilts to protect from flooding.

She stopped the golf cart under a tree so her suitcase would have some protection against the weather and she slipped off her sandals. They'd do nothing but sink into the sand. Plants had overrun the yard so some of them came waist high and the tree that grew closest to the house looked like it might fall on the roof at any time.

The rain soaked her to the skin the moment she left the shelter of the golf cart and she made her way to the middle of the road so she faced the house like a gunslinger.

Jessie tried to tell herself it was a house like any other. That it was wood and glass and it had given her a place to sleep and a desk where she could do her homework. But it would've been a lie. A home was supposed to be safe. It was supposed to give shelter and comfort. And the people inside the house were supposed to love.

She didn't remember that kind of love after the age of five when her mother died. The house that stood before her was nothing but a mockery, and she'd see it burned to the ground before she would ever step through the door again.

The rage inside her built in speed and intensity until she thought she'd explode if she didn't find an outlet. The animalistic sounds that tore from her throat went unnoticed and the scalding tears went unchecked. She searched the ground for something—anything—that would do the kind of damage she envisioned.

Triumph roared through her as she found broken pieces of brick where old Jesse had tried to lay a sidewalk. Her arm reveled in the weight as she hurled it toward the front window, and with every brick she threw, every shattering sound of the windows, the rage ebbed to a quieter storm.

***

It was barely a fifteen-minute walk to old Jesse's place, a little quicker if one knew a shortcut. And even faster still if a scream loud enough to pierce through the raging storm could be heard.

Luke reached the edge of the clearing just in time to see her launch the first brick. His mouth dropped open in shock and he stood frozen as he watched the destruction. The pain on her face and the screams that sounded as if they were ripping from her soul made his heart ache for her.

"Jesus," he whispered. And when her foot caught on something and she went to her knees he started to run.

She was huddled on her knees, her arms over her stomach and her face buried against them as sobs wracked her body. He didn't know where to touch her, how to hold her. He was out of practice on knowing how to take care of anyone but himself.

Luke finally knelt down in the rising water and picked her up to pull her into his lap. He wasn't expecting the wild cat that greeted him. Fists and elbows came at him followed by cries so wounded he couldn't even imagine that sort of pain.

"Ssh, baby. I've got you." He held her tight and waited her out until he felt her strength begin to wane. "God, Jess. Tell me what to do. Tell me how to fix it."

She didn't answer him but finally lay limp against his chest, her tears mixing with the rain. He felt her heart pounding and noticed the scrapes on her hands that were bleeding sluggishly.

"Let me go." He could barely hear the words her voice was so hoarse.

"Not until you tell me what the hell is going on."

She pushed against his chest but she was as weak as a kitten so she didn't budge from his grasp.

"Let me help you, Jess. I'm not an idiot. I've obviously missed something that happened. Missed the real reason you left. Talk to me."

Her head tilted back and she looked at him out of the saddest eyes he'd ever seen. "I'm fine. I just needed to get rid of some stress."

Disappointment speared through him that she didn't want to confide in him, and he couldn't exactly say he blamed her. But she needed someone to be there when she was ready, and he decided he was going to be that person. They'd both made mistakes in how they'd handled life apart, and it was obvious from the moment she walked back into his life that he couldn't let her go again. She was his heart, and she'd been missing for much too long.

"You can't stay here," he said.

She hiccupped out a small laugh. "No kidding. I'm going to get a room at the inn until I find a place of my own."

"You'll be lucky to find an empty closet. It's high season and every cabin and hotel room is booked solid. Seeker's Island is a lot more popular than it used to be. They featured the springs on one of those Travel Channel shows and we've been overrun with people ever since."

"Good for business," she said, pushing out of his arms.

Luke helped her to her feet and they stood facing each other while she pretended nothing had just happened.

"Yeah," he sighed. "Good for business. Lousy for privacy. You can stay with me until you find your own place."

"I don't think so," she said, making her way back to the golf cart.

"The other option is for you to ferry over from the mainland every day. Seems like a waste of time to me. Especially now that you have a business to help run."

She narrowed her eyes at him and he knew he'd won. At least this round. "Do you have an extra bedroom?"

"One or two. We'll barely see each other. I pretty much work all the time."

"I'm here to stay, Luke." The seriousness in her voice made him look closer, to see if he could read her moods and feelings like he used to. But it was no use. This Jessie James was a stranger in some ways, while in others she was as familiar as his own hands.

"I believe you, Jess."

CHAPTER FOUR

More than two weeks went by without a mention of what had happened her first day back on the island. She and Luke had managed to coexist with only minor bumps along the way. The biggest bumps were that they'd been dancing around each other in the confines of Luke's home, pretending the tension wasn't growing hotter and thicker between them with every passing day.

The kiss had been a mistake, but it was all she'd thought about since it happened. And she recognized the signs that he'd been thinking about it too. The way his eyes lowered to her mouth whenever they were talking. The way he shoved his hands in his pockets so he wouldn't touch her.

Not the she hadn't been having fun teasing him whenever possible. It wasn't her that was against rekindling the flame that was obviously still burning bright between them. It was all Luke. He'd been avoiding her whenever possible. Tolerating her whenever the business threw them together. And the way he'd been looking at her made her wonder if he was starting to put together more of her past than she was comfortable with. But he still wanted her. He couldn't hide that.

"I'm just saying there's nothing wrong with a little atmosphere," she said for the thousandth time. "There's nothing wrong with candlelight or flowers. No one is going to question your manhood."

It was after two in the morning and the last of the customers had already staggered home or back to the hotel. She'd already wiped down each table and stacked the chairs on top, but she still needed to damp mop the floor. Her back ached and the lull of the ocean made her want nothing more than to lay down where she was and fall asleep.

She wouldn't admit it to Luke, but she loved what she was doing—

serving customers and cleaning up at the end of a long night—learning how to place orders for enough food for the week and how to negotiate orders of the liquor so they wouldn't get overcharged. She loved it was because it was hers. She'd never had anything else she could say that about.

"We have plenty of atmosphere." Luke swung out of the kitchen carrying a box of napkins and straws so he could replenish the shelves under the bar. "We've got moonlight and the ocean. It doesn't get any better than that. And the crazy thing is they're both free."

"I mean, the live band is nice," she said, pretending like he hadn't spoken. Jessie rubbed the small of her back and looked around the wide-open space as visions of what Seeker's Paradise could be filled her head. "But it would be even better if it was music people could dance to. I'm not sure "Stairway to Heaven" is the best way to get people on the dance floor."

She looked over in time to see his lips twitch.

"Hmm, is that what that was? I didn't' recognize it," he said, turning back to his task.

Jessie moved behind the bar and just watched the way he moved. Muscles rippled in his back as he bent to restock. Relaxed and methodical. Luke never got in a hurry for much of anything. The memory of those slow hands made her blood heat and her skin tingle. He could do amazing things with his hands.

"Why did he do it?" The words came out of her mouth before she could stop herself. But there was no going back now. "Why did old Jesse give you money for this place? We know it wasn't out of the goodness of his heart."

Luke stood and turned around so he faced her, and he crossed his arms over his chest. "Believe me, I was pretty surprised myself. It's not like there was ever any love lost between the two of us. He never approved of you and me together."

"That's an understatement," she said, her laugh brittle.

Luke stared at her like he'd been doing a lot lately—as if he could see more of her than she wanted. "I'd just turned twenty-one and was in my last semester of college when my grandmother died and left me some money. I'd had enough of school and had already decided I didn't want the kind of job or life it was steering me toward. So I packed up and came home and told my dad I wanted to open a restaurant and bar on the island so tourists didn't have to keep ferrying to the mainland. And I asked him to invest the other half of grandmother's inheritance with mine and go in with me."

Her brow raised in surprise. Luke's parents had always been very supportive of him in anything he'd wanted to do. "I take it he said no?"

Luke smiled slow and lazy and rubbed a hand behind his neck. "He was pretty pissed I didn't finish the semester and graduate. He told me he'd do it as soon as I got my diploma and wouldn't back down. Things got pretty heated for a while there and my mom said I'd gotten my hard head from somewhere when I told them I wasn't going back and I'd find another investor on my own.

"Dad probably would have given in once he'd had time to let it all cool down, but your dad showed up at my door out of the blue one day and told me he thought it was a good idea and wanted to go in as a silent partner. I was young and stupid enough to do it without asking why. I just wanted what I knew was mine."

"I wonder where he got the money. God knows we never seemed to have an extra penny when it was needed. Not unless he needed a bottle of Jim Beam."

"Why didn't you tell me what was happening?" His gaze was so serious she knew she couldn't pretend to misunderstand his meaning.

Jessie took a step backward and moved to make her way around to the other side of the bar to put more distance between them. She needed space and time to think about what she should say. And she was almost positive she didn't want to have the conversation right now, when her mind was tired and her body yearning for something else.

He caught her before she'd taken the second step. It looked as if he could move fast enough when he wanted to.

"Stop running," he said, the frustration coming out a low growl. His hand clamped on her shoulder and he spun her around, moving quickly to trap her against the bar, exactly as he'd done the first day she'd come back to the island. "You should have told me what was happening. What he was doing to you? I would've helped you."

"He would have killed you," she yelled, pushing against his chest. But he didn't budge an inch. "He would have killed you and taunted me with it while he beat me. Is that the truth you think you know?" Tears she'd told herself she wouldn't shed coursed down her cheeks as her fists pounded against him. "If I'd stayed here you'd be dead. Because eventually you would've found out what was happening. And your death would've been my fault and I couldn't live with that."

Her head dropped to his chest as the strength seemed to go out of her all at once. She'd never actually said the words out loud before. Never confessed her darkest secret to anyone. Aunt June had known what had happened but they'd never spoken about it.

"If you'd told me what you had planned I would've left with you." His hands cupped the side of her cheeks and he tilted her face up.

"Bullshit. I left you a note." She managed to slip out from under his arms and put distance between them. "I waited for you to come after me. To call. For something. Did you think about me at all after I left? I know he never did. But did you?"

"I've thought about you every moment of every day for fifteen years." The look of his face was so tortured she lost her breath. He came toward her slowly but didn't reach for her. "I never found a note, sweetheart. If I had I would have been after you on the next ferry out of Seeker's Island."

"I was so scared." Admitting that was one of the hardest things she'd ever done. "And I'm sorry I had to leave. My fear of him, and my fear of what he'd do to you, was greater than what we had between us. Or at least I thought so at the time."

"All that matters is the here and now. The past can stay where it is."

He leaned down and took her mouth in a scorching kiss she felt all the way to her toes. His mouth was hot and hard on hers—a branding—letting her know in no uncertain terms that she belonged solely to him.

His hands clamped at her hips and he jerked her against him so she felt the hardness straining behind the zipper of his shorts, and when he lifted her she wrapped her legs around him and whimpered as he tortured her in just the right spot.

A jolt of need so powerful it made her whimper shot straight to her core, and she answered the demand of his kisses with demands of her own. Need wasn't the right word. She craved him. Her body hadn't been whole for years. Not since the last time they'd been together.

Her hands slipped beneath the thin cotton of his T-shirt, her fingers trailing over the taut ridges of his abdomen as he shuddered beneath her touch. With one motion, she yanked at the shirt and had it over his head and sailing across the bar.

"God, Jess. I can't wait to get you in a bed." Desperation tinged his voice.

"Don't wait. Here and now."

He sat her on the edge of the bar as his hands pushed her shirt above her breasts and then over her head, and his gaze was molten as he took in the sight of the white lace bra she wore. She leaned back, her torso long and limber, and his lips trailed down the long column of her neck to the swell of her breasts and she saw stars as his hot mouth clamped over her lace-covered nipple.

"If we keep going at this pace I won't make it thirty seconds."

"It's okay," she panted. "I won't hold it against you. You can make it up to me the second time. Or third time."

"You always were ambitious," he said, laughing.

Her breath caught as his hands moved up, molding her, cupping her breasts and weighing them in his hands before he released the clasp in front and let them free.

He groaned and the sound sent chills of anticipation over her skin. "I've always loved your breasts."

"They're small."

"They're perfect." He pushed the cups out of the way and the skimmed his thumbs over the dusky pink nipples that spiked beneath his touch. "See how well we fit?"

Before she could answer his tongue traced the same path as his fingers and her head dropped back on a moan. His mouth was hot against her fever skin, and his cheeks hollowed as he began to suckle. She felt every stroke and every flick of his tongue at the moist center between her thighs, and she tightened her legs around him, searching for the release she wanted.

He flipped open the button of her shorts and teased them both as his fingers dipped just inside the elastic band of her panties.

"Hurry," she begged.

"Not this time, sweetheart."

He tucked his hands under her bottom and pulled at the denim cutoffs she wore until she was force to uncurl her legs from around his waist. They fell to the floor so she was only left in the matching lace thong she wore.

"Those are very nice, but they're going to have to go."

"I hope so. And the sooner the better." Jess whimpered as his fingers trailed over the damp lace and teased the hidden bud within. And then his thumbs tucked beneath the elastic and he pulled them of in one fell swoop so she was completely bared to him.

"Impatient, aren't you?"

Her fingers tugged at the button on his shorts and they trembled as she lowered the zipper. She pushed down his shorts and underwear until they caught at his hips and he sprang hot and heavy into her hand.

"Oh, yes. Very impatient." She stroked him once before he grabbed her hand and pulled it away.

"I get to touch first," he said, kissing her belly as his lips trailed a damp path down her hipbone and farther down to her inner thigh. Her breath caught in anticipation and her hips arched as his mouth covered her sex. She went blind and deaf as his tongue zeroed in on familiar territory and she tried to hold back a scream as he sent her flying.

When she came to he was lifting her from the bar and setting her on her feet. Her legs felt like jelly and she was past the point of desperate to feel him inside her. Her muscles trembled and she caught herself against the counter to keep her balance.

***

Luke almost smiled at the dazed expression on her face. The taste of her was like a drug to his system and he was addicted. He'd thought he could take her here where they stood—a fast and furious coupling to ease the pain and loss they'd both experienced. But after he'd felt her go liquid beneath him he knew it needed to be more.

He flipped the switch at the wall and the bar went dark, leaving only the soft glow of the nightlights he left on at each entrance. And he took only a few precious seconds to lock the liquor cabinet. Luke grabbed a white cotton tablecloth from beneath the counter.

"What?—"

"Think back to when you lived here before. What used to be in this spot?" he asked, interrupting whatever she'd been about to say.

She bent down to pick up her clothes, but he stopped her by

scooping her up in his arms and heading out to the beach at the backside of the restaurant.

"We're not done. Don't even think of putting on clothes for the next thirty or forty years."

"Is Seeker's Island turning into a nudist colony?"

"Surely you remember Amos? He's almost as much of a tourist attraction as the springs. The sheriff doesn't even bother giving him public indecency citations anymore."

She giggled against his chest and he tightened his arms around her. "I'd forgotten about Amos. Though he's got to be close to a hundred now."

"He says he's going out of the world the same way he came in. I guess he's just getting ready."

The breeze was cool as he carried her down the sandy path to the beach. Technically this stretch of land was his. And now Jessie's as well. Though he knew there was the occasional group of college kids who liked to sneak out and get drunk once in a while.

He set her on her feet and then stood behind her, resting his hands on her shoulders so they faced the water, the moon a dim sliver of silver in the sky, but just enough that he could see her profile.

"You never did answer my question," he said, kissing the back of her neck so she shivered.

"I didn't remember until you brought me to this spot. So much of the island has changed, but not this place. The docks are gone."

"I had them taken out once I bought the place." He kissed her neck against and skimmed his hands over her belly and up so they cupped her breasts. "Too many memories of laying there with you. Taking you in the moonlight like I'm about to do now."

"Is that what you're about to do?" He heard the smile in her voice along with the sadness.

"I built the bar here because this place holds the best of my memories of you. We've come full circle this time." He left her long enough to spread out the tablecloth on the sand and then he took her in his arms, building the heat back to where it had been before.

The waves crashing in the background was the only music they needed. Blood pumped and pulsed beneath their skins and every touch drew moans and gasps of pleasure. Luke pulled her down so they were on their knees and when she took him in her hand and pushed him to his back he wanted to shout with the pleasure.

She came down on top of him, straddling his hips, poised to take him inside when he flipped their positions and she ended up on her back as he leaned over her.

"Not fair—"

The words trailed off into a moan as he slipped inside of her. She closed around him like a fist and his lips crashed down on hers to swallow her cry of pleasure. Hands clasped and held as her hips rose to take him farther, deeper inside of her. Her body shimmered in the moonlight as he took her higher and higher, until he felt the ripples of her release and the liquid heat of her clamping around him like a vise.

He was powerless to keep himself from following her, so he closed his eyes and gave her his heart, soul and seed with a final thrust.

***

Pulses slowed and perspiration cooled on their skin as they lay wrapped in each other's arms. They'd have to move eventually, but for now he wanted the moment to last as long as it could before reality intruded. And it would soon enough. They had a lot to talk about. A lot to work through—Jessie especially. And it wasn't something that could be done in a day. Or maybe even a year. But he knew what they felt for each other would only grow stronger over time, so they could take their time reacquainting themselves with one another. Filling each other in on the years they'd missed.

Her hand was warm against his chest and her head nuzzled between his shoulder and neck.

"What are you thinking?" she asked.

"That I want to stay right here forever. At least until the tourists start taking pictures of us." He felt her laughter and realized he was smiling too. The locals were going to be in for a surprise in just a few hours since smiling wasn't something he did often.

"I was thinking I'm glad old Jesse decided to break his promise to you and left me his share. I wanted to come home and it gave me a reason." The sigh against his chest was soft and warm. "Maybe he was trying to do something right. To make up for all the wrong."

"More likely he was just trying to piss me off and make things awkward for you, but I like that you try to see the best in everyone. I'm glad you're the kind of person you are, despite what you had to live through. And I'm glad you came home."

She leaned up so she could look down at him and she kissed him softly on the lips, a slow melding that had the embers of a banked fire stirring inside him once more.

"I'm glad you said that. Because I've got a lot of new ideas and changes for the bar."

They were both laughing as he rolled her to her back, but the laughter turned into moans as he slipped slowly inside of her. His lips touched gently to hers before he started to move.

"Welcome home, Jess."

Angel In Paradise

Debra Holland

CHAPTER ONE

Rafe stared down at the cream-colored envelope in his hand, the sixth one in the last five months. This one had his whole name written out, *Mr. Raphael Nicolas Thompson Flanigan,* as if the formal address would make him open the flap. He glanced at the trashcan next to his desk about to toss away the letter. Instead, he leaned to the right and shoved the envelope along five identical ones slotted into the square cubby.

He sat back in his chair, laced his hands behind his head, and put his feet on the desk in his favorite position, staring out the window at his fabulous view of the beach, the coconut palm branches swaying in the breeze, and the turquoise water beyond. Instead of seeing the fishing boat plying the tropical ocean, Rafe was swept back fifteen years in time to a warm Montana night.

His grandfather Harry Flanigan stood, fists clenched, hurling words as if they were weapons at eighteen-year-old Rafe.

Rafe's older brother, Gabe–the catalyst of the explosion–cringed on the couch. Why had Gabe snitched to their grandfather...?

"Why the hell would you go near the McCurdy's?" The old man's voice cut. "Have you no brains, boy?"

Apparently not, or Dustin McCurdy wouldn't have swindled me.

The truth of Harry Flanagan's accusation stung. Earlier, his grandfather had cut off Rafe's attempts to explain, leaving him to bottle up his frustration.

Rafe's gentle mother sat in her wing chair by the river rock fireplace weeping. Her tears wrenched at him in a way his grandfather's yelling and threats couldn't.

"That Howard girl's got mongrel blood," said the old tyrant, moving on to the second topic that had enraged him tonight.

"Angel's blood's red," Rafe fired up. "The same as the rest of us."

Harry narrowed his eyes. "She's not good enough for a Flanigan."

"Her dad's a respected attorney," Rafe retorted. "They probably have as much money or more than we do, and Angel's going to Harvard. What's not good enough about that?" An unacknowledged insecurity chose that moment to surface. "Maybe it's the other way around. I'm not good enough for Angel."

His grandfather's craggy features reddened, but his gray eyes remained as chilled as ice. "Your parents should have named you Lucifer instead of Raphael," he said in a bitter tone.

His mother made a sound of protest.

His grandfather ignored her, focusing his wrath on Rafe. "Stealing a horse from the McCurdys, of all people!"

"I didn't steal that stud!"

"I can't believe a grandson of mine is a horse thief!"

Rafe's control snapped. "Fine!" Like a knife, he threw the word at the old man. "Then I'm no grandson of yours!"

He stormed out of the family room and up the stairway to his bedroom. Slamming the door, Rafe grabbed his big duffle out of the closet and started throwing in clothes, then took cash from the dresser drawer as well as the folder of notes about his horses. In the bathroom connecting the bedroom to his brother's, he scooped up toiletries and shoved them into his leather traveling case, a gift from his mother last Christmas. He didn't let himself think of the warmth of that holiday.

Once packed, he carried his duffle down the stairs and encountered his mother in the entryway.

Her pale skin was red from crying. "If you'd just stop fighting with your grandfather, I'm sure you can make this right. He'll pay off Dustin McCurdy." She noticed his bag and her eyes widened. "Raphael, where are you going?"

The fact that his mother, his staunch supporter for all his eighteen years, didn't believe him hurt harder than a strike to the stomach. "I'm going straight to hell," he said, using the words to punch, to damage.

Her face whitened, and she stepped back as if he'd really hit her.

"Don't talk that way."

Shame curled around the edges of his anger, and he hesitated, wanting to explain that McCurdy must have set him up. But then his grandfather stepped into the doorway from his study, his face implacable. Without saying a word, the man inflamed Rafe's rage, making him stiffen his spine and square his shoulders. Turning his back on his family, he strode toward the kitchen door.

"If you leave, boy, don't ever come back," his grandfather yelled after him.

Rafe shrugged and kept on going, through the kitchen, out the door, and into the warm night air of summer. He threw his duffle into his truck.

Bear, their burly mutt, trotted out of the barn and nudged Rafe's leg.

He crouched and hugged the dog. "I have to go, boy." Grief threatened to surface. Swallowing the emotion, he stood resolutely for a moment and then got to work.

Rafe hitched his truck to the horse trailer, a graduation present from his grandfather, then stomped into the barn. He loaded his gelding, two pregnant Paint mares, and three miniature horses, also in foal, into the trailer, along with their gear and some feed.

In five minutes, he was idling the engine at the corner of the Flanigan land, the boundary separating their spread from the McCurdy's ranch. He scribbled a note to Angel on a piece of paper telling her where he was headed, got out of the truck, and shoved it into the hollow of the oak—their own personal mailbox. He hoped that when she read it, she'd understand.

Lucinda McCurdy sped by in her Mustang convertible, her long blonde hair flying. She flipped him off.

Rafe scowled and waited until her car passed before pulling the truck and trailer onto the road.

He drove though Sweetwater Springs, the town where his roots grew deep into the land, a place where everyone knew everybody, and stories about someone's great-grandparents could be dropped into gossip as easily as what had happened that afternoon. Rafe could almost hear the ripping sound as he tore those roots out of the beloved ground.

He'd vowed to shake off the town's dust, drive as far from Montana as he could and never look back.

Rafe shook his head, trying, but not entirely succeeding, in bringing himself back to the present. While he hadn't ended up in hell like he'd threatened, he'd landed in Seeker's Island, Florida—the legendary place where his parents had met and fallen in love.

And ever since, he'd ruthlessly squelched any thought of homesickness for the sight of the purple mountains and grassy valleys, the crisp air and the luminous light of the prairie, the howl of a wolf or screech of an owl, the scent of pine, or the sweet taste of Angel Howard's lips when he kissed her.

With a quick, dismissive glance at the unopened letters, Rafe thumped his bare feet to the ground and stood, determined to forget the past. After all, he had fifteen years of practice. He pulled on socks and work boots and strode out the back door of the office and down a path made of crushed shells until he reached the stables. From experience, he knew hard labor might help take his mind off things he didn't want to recall.

He opened a stall door, took in the familiar scents of horse and hay, and rubbed the nose of Abigail, the Paint mare, inside. He slipped on Abigail's halter, led her outside, and tied her up in the shade. Then he pushed the wheelbarrow next to the door and grabbed a shovel. But as Rafe mucked out the stall, he realized he had chosen the wrong occupation to help him forget all he'd loved and left behind in Sweetwater Springs.

Some things didn't change. Horse shit smelled like horse shit no matter where you were in the world.

CHAPTER TWO

Angelina Howard walked down the hallway of Elland & Kirkus, trying to remain stoic, to hold back the tears and contain the ball of shame and anger burning in her stomach. In the outer office area she shared with another attorney, she managed a smile for her legal assistant. At least Angelina hoped the turn of her lips resembled a smile more than a grimace.

Crossing the threshold of her office, Angelina ever-so-carefully shut the door behind her. If she slammed it closed the way she wanted, the reverberations would echo through the hushed corridors of power. Maybe even the senior partners in the penthouse offices would hear. Not that it mattered. Soon enough, everyone would know Angelina had just slipped *down*, not *up* as expected, the corporate ladder.

Inside her tiny office, Angelina stalked between the two client chairs and behind her L-shaped desk. She flung herself into her chair so hard the force propelled her several feet into the side of her desk.

What am I going to do?

Springing back to her feet, she paced five steps across the area between the chairs and the combination of open shelves and file cabinets. The phone on her desk rang, and she snarled at the instrument. Angel wasn't about to answer, to have to *talk*.... But she glanced at the screen and recognized her father's cell number.

Concern shafted through her. Daniel Howard had suffered a heart attack two weeks ago, then surgery. She'd flown to her hometown of Sweetwater Springs, Montana, and stayed by his side for a week before returning as soon as the doctor had assured her family that her father was on the mend. Four days ago, Angelina had returned to New York, not only to wrap up the big case she'd been working on for months, but also to attend today's meeting where she thought it'd be announced that she'd made partner.

She grabbed up the receiver. "Dad?"

"Hi, Angel Baby."

She couldn't get used to her powerful father sounding so weak. "How are you feeling? Is everything okay?"

"As good as can be expected, healthwise. Now I want you to stop worrying about me."

Easy for you to say. "I'm your daughter. I'm entitled to worry about you for a while longer." She walked back around her desk and sat, deciding not to relate her bad news. She'd wait until he was stronger.

"Angel Baby, I need your help with something."

She'd broken him of the childhood nickname when she'd gone through her independent adolescent stage. Then, in intensive care, he'd whispered the endearment when she'd first walked in... Just remembering made her swallow a sudden lump in her throat. "Anything, Dad. Do you need me to come home?" As she spoke, Angelina thought through her schedule, what she'd have to do to leave again...

"I need you to fly to Florida, to Seeker's Island."

"What's on Seeker's Island?"

"Rafael Flanigan must sign some important documents."

Oh, no! Anything but an errand that involved an encounter with Rafe Flanigan.

"Dad, I'm in the middle of a case." Not quite true. She'd just closed the file. But there was always another case...another ten cases...whatever she needed to avoid Rafe Flanigan. "Sorry, Dad." She tried to project some remorse into her voice.

"It will only take you a day. I've already couriered the documents. In fact, you should have them on your desk."

She glanced at her desk and saw a big envelope sitting in front of her computer. "You're not supposed to be working!"

He chuckled, the sound a pale version of his normal belly laugh. "I have an excellent assistant."

"Then let your excellent assistant do it. James is more than capable."

"James has a crippling fear of flying. He refuses to set foot anywhere near an airport."

"Guess he's not so excellent, is he?"

Her father ignored her snarky comment. "It's just for the day, Angel. Fly down, get Rafe's signature, courier the documents back to me, fly back to New York."

"Can't this wait?"

"The deadline is Friday."

Five days!

"I'd planned to go myself, but then…" His voice turned urgent. "This is important, Angel. Millions of dollars and the fate of the Flanigan Ranch."

"Why the last-minute rush?"

"Rafe Flanigan has ignored my previous letters and phone calls."

Figures.

"Harry Flanigan stipulated in his will that if Rafe didn't return home within six months of his death, as well as sign the agreements for future arrangements about the estate, the ranch would be sold to the McCurdy's."

"What!" The word burst out of her. "I can't believe he'd do that!"

"It's Harry's way to force Rafe to bow to his will, even after he's dead."

"And what about Gabe?"

"Gabe will lose the ranch he's worked on all his life. He'll see his family's land go to their rivals."

Rivals. More like *enemies.* "Rafe couldn't possibly want that...But Harry hated Old Man McCurdy."

"If Arn McCurdy hadn't died before him, I don't think even Harry would have gone this far."

"I can't believe he'd do such a thing."

"I tried to dissuade him, Angel. But Harry Flanigan had a bull-headed need to control his grandsons...well, control everyone around him. I'll require Rafe's signature, already have Gabe's, to avoid the ranch falling into McCurdy hands. You know what a disaster that would be."

The Flanigans weren't the only ones who'd carried old generational wounds caused by the McCurdys. Some acts, even after more than a hundred years, would never fade from her family history.

Her father sighed. "Dustin McCurdy is talking with a developer, who plans to cut their ranch into little parcels and throw up a lot of cheap houses. The plan's not well received by most in town. If the McCurdys also get their hands on the Flanigan land..."

She thought of the pristine, beautiful place where she'd fallen in love with Rafe. *The secret waterfall, a Flanigan treasure exposed to all and sundry...*

Angelina's mind reeled. She was unable to wrap her mind around what a disaster this would be for the brothers...for the boy she'd once loved.

"I'd go myself, Angel, but the doctors won't let me out of this place."

Just thinking of her father flying to Florida in his condition made her blood run cold, spurring her grudging agreement. "All right."

"I knew I could count on you!" His voice sounded stronger.

Angelina wondered if she'd just been played.

"You'll find the plane ticket with the documents. You'd better get going, Angel. The flight leaves in three hours."

Three hours! Angelina held in a shriek.

"Thanks, Angel Baby." Her dad hung up before she could protest.

Angelina glanced at her Rolex. At this time of the day, she'd need an hour, maybe more, just to get to the airport. She didn't even have time to change. Grabbing her roomy leather briefcase from underneath her desk, she slid in her father's envelope, adding some of her own paperwork for good measure. *Might as well work on the plane.* She tucked her small purse in the corner.

She looked around the room and caught sight of her gym bag on a bottom shelf, holding her workout clothes. She unzipped the top and pulled out shorts, sports bra, an extra pair of panties, socks, tennis shoes, and a couple of protein bars, and tossed them into her briefcase, arranging everything to fit—barely.

I can do this, Angelina gave herself a pep talk, but had trouble believing her own words. She took a deep breath, then strode out the door to meet with the man who'd broken her heart fifteen years earlier.

CHAPTER THREE

His feet propped on his desk, working on his iPad, feeling the breeze from the half-open door, Rafe didn't pay any attention to the familiar sound of the gate opening. But the click of high heels on the boardwalk outside the office did catch his interest. Not too many ladies visited the livery stables wearing heels. He set his iPad aside.

The woman walked to the door, pushed it open, and stepped inside into a pillar of sunlight. She wore business clothes and carried a black briefcase. He had to blink several times to make sure she wasn't a figment of one of his fantasies, conjured up by those damn letters from Sweetwater Springs.

She's real, all right. Rafe tried to conceal his shock over seeing Angelina Elizabeth Carter Howard all grown up and standing in front of him, more vivid than any of his dreams of her. He'd shoved the memory of their young love, along with everyone and everything in Sweetwater Springs, into a small mental box he kept locked. But he couldn't control what happened when he slept...

The light played over her curves and revealed the expression of annoyance on her beautiful features. Her oval face, with the high cheekbones, was the same as in his dreams—perfect features, golden skin courtesy of her part Sioux grandmother and her African-American great-great-grandfather, except for some fine lines around her big whiskey-golden eyes. He was glad to see she hadn't cut her long curly hair, which she wore up in a bun with two sticks through it.

Fifteen years hadn't changed her much—filled her out some—which was all to the better. At eighteen, she hadn't lost her adolescent coltishness, but now... With a black jacket tucked under one arm, her purple sleeveless blouse showed trim, smooth arms and her black several-inches-above-the knee short skirt and high-heeled pumps revealed long legs. He'd seen her in less—bathing suits when all the kids came over to the ranch to swim on hot summer days, the tiny bikini she'd worn on the day he'd taken her to the Flanigan waterfall before all hell had broken loose... But not with a woman's figure.

The sight of her sent a buzz of attraction through his body. Rafe wanted to jump up and hug her hello, then kiss her like crazy and sweep her off to his house on the beach. But the fact that Angel Howard, the descendent of generations of lawyers... He eyed her business attire, the leather briefcase--hell, she was probably an attorney herself, just like she'd planned. That didn't bode well for his peace of mind.

So, he restrained himself, giving her a purposely lazy smile. "Hello, Angel Howard. Vacationing on Seeker's Island, are you?"

"Do I look like I'm playing tourist, Raphael Flanigan?" she said with a snap to her tone.

"Well," he drawled, baiting her for the pleasure of watching her color rise. "You do look a mite overdressed for our little island. I hope you brought a bikini. I recall you looking mighty sexy in one. Why don't you go change, and we'll—."

"I'm quite comfortable, thank you," she said crisply, pulling a folder from her briefcase. "I've brought something for you to sign. "

Yep, part of the family business.

"As soon as you do, I'll be out of your life."

Maybe I don't want you out of my life. The thought shocked him. To buy himself time, Rafe held up a hand in a stopping motion. "I'm not signing anything."

"But, Rafe, this is important. Your family— "

"I don't want to hear about it. Not one more word, Angel. Or I'll toss you out of here on your pretty little ass."

"My ass isn't little," she muttered.

"Turn around and let me see."

Pink flooded her dusky cheeks.

Well, one thing hadn't changed. Rafe could still make her blush. The rose color seeping into her skin did something to his innards—an effect she'd often had on him. He wrenched his gaze from her and stared blindly out the window, memories and old longings flooding him. God help him, now she was here, he couldn't let her go again.

***

At the first sight of her former love, Angel caught her breath on a skipped heartbeat.

Rafe wore a loud Hawaiian shirt patterned with hibiscus flowers, shorts, and flip-flops. He wore his dark hair long and loose to his shoulders, looking like a throwback to the photo of his great-great grandfather that hung in the town library.

He sat in a chair, his long, tanned legs stretched out on top of the desk, looking at a view of the ocean instead of at her. Granted the view was a beautiful sight, but Angelina didn't have time to wait. She wanted to be on the next ferry off the island, signed documents in hand.

At Rafe's bikini comment, she struggled to suppress the sudden memory of them swimming in the pool at Flanigan Falls, their passionate embraces. "Rafe," she said, keeping her tone even. "I need to talk to you."

"I'm busy."

"You don't look busy," she said with a pointed look at his legs.

"I'm working."

He might be right. In school, Rafe was prone to stare out the window during most of class. She couldn't even count the times an exasperated teacher would snap a question at him, and Rafe would fire off the correct answer, then return to window gazing. She'd always admired his nonchalant attitude. But now, hot and sticky, overdressed in her suit, she felt a belated sympathy for their teachers and made a mental note to send them all cards of appreciation when she returned to New York.

The phone on his desk rang. Rafe ignored it.

"Aren't you going to answer that?"

He didn't even look away from the window. "No."

"Why not?"

"If it's important, they'll leave a message. I might, or might not, listen and get back to them...eventually."

No wonder he hadn't returned Dad's calls. She gave an exacerbated shake of her head. "I can't believe you."

He flicked her a glance. His face was leaner than he'd been at eighteen, more chiseled. His eyes, those Flanigan eyes, gray with a black circle around the irises, looked inscrutable, although his tone sounded friendly.

Inexplicably, Angelina missed the affection she'd always seen when he'd looked at her—at least, when they'd grown old enough to have a crush on each other.

She glanced toward the cubbyholes on the sidewall above his desk and saw a stack of familiar envelopes. Ire rose in her. Angelina walked to them, heels clicking on the white tiled floor, and pulled out the envelopes. A glance revealed her father's stationery. She waved them in his face. "I can't believe you didn't at least open these so you'd know *what* you're ignoring."

"Not interested." His gaze heated, traveled over her.

But he's definitely interested in me. Angelina wondered if she could use that to her advantage—charm the signature out of him.

"I'm serious, Angel." He softened his voice. "Why don't you stay a while? Look at you," he said gently. "You look stressed out and pale."

"Raphael Flanigan," she said in a warning tone. "I don't have time for this. I have to get back to my office in New York."

"New York?" he said, surprise in his tone.

"I work for Elland & Kirkus. I'm here as a favor for my father."

"No wonder you're so pale. What do you work? Sixty hours a week?"

Her laugh held no humor. "More like eighty."

"What happened to working with your father?"

"I became ambitious." *And look where it got me.*

***

Rafe had distanced himself from memories of Angelina, or so he'd thought. When he'd left Sweetwater Springs, almost a year had passed before he'd reconciled himself to the idea she'd cut him off; more years than that to get over the hurt. But seeing a flash of pain in her eyes at the mention of her job softened him. He wasn't about to sign those papers, but Rafe sensed Angel needed Seeker's Island. "Sounds like you've come to the right place," he said in a light tone. "Do you know we have a magical pool on this island?" Not that he believed the tale. But he needed to do something about her sadness. "Grants your wishes."

"Rafe, be serious. I have to get back."

"All right, not your *wishes*, your *heart's desires*. And not to everyone. Just *special* people." He slung his feet off the desk and stood. "I'll take you for a drive, Angel. On Seeker's Island, we don't talk business until after the sun sets."

Angel glanced at her watch.

Rafe could almost see the wheels turning in her brain as Angel estimated how long she needed to persuade him to sign her paperwork. *You're in for a long stay, Angel, baby*. But he knew better than to say anything. He'd have to toss out breadcrumbs in such a way as to make Miss Smarty Lawyer fall for his trick. For although he didn't want to examine why, Rafe wanted to keep her there.

CHAPTER FOUR

Angelina closed the door to the bathroom, shutting out the sight of Rafe. She leaned back against the wood to catch her breath and still her heartbeat where that infuriating man couldn't see the impact he had on her. The bathroom was surprisingly roomy, with a white quartz counter edged in navy-blue tile, over a mahogany cabinet containing an oval sink, and a toilet in one corner and a shower in the other.

I'm still dangerously attracted to him.

That thought was enough to make Angelina push away from the door and strive for control—or at least a semblance of control. After Rafe had left her, she'd worked too long and too hard healing the aching wound he'd dealt her—trying to, if not forget, then file him away.

I'm here on business. As soon as Rafe signs those papers, I'm leaving.

She set her briefcase on the sink. *Might as well get comfortable.* Casual and relaxed might work better with Rafe than formal lawyer. *Not that I can relax around him.*

Stepping out of her heels with a sigh of relief, Angelina stripped off her clothing and neatly folded the suit, leaving them neatly on the counter. The cool tile soothed her sore feet. She donned her shorts and a tank, then pulled on the ankle socks and tennis shoes.

A glance in the mirror made Angelina wrinkle her nose. Rafe was right about her being paler than normal. She appeared drained, haggard. Had he seen her that way? Old taunts about her "mongrel" heritage tried to burrow into her thoughts, but she squelched them with a shake of her head.

Well, since she'd be staying a little longer on this tropical island than she'd planned...catching the evening instead of the afternoon ferry, she'd get a little time in the sun. Showing up at the law firm tomorrow with some color wouldn't be bad.

Yet if ten minutes with Raphael Flanigan had shaken her, broken open a tightly contained core of pain, what might several hours do?

I can do this! Angelina took another bracing breath, then opened the bathroom door, and stepped out.

Rafe was just hanging up the phone, and the sound of the door made him look her way. His eyes widened and his lips turned up, just the tiniest bit. "That's better."

Angelina was immediately lost in his compelling gaze. She looked away, unwilling to get pulled back into their attraction.

"Let's head for the inn. Have you been there yet?"

She shook her head. "I came straight here. No need to check into the hotel. I won't be here overnight."

He shot her a grin. "Won't matter anyway. The Sunseekers' Inn is filled up. A big, fancy wedding."

Another reason to catch the evening ferry, or I might end up staying with him.

"One of my carriages is parked in front of the inn. I just called the driver to wait for us."

They strolled out the door and down the wooden path she'd walked up earlier, but instead of turning toward the ferry, he led her in the opposite direction.

Her gaze fell on a sign obviously posted as a warning for ignorant tourists.

BEWARE!
HORSES, EVEN THE LITTLE ONES,
MAY KICK OR BITE!
THANK YOU!

Rafe hadn't strayed far from his roots, she decided.

The livery consisted of a weathered gray wooden barn painted with cobalt blue trim, some small outbuildings, and a tiny cottage in the same color. She looked up at Rafe, whose sunglasses covered his eyes. "Cobalt? A little unusual for a stable, don't you think?"

A smile played at the corner of his mouth. "Not on Seeker's Island.

When I first arrived, the livery was turquoise...*faded* turquoise. Now *that* was a little much."

Angelina chuckled, then realized she couldn't remember the last time she'd laughed. Certainly she must have smiled recently, but she'd been too worried about her father and caught up in the stress of work to feel light-hearted.

"I converted the chicken house to staff quarters for my driver. Two college girls who work for me in the summer live in the cottage. They're in charge of the kids' parties with the miniature horses and also during the hours of the petting zoo."

"Petting zoo?"

"Not quite a zoo. But kids sure do like the minis."

"I remember. When you're small, a horse that's your size is just perfect."

Rafe took her hand, as if casually leading her past the stables, and walked toward the direction of town. But the touch of their hands felt anything but casual.

Not wanting to make a scene, Angelina didn't pull away, although she couldn't help liking the feel of her hand in his calloused one. She had an increasingly hard time keeping an emotional distance and wondered if she had the same effect on him that he did on her.

They reached a large corral edged by trees. Five sorrel-and-white Paint horses and two foals, interspersed with six similar patterned miniature horses, lazed in the shade. Their coats gleamed more orange than dark copper.

Angelina caught her breath at the sight. "You still have your Paints?"

"At least I held onto part of my dream." Rafe's tone was wry. "Stuck to producing orange Overos."

"I'm glad," she murmured, thinking about their last conversation so long ago, when they'd shared their cherished dreams, only to have them shattered hours later.

"What about you, Angel?"

"I guess you can say that I held onto part of my dreams—the lawyer part—too."

They reached the wooden corral and stopped to observe the horses.

"Took awhile to get that light color for the minis. I still breed for confirmation, personality, and color."

"They're so bright and cute." She was especially taken with the mini stallion. The small horse faced her direction, his light-colored tail and mane blowing in the breeze, two blue eyes fixed on Angelina as if hoping she'd produce a treat. "I don't think our ancestors would recognize them."

"Nope. The minis are no longer the Falabellas breed that came from Argentina." He pulled on her hand. "If we stop to say howdy, we'll never leave."

Would that be so bad? Angelina banished the traitorous thought. She gave him a rueful smile. "I guess you're right." Reluctantly, she walked on.

They reached a road, and the wooded walkway turned into a concrete sidewalk. They passed quaint stores, the buildings looking as if they'd been on the island for ages. Probably had.

Rafe pointed to a two-story building with a porch and a balcony. The sign said *Paradise Ice Cream Parlor*. People sat at bistro tables on the broad, white porch. One skinny man leaning against the carved support post had an ice cream cone in each hand.

Watching him lick first one cone then the other gave Angelina an immediate craving for chocolate. She wished for the skinny guy's metabolism.

Rafe nudged her. "The former whorehouse. Now the ice cream parlor's downstairs and living quarters are upstairs."

"Still housing wicked indulgences."

Rafe chuckled. "That they are. The ice cream here has won awards. People come from the mainland just to get a sugar high." He steered her inside and held open the screened door. "You'll have to taste for yourself."

Angelina stepped across the threshold and was assaulted by the smell of sugar. A long Formica counter ran across the right side of the room. People perched on high stools in front of it. The left half held the glass-fronted freezer with the ice cream. A staircase to the upper floor was in the back.

Rafe slid his sunglasses on the top of his head and leaned closer. "An ice cream cone is mandatory when you visit Seeker's Island. It primes you for the magic."

She nudged him, trying not to giggle. "Don't be silly."

He approached the gangly teenager behind the freezer and told him, "One Rocky Road for the lady, and one Pumpkin Spice for me."

He remembered. Angelina was amazed. *Odd how some things hadn't faded over the years.* She didn't know how she felt about that...what she wanted Rafe to recall about her.

Rafe handed over some money, accepted the two cones, and gave Angel hers.

She took a lick and almost moaned at the taste of the rich sweetness. How long had it been since she'd eaten ice cream? At least a year.

Rafe's gaze didn't leave her face. His tongue slid around the side of the ice cream ball. As Angel watched in fascination, shivers raced down her spine, and not from the cold of the Rocky Road. Rafe made eating an ice cream a sensual experience.

Angelina decided to give him a taste of his own medicine, or in this case, ice cream. She looked at him from under her eyelashes, sending him a seductive smile. Her tongue played over the top surface, then she bit into a marshmallow with her front teeth,

His smoky gaze smoldered.

She held in a smile and lowered her eyelids, feeling the power of her femininity.

The screen door banged open. Several teenage boys entered, jostling each other.

Rafe took Angelina's free arm, steered her around the gang, and escorted her outside.

They continued down the sidewalk, past a surf shop and a bakery, the yeasty smell of bread drifting into the air. They strolled across the driveway of Sunseekers' Inn. The yellow Victorian, with a turret on each side and tropical-print cushions on the porch furniture, beckoned her to linger for a while.

If only I were here on vacation. She slanted a look up at Rafe. *Without the company of a stubborn Flanigan.* But even as she thought the words, deep down Angelina wished she could be here under entirely different circumstances—featuring hot sun, a cool ocean, and Rafe's strong hands on her body.

Stop, she chastened herself. *I have a job to do.*

A white carriage with turquoise leather seats was parked in front of the white picket fence under the shade of the trees, the top folded back. Instead of the expected brown or black horse, a Paint stood between the shafts. She admired how the orange coat, splashed with white, gleamed like a new penny in the sun.

"He's a descendant of Sassy and Cass."

Nostalgia caught Angelina in a grip. She and Rafe had taken many a ride over the ranches and wilderness of Sweetwater Springs, part of a posse of close-knit friends from the time they first put a headstall on their ponies. "They're beautiful. I'm amazed you kept up with your breeding program."

Pride lit his face. "Albeit on a smaller scale than I'd planned. Don't have the expanse of land here. I sell the Paints to the rich on the mainland."

"They look valuable."

"More so than in Montana. Course, with the Internet, we can sell all over. But I don't like to ship my stock long distances. Travel's hard on them."

They reached the carriage. The driver, an attractive man with sun-streaked brown hair, bottle-green eyes, and a rich tan, looked to be in his late twenties. He sketched Rafe a salute.

Rafe nodded. "Meet Chip Brockman. Driver and groom. He's been with me for the last three years. Chip, this is Angel Howard, an old friend of mine."

"Angelina," she corrected.

One of Rafe's eyebrows pulled up. "*Angelina* Howard."

Chip flashed a cocky grin. "Didn't think you had any old friends, boss. Especially pretty ones."

"I didn't either." Rafe led her over to the horse and ran a hand over the white patch on the animal's neck. "Meet Abigail."

"Abigail?"

"For the last few years, I've used names of the First Ladies."

"Do you have a Martha?"

"I did. Martha now lives in Washington," he said deadpan, but his eyes twinkled.

She burst out laughing and had to hold her stomach.

"D.C."

Angelina couldn't help another bubble of laughter escaping. She took a deep breath, surprised to feel the constriction which banded her chest for who knew how long had eased. *I knew I was stressed, but not that my body was so tight.* The knowledge shook her. Sadness surfaced for what she'd gone through...no *put* herself through. *All that work, everything I sacrificed, and I still didn't make partner.*

"I'll take over, Chip," Rafe said.

The driver glanced at his watch. "I have a couple scheduled in a half an hour."

"Get the other carriage. I'll bring this one back to the stables."

"You got it, boss." Chip jumped down in a smooth motion.

His hand on the small of her back, Rafe guided Angelina around the carriage. "Sit in front with me, Angel*ina*." He extended his hand to help her up.

She slid her fingers into his callused palm. "Sure, boss."

He grinned.

So did she.

He handed her up to the seat.

Although Rafe touched her with the same impersonal courtesy he must give any woman climbing into the vehicle, his hands didn't feel at all impersonal. Warmth trailed where he touched. She couldn't help the sensations thrumming through her body.

Raphael Flanigan. Achingly familiar, yet different, perhaps because she had an adult's awareness of him. She glanced away, afraid of what he'd see on her face, and stared at the flowers lining the driveway.

Angelina felt the seat cushions give beneath Rafe's weight, heard the slap of reins, felt the jerk of the carriage pulling forward, listened to the clop-clop of the horse's hooves. But she couldn't turn her head to look at him. Not until she'd banished the impact he had on her, or at least controlled herself enough so he wouldn't guess.

"My father said…" Angelina began.

"Uh, uh. Relax. You're on island time."

Angelina backed off, biding her time.

While he took them through the streets of the town, they kept to the safe topic of horses, although she itched to get his agreement to sign so she *could* relax.

A pretty woman standing in front of a jewelry store waved at Rafe.

He smiled and nodded in acknowledgment.

They drove past wooden cottages in pastel colors. Some looked like simple shotgun homes, others were Craftsman bungalows. From time to time, a stately Victorian with lacy trim would tower over the neighbors.

Flowers spilled out of window boxes, grew alongside the walkways, and flourished in shell-lined beds. Their scent perfumed the air.

The beauty of Seeker's Island charmed Angelina, and some of the tension seeped from her tight muscles. She caught herself imagining which house she'd choose for a vacation home—perhaps one in need of renovations that she could lovingly restore. Then she remembered being passed over for partner, the lack of extra income her new position would have brought, and her good spirits crashed.

CHAPTER FIVE

Sensing her inner turmoil, Rafe allowed Angel to sit in silence for the first twenty minutes of the ride, but studied her from the corner of his eye.

Finally, she gave a tiny shake, as if rolling something off her mind. She glanced up at him, her gaze friendly but impersonal. "Tell me about your business. How long have you been on the island?"

He decided to play the conversation her way. At least for now. "Fifteen years."

She gave him a wide-eyed look.

"When I lit out from Sweetwater Springs, I wanted to drive as far away as possible and still be in the states. Florida, believe it or not, is good horse country. Lots of rich retired people who like to ride."

"But you ended up on an *island*."

"My parents met here, and my mother told us enough stories about the place…." He shrugged. "Sort of felt familiar."

"I never knew that about your parents."

"Imagine a soldier on leave. He's from a wealthy ranching family with roots dating back a hundred and twenty-five years. He meets a shy eighteen-year-old orphan who grew up shuffled from foster home to foster home. They tumble into love and get hitched before his leave ends."

"I imagine that marriage didn't meet with your grandfather's approval."

"Nope. The two stayed away from Sweetwater Springs. By my mother's account, they were deliriously happy."

"Named their babies after angels," she teased.

He slanted her a glance. "Look who's talking, *Angelina*."

She laughed.

"Then my father was killed, and everything changed. With a babe in arms and pregnant with another, my mother had no place else to go…and my grandfather never let her forget it."

"What a mean old man."

"I remember riding with him around the ranch...his pride in our land, a pride he passed on to Gabe and me. Learning to be cowboys... He wasn't all bad." Rafe shook his head. "Stubborn, though."

Angel laughed. "He's not the only stubborn Flanigan."

Ah, I've coaxed her out of her shell. Rafe raised his eyebrows. "How about narrow-minded? Or ruthless and controlling?"

"You're not any of those!" Her response was obviously instinctual.

Hope rose in him.

Angelina paused. "Are you?"

He narrowed his eyes. "You couldn't accuse me of anything worse than being like my grandfather."

"Have you any idea what he had in mind for you and Gabe's legacy?" she asked, daring to bring up the forbidden topic.

Something hot went through him, an old anger. "Leave it, Angel," he said more sharply than he wanted. "Don't ruin this...the little time we have."

She sat back in the seat. "All right, Rafe. But I will be heard. *Soon*."

***

The tables on the waterfront deck of Joe's Cajun Seafood crowded each other and overflowed with locals and tourists alike. Rafe knew Angel wouldn't try to talk business where they could be overheard, and he'd be safe to enjoy her company for a few hours, without the stress of having to deal with whatever brought her here.

Angel had never participated in a crawfish boil, and he taught her how to pinch off their heads and suck out the meat. After a squeamish attempt or two, she was soon peelin' and eatin' like a local.

They stuck to neutral topics such as their favorite books and movies, finding many in common and arguing amiably over others. They shared about their travels to different parts of the world, mostly for business—Angel on quick trips to Europe for her law firm, he on the delivery of his

Paints to their new owners in various parts of the southeastern U.S.

The more they talked, the more he saw her shoulders relax. The fine lines around her eyes crinkled when she smiled. He even coaxed a laugh from her a couple of times.

Stuffed, they waddled, as Angel said, although she walked as gracefully as ever to the carriage.

He helped her into the driver's seat.

She cajoled him into letting her handle the reins, and he lounged against the seat, watching her profile. No one seeing her now would know this sweet-looking woman, wearing a tank and shorts and driving the carriage, was the same one who'd earlier been dressed in the conservative business suit.

But the change went deeper. As Angel had relaxed, she'd shed her proper attorney attitude, became more the friend he remembered.

The night deepened. Stars speckled the blackness above them. The lights of the carriage illuminated their path. A fat pearly moon drifted into the sky.

It must be getting late. Rafe glanced at his watch. "You've missed the last ferry. Left five minutes ago."

She gasped.

Even though he did want her to stay, Rafe hadn't realized the time. "You can bunk at my place. I have a guest room."

"I'll have to text my boss." She made a face. "He won't be pleased."

"Just work a ninety instead of eighty-hour week when you get back to compensate."

She sighed. "I don't want to think about my job."

He pulled the carriage into the yard in front of the stable.

The door to the chicken house opened, and Chip shuffled out, muffling a yawn with one hand.

"Little early to be fallin' asleep, don't you think?" Rafe teased, setting the brake and handing Chip the reins.

"Late one last night. Pretty college student from the mainland."

"Pretty college students usually lead to late nights," Rafe agreed.

Beside him, Angel stiffened.

Rafe climbed off the seat, hurried around the back of the carriage, and reached for her just as she started to step down. Slipping his hands around her waist, he swung her to the ground. He wanted to let his hands linger, but knowing they had an interested audience, he forced himself to step back.

Angel's expression closed.

Rafe wondered what she was thinking. He used to be able to read her so well and didn't like how she'd shut herself off to him. Although, when he took her hand to lead her into the stables, Angel didn't pull away. "Night," Rafe told Chip.

The driver led Abigail into the livery.

Rafe felt unaccountably nervous escorting Angel to his bungalow. The two-bedroom wooden cottage was a far cry from the big Flanigan ranch house or the stately Howard mansion in Sweetwater Springs. He imagined her apartment in New York was as sleek and sophisticated as Angel herself.

Yet, he took pride in his home. He'd lovingly renovated the dilapidated house, doing much of the work himself, until the place shone like a jewel. Over the years, when he enjoyed a liaison with an attractive tourist, he'd never brought the woman home, although he was very familiar with the bedrooms in the inn and the bed and breakfast.

The front of the house had a broad porch on the first floor and a balcony on the second, both overlooking the ocean. He led her up the steps and opened the door.

"No lock?"

"This isn't New York, Angel."

Her brows drew together, forming a crease in her forehead.

He wanted to drop a kiss on that little dent. "Don't worry. I'll lock up tonight, so you don't have to worry about marauders disturbing your sleep."

"It's not the marauders I'm worried about," she said dryly.

He flashed a seductive grin. "I can't make any promises, Angel."

Apprehension sparked in her eyes, only to be replaced by a bland gaze and a slight lift of her chin. "I'll put a chair against my door."

"No need. The guest room has a lock." Rafe didn't mention he had the key. "You're safe with me, Angel." He gestured for her to enter.

"So I used to think," she murmured, stepping into the house.

Wondering if he'd heard correctly, he followed her inside. He should explain what happened, but that would mean tearing open an old wound that he'd worked long and hard to close. And it wouldn't change the past. Angel had cut him off, and that had been as painful as his family disowning him. Not to mention talking about that subject would open the door to the conversation of why she was here.

Rafe didn't want to fight about documents he had no intention of signing. Something much more pleasurable was on his mind. He speculated if she, too, considered letting the spark between them ignite once again.

They walked into the room, and he tried to see the place through her eyes. He'd opened up the downstairs, so the main room and the kitchen flowed together. He'd stained the original wide-planked flooring a dark mahogany and then coated it with marine sealant to withstand the sand that constantly made its way into the house. He'd adapted the built-in shelves to fit his big-screen television, had decorated with a comfortable couch and loveseat covered in soft navy canvas-like material, and hung several seascapes by native artists on the walls.

Rafe watched Angel glance around, taking in everything. Her presence changed the energy in the room, softened the masculine feel and made the house feel alive. *Or maybe that's just her effect on me.*

She smiled up at him. "Nice. Comfortable looking. How long have you lived here?"

"Ten years. Spent the first two on a cot while I made the place habitable."

"You did the work?"

Rafe had to laugh at her tone. "Yep. Part of the reason it took so long. Learned as I went."

"I'm impressed." She set her briefcase on the coffee table.

He tilted his head toward the kitchen. "Would you like a house tour?"

"Certainly."

He led her through the contemporary kitchen with the granite countertops and stainless steel appliances, showed her his office, the small bathroom he'd tucked under the stairs, then the back porch. Upstairs, he first took her to his bedroom that looked over the ocean.

She candidly surveyed the king-sized bed and crossed the room to the balcony, opening the French doors and stepping outside.

Rafe followed her.

"Ahh," Angel breathed a sigh of pleasure. The tropical breeze danced around them, the air warm and heavy, scented of the sea and the flowers growing in his yard. Ocean waves made a gentle whooshing sound in the background. The full moon illuminated white foam on the waves cresting over the obsidian black water.

She leaned on the rail. "I can't believe how beautiful this is, Rafe. Pure paradise. I can see why you've stayed here."

Rafe had no eyes for the view he usually enjoyed, for he couldn't take his eyes off Angel. Moonlight coated her in silver light, a Grecian goddess come to Earth. Maybe it was moonlight madness, maybe just Angel Howard herself, but he could no longer resist.

He drew her toward him, leaned in for a kiss.

Angel stared at him, eyes luminous. She tilted her face up, but when their lips almost touched, she made a resisting sound. Shaking her head, she stepped back. "I can't do this."

Disappointment stabbed him, but Rafe spread his hands in an "it's all right" motion. "Let me show you your room." He tried to sound matter-of-fact. "You can have one of my T-shirts to sleep in. I have an extra toothbrush and toothpaste you can use."

Relief crossed her face.

Feeling far more hurt than he should have, Rafe strode into the bedroom. He opened a dresser drawer and grabbed one of his roomiest T-shirts.

Angel had followed him, standing stiffly about three feet away, as if needing to be out of grabbing range. She took the T-shirt he held out.

He strode into his bathroom, searched in a cabinet for a new toothbrush and toothpaste, walked out, and gave them to her.

In the hallway, he opened the linen closet and took down a fluffy blue towel and washcloth. Carrying them, he led her into the guest room.

This room was smaller than the master because he'd added a private bathroom. On the back wall, French doors opened onto a balcony overlooking the garden. The queen bed took up much of the space, with a nightstand on both sides. A small chest of drawers and a tiny desk and chair were the only other pieces of furniture.

He laid the towel and washcloth on the bed. "The sheets are clean. The bathroom is private. Set your clothes outside the door, and I'll toss them in the washer."

Her smile was polite. "Thank you."

"Sleep well, Angel."

She gave him a slight duck of her chin. "Good night, Rafe." Angelina gently shut the door in his face.

A few minutes later, from his bedroom, he heard the sound of her door open and shut again. Rafe walked down the hallway, scooped up the neatly folded pile of Angel's clothes and trotted downstairs to the small washroom next to the kitchen. Once he'd started the machine, he wandered back to the kitchen, grabbed a bottle of beer from the refrigerator, and popped the cap. From where he stood, he could see Angel's briefcase containing her precious documents.

Rafe took a swig of the beer. *I could always burn them.* Not that he would. *There's more where those came from.* But maybe the act would buy him more time with her. *And make me look as childish as a five-year-old.*

To avoid temptation, he climbed the stairs and passed her room. The sound of the shower made him imagine Angel naked under the running water, and Rafe felt an answering response in his body. *Joining her probably wouldn't be a good idea.*

He quickened his pace into his room and onto the balcony, where he stretched out on his lounge. Taking another sip of his beer, Rafe stared at the water.

Tonight, the sound of the waves didn't lull him into relaxation. Instead, his body was strung tight, his emotions turbulent, and his thoughts in a whirl. Angel's abrupt appearance today had torn away his contentment with his life in paradise.

For years, he'd lived in this house without feeling lonely. Could probably have gotten along just fine for a long time, maybe forever. But tonight, Angel's presence had broken open a deep-seated loneliness within him, old and bitter. He didn't like the feeling.

Taking the last swig of beer before setting down the bottle, he leaned his head back against the cushions to do some serious thinking. Rafe knew he stood at a crossroads. He could continue on as he had been, avoiding his past, his pain, his family. But he doubted, after today, he'd have success with that decision. The only choice really was to open up to Angel. Face his past. Hear what she had to say.

But...if they talked in the morning and she convinced him to sign whatever the heck those papers were, he knew she'd leave on the next ferry. If he absolutely refused to sign them, she'd still leave on the next ferry. The thought struck him. *The papers be damned. I want her.*

Rafe realized he needed to ask Angel for more time, for her to remain just long enough so he could hook her into staying for good.

He began to plan his strategy—Operation Angel.

CHAPTER SIX

The next morning, Angel awoke feeling surprisingly refreshed. She'd expected to toss and turn all night, thinking about her life, especially Rafe. Indeed she had for a while before crashing into a deep sleep, soothed no doubt by the sound of the waves through her open windows and balcony door.

She stretched, then made her way to the bathroom, using the toilet and brushing her teeth. When she opened the door to the hall, she saw her clothes in a neat pile next to several boutique shopping bags. Intrigued, she scooped up everything and brought them inside, dumping the armful on the bed.

Rummaging through the first bag, Angelina pulled out five bikinis in various colors and styles, which all looked about her size. She held a gold top to her chest, wondering if she'd dare wear the tiny scraps of material in public. Just imagining wearing the bikini in front of Rafe made heat flush through her body.

Angelina set down the bathing suit and opened the other bag. This one contained three pairs of jeans. Again, he'd guessed her size.

The warm breeze blowing through the windows made her decide on the clean tank and shorts from yesterday. She dressed and combed out her curly hair, but left it free, flowing to her waist. Rafe had always loved her hair. She put on a little makeup and made a mental note to ask Rafe for sunscreen.

Angelina paused at the door, wondering how she could pin him down to talk. *I'll find a way,* she promised herself.

Barefooted, Angelina padded down the staircase, eager to see Rafe. She heard the ice-crushing sound of the blender and followed the noise into the kitchen, where she found Rafe whipping up a smoothie. Dressed in a faded gray T-shirt and running shorts, with his hair rumpled, he looked far too attractive for her peace of mind.

"Ah, just in time." Rafe smiled, poured the smoothie into two tall glasses and handed her one to. "Good for what ails you."

You are what ails me. But Angel didn't say anything, just took a sip, enjoying the tropical flavors.

He watched her drink. "Mango. Papaya. Pineapple. Vanilla protein powder. Ice cubes. Liquid vitamins and minerals and other good-for-you things."

As opposed to bad-for-me Rafael Flanigan. "I found some interesting articles of apparel outside my door this morning. A bit early for shopping, isn't it?"

He flashed the charming Flanigan smile. "A few phone calls, and the deliveries arrived on my doorstep." He snapped his fingers. "Magic."

She took another sip of her smoothie.

"On Seeker's Island, the locals aren't strangers," Rafe explained. "We help each other out."

Angelina wondered just how well he knew these shop owners.

"You can return anything that doesn't fit."

"I won't be here long enough to use them." Regret followed the words.

"Don't go, Angel. Give me today. Later, I'll listen to your proposition, sign the damn documents if I think it's right to do so. But I want you to spend some time relaxing on Seeker's Island."

Why? Because she was pale? Or because he wanted her? Angelina thought of, and then dismissed, her boss's reaction. She'd send him another text. "You'll cooperate?"

His grin was wicked. "You could call it that."

"Rafe…" she warned.

He held up a conciliatory hand. "Here's the plan. I want to go for a run on the beach, and I hope you'll join me. Then, breakfast and a ride to the falls for a swim in the magical pool. Then lunch. After that, whatever you want to do, even if it means talking about things I'd rather avoid. Deal?"

Angelina studied Rafe's face, searching for his level of sincerity. What she saw reassured her. "Deal."

***

Wearing wide-brimmed straw hats and bathing suits under their jeans and T-shirts, they rode two of Rafe's Paints around the island to the falls.

Angel missed being on horseback. *How did I stray so far from my roots...from what I loved?* Even as she thought the question, she knew the answer.

Sweetwater Springs had been too full of painful memories of Rafe, so she'd stayed away from her home as much as possible. Her family had made her avoidance easy, for they'd frequently visited her at college and law school and later in New York.

Angelina forced herself to concentrate on the present. To enjoy the beauty of the white sand beach; the turquoise water that deepened into dark blue; the mangroves anchored on the edge of the water; the sandpiper that skittered across their path—and the sexy man who rode beside her, though she fought the attraction.

They passed a thatched roof, open-sided tiki hut. *Seeker's Paradise Bar* read the sign out front. The man behind the bar saw Rafe and waved.

Rafe waved back but didn't stop. "Only another few minutes."

Up ahead, the sandy beach changed to rocks. Rafe pointed inland to a grove of trees. "The nature preserve. The falls and pool are there."

They headed their mounts off the beach and onto a path leading through the mangroves with their stilted roots burrowing into the moist soil. Shade provided welcomed relief from the sun. Farther in, the mangroves gave way to white cedars, tall palms, and gnarled oaks dripping with Spanish moss. Here and there, Angelina spotted a tree with small orange-red flowers or an orchid peeking through the thick ferns.

An old man, wearing overalls and no shirt, stepped between two oaks. Spanish moss dangling from the tree limbs framed his head. His face was brown and wrinkled, and his gray hair waved to his shoulders. A squirrel monkey rode on his shoulders.

Rafe shot the man a dark look. "Amos, you have the worst timing."

The old man saluted and backed away. "Just checking things out, Rafe. I'll head back to my place. Leave you two alone."

Rafe watched the man go and winked at Angel. "I supposed we should be glad he had clothes on."

Her eyes widened.

"Yep. Amos likes to soak naked. Not a pretty sight. And Chachi, the little devil monkey...nothing's safe around him. He'll steal you blind. I know from experience...never, ever leave your clothes lying around while you skinny dip." He urged his mount on.

Angelina followed, chuckling at the image of Rafe running around naked to catch a monkey and retrieve his clothes.

As they neared the pool, the distant sound of a waterfall grew louder. Instead of cascading over a cliff like the Flanigan Falls, here the water spilled down a hill of jumbled rocks, lush with ferns and other greenery, and divided into several streams before splashing into the turquoise pool. The water looked deep near the falls, but became shallower on the other side, and she wondered why no one was around.

Angelina sat on her horse watching the hypnotic dance of the water and feeling the sadness for a girl who'd once happily ridden to another waterfall, excited and in love. The hurt that lay in store for her... She glanced at Rafe. *Would history repeat itself?*

***

Rafe watched Angel, wondering what she was thinking. Like him, was she remembering the past?

They dismounted, and Rafe short-tied the reins to a limb of a towering sand pine. A long time ago, someone had trimmed away the lower branches, except for one used as a hitching post, the scaly red bark worn smooth from generations of use.

Rafe sat on a rock to pull off his boots and socks, then shucked off his outerwear.

Angel took her time undressing. But when she bared her body, her golden curves barely concealed by small triangles of shiny fabric, Rafe did everything he could do to keep his hands off of her. Over the years, Rafe had probably seen thousands of women in bathing suits, but none affected him like Angel.

To distract himself, he rolled up his clothes and tucked them in the saddlebag he'd brought for that purpose. "To keep them safe from Chachi. I can't guarantee the safety of our hats though."

Angel folded up her clothes and handed them to Rafe.

Once he'd secured them in the saddlebag, he pointed at the pool.

"The water's warm." He raced the few steps to the pool and dived in, swimming deep to touch the bottom before pushing off to the surface. The water was crystal clear and almost too warm from the hot springs combining with the cold waterfall on a hot summer day. Definitely not chilly enough to cool his reaction to seeing Angel in a bathing suit. He had a moment of wishing for a cold Montana pool to quench his ardor. He came up for air and waited for her to join him.

Her hair was loose in a mass of curls that bounced when she followed his lead. She dove in next to him, emerging with the water shining on her skin, her thick eyelashes clumped together.

Rafe tipped his head, indicating they swim to the other end. Side-by-side, they stroked to the shallow end. When he knew the water was waist high, he stood.

The weight of the water pulled Angel's hair into long waves, which flowed all the way to her waist. Rafe fingered one tendril, then in an instinctive reaction, wound the strand around his wrist, twisting until his hand reached her face. He used her hair to gently reel her closer. With his other hand, he cupped the back of her head and tilted up her face.

Her lips parted. In that moment, Rafe remembered doing this very gesture in a snowmelt pool under a blue Montana sky, with the sound of Flanigan Falls in the background. Their first kiss on a magical day.

The memory surged through him, unbelievably sweet and nostalgic. A time as different from now as could be. Yet...the promise of *more* was there, as strong as ever.

CHAPTER SEVEN

Rafe's heavy-lidded eyes gazed knowingly into hers.

Tethered by her hair, Angelina found herself fighting the ache in her throat. Was this really happening? Was she going to allow herself to become intimate with him?

Angelina felt torn, as if she were two different people. One was the detached and rational lawyer. The other ached for Rafe, wanted and needed him, and knew this encounter had been inevitable from the moment her father asked her to fly to Seeker's Island.

Passion darkened Rafe's smoky eyes. Dipping his head, his lips only a few inches away, he paused, giving her time to reject him as she had the night before.

Angelina arched her back to close the distance, longing for the feel of his lips on hers, a return to an earlier time of innocence.

But Rafe wasn't a green boy, and this kiss wasn't gentle, tentative. Instead, his mouth claimed hers, his lips possessive, demanding her passionate response.

Angelina wrapped her arms around him and slid her hands up his wet back, the muscles strong and sleek under her palms.

The kiss deepened. Tongues touched. All her senses heightened. The feel of his lips, their shape and texture felt so familiar, so *right*.

The kiss ended as suddenly as it began. She pushed Rafe away at the same time he pulled back.

They stared at each other, breathing raggedly, before Angel leaned away.

Rafe seized her wrist and towed her over to a flat rock submerged in the shade of the overhanging trees. He gently pushed her onto the wide surface—a comfortable seat.

"Rafe…Rafe, wait—"

"I know," he murmured. "We need to talk before we..."

Angelina lifted her chin. "I agree." She brushed her fingers across her lips. They still tingled from Rafe's kiss, sensitive and swollen under the pads of her fingertips. She thought they might tingle for hours–no, days–from that kiss. Maybe they'd never recover. Maybe *she'd* never recover.

"Who's going first?" Without waiting for a response, Rafe cocked an eyebrow. "I brought up the topic of *talking,* an unmanly thing to do. Therefore I get huge points, and you should be so impressed you'll spare me further masculine humiliation by plunging right into the conversation."

Angel gave him a half smile, withdrawing even though she didn't move. "I waited for you, Rafe. Waited for the phone to ring. Ran to the mailbox for months, hoping for a letter. I couldn't believe you'd left without saying goodbye. Then the rumors started circulating…" Her voice broke.

"What rumors?" But Rafe knew. *Horse thief.* He closed his eyes, as if he could turn off the sound of the words by shutting out his vision. *The McCurdys hadn't kept that bit of slander to themselves.*

"Mongrel." Angel spoke the ugly word in an even tone.

Rafe could see the shadow of pain in her eyes. "*What?*" Her response was so unexpected that it threw him. "How did you know Granddad called you that?"

She made a rueful turn of her lips. "Gabe told one of his friends what your grandfather said. Then he told one of his—"

"Gabe talked?" Rafe couldn't believe it. He and his brother had always abhorred tattling and gossip. They had a pact to never betray each other to their grandfather, no matter what punishment they suffered. After many years had passed, Rafe had figured out that Gabe had only gone to their grandfather that night because he'd believed the old man would take care of the situation with Dustin McCurdy. And he did. But not in the way his brother expected.

"Gabe confided in Ben Grayson. Remember how they became buddies because of football?"

He grimaced. "Never liked the guy."

"Gabe beat up Ben for talking, and that was the end of their friendship."

Good for Gabe. Rafe had a surge of missing his brother. He cupped Angel's neck. "I'm sorry. My grandfather was wrong to judge your family's heritage, to *say* such an ugly thing about you, and I told him so. It was one of the things we fought over."

She looked down. "I thought you must have believed him. Why else would you have left me?"

Rafe gave her a little shake. "Because I was young and stubborn and stupid. Because I'd vowed never to return to Sweetwater Springs, and I knew you dreamed of practicing law with your dad. Because if I allowed myself to miss you, then I'd miss my friends, my family, the ranch, and I couldn't...*wouldn't* go crawling back. Came here, put my mind and my back into creating a new life. When I wasn't working, I stayed drunk and numb for a long time. But by God, Angel," his chin rose "I was no horse thief."

"I know," she whispered, cupping the side of his face with one hand. Her eyes filled. A tear spilled over, sliding down her cheek.

Rafe couldn't bear to see her cry. Remorse welled up, clogged his throat like someone had shoved a fistful of sand into his mouth. He took a minute to fight for control, to find the words. "I'm so very sorry, Angel," he said, his voice thick. "I shouldn't have been so damn stubborn. When you didn't answer my note, I should have written a letter, written a hundred letters."

Her eyebrows pulled together. "What note?"

He leaned forward and kissed the teardrop before it could fall, tasting the salty trail. "The one I left in the oak."

She stared wide-eyed and slack-jawed. "There wasn't a letter, Rafe. I went there the next day. Made sure I felt every inch of that hole in the trunk. Went back every day for months, just in case you returned or were around, but in hiding."

"I did leave you a message, Angel. I swear. Told you I was coming here. Told you to write me care of Seeker's Island Hotel." Then he remembered Lucinda McCurdy driving by. "Lucinda must have taken it. I was pulling out when she passed me. She must have wondered why I'd stopped there at night, and being a McCurdy had to investigate and make trouble."

She pressed a hand to her heart. "I can't believe this, Rafe. All those years of pain."

"It's the truth."

"No, no. I believe you. I mean that I can't believe we've wasted so many years."

Time for my confession. "I thought you believed McCurdy's lies about me stealing his stud."

She made a raspberry sound. "Never in a million years would I believe one of Dustin McCurdy's lies. Besides, I heard almost a day-by-day recounting of you saving the money, paying Dustin, bringing your mares there... And so I told everyone. Some people might have believed the McCurdys, but most didn't."

"Why didn't my family get in touch with me?"

"I'll bet your grandfather was too damn stubborn to admit he was wrong. As for your mom, she was so downtrodden by that old man. She and your brother, they're too much alike—both gentle souls, even if Gabe has a hunky cowboy body."

"What!"

"Just saying." She grinned and kissed his chin. "Not as hunky as you, though."

"So, they knuckled under. But what about after he died?"

"They knew you weren't responding to Dad's letters. Probably figured you didn't want to talk to them."

He kissed her nose. "They figured right."

Her expression turned serious. "Rafe, your grandfather died a year ago."

"I assumed something like that." Maybe in the future when he'd worked through things, he'd be able to mourn the loss of the old man. Right now, he didn't feel anything.

"His will stipulates that if you didn't return to Sweetwater Springs, the ranch is to be sold to the McCurdys. I have no doubt, they'll break the land up into parcels for developing."

Rafe swore. He sat a few minutes, watching the breeze dry Angel's hair, seeing the curls spring back around her face, thinking though the implications of her revelations. "Did he expect me to live there? Run the ranch with Gabe?"

"No. Just visit for one month a year. Your stay doesn't even have to be continuous."

"That's it? He went to all that trouble for that little bit? I'd have thought he'd not only want me tied down, but also my progeny for ten generations."

"Deep down, your grandfather must have known he was in the wrong. He wanted to force your hand to make you come home, make peace with your family."

"Good." He pulled her into his arms. "Because I'm staying here on Seeker's Island." He dropped a kiss on her lips. "Unless you'll make me move to the big city."

"You'd do that for me? Relocate to New York?"

"We'd have to raise the Paints in your apartment," he teased. "Is it big enough?"

"Oh, Rafe," she breathed, her eyes starry.

He touched his lips to hers, longer this time, putting all his love for her into the kiss before coming up for air. "I should never have left you, Angel. When I did, I broke my heart in two and left half with you." He took her hand and pressed her palm to his chest. "It's never been the same since. *I've* never been the same." Rafe tried to grin. "Did I tell you I'm stubborn and stupid? Only now do I see what I've done to myself." He brushed a tendril of hair out of her face. "To you."

"I guess you're not the only one. I should have believed in you. Trusted in our love. Tracked you down." She felt the beat of his heart under her palm. "Since I've been here, I've realized I'm not happy in New York. I thought that's what I wanted. I sacrificed everything to make partner in my law firm. Then they chose someone else anyway."

Rafe took her hand from his heart and kissed the top. "You could open a practice here. We don't have a lawyer on the island. Course, you wouldn't have a lot of work, which is just the way we like it."

"I could handle that. Plus, I want to help my father. Lighten his caseload. Nowadays, much of the work doesn't have to be done in the office anyway." She let out a happy sigh. "I didn't know when I came here that I'd find what I was seeking. I didn't even realize I was looking."

He tapped her nose with his finger. "Your heart's desire."

She captured his finger. "And yours."

Rafe made a little splashing sound. "Took the magic long enough. I've been swimming here for years."

"We had to be ready, Rafe. I don't know that I was before." She looked at him with love. "But I am now."

"That's settled then. We'll fly home to Sweetwater Springs. I'll patch things up with my family. But we're *not* leaving until tomorrow. We'll be a bit busy today."

Angel leaned forward until their lips almost touched. "We will?" she murmured.

"Definitely." Rafe drew her toward him for a kiss.

CHARMED

DORIEN KELLY

CHAPTER ONE

Siobhan O'Brien frowned at the antique clock on the back wall of her jewelry shop. If the bloody thing would chime six, she could shut down and maybe outrun the trouble she sensed approaching. She was, after all, a prodigy at running. Last time she'd bolted all the way from Castlequin, Ireland to Seeker's Island, Florida to start a new life...one she loved and refused to see disrupted.

"You might as well start closing out the register," she said to Anna, one of the three part-time employees she'd hired when she'd opened Fadó Jewels a year ago. "I think we've seen the last of our customers."

"But it's not six," Anna replied with an open sincerity that matched her surfer girl blonde hair and wide-set blue eyes.

"Close enough," Siobhan said while flipping the sign in the shop's front window to *Dúnta*, which was Irish for *Closed.* Then she stepped outside, drew a deep breath of rich tropical air and told herself to calm down. She'd been at peace for months. Her premonition was likely nothing more than a ghost of troubles past. She could exorcise it as she had those last, unhappy days in Castlequin.

This island was her world now. Siobhan loved the quaint feel of Main Street with its lack of cars and improbable mix of Victorian and island architecture that shouldn't work, but did. She was endlessly thankful for a tourist season that ran a full twelve months instead of the brief four she'd had back home. But most of all, she was grateful that the people of Seeker's Island had accepted her—no questions asked—when she'd arrived here reeling from a betrayal that had run soul deep. The island's slow pace and unassuming beauty had healed her, and so she'd stayed.

Smiling, Siobhan returned Rafe Flanigan's friendly nod with a wave as he clip-clopped by atop his white tourist carriage packed with a mother, father, and three excited children. The orange-and-white Paint horse pulling it snorted as it passed. As always, Siobhan gave the mare a wave, too. This and a dozen other small daily rituals made her a part of Seeker's Island. She could have landed in no better place.

Siobhan reached up to pull the shamrock banner that hung outside the store during open hours. She'd set the bracket high enough that the flag wouldn't tangle with customers in the island's strong sea breeze, which meant it was too high for her to comfortably take down. Mam had always said the O'Brien women's lack of stature was nature's way of being even-handed since they'd also received the Gift. Siobhan would have gladly given up her second sight for a few more inches. After all, what good was the Gift when she remained frustratingly blind about her own life?

Weary of fighting with the flag, she went up on tiptoe for better leverage and gripped the flagpole with both hands. Then a broad hand reached from behind her and settled just above hers. Despite the warmth of the evening, a shiver rippled across her skin and her hands fell away, nerveless. Trouble had arrived, and Siobhan turned to face it.

"You looked as though you could use some help," Mac Scanlon said.

It had been over a year since she'd heard Mac's deep voice, and it was as roughly appealing as ever. She'd never been this physically close to him. He stood a foot and more above her scant five feet, smelled of sandalwood and made her heart beat so quickly that she felt as though she couldn't catch her breath. Of course, that could be fear he was about to set the police on her, which she richly deserved.

"Thank you for the offer, but I get by well enough on my own," she replied, relieved that she sounded a fair approximation of herself since she wasn't feeling that way.

"No doubt you do," he said. He pulled the flagpole and rested its butt end against the concrete walk.

Siobhan scrutinized his face for some sign that he was mocking her, but could find none. "What are you doing here, Mac?"

"I'm on holiday," he replied.

He was dressed the part. A white polo shirt clung lovingly to his muscled chest, and a pair of khaki cargo shorts and flip-flops completed his tourist's uniform. It wasn't as though the Irish didn't come to Florida, but for Mac to take a holiday in the summer when the Scanlon family businesses were at their peak? Impossible. He was far too wedded to profits to stray.

"Right, you are," she said, letting her skepticism color her voice.

"Even Scanlons need a break."

She hated being lied to. "I might have been fool enough to think myself in love with your thief of a cousin, but don't take me for an idiot. Three things never rest...rust, the devil, and male Scanlons."

His green eyes lit with a humor that made him seem less the stern businessman she was accustomed to seeing. "Then you concede that the devil and male Scanlons aren't one and the same?"

"It's a slight distinction since you're all sons of Satan," she said, taking her flag from him. "Have a grand vacation, Mac. And for both our sakes, stay away from me."

Siobhan slipped back into the shop and found Anna waiting just inside the door.

"Who was *that*?" she asked in an awestruck tone usually reserved for rock stars and Hollywood royalty.

Siobhan leaned the flag against the wall and turned the deadbolt on the old oaken door. "No one at all." Without another glance out the front window, she set about her night's usual business of removing jewelry trays from the display cases to tuck into the safe.

"Okay, but he's a really super-hot no one," Anna said.

Siobhan worked up a dismissive shrug. "If you like that sort."

"I don't know a woman with a pulse who doesn't like tall, dark, and handsome. Do you know him?"

"No."

Anna smiled. "He seems to want to know you. He's still out there."

Siobhan swung around, marched to the window and pulled the jewelry displayed there.

"*Go hifreann leat*," she said through the glass to the unwelcome Irishman.

Mac Scanlon didn't mistake her words. He tipped back his head and laughed.

"What did you just say?" Anna asked.

"The hell with you," Siobhan replied as she turned away from Mac. "Where else would one send the devil?"

Anna's perfect brows arched skeptically. "And you don't know him, right?"

"Not at all." Siobhan had once thought she did, but she'd been wrong. And because of that, she would never trust him again.

CHAPTER TWO

Later that evening Mac sat at the only bar he'd been able to find—an outdoor palm shack of a place named Seeker's Paradise. And given its location by the water, paradise it might be if the bartender could motivate himself to bring Mac another beer. The man seemed in no particular hurry. Mac shouldn't be, either. He would be on this island for as long as it took to persuade Siobhan O'Brien to bring her talents back to Scanlon Enterprises.

Mac thought it madness to believe that Siobhan—or any other one person—was critical to Scanlon family success, as his grandda, chairman of the company, believed. A record-setting poor Irish economy was affecting business, not Siobhan's absence. No matter, though. Mac had to get her back. Otherwise, Grandda had decreed that Mac would find himself as unemployed as Eddie, his git of a cousin who'd precipitated this mess.

Honestly, Mac couldn't believe that feckless Eddie had even found the balls to cross a woman like Siobhan. It wasn't just that she was beautiful, though she was. In fact she was beautiful enough that Mac's fingers had nearly twitched with the need to touch her when she'd been close. She was small but had curves a dead man couldn't miss, and a mouth made for kissing. Still, there was something more about her...an internal light that made the amber flecks in her brown eyes glow.

Mac snorted at his own thoughts. Glowing amber, his arse. In her case, the light should be more like an arsonist's match. And yet he was making the woman sound as though she were one of the *Sidhe*, or faeries, that played into the tales Grandda loved to spin. As a child, Mac had enjoyed those stories of how the Scanlons had their own protector *Sidhe* forever linked to the family, but now he was grown and knew that magic did not exist. He anchored his world in what could be tallied on a spreadsheet and deposited in a bank. And those numbers were declining daily.

The bartender set a fresh bottle in front of Mac, and he had it half gone in three thirsty swallows. He was thinking about asking for a third when a blonde-haired girl and a skinny, dreadlocked guy took the two tall woven rattan-backed stools to Mac's left.

"I'll have an Italian Surfer, Luke," the girl said.

The bartender muttered something under his breath, probably about the taste of a drink with a name as suspect as Italian Surfer.

"The same," Dreadlocks announced, earning an eye-roll and a blunt obscenity from the bartender.

Mac covered his laugh with a cough, gaining the attention of the girl, who looked him up and down.

"Hey, you were outside Fadó Jewels earlier, weren't you?" she asked.

"I was."

"And you're Irish, too."

"I'm guilty of that as well," he admitted.

"Just like my boss," the girl said. "And she said she didn't know you."

Mac smiled. "While it's possible that two Irish people don't know each other, in this case we do."

"I knew it! Are you her ex? I know she has to have one even though she doesn't talk about it. There's something so tragic about her being all alone. I don't know what I'd do without Woody," she said before leaning over to give Dreadlocks a kiss on his tattooed arm.

"Some people prefer to be alone," Mac replied. In fact, he generally preferred that state.

The girl laughed as though he'd told a side-splitter of a joke. "Okay. Sure." She held out her hand and Mac shook it. "I'm Anna Parker, by the way. Right now I'm Siobhan's part-time shop assistant, but I want her to take me on as an apprentice."

"You work in gold, then?"

"Not since I graduated from art school last year."

"Siobhan would be a fine teacher." For all her anger issues, she was prodigiously talented.

"Yeah, right, you know?"

Though Mac hadn't spent enough time in America to be sure, he figured that was longhand for a yes.

"How long have you known her?" Anna asked.

"Forever. We're from the same town in County Kerry."

"She never talks about anything in her life that happened before she came to Seeker's Island," Anna said as the bartender slid a tall glass garnished with a slice of pineapple in front of her. Mac swore he could smell sugar fumes. He'd stick with his beer.

"So, *are* you her ex?" Anna asked.

Mac could have gone with the truth that he had most recently been her employer, but he didn't think that would play quite as well with romantic Anna as a hint of lost love.

"I've always cared for her," Mac said, and it wasn't a lie. "And I'd like the chance to talk to her away from her shop." Which was also true. He knew Siobhan well enough to be certain she'd bar the door every time he arrived, and she had good reason to do so. "It's deeply personal."

"I'd give you her cell phone number but she never answers it, so that won't do us any good," Anna said.

Us, eh? It seemed that Anna had just fallen squarely on the side of Team Unrequited Love. "Then her address, perhaps?"

"I don't know..." She sat silent for a moment before whispering in Woody's ear. He nodded his head, pushed back his stool and ambled over to Mac.

"Hang on there, boyo," Mac said warningly when Dreadlocks settled his hands on Mac's shoulders.

"It's okay," Anna said. "Woody reads soul vibrations. I asked him to tell me whether you're a good guy or a bad guy. I mean, you're pretty hot for an old guy and all, but that doesn't mean you're not a psycho stalker."

"I'm only thirty-five," Mac said, feeling mildly offended, though he supposed that seemed eons old to a recent college graduate.

"Note that you didn't deny being a psycho stalker," Anna pointed out.

"Vanity at work," he replied with a smile. "The age misconception concerned me more."

"Huh..." Woody said as he moved a hand from Mac's left shoulder and settled it on top of his skull. Woody began to hum like a low-pitched tuning fork.

Mac was fairly certain he'd landed on an isle of lunatics, but to the extent he even had soul vibrations, he willed them to be as pure as the water tumbling down a Castlequin mountain stream to the town below...though he supposed that stream might have a fair amount of bull shite in it, too.

"The dude means good," Woody announced. "Even if he doesn't really wanna be good."

Anna nodded, seemingly content with the mixed verdict.

"Tonight's a full moon, right?" she asked her boyfriend.

"Totally," Woody replied as he sat down in front of his drink.

"Okay," Anna said to Mac. "Here's the deal. Siobhan goes to the hot springs every full moon. She says she does her best design work out there. So if you happen to take a midnight stroll, you should find her."

"What hot springs?" Mac asked.

"At the end of the island," the bartender said while reaching for the beer that Mac hadn't quite gotten around to finishing.

Mac pulled it back. "Which end?"

"Instead of heading into town, take a right on the trail in front of the livery stable. Keep walking until you find water. Ignore the signs about the area having closed hours. That's crap. And just for the record, before woo-woo boy, there, says anything, all the talk about the springs being magical is total crap, too."

"Grand," Mac said before downing his beer and asking for that third.

He'd finally found someone on this island who made sense.

CHAPTER THREE

"A full, midnight moon, magical waters...and a fat lot of nothing," Siobhan said as she set aside her sketchpad and pencil before rising from her inspiration spot beside the hot springs.

This place had never failed her before, and she'd be damned if she'd let it this time. After she'd fled Castlequin and that thieving bastard Eddie Scanlon, she'd been in survival mode, looking only to find a way to earn money and spite all Scanlons. Never mind that the Scanlons were an Irish arts, dining, and lifestyle empire, Siobhan would outdo them. After all, she'd even taught Eddie her craft, turning him from the spendthrift playboy of the Scanlon family into a really rather adept goldsmith. If she could work that sort of alchemy, she should be able to do anything. But hurt and fury had burned her imagination to ash, leaving her unable to design a single piece worth crafting in wax, let alone gold.

Then one night about a week into her stay on the island, something—and she refused to believe that it was the same fickle Gift that had sent her visions of bliss with Eddie—had urged her to come to the hot springs. The place had been breathtaking in its beauty, with the springs welling up into a fern-bordered pool and a waterfall spilling from above, cleft in two by a boulder. For the first time in too long, peace had come over her.

With the noisy jangle of anger gone, Siobhan had sat on a log at the pool's side and sobbed out her pain over having both her heart and her best work stolen from her. When she could cry no more, she'd swum in the pool until exhausted, then slept at the water's side until awakened by a new idea that refused to leave her alone. She'd gone back to her little vacation cottage and sketched a sinuous sweep of gold symbolizing the waterfall that tumbled into her magical pond. And after that, ideas for other pieces had flowed as freely as those falls. In the space of three days, she'd filled all the sketchbooks she'd packed.

Operating on pure faith, Siobhan had emptied what was left of her savings account in Ireland and opened Fadó Jewels. She'd not been let down, either. Charms and pendants of that first design now earned enough to pay both the upkeep on her shuttered home in Castlequin and the rent on the Seeker's Island shop. Not one to turn her back on tradition, each full moon she returned to the hot springs, both in thanks for being able to let go of her past and in celebration of who she'd become.

While Siobhan wasn't the same fanciful and open woman she'd been before tangling with the Scanlons, she'd grown wiser and stronger—both as tempered as fine steel and as sharp. But here she was, edgy and empty all over again, and she knew why. Maybe if she let her feelings go, as she'd done a year ago, she'd be freed.

"Bloody Mac Scanlon, showing up where you're not wanted. Give me back my peace," she shouted to the golden moon hanging in the sky. Somewhere in the distance a night bird screeched its approval, the sound shrill above the steady splashing of the waterfall. But Siobhan felt no different.

"What's it going to take?" she asked, but not even the bird weighed in.

She gazed at the pool in front of her. Moonlight played across the ripples fanning outward from the waterfall, drawing her in. And that, of course, was her answer. Siobhan began to shed her clothes, toeing out of her hiking sandals, unzipping the fleece hoodie she'd pulled on over her tank top, and eventually working her way down to bare skin. She stepped into the pool without hesitation; its source was far beneath the earth and the water warm from its travels. Local legend held that swimming in the pool would bring one his or her heart's desire. Siobhan knew this to be true—if not in quite the manner the story contemplated—because the springs had replenished her creativity.

The breeze picked up. Seeking the water's warmth, Siobhan waded deeper and then swam to the center of the pool. Playing mermaid, she dove beneath the surface to revel in the utter silence below. When she could hold her breath no longer, she floated to the top and slicked back her hair. Already she felt better, but far from whole.

Siobhan floated on her back and counted the stars until time lost meaning. She was sure she'd look like a raisin by the time she left the hot springs, but that was a small price to pay for peace. And maybe by then, she'd be ready to deal with Mac Scanlon. She knew he wasn't through with her. Scanlons not only never rested, they also never quit. Except Eddie. Though he was the most handsome of the Scanlons, it had turned out that he was also the most dishonest and the shallowest. Mac, on the other hand, was the pack leader, strong and sure. *And drop-dead sexy,* added a wee voice that Siobhan dove underwater to escape.

Suddenly she had the sensation of not being alone. She swam to the surface and began to tread water. It was difficult to pick up subtle sounds above the noise of the waterfall, but she could swear she heard twigs snapping.

"Amos?" Siobhan called. "Are you out there?" Offbeat, elderly Amos was the hot springs' caretaker. Siobhan had never quite figured out if his was an official position or one to which he'd elected himself. Either way, she didn't want to be caught without clothing. It was bad enough she'd stumbled upon him naked and in the pool a time or two.

"Amos?"

No one replied. Siobhan treaded water a little more frantically as she tried to recall whether anyone had ever mentioned the existence of man (or woman)-eating animals on Seeker's Island. She didn't think so.

Another twig snapped.

"Damn it all," she muttered to herself before calling to the approaching person/monster/figment of her imagination. "Amos, if that's you, this is Siobhan O'Brien. I'm in the water but will be on my way if you give me a moment to grab my clothes."

Siobhan peered down the moonlit trail that led to the hot springs. A human form rounded the bend, one too substantial to be Amos.

"Don't be grabbing your clothes on my account," Mac Scanlon called.

"Grand, and double feck it all," Siobhan said. It seemed that by thinking of him, she'd accidentally summoned the devil.

Seeking cover, she paddled until she reached a point that was both far from the side of the pool that Mac was approaching, and as deep as possible. Even though the full moon shone brightly, she doubted he could see much of her beneath the water's surface. All the same, she'd never felt more naked in her life.

"Sightseeing in the dead of the night, are you?" she asked Mac, who now stood by the log on which her sketchpad—and her clothing, dammit—sat.

"Some folks at the tiki bar told me about this place. I couldn't sleep, and town is buttoned up tight with nothing to do, so I decided to take a stroll."

"Possible, but not probable," Siobhan replied tartly.

Mac sighed. "Can we not be friends? We were once, you know."

"That was a very long time ago." She'd wanted to sound as though she had no regrets, but she'd failed. Hurt and a silly, poignant yearning for those simpler days before she'd gone to work for the Scanlons had squeezed her throat until she could scarcely get the words out.

"Castlequin misses you," he said. "Your house sits like a ghost."

"I'm sure Castlequin is doing fine enough without me. My mother told me you've opened a gallery and studios in the old stone grain house on the edge of town. You've artists aplenty out there."

"But we don't have you."

"I'm replaceable." She languidly waved her arms in the warm water. "And I have Seeker's Island and a new life."

"I can see that," he said. "This place suits you. You're looking quite well from what I can see."

Siobhan glared at her trespasser. Nervy man! Just how much *could* he see? And what would it take to make him leave? Even before taking over the day-to-day operations of Scanlon Enterprises, Mac had been the proper businessman sort. If she could push him past his comfort zone, she might regain her solitude.

"You Scanlons never were much for playing fair, were you?" she asked. "If you're going to stand there and chat me up, the least you can do is take off your clothes, too."

"Fair enough," Mac replied with no hesitation. He shucked off his T-shirt.

Siobhan's mouth went dry. Her bluff had been called, and there was an excellent chance she wasn't sorry at all.

CHAPTER FOUR

Every single thing about Siobhan O'Brien was driving Mac mad. It was bad enough that he was as hard as a spike from looking at what little of her he could see and speculating about the rest. But now he'd allowed her to goad him into a midnight strip-down, which meant he was going to lose what leverage he still had.

Mac sat on the log and pulled off his trekkers, then stood and paused with his hand resting against the button at the top of his denims.

"Move it along, Scanlon, or have you got something to be ashamed of?" Siobhan asked, sounding like a particularly imperious queen.

He had a few things in life he deeply regretted, but none of them had to do with his body. "No, but at this moment, a certain part of me might be putting that log to shame."

She laughed. "Again, possible, but not probable."

Mac stripped off the rest of his clothes. "Now at least you know I've nothing to hide from you."

She cleared her throat before saying, "And I'll be rethinking the laws of probability."

He laughed as he stepped into the pond. "Flatterer."

Mac rounded a few flat rocks that sat half submerged at the water's edge.

"What are you doing?" Siobhan asked in a voice that sounded a little thin to Mac's ears.

"Coming in, of course."

"You can stay on dry land, thank you very much."

"Only if you're coming out," he replied. "An eye for an eye, and a—"

"Oh, all right, in with you," she said before he could offer up another body part.

Mac forged ahead. He'd been thinking the pool's bottom would be weedy, as was Loch Gill's, just north of Castlequin. But the water was warm, and mostly sand met his feet. Once he was waist-high, he dove in and came up just short of Siobhan.

"Not any nearer," she warned, using her arms to pull far enough away that she was at risk of ending up beneath the falls.

"Don't be drowning yourself in that wee waterfall."

"Over a Scanlon?" she scoffed. "Not bloody likely."

She swam closer—close enough that he could see some of the secrets the water had been hiding—and she was indeed beautiful all over. A humming sound, much like what he'd heard come from Dreadlocks at the bar, echoed in Mac's ears, and for a second he couldn't tell up from down. He shook his head to rid himself of the odd sensation.

"Are you not liking the water?" Siobhan asked.

He was liking it—and her—too much. He'd always thought she was lovely, but had done so as an objective observer. Now he wanted to take her to the edge of the pool, make her hunger for him as he did for her, and then lose himself in her slick heat.

"The water's fine," he said. This time he was the one to put some distance between them.

Apparently, Siobhan wouldn't allow it. She dove under the surface and appeared even more closely to him. "Tell me why you're on Seeker's Island, Mac, and don't be handing me another tourist tale."

"I'm here to see you."

"Fine, but for the time being, eyes no lower than the nose, if you please," she said crisply.

Mac smiled. "My eyes are always above my nose."

"I meant *my* nose, as you well know."

He'd forgotten just how much he liked talking to her. She wasn't the sort of woman to take grief.

"Now, why are you here to see me?" she asked.

"Do you miss Castlequin?" he asked in return.

"Of course I do," she replied. "My family is there. If we didn't get the chance to visit with each other online, I'd likely go mad."

"Then come home. We'd like to hire you back."

She blew out an impatient huff of a breath. “I melted down every single piece of gold in Scanlon Jewelers and tried to torch Eddie’s car. That’s not the sort of behavior that earns one a repeat appearance.”

“I’ll allow you have a bit of a temper issue, but you weren’t without provocation. And you did pay for the Volvo,” he added.

“True enough, but that barely pulls us even. So why have me back?”

Mac refused to tell the woman that his grandda believed she was the Scanlons’ living and breathing lucky charm, so he focused on the business reasons. “Because you’re already the most talented designer and goldsmith in Ireland, and you’ve barely even begun your career. Because every time you appear on Nuala’s show, ratings go up,” he said, referring to *Simply Irish*, his sister’s weekly program on the BBC. “Because you’re a natural at everything you do, and with the Scanlon name behind you, you can do whatever you want.”

“Maybe this is all I want.”

“I know you, Siobhan, and have for your entire life. You want more than a shop on Seeker’s Island. If you didn’t, you wouldn’t have come to us and offered your services in the first place.”

“Ha! And look how well that worked out.”

“It could have been worse,” was the best he could think to offer.

“I can’t imagine how,” she said. “Your cousin...*my* former fiancé...stole my private design work and registered it with the Patents Office under his name. And when I came to you with what he’d done, you took his word over mine.”

That moment was one of the few events in Mac’s life that shamed him. Even knowing Eddie to be the shiftless sort, Mac had allowed himself to be persuaded that thanks to Siobhan’s stellar training, his cousin had finally tapped into his own creative wellspring. Mac had been wrong, of course. The only tapping Eddie had been doing was of a more base nature.

Mac never had the opportunity to apologize to Siobhan after Eddie, in a fit of rage over his half-burnt car interior, slipped up and admitted that the design work had not been his. She’d already left Castlequin. Now he could share the long overdue words. Wrapping one hand around her upper arm, he drew her closer. Something like electricity jolted through him, and judging by the way her eyes widened, she felt it, too. Mac let go and moved ahead with his apology.

"I made a huge mistake that day. I'd like your forgiveness. Trust my family to do right by you this time," he said. "Trust *me.*"

She watched him silently. He got the sense she was measuring the truth in his words as she would gold on a scale.

"Trust is earned," she finally said. "You've lost mine, and I'd have to say that after my wee rampage before leaving Castlequin, you'd have little reason to trust me."

"We'll call your rampage situational. I know I can trust you so long as I don't steal from you, which I'd never do. But I violated your trust by believing Eddie. What can I do to earn it back?" And he wasn't asking simply because he wanted her on the company payroll. His manipulative words to Anna earlier in the evening had become real. This now mattered to him. Deeply.

"I'm not so sure earning it back is possible," she said.

"You know that Eddie is no longer with the company?"

"Yes, my mother told me, but this isn't about Eddie anymore," Siobhan replied. "I should never have been with him in the first place."

Mac couldn't have agreed more.

"And it's not about you handing me something or doing something for me," she said. "Trust runs deeper than that."

"Tell me what you need, then."

"To begin with, if you want me to trust you, you'd do well by not trying to seduce me." Mac noted that as she spoke, her eyes were traveling far below the nose level she'd mandated. "Because I'm tempted," she said. "It's clear I have an inexplicable weakness for Scanlons. But I've already been seduced by one. And sadly, a much lesser one, at that. As for the rest of it, all I know is that you've muddled my mind enough for one night."

She swam in three easy strokes toward the shallower water by the edge of the springs, where both her and Mac's clothes waited. "I need to go home and sleep."

As she rose from the pool, she looked a perfect Venus in the moonlight with her narrow waist and round bottom. This was a sight Mac knew he'd never forget. She looked over her shoulder at him.

"I'm trusting you not to watch me as I get dressed," she said. "But I'm betting that you will."

Mac grinned; she knew his mind too well. He turned and swam

beneath the falls so that he couldn't watch. Besides, there was nothing like being pummeled by falling water to take a wee bit of starch out of a man. He put up with it as long as he could before escaping to the falls' outer fringes.

"You can turn around now," Siobhan called.

Mac did, and immediately noticed she had something in her arms.

"Just so you know, I'm taking your clothes," she announced. "But I've been kind enough to leave you the key to your room at the inn. We wouldn't want you scaring the tourists, come morning."

"That's grand of you," Mac said, thinking it wasn't grand at all. But he did feel a grudging measure of respect that she'd thought of doing this. "And I hope it brings you a good, long way toward trusting me."

"It does nothing for the trusting, but it's bringing me closer to forgiveness," she said in a cheerful voice. "*Slán*, Mac."

CHAPTER FIVE

When Siobhan arrived at her shop to open it the next morning, she wasn't surprised to see Mac standing out front in full tourist uniform. The man had always defined determination, which made him all the sexier to her. However, considering the way she'd left him the prior night, she was startled by the broad smile on his face.

But it was yet another perfectly warm and sunny Seeker's Island morning, with the mockingbirds singing their tunes of choice and tourists strolling back from breakfast before a day of fishing, kayaking, horseback riding, or doing nothing at all. Why not be happy?

"This island has mosquitoes the size of sparrows," he said conversationally as he held out a cup to her. "They came near to draining my blood last night. I've got bites in places that never see the sun."

And then there was that.

"Mosquitoes are the state bird," she said. "If you'd had the forethought to be carrying insect repellent, I'd have let you keep it." She dug into her purse for her fat key ring with the shop's front door keys. As usual, it had sunk to the very bottom.

"That's generous of you. Don't you want your drink?"

She gave up on the key search and scrutinized the brown recycled-paper cup for obvious signs of tampering. Mac would likely have been subtle, though. "I'm not sure."

"I didn't doctor it," he said. "It's a soy chai latte, which is exactly what the very nice lady at the coffee house says you order every time you're in there. I'm not after retribution for my off-the-beaten path excursion last night, but I am wondering if we're at least even, now?"

"Yes, we are," she said. "I don't have much of an appetite for revenge."

Mac gave her a crooked smile. “That sounds ripe coming from the Castlequin arsonist.”

“Well...about that,” she said as she set her purse on the walk and accepted the latte. “I can’t quite explain what came over me. It was an out-of-body experience, me looking down on myself as I went insane.”

“Luckily, you were none too efficient. Hand sanitizer isn’t most arsonists’ accelerant of choice.”

“It was a spontaneous thing,” she said. “I was going with what I had in my purse. It was that or lip gloss.”

Mac laughed. “It’s a good thing you gave up a life of crime.”

“Honestly, I do feel remorse about the Volvo, if not for melting down the shop’s gold. I figured Scanlons shouldn’t profit from my work if I wasn’t allowed to. But I do hope Eddie wasn’t fired only because he took my designs.”

“Trust me, that was far from Eddie’s first cock-up, but it was the one Grandda couldn’t let slide. He has a soft spot for you, Siobhan.”

She smiled. “I know. And I adore Eoghan. He’s a fine man...especially since he wouldn’t let Eddie call the Gardai on me.”

“Never would have happened,” Mac said after taking a swig of his coffee. “Everyone was far too worried that you’d start a fraud claim. Which reminds me...” He set his coffee cup on the windowsill and shrugged off a dark blue nylon backpack. He unzipped it, and after a bit of rustling around pulled out an envelope. “This is for you.”

She put her latte next to Mac’s cup and looked at the envelope. It was from Patents Office in Dublin. Her hands shook as she opened it. Inside she found a letter revoking Eddie’s design registrations.

“Really?” she asked Mac after she’d read the document through twice just to be sure.

“Absolutely.”

“I thought I was going to have to wait the statutory five years to get them back,” she said as she bent down and tucked the letter safely in her purse.

“They’re yours and should have been all along. I was happy to take care of it. Now you’d best file your papers so you can make the pieces.” He smiled. “I like the *Faerie* design best of all. It reminds me of you.”

She had no idea what Mac did to get the design registrations revoked, but whatever it had taken, she was thrilled. She went up on tiptoe thinking to hug him, but as soon as they touched, a kiss seemed a far more tempting choice. She tugged at his blue polo shirt to urge him down to her mouth level; thus was the love life of a short woman. Then it happened again...that power surge unlike anything she'd ever felt, not that Siobhan had vast grounds for comparison. Other than an apathetic affair with a fellow art student, and then the disaster with Eddie, she'd only casually dated.

Mac muttered a low, blunt word and hauled her up against his body. She'd found that first kisses were awkward, often embarrassing things, but clearly she'd been kissing the wrong men. Mac kissed like a man who knew exactly what he wanted—just enough pressure that her lips weren't crushed, and just enough demand that opening her mouth to the sweep of his tongue was the most natural thing in the world. She twined her arms around him, holding fast against the electricity that arced between them, and didn't give a rip what passersby might think when his hands settled against her bottom. She'd waited a lifetime and maybe longer to feel this sort of passion, and she didn't plan to stop.

Mac, though, did. He set her down and looked to either side of her as though someone else might have joined in.

"What's wrong?" Siobhan asked.

"You heard that, didn't you?"

He still didn't look quite right, and she was sure her response wasn't going to help. "Heard what?"

"The humming."

"Humming?"

He ran a hand through his hair. "Yes. A humming sort of noise. The closest thing I can compare it to is a tuning fork. Or honeybees, maybe."

"I didn't hear a thing, but I felt the jolt."

"I felt the jolt, too," he said. "That, I can wrap my mind around, but aren't you hearing the humming?"

She gave an apologetic shrug. "Sorry, but no."

"You're not having one over on me, are you?" he asked hopefully.

"No, I'm not joking. Honestly, I didn't hear it."

He scooped up his backpack, slung it over his shoulder, and grabbed his coffee. "I've got some business to look after. I'll be back later...maybe I can gather you up for dinner?"

"Of course," she said. But after Mac's paranoid looks and talk of honeybees, Siobhan wondered instead if she might not be gathering him up in a very large net. These Scanlons were turning out to be an odd lot, indeed.

CHAPTER SIX

Twenty minutes later, Mac sat in his lodgings at the Sunseekers' Inn. He'd set his laptop computer on top of the wicker dresser, the only spot in the room not covered with white eyelet or mint green ruffles. Ignoring the frippery around him, he typed one word into a search engine: *Sidhe.* He felt ten times a fool to be researching Grandda's stories as though they were cold fact, but too many strange things had happened over the last day for him not to. Either Grandda had been telling the truth about his faerie friends or Mac was going mad.

Mac's search results came back lightning fast. He clicked the first link and landed on a page adorned with faux-Irish script and drawings of lissome, longhaired females who he supposed were meant to appear other-worldly but really just looked like bored suburban girls dressed up for a folk festival. They weren't inspiring much confidence in the academic credibility of the page's creator...not that facts and faeries often mixed.

Mac let his eyes skim the talk of the *Tuatha Dé Danann,* who, according to the Irish Myth and Legend class Mac had been unable to avoid on his way to a business degree, had settled Ireland before the beginning of time. He ignored the chat of fae in Scotland. All he wanted to do was know how to spot a true Irish *sí,* or singular female fairy, for he suspected one was running a jewelry shop on sunny Seeker's Island.

What Mac saw next stopped him dead: *The Sidhe are talented metalworkers who, given their wealth and high standing, have a fondness for gold. They have been known to share their skills with favored mortals.*

After that, more phrases jumped out at him: *generous to mortals until crossed by a fool...the sound of a thousand bees buzzing with the coming of the Sidhe* and *tall and elegant.*

"Well, forget that last one," Mac muttered. Siobhan would be tall only on stilts.

Mac closed down his computer and paced the confines of his frilly room. Only a madman would believe he'd found a *sí* walking among mortals, and yet here he was—with post-graduate degrees from two universities and the skills to run a multi-million euro company—thinking just that.

"A madman or an Irishman," he told himself. And the line between those two beings was often erased altogether...

***

Siobhan shifted restlessly at her desk in Fadó Jewels' back office. Much as she wanted to focus on the inventory-tracking program on her computer screen, she kept having unsettling flashes of visions. The Gift had never been a precise sort of thing. Siobhan couldn't predict lotto numbers or make a killing in the stock market. Generally, she was adept at forecasting nearby natural disasters or the marriages of good friends, which sometimes had more in common than she cared to see.

When she'd first met Eddie Scanlon—who hadn't grown up in Castlequin, but had moved there as an adult to work with the family—she'd kept seeing a hazy image of herself being made love to by a man with Scanlon green eyes. As Eddie's life and hers had begun to merge, the vision had come to her less and less. She'd assumed it was because she'd chosen the correct path. But now the vision had returned, and this time it was more finely detailed, if sharing no surprising news: she'd been with the wrong Scanlon all along. Aye, the Gift in exchange for some height would be a useful trade indeed.

Telling herself to concentrate on the work at hand, Siobhan settled her computer's mouse over the Create Inventory Report button and was about to click on it when the office door opened and Mac entered. She wished she could say he looked a little more put together than he had when he'd left forty minutes earlier, but she'd be lying.

"There's no chance you're immortal, is there?" Mac asked.

Grand, so he'd gone around the bend.

"With the lines that are beginning to creep from the corners of my eyes, I'd guess not," she replied.

"Good," he said. "I'd hate to be falling in love with a woman who was going to look perfect while I fell slowly and inevitably apart."

Love? She supposed if he were going mad, at least it was of a good variety.

"Mac, are you feeling all right?"

"Better than I have in my entire life, but let me get this out first," he said. "Then I'll answer your questions."

Siobhan nodded. "Fair enough."

"Yesterday, when you asked why we want you back with the family business, I only gave you half the truth, and that was wrong of me. You deserve the whole of everything, Siobhan...of honesty, commitment, and of love. If I had looked up from the company books more frequently, I would have discovered how deeply I feel for you much sooner. And I would have spared us both the pain of dealing with Eddie. But I'm looking at you now and promising that from this day forward, you'll get both love and the truth from me. And the truth of it is that Grandda issued an ultimatum. Either I'm to get you back working for Scanlon Enterprises or I'm to lose my job."

"Eoghan couldn't mean that," Siobhan said.

"He could and does," Mac replied. "He's got it into his head that your absence is the reason that our revenues are declining, and not the overall economy. He feels that you're our good luck charm, for lack of a better term, and that without you, we'll fail."

Siobhan knew she was small, but she was hardly charm-sized. "That's nonsense."

"Maybe not so much. Grandda loves telling the legend of the *Sidhe*. Do you know it?"

"Well, of course," she said. "In fact, I know more of the *Sidhe* than most. My mother claims that her people are descended of an affair between a mortal and one of them. That's where our second sight is supposed to have started." Siobhan smiled. "I think that's a fat lot of nonsense, too. The Gift is nothing more than a genetic quirk in brain wiring that lets us tap into a part that others can't. But the legend did get me interested in metalwork, so even if I don't believe, I have it to thank for a career that I love."

"That's all highly practical, but you're wrong," he said. "Now stand up."

Siobhan did so hesitantly. Mac took her hands in his larger ones, and a shiver of pleasure immediately danced through her.

"You felt that, right?" Mac asked.

"Yes."

"That is the magic of attraction. It's chemical, elemental and perfect. It makes me want to strip that little red dress from you and make love to you until we're both too tired to move."

Siobhan swayed a bit at the image he'd painted in her mind, one very close to the vision she'd been having for years.

"I see," she managed to say.

He smiled. "You see half of it."

When he let go of her, she felt bereft of his touch, but only for an instant because he cupped her face between his broad hands, leaned down, and thoroughly kissed her.

"And did you hear the buzzing?" he asked when he let her go.

"No, still no buzzing." Though the room was spinning a bit.

"That's because you're of *Sidhe* blood, Siobhan O'Brien. Only a non-*Sidhe* can hear the sound. It would drive the *Sidhe* mad to hear it every time they were near one other."

She laughed. "And how would you be knowing all of this?"

"I just do," he replied. "And I've also figured out that life is better with a little magic in it." He took her hands in his again, and his eyes were alight with what Siobhan could only call tenderness. "I'd like you to be the magic in my life, if you can trust me enough to do me that honor."

"If you can take fairies on faith, I can certainly take you," she replied. Still, a thousand thoughts whirled in her mind. *What about her business here? And his job? Did he truly expect her to...?*

"Stop thinking so hard, my love," Mac said. "I can hear that practical brain of yours spinning."

Then all her worries disappeared as Mac kissed her again. Soon enough she'd locked the office door, and he was easing down the zipper of that little red dress he wanted gone.

Siobhan smiled to herself and then asked, "Mac, did you know that swimming in the hot springs is supposed to bring you your heart's desire?"

"Nearly true, my love," Mac replied. "Technically, an airplane brought you yours."

Siobhan laughed with joy as he whisked her dress over her head. Yes, life was much better when one embraced the magic in it...and love was the most powerful magic of all.

I Will Wait For You

Theresa Ragan

CHAPTER ONE

Thirty-year-old Isabella Mina Kelsey lived with her eight-year-old son, Liam, on Seeker's Island off the Florida coast, population 2,301. She ran a daycare, and every once in a while, she brought some of the kids on a field trip to the hot springs.

It was summer vacation and today, six-year-old Addison sat to her left, while Christopher, Bonnie, and her son sat to her right, everyone dipping their feet in the warm water.

The tropical setting, complete with waterfall and lush green palm trees, usually soothed Isabella, but not today. Her best friend Jane would be getting married soon and every time she thought about the upcoming wedding, her heart twisted and she saw images of Steve Brennan, the only man she'd ever loved. All she had to do was shut her eyes to see his broad shoulders, perfectly chiseled jaw and intense blue eyes half covered by dark windswept hair.

A squeal of laughter brought Isabella back to the moment as the kids splashed one another. Addison had been rubbing water on her arms ever since they arrived. "If you put water on your body," she explained, "a new wish comes true every time."

"You're not s'posed to use the water to make wishes," Bonnie scolded. "My mom says the water is dirty."

"If you swim around in the water," Christopher cut in, sounding fifteen instead of eight, "you get your heart's desire, but *only* if you know what your heart really wants."

Isabella tried not to laugh at the seriousness of their conversation.

The kids' differing opinions about the infamous springs' magical powers should not have surprised her. Isabella had grown up on the island. Everybody had his or her own ideas about the legendary hot springs. Some believed the springs made miraculous things happen. Some did not. Isabella's nana used to tell her the island itself was magical, using its tropical breezes to seek out those who needed the most help and then use its powers to help lost souls find true happiness.

"I don't think it works," Liam said.

"It works," Addison assured him, nodding her head vigorously enough to make her red curls bob. "You will know when it's working, too, because your feet and ears will tingle and then your heart will swell with goodness."

"If you really want it to work," Christopher cut in, "you need to dunk your head all the way under the water."

Liam's eyes widened.

"You don't have to dunk your head in the water," Isabella assured him.

"Do you think the hot springs are magical, Ms. Kelsey?" Bonnie asked.

Before Isabella could answer, one of the kids shouted, "Look! There's Chachi!"

As the children watched the island's squirrel monkey fly from tree to tree, Isabella looked at her son. Sadly, she didn't have to ask Liam what his heart's desire was. Nobody did. Everyone knew Liam wanted nothing more than to find his father.

Isabella stood and began packing half-eaten snacks and towels as her thoughts returned to Steve Brennan. It had been almost nine years since she'd seen him, and yet she still couldn't think about him without getting a queasy stomach. They had both been juniors in college when they met in culinary class. While chopping onions, their gazes had locked, and sparks not only flew, they hit the walls and started the curtains on fire. Literally. Thank God for the fire extinguisher and the student next to them who saw it all happen and put the fire out.

Steve asked Isabella out and she didn't hesitate to say yes. Steve was funny, smart, and beyond handsome. He was also romantic. He would throw pebbles at her dorm window three stories up and then sing to her from below.

Isabella fell instantly in love and for the next six months they talked, they laughed, and they had lots of crazy, hot sex. They used protection, too—every single time. But something had gone wrong. A bad condom: there was no other explanation. She missed her period and the next thing she knew, she was pregnant.

And it was all so déjà vu from that moment on. Her father and mother had also met in college. They had married soon after Isabella's mother realized she was pregnant. Her parents then proceeded to spend the next few decades fighting, each blaming the other for unrealized dreams.

Panicked out of her mind, Isabella did what she felt she must to save both her and Steve from a life of misery. She ran. She flew back to Seeker's Island to have her baby. Her parents had divorced and moved away from the island within days of seeing Isabella off to college. But Seeker's Island was all she had. Nana lived there and so did her best friend Jane.

For the next eight and a half months, Isabella took long walks, she whined to Jane, and she cried on Nana's shoulder. And then Liam was born.

And the moment she held her little boy in her arms, she realized what a colossal mistake she'd made.

"Ms. Kelsey," Bonnie said, tugging on Isabella's sundress. "Liam's going to get an eye infection."

"Why is that, Bonnie?"

"He's been under the water for a long time and his eyes are open."

Isabella looked over her shoulder, and then dropped the towels she was about to load into the golf cart. The kids were standing at the edge of the hot springs, pointing and looking seriously concerned. Liam was nowhere to be seen. Liam couldn't swim, which was why he never left the safety of the shallow end of the hot springs.

As she ran around the springs to the deeper part of the water where Addison pointed, her heart exploded inside her chest, even before she saw Liam's limp body sinking to the swampy bottom of the hot springs.

How had he managed to get so far out there?

Everything felt like it was happening in slow motion. Addison was crying. Bonnie was shouting for someone to do something, and Christopher held out a long stick over the water, telling Liam to grab onto it.

Isabella couldn't get there fast enough. It was as if her feet had become heavy blocks of cement. But somehow she must have jumped into the water because the next thing she knew, she was swimming toward her son.

***

After checking in on his cousin Raymond, who was suffering from food poisoning, Steve Brennan headed outside to soak up some sun.

Six months ago, Raymond had asked Steve to be the best man at his wedding. Although Steve was busy as head chef at a popular restaurant in New York, Steve knew he'd never forgive himself if he didn't say yes to Raymond's request. Steve had met Raymond for the first time at the age of fourteen when his parents sent him to Missouri to stay with Raymond's family for the summer. Steve had been more than worried when he learned Raymond's idea of fun was walking the neighbor's dog or standing outside the grocery store and helping people with their groceries. Steve's idea of a good time was playing street football or hanging out at the mall to meet girls.

Surprisingly, what could have been the worst summer of his life turned out to be one of his best; it turned out to be a summer of compromises.

One day he and Raymond would visit museums and the next day they would hang out at the mall. Raymond learned how to converse with girls and Steve discovered a newfound appreciation for helping others. The moment Steve returned home, he signed up to work at a local food kitchen.

The memories made Steve smile as he headed away from the pier, down the center of Main Street, and toward the southeast side of the island. Fifteen minutes later, he realized he hadn't been paying close enough attention to the markings that were supposed to lead tourists to the mythical hot springs. Instead of discovering the trail Raymond had talked about, he found himself hiking through a dense patch of forest intermingled with tall white cedars, giant palms, and old gnarly trees, their branches dripping with Spanish moss. Birds squawked above his head and in the distance he could hear the low continuous rumbling of a waterfall.

The air was humid, but not unbearably warm, as he pushed his way through a thick copse of ferns, continuing past palms, colorful flowers, and more trees adorned with Spanish moss.

For the past six months, his cousin had been keeping him updated on the wedding. Every time Raymond mentioned the fabled hot springs, something zipped and zinged inside Steve's head, telling him he'd heard about the mythical springs before. But when? He'd never been anywhere near the Florida Keys.

As he grew closer to a clearing, he could hear kids shouting loud enough to be heard over the sounds of rushing water. Quickening his pace, Steve pushed his way through thick brush. Three kids pointed at something in the water. The children were too young to be left on their own. Where were the adults?

At closer view, he saw the silhouette of a child sinking to the bottom of the hot springs. Running now, Steve pulled off his shirt, kicked off his shoes and dove in. He reached the child at the same time as a woman, but he already had the child in his arms, so she backed off.

Steve swam toward the edge with the boy in his arms, making sure to keep his head above water. He stepped out of the water, the child lying thin-boned and pale in his arms before he laid him on the grass. The boy's face was as white as the clouds above, his lips blue.

Thankful for his time as a lifeguard, Steve turned the boy's head to the side and allowed water to drain from his mouth and nose before beginning mouth-to-mouth resuscitation. He gently pinched his nose to help air get past any water that might be clogging his passageways. After four breaths, Steve put his ear to the boy's mouth and then watched the chest for any movement.

The child didn't stir. No water discharged from his mouth. Nothing happened.

"Please save him," the woman cried.

"Is he dead?" one of the kids asked.

The child's face was turning a light shade of blue.

Steve continued to breathe air into his lungs. No way in hell was he going to let the kid die under his watch. When he was eight years old, he'd watched his best friend drown in a river as he tried to save another. More determined than ever, Steve blew four more breaths into his mouth, then used his hands to gently but firmly press into the boy's chest beneath his ribs. Another four breaths…massage…four breaths…massage.

The beat of his own heart thumped hard against his ribs. Water dripped from his hair and onto the child's face. He stopped again to listen for a pulse.

Four more breaths…massage...and then a miracle.

Thank God.

The boy twisted to his side, clutching his abdomen. He coughed and spit up dirty water, his face turning a deep red.

Consumed with relief, Steve finally looked at the woman hovering over him. Recognition hit him like a fist to the chest. "Isabella?"

Her eyes widened.

It couldn't be?

Steve blinked, hoping to clear the apparition standing before him, but it was no use. *What the hell is she doing on Seeker's Island?*

And then it struck him like a bolt of lightning to the head. Isabella was the one who used to talk about the mythical hot springs.

More important, she was also the woman he'd intended to propose to the night she disappeared, never to be seen again.

When the boy tried to sit up, Isabella plopped to the ground and took the child from him. She cradled the child in her arms and whispered words of comfort.

"It worked," the boy told Isabella, his voice weak and gravelly sounding.

"Are your feet tingling?" a small girl with the curly red hair asked excitedly.

The boy nodded with wide-eyed excitement as if he had no idea how close he'd come to losing his life. "My ears and my feet feel funny. My whole body is tingling and my heart feels good."

"What's he talking about?" Steve asked.

The boy in Isabella's arms pointed a wobbly finger at Steve and said, "I think you're my dad."

CHAPTER TWO

All the way from the medical clinic lobby to the parking lot, Addison's parents hugged her tightly, leaving Steve to wait in the lobby alone while Isabella stood in the hallway talking to the doctor.

He hadn't seen Isabella in nine years and yet she'd hardly changed—a little thinner, a little older, but just as beautiful as the first time he laid eyes on her—blonde hair and hazel eyes. She couldn't be an inch over five foot two, but she packed a lot of curves into such a petite package. A slideshow of images from the past flashed through his mind's eye, making his heart twist. He'd been so sure she was the one, the girl he'd marry and spend the rest of his life with.

But it had all ended as quickly as it had begun.

Two days before she disappeared, her cell phone had been stolen, leaving him no way to contact her after she disappeared. Worried about foul play, he'd run to her dorm room. And it took one glance into her roommate's eyes to realize Isabella had left on her own accord and would not be coming back. Unfortunately, nobody knew where she had run off to.

I think you're my dad.

He couldn't get the boy's words out of his head. The instant the kid had pointed at him, he'd known the truth. And yet, even now, as he headed down the hallway toward Isabella, his imagination worked triple time trying to come up with a million different scenarios.

The doctor finished talking to Isabella, leaving her alone in the hallway.

Perfect.

A few long strides brought him to Isabella's side. His heart beat like a drum against his chest as he gestured toward the room where the little boy was sleeping. "Is that your son in there?"

She nodded.

"How old is he?"

"Eight."

"What's his name?"

She swallowed hard before saying, "Liam."

"What did the doctor say?"

"He's going to be fine. They'll be keeping him overnight, but just for observation."

Steve nodded, then turned and walked away. He was scared, much too afraid to ask the question at the forefront of his mind. The question he already knew the answer to. Maybe tonight, maybe tomorrow, but not now. The notion that he had a son refused to compute.

"Steve!" she called out behind him.

He kept walking.

Isabella came running after him, grabbed his arm to stop him from taking another step.

When he stopped, he looked down at her hand and closed his eyes, trying to block the memories still spewing forth, but it was no use. That one touch transported him right back to the first time he'd felt her fingers sliding across the back of his neck as he brushed his lips over hers. They had set up a picnic in a meadow. The sun was shining and birds were chirping. Her soft lips had tasted of honey and sweet promises of so much more.

He opened his eyes. "What do you want, Isabella?"

"We need to talk."

"Okay. Fine. Talk."

She shifted her weight from one foot to the other, even dared to show off her straight white teeth as she bit down on her full bottom lip. "Leaving you without talking to you first was the biggest mistake of my life."

"And…I'm supposed to feel bad?"

"No, of course not. I'm just stunned to be standing here now…talking to you." She took a breath and added, "There's so much I need to tell you."

That's what he was afraid of. Not here. Not yet. He wasn't ready for the truth. "There's no reason for either of us to relive what was nothing more than a tiny blip in our lives."

"A blip?" she asked in disbelief.

"I'd say I was being generous."

"I loved you," she said, her expressive gold-flecked eyes widening, everything about her just as he remembered. "And you loved me."

"Spare me, Isabella," he said, pulling himself out of what he considered to be some sort of weird trance every time he looked into her eyes. "That was more than eight years ago."

"So you're just going to walk away and never talk to me again?"

His hands itched to touch her. His heart continued to beat erratically. He'd dreamt of this moment for so long, saw her in his dreams, felt her in his arms. It irked him to realize some sort of crazy chemistry pulled him to her. It was more than lust he felt, but he was angry and hurt and he wanted nothing more than to take her right here, right now, flat against the wall, see if his memories were as good as the real thing. Instead he said, "That's the plan."

"If our time together was nothing to you, why are you so angry?"

He snorted and shook his head at her audacity. "I don't have anything to say to you."

"And you won't let me explain?"

"You'd be wasting my time and yours," he said before he began to walk away again, quickly, before he melted in the palm of her hands.

"Go ahead. Walk away," she said, her tone wavering. "But please don't leave the island without saying goodbye to your son."

Steve stopped, catching his breath before he turned back to face her. He wished she had let him go, let him walk out of there so he could have time to think, just an hour or two to gather his thoughts. But she didn't, and all he wanted to do was hurt her back. "How do I know this isn't a trick?"

She held her chin high, refusing to back down. "I guess you'll just have to take my word for it."

His back straight, every muscle taut, he walked toward her until they stood inches apart. "If that's true," he said calmly, "if Liam is my son, I will never forgive you."

***

Four days had passed since he'd pulled his son from the springs.

Feeling rejuvenated, Steve exited the hotel where he was staying and breathed in a lungful of tangy sea air.

Raymond's fiancée had called the wedding off. Steve had a long talk with Raymond this morning, telling him the age-old story of there being lots of fish in the sea, but he wasn't sure how convincing he'd been since he knew as well as anyone what it felt like to have your heart trampled on and then ripped in half. It sucked.

Today, Steve would officially meet his son. The morning after pulling him from the water, he had called the clinic and talked to the doctor in charge. Liam was fine.

After discovering the wedding had been called off, Steve wanted nothing more than to take the first ferry off the island, but he wasn't going anywhere without his son. The truth was he'd known Liam was his son the moment the kid pointed at him and told him he was his dad. Liam looked identical to the pictures he had of himself at that age. The likeness was uncanny. But he'd needed time to process everything. He *still* needed time, but time wasn't a luxury he had. What was he supposed to do?

Within forty-eight hours of stepping foot on Seeker's Island, his entire life had drastically changed. Suddenly he was a dad. He'd always told himself if he ever had children, he'd be a better father than his own.

And there was the answer to his dilemma.

Not only did he need to spend time with his son, he needed to let Liam know he was proud to be his dad and that he would always be there for him.

The question remaining was how was he going to deal with Isabella? He wanted nothing to do with her. Some might consider the entire incident water under the bridge, spilt milk, whatever. But the day Isabella packed her bags and left San Francisco without a word was the same day his heart had been ripped to shreds. He'd been trying to piece it back together ever since. She didn't know he'd spent every dime he had at the time on a diamond ring. He'd gotten all spiffed up, too, and put on a suit and tie. With a ridiculous grin on his face, he'd told everyone in the restaurant he was going to propose to the most incredible woman in the world. By the end of the night, all of the other patrons knew he'd been stood up.

And now to learn she'd been pregnant with his child?

The anger he'd felt yesterday was gone. In its wake was a cold, empty void. He felt absolutely nothing for Isabella Kelsey, nothing at all. But for Liam's sake, he would try to be cordial whenever he and Isabella were in the same room.

As he headed down Main Street, people smiled and waved—everyone on the island was happy-go-lucky. A quaint town filled with cheery people. Despite his contrasting mood, Steve smiled at the postman and held a shop door open for a woman with too many packages. Nothing was going to stop him from enjoying the day with his son.

***

Isabella saw him coming their way. Steve Brennan was by far the sexiest man she'd ever laid eyes on. He wore a pair of dark shorts and a collared T-shirt, the sleeves snug against his well-muscled arms. He was tall and broad shouldered and he exuded confidence. With his thick dark hair and strong jaw, he was everything she remembered him being. What a fool she'd been to run away. If only he'd let her explain. Clearly, though, that wasn't going to happen. He wanted nothing to do with her. He could hardly look her way without frowning.

Isabella glanced at her son and realized he was watching Steve, too. The doctor assured her Liam was fine and could play baseball today, but he looked pale and nervous.

"Are you okay?"

Liam nodded as he kept his eyes on Steve.

Steve gestured with his chin toward Isabella before walking toward Liam. Steve knelt down so he and Liam were at eye level. "How's it going? Are you feeling better?"

Liam nodded. "Are you really my dad?"

"I am."

His declaration surprised Isabella since he'd hardly said two words to her when he called to ask her if they could set up a meeting time. She wasn't sure if he was going to insist on a blood test.

Steve pulled a folded piece of paper from his back pocket and handed it to Liam. "I asked my mom to e-mail me a picture of myself when I was your age. We could be twins."

Liam unfolded the paper and examined the picture for a long while. When he finally looked back at Steve, he had a huge grin plastered on his face. After a moment, Liam added, "I'm a lot smaller, though."

"I didn't grow much until I was in high school."

Another wide smile. "I might be tall?"

Steve smiled, too, making Isabella's insides flutter, wishing he would smile at her like that.

"I think you will be," Steve told Liam.

This time Liam flew into Steve's arms and hugged him tightly as he said, "I'm glad you found us."

"Me, too."

"The game starts in twenty minutes," Isabella said, her voice cracking slightly. "We better get going."

"So what position do you play?" Steve asked as they headed back down Main Street toward the baseball field.

"Left field. I'm not very good."

"Who says so?"

"Me. My friends. The coach."

Concerned, Steve looked at Isabella.

"Liam is a team player," Isabella said. "He always gives one hundred percent," she added zealously, making Liam sigh with embarrassment.

Within five minutes, they were at the field. Fans, mostly parents, had taken seats on the metal bleachers. Some mothers and fathers remained on the field giving their Little League player a pep talk before the game.

Once again, Steve knelt in front of his son. This time, he put his hands on Liam's shoulders. "You can do this. All you need to do is focus." Steve pointed two fingers at Liam's eyes and then swept those same fingers toward the ball. "Keep your eye on the ball and there's a good chance you'll hit it every time."

"What if I strike out anyway?"

"No big deal. You just try again next time."

"You won't be sad?"

"Me?" Steve pointed at his own chest. "Why would I be sad?"

"You know…disappointed in me."

"Not in a million years. I'm already proud of you, Liam. You're playing because you love the game, right?"

Liam nodded.

"That's all that matters," Steve said.

Once again Isabella felt herself getting all choked up with emotion. So many times she'd imagined what it would be like to see Steve again and finally have a chance to tell him he had a son. Seeing the two of them together made her heart soar. Liam's dreams were coming true and she couldn't be happier for her son. She only wished Steve would give her a chance to explain that she'd been looking for him for years. But he wasn't ready to hear anything from the likes of her. Not yet. She needed to be patient and give him time to adjust to the fact he had a son.

They both watched Liam head off to huddle with his teammates, who were all gathering around the coach.

"That was beautiful," she told Steve.

"What was?"

"Your pep talk."

The look he gave her was unreadable, but then he chucked her under the chin and said, "I forgot how emotional you could get."

Steve headed off for the bleachers without another word. As she followed him to the stands, Isabella wondered what it would take to get through to him. At the very least, she hoped they could be friends. But two hours later, Steve continued to sit stiff and unyielding beside her, unwilling to give an inch, answering her questions with a nod or a shake of the head. Every time Liam got up to bat, he would glance at Steve and then proceed to strike out.

The game was tied now, the score two to two and Liam was up to bat next. If the batter struck out, Liam would be up to bat…he would be his team's last chance. The thought of Liam having all that pressure made her feel sick. They had never beaten the Bulldogs before and after explaining as much to Steve, he suddenly rushed to the dugout and had another talk with his son.

When Steve returned to his seat, Isabella worried he might have put additional pressure on Liam. Liam was nervous enough and trying so hard to please a father he'd only just met. This couldn't be easy on him.

The batter hit a fly ball to center field and the Bulldogs caught the ball. A murmured sigh/groan erupted from the crowd.

Liam walked slowly to the batter's box.

It was so quiet the chirping of the birds could be heard in the distance.

Isabella held her breath as the pitcher made eye contact, daring Liam to go ahead and try to hit one of his fastballs or breaking balls or whatever the heck they called them.

The pitcher let loose.

Liam swung and missed, but instead of looking back at Steve, this time Liam took a step back and stretched a little before returning to the batter's box. The stare-down between pitcher and batter lasted a little longer this time and it was all too much for Isabella to handle. She shut her eyes and no sooner than she had done so, she heard a piercing crack that sounded like a baseball making contact with a bat, her son's bat!

Her eyes shot open as the crowd came to their feet, everyone shouting, "Run, Liam, run!"

Adrenaline pushed Isabella out of her seat. Her heart drummed against her chest. The ball slipped right through the hands of the second baseman. Liam didn't get to run often and he wasn't the fastest kid on the team, but he just might be the most determined.

Dropping the bat, Liam ran toward first base, his feet kicking up dirt as he went. The outfielder ran for the ball. The first baseman kept one foot on the base, his gloved hand stretched out and ready.

Liam must have seen the outfielder pick up the ball because he dove for the base, his small body sliding across the dirt, his hand reaching, stretching.

"Safe!" the umpire called.

Stunned, Isabella couldn't believe what had just happened.

She turned to Steve, and he lifted her in his strong arms, his eyes bright, his smile brighter, and that quickly, in one glorious moment, Isabella realized she was still in love with this man, always had been, and always would be.

Their gazes held, her insides doing somersaults as she recalled being held in his arms the first time they had made love. He'd been caring, gentle, exhilarating.

Too quickly, Steve set her down, his attention back on the game as the next hitter batted one to right field, taking Liam all the way to third base. Frustrated, the pitcher wound up for the next batter, his face grim.

Their best hitter was up to bat. Liam's team might have a chance.

It was just a game, Isabella reminded herself, a silly game. No reason to feel faint.

The first pitch was a fastball and the hitter got a piece of the ball, but the ball rolled out of bounds. Strike one. The next pitch sent the ball wobbling through the air. The ball hit the tip of the catcher's mitt and rolled toward the dugout.

Suddenly, Liam was running toward home base.

People were on their feet again, only this time they shouted, "Go back, go back," but Liam wasn't listening. He was focused on one thing and one thing only.

"What's he doing?" Isabella asked Steve.

"He's doing exactly what I told him to do. He's using his instincts."

The Bulldogs hadn't seen it coming. Panicked, the catcher ran for the ball, tripping over his own feet.

For the second time, Liam dove, his body sliding through dirt as if it were water, all five fingers reaching for home plate.

"Safe!"

The crowd took a moment to catch their breath and quiet down. Liam headed to the dugout. The next pitch was a good one and the batter put the ball in the air. The Bulldog's right fielder easily caught the ball and the game was over.

The Gators won.

Liam was a hero, and his teammates, along with their coach, carried him across the field in celebration. Parents rushed for the field, many of them giving Steve congratulatory slaps on the back as they left the bleachers.

When Steve glanced at Isabella, she stood on the tips of her toes and kissed him on firm, unforgiving lips, causing any sign of cheerfulness to leave his face.

With a sigh, she watched him follow everyone to the field, eager to find his son. Standing alone on the bleachers, Isabella looked heavenward. A gentle breeze swept over her, caressing her face and reminding her that forgiveness didn't come easily.

CHAPTER THREE

Isabella was watering plants in the backyard when she heard the doorbell. A lot had happened in the past two weeks. Her best friend Jane had called off the wedding after realizing she was still in love with J.B., a boy who had grown up right here on Seeker's Island. And Liam seemed like a new kid—confident and happier than ever. He and Steve had bonded quickly. Since it was summer and school was out of session, the two of them had spent every day together. Today Liam was at Christopher's house, though, and she wasn't expecting anyone.

She opened the door, surprised to see Steve standing on the other side. Ever since kissing him at the baseball game, she could hardly look at him without feeling sort of stupid for getting carried away. More than anything, she wished the two of them could pick up where they had left off, but clearly Liam was the only reason Steve Brennan was still on the island.

Isabella was happy for her son. She only wished Steve could find a way to let go of the anger he felt toward her. She was done trying to explain to him what had happened. She just wished her insides would stop fluttering about every time he came around. It was ridiculous. Due to badgering by well-meaning friends, she had gone on a few dates over the years, but nobody managed to fire up her libido like this particular man. But it wasn't just his good looks and amazing body that drew her to him. During those six months they were together, he'd given her everything. Not only had he confided in her, telling her about his difficult childhood, he'd trusted her and gave her his heart on a platter. And what did she do in return? She'd left him high and dry without a word. She deserved his anger and resentment.

Today he wore a button-up shirt. The top buttons were undone, revealing just enough of his bronzed chest to tease and tantalize. Sure, he was great fun to look at, but there was so much more to Steve Brennan than met the eyes. At least there used to be.

He looked over her shoulder and into the house. "I'm here to pick up Liam to take him to his game."

"He doesn't have a game today," she said. "He's at Christopher's house. Why don't you come inside and I'll give Christopher's mom a call and see what's going on?"

Isabella pushed her hair out of her eyes and headed for her cell phone on the kitchen counter. As she made the call, Steve took a seat on the sofa.

Isabella said goodbye and clicked her cell shut after Christopher's mom promised to send him right home. Steve flipped slowly through the pages of a picture album she kept on the coffee table, photographs starting with Liam's birth up until present time. Taking a seat on the arm of the sofa, Isabella chuckled at the picture of Liam on his second birthday. His entire face was covered with chocolate cake.

"Was he a good baby?" Steve asked, his tone flat.

"The best."

He flipped through a few more pages and stopped at the page where three-year-old Liam stood at the door in his baseball uniform. "He's always liked baseball?"

"That would be putting it mildly. He has loved baseball since he was two and got a plastic bat for Christmas."

"He seems like a happy and well-adjusted kid."

Although she could tell he wasn't complimenting her—just stating the obvious—her heart swelled.

"I ran into Jane the other day," Steve told her. "She didn't have much time, but she told me you've worked hard to be a good parent, always being truthful with Liam and never babying him too much. It probably wasn't easy being a single mom."

"I tried to do the dad thing, too," she told him. "I took Liam fishing once, but that was a disaster. I couldn't get the hook out of the fish's mouth. The poor thing was flapping all over the place. I broke down and cried before I finally managed to get the hook out and throw the fish back into the water. Needless to say, Liam doesn't like to fish."

Steve nodded as he looked around at all of the shelves in the room lined with books. "He likes to read, though."

She nodded. "He likes to write, too. He's very smart."

An awkward moment passed between them before she stood and rubbed her hands together. "Christopher's mom said she would send Liam right home. Can I make you something to eat?"

Steve stood, too. "I will admit I'm having a difficult time adjusting to the fact that I have an eight-year-old son. It kills me to know I've missed seeing him grow up."

She sighed.

Liam burst through the door before either of them could say another word. "Dad! The Summer Festival started today! Can we go? Please?"

"That sounds like a lot of fun," Steve said, his voice suddenly animated.

"What about you, Mom? Want to go with us?"

"Oh, I don't know. It's Saturday. I've got laundry to do, furniture to dust, plants to water. Besides, I think your dad would prefer to spend time alone with you, Liam."

"Can she come, Dad? She's not that bad to be around."

"Thanks, Liam," she managed.

Steve looked at her and said, "It's up to you."

"Yeah, come on, Mom! It's going to be fun! Christopher's sister said there were going to be clowns walking around on ten-foot poles and a dunking pool and cotton candy. I've never had cotton candy before!"

"You've never had cotton candy?" Steve asked. He looked at Isabella again and this time he conjured up a lopsided grin and said, "Get dressed, Isabella, so we can get the boy some cotton candy."

"Okay," she said. "I'll go. Give me five minutes to change."

***

Steve kept his eye on Isabella as she walked ahead with Liam. It didn't matter if Isabella was wearing a sweat outfit or cut-offs and a T-shirt, she always looked beautiful. She smiled easily and was a positive force, making it difficult for him to keep his distance. When she'd kissed him at Liam's baseball game two weeks ago, he'd been taken aback, never expecting he would experience such a jolt of raw emotions and lust, confirming there were indeed lingering sparks from all those years ago. It had taken every bit of willpower for him not to take her in his arms and kiss her back. Despite his annoyance with her, he couldn't deny the sizzling attraction he still felt for her.

Her friend Jane had also told him about Isabella's parents and how they had married after Isabella's mom ended up pregnant. Isabella's parents had a miserable marriage and Isabella grew up feeling as though it was her fault her parents weren't happy.

The tropical air lightened his mood as they went along. He didn't want to place blame or hold onto the anger any longer. And yet, sadly, he didn't trust Isabella. For now, he figured it best to focus on Liam. He and Liam had spent too many years apart and he needed to make up for lost time.

Seeker's Island was in full festival swing and despite a few clouds dotting the sky, the sun's rays managed to warm his back. There were jugglers and clowns on unicycles. Food sizzled on barbeques and the smell of hot dogs and burgers on the grill made his stomach rumble. Caribbean music blared and a line of merrymakers kicked up their feet as they danced to the beat of bongo drums.

Liam used his right hand to grab hold of Isabella's hand and his left to reach out to Steve.

"Are you going to move here, Dad?"

Liam had been calling him Dad for weeks, but it still managed to surprise him in a good way every time Liam said it. Steve certainly hadn't thought about moving to Seeker's Island, but it made sense that Liam would have wondered what was going to happen next. "I have a house in Brooklyn, New York," Steve told him. "I have friends, too. Friends I would love for you to meet."

"Do you have a job?"

"As a matter of fact, I do. I own a restaurant with other people and I'm head chef."

***

"You opened your own restaurant?" Isabella asked.

"I did."

Back in the day, they had shared many nights experimenting with roasting duck, filleting fish, and scoring chicken.

"Do you make macaroni and cheese?" Liam asked, his eyes wide.

"I do," Steve said as he rubbed the top of Liam's head. "I'd like to bring you home with me and show you around. That is, if your mom will let you go with me for a few weeks."

"Can I go, Mom? Can I?"

"Oh, I don't know. You have an art project to finish before school starts and isn't Bonnie having a birthday party next week?"

"We could wait until after Bonnie's party," Steve said. "My neighbor, Pamela, is an art teacher. She'd be happy to help Liam out. I'll have him back with time to spare before school starts up."

Just breathe, Isabella told herself. This was all so sudden. Having Steve Brennan back in their lives was one thing, but the idea of him taking Liam off the island was difficult to comprehend. And who was Pamela? Just because he wasn't wearing a ring on his finger didn't mean he didn't have a girlfriend. She felt like thumping herself on the forehead for being such an idiot. Of course, he had a girlfriend. Not only was he easy on the eyes, it was easy to see, judging by the way he treated Liam, that he was still the same sweet man she remembered. Some girls had all the luck. She'd had her chance and she'd blown it.

"Look at that, Mom!"

A clown on a five-foot unicycle rode by, juggling an assortment of fruit. Isabella looked up, past the clown, and toward the sky. She felt a warm tropical breeze brush across her cheeks and for the first time since she was a little girl, she thought about the hot springs and about all of the years spent wishing and praying that someday she would have a family of her own, a happy household where her children would be excited to walk through the door after school each day. She loved Liam. They were happy. For years now she'd had her heart's desire. She just hadn't realized it until this very moment. If Steve never found it in his heart to forgive her, she'd be all right. For Liam's sake and her own, she would find a way to move on.

***

They didn't arrive home until ten o'clock. All the excitement of the day had worn Liam out and he'd fallen asleep in Steve's arms.

Steve carried Liam to his bed and Isabella watched from the doorway as he gently tucked his son in for the night. He quietly shut the door and when he turned around, she looked up at him. "Thank you for today. I had a good time."

"I've never forgotten the first time I laid eyes on you."

Shocked by his confession, she couldn't help but smile. "I believe I saw you first. The professor was late to class so you took it upon yourself to teach the class."

"That's right," he said. "I'd forgotten that part. I just remember your laughter. Once you caught my eye, I couldn't look away."

"I didn't want you to look away," she said. "We shared so many special moments."

For the first time all day, he gazed deeply into her eyes, his heated expression filled with confusion and lust as he leaned toward her and brushed his mouth over hers. Angling his head, he deepened the kiss, making her body tingle and her legs wobble.

This was no ordinary kiss. It was hot and fiery, filled with years of repressed emotions—a make up kiss like no other.

She ran her fingers through his hair and then downward over his thickly corded neck and onward to his chest. Her breathing was unsteady. She wanted him, needed him. She took a handful of his shirt and pulled him close, insisting on more.

He gave her what she wanted. His mouth covered hers completely and his hand cupped the back of her head, bringing her mouth impossibly closer. Backed up against the wall, his body pressed close as she squeezed her hand between them and unbuttoned his shirt, hoping to strip him bare, but he stopped her before she got his shirt off.

"I can't do this," he said.

He took a moment to catch his breath and then he said he was sorry before he turned and walked away.

***

Steve was back at the hotel lying in bed. It was seven in the morning and he'd hardly slept. Shit. What the hell had he been thinking? He never should have kissed her. Nine years ago, he'd known Isabella for all of six months before he was ready to get down on bended knee and propose.

Now, all of these years later, he wanted nothing more than to carry her to bed within two weeks of seeing her again.

Absurd.

The mere idea of it made him question his sanity.

Yes, Jane had told him all about Isabella's vow to never marry for the wrong reasons after what had happened between her parents, but Isabella hadn't thought to give him a chance to have a say in the matter before she ran off. And no matter how hard he tried to put it all in the past and get over it, what Isabella had done felt like a sharp knife to his heart every time he looked at her.

He already loved Liam. In such a short time, Liam had become the most important thing in his life. And that was the crux of the problem. He'd missed out on the first eight years of his son's life. Looking through the picture album hadn't helped. Seeing all of the things he missed had only served to reignite his frustration toward Isabella. He was trying hard to understand what might have been going through her head at the time. They were young, they were impulsive, but he had been so sure of their love back then.

In anger, he'd told Isabella that their time together was merely a blip on the radar, but those six months had been much more than that. It had taken him years to get to a point where he could live day to day without being eaten alive by her abrupt disappearance. It had taken him years to finally get to a place where he felt he could forget about the woman he'd fallen in love with. But in the blink of an eye, all of that changed.

Again.

And this time he had no one to blame but himself.

His body began to shake, his heart pounding. He needed to get off the island.

He grabbed his luggage and blindly began shoving clothes inside. He'd stayed on Seeker's Island long enough. It was time to head back to New York.

And he wasn't going anywhere without his son.

***

"Hey, Mom?"

"What's on your mind, Liam?"

"Are you still mad at yourself for leaving Dad?"

Isabella stood at the kitchen sink, washing dishes while Liam ate his cereal. Liam was young, but not young enough to keep the truth from him. They talked about everything and she had always been truthful with her son. As she wiped her hands on a dishtowel, she said, "What makes you ask?"

He shrugged. "I was just wondering."

"If I stop to think about it, yes, I'm disappointed in myself and I wish I had handled it all differently."

Liam took a bite of his cereal, chewed, finally swallowed and said, "I'm not mad at you anymore."

Isabella leaned over the table so she could look Liam square in the eyes. "I'm glad, Liam. It takes a lot to learn how to forgive. Some people never do figure it out, but you have, and you're only eight."

"My teacher said everyone makes mistakes and sometimes there's nothing you can do to change things back to how they were. You can just feel bad about it and that doesn't do anyone any good."

Isabella felt tears come to her eyes, but she sucked in a breath and said, "I love you, Liam. I'm proud of you, too."

"How come?"

"Because I see the way you treat your friends. I see you smile at strangers and how respectful you are of other people. You're one of the good guys."

He took another bite of cereal and seemed to ponder that. After a while he said, "You believe in the power of the hot springs now, don't you?"

"If I say yes, you're not going to jump into the deep end every time you want something, are you?"

He laughed. "Nooo way."

"I signed you up for swimming lessons."

Liam groaned but before he could protest further there was a knock on the door. He jumped off the stool and ran to the door.

Steve stood on the other side, the sky-blue of his short-sleeved shirt matching the color of his eyes. As always, her heart skipped a beat. She had been sorely disappointed when he stepped away last night, abruptly ending their kiss and then leaving without saying goodbye.

She'd hoped he just needed to think about things before realizing they owed it to their son to give each other another chance. He stepped inside, and at closer view, she could see something was definitely wrong. Dark circles shadowed his eyes and his hair was disheveled.

"Want some cereal?" Liam asked.

"No thanks, kiddo. I already ate." There was something in the tone of his voice that worried her. His hard, set jaw echoed his strange mood.

Steve looked at Isabella as he said, "Liam, do you mind giving me and your mom a few minutes alone? I need to talk to her for just a little bit."

"Okay," Liam said, jumping off the stool and running to his room, seemingly happy to give his parents time alone.

"What's going on?" she asked.

"I'm leaving for New York first thing tomorrow morning and I want to take Liam with me."

Her stomach clenched with dread. She didn't know what to say, so she said nothing.

"I talked to Bonnie and her mom, and they both said it was fine if Liam missed her party because apparently Bonnie missed Liam's party last year."

"Oh." She wrung her hands. "I need more time to think about this."

"There is no time, Isabella. I'm not asking for the moon. I promise to have Liam back before school starts and I already talked to Pamela and just as I suspected, she'd be happy to help Liam with his art project."

"Is Pamela your girlfriend?"

"She likes to think so, but she knows it could never work. She turned eighty last month."

Feeling silly, she turned toward the sink and looked out the window. "Liam has never left the island without me. This is all so sudden."

"I have a life, too."

She turned back to him. "I never insinuated you didn't."

"No," he said, "I guess you didn't. I've stayed on the island much longer than I planned and I have things back home that need my attention."

"Why the sudden hurry? Is it because of the kiss?"

His eyes dropped to her lips. He was staring at her mouth and yet his stubborn pride would not allow him to admit that they had so much more to discuss.

"No," he finally said, his eyes back on hers. "This is about me doing what's right for me."

"I see."

She came back to where he stood and put a hand on his arm. He was so physically powerful; just that one simple touch made her feel things she couldn't explain.

He flinched, but didn't pull away.

"You're still angry with me for leaving."

"I'm trying hard not to be. I need time, Isabella."

She dropped her hands to her sides.

"If you agree to let Liam come with me, we'll be leaving first thing in the morning. I checked the schedule. The ferry leaves early on Mondays."

"I still love you, Steve." She knew it sounded crazy, but it was the truth. "I've never stopped loving you."

He brought his hands to her shoulders, his eyes brimming with emotion, making her see how much pain she'd caused him.

"I'm so sorry," she said.

"I'm sorry, too," he said sadly as he released his hold. "How long will it take to pack up Liam's things?"

"Does Liam have any say in the matter?"

"Of course, but I wanted to get your permission before I asked him."

"Thank you for that." She didn't want to let her son go, but it was only for a few weeks. She trusted Steve to take good care of Liam. She gestured toward Liam's room. "You know where to find him. I'll be in the backyard when you've finished talking with him."

Isabella wanted to kick something, preferably Steve Brennan's shin, but she straightened her spine and held her chin high while she headed for the backyard. Although she loved Seeker's Island, a small part of her had hoped Steve might ask her and Liam to join him in New York for a time and give them both a chance to see where he lived—maybe bring them to his restaurant for a meal. But obviously Steve wasn't even close to getting over what he saw as her ultimate betrayal. Payback was a bitch. She'd made her bed and now she would need to lie in it for the rest of her life, it seemed.

***

The next twenty-four hours were tortuous for Isabella. Of course, Liam had been thrilled at the prospect of going off on a wild adventure with his newfound dad. So Isabella had told Steve she'd like to spend some time alone with her son before they left in the morning. After Steve headed back for his hotel, Isabella and Liam rode their bikes to the park and had a picnic, something they used to do a lot when Liam was younger.

After dinner, they packed Liam's things and Isabella forced herself to keep a smile on her face. How could she not? Liam was beyond excited and rightfully so. Morning came too fast and within the blink of an eye, it was time for Isabella to say goodbye to the two loves of her life. She'd never been away from Liam for more than one night. School wouldn't start for another month and a half. She couldn't stand the idea of not seeing Liam for that long. For a moment, she'd considered pulling Steve aside and begging him not to do this, but Liam was so animated, so eager, she couldn't do that to her son.

She had to be strong. She *would* be strong.

And so before the sun had yet to rise, she watched Liam and Steve climb into a golf cart and head off to catch the first ferry off the island.

***

Steve sensed Liam's apprehension, which was understandable. He knew Liam had only been off the island a few times in his life and never without his mother. The sun was only just beginning to rise as they made their way along the quiet street, the low hum of the golf cart engine the only sound. Steve knew he wasn't being fair to Isabella. He didn't like seeing the hurt in her eyes, but this wasn't his fault. Was it? A part of him wanted to go back and tell Isabella everything would be okay. He understood perfectly well that she'd been scared all those years ago. They were young back then, but something else stopped him from telling her all of that.

They made it to the pier with time to spare. He grabbed Liam's duffle bag and waited for his son to climb out of his seat. Hand in hand, they walked to the loading area.

Yesterday, he had bought tickets for two. The ferry had yet to open the gates. Other people waited, too. Suddenly a strong gust of wind swept over him and took the tickets right out of his hand. He reached out, but then he looked down at his son and saw one lone tear sliding down his cheek. Liam raised a hand to his face and quickly wiped the tear away.

Forgetting about the tickets, Steve set the luggage on the ground and knelt so he could get a better look at Liam. "Is something bothering you?"

Liam shook his head, his mouth trembling, his eyes watery.

"You can tell me whatever it is. I'll understand. I promise."

"I don't want to leave Mom."

And in that moment, maybe even an instant before, Steve realized he'd messed up big time. He'd always been stubborn, but just like his father, he'd let his stubborn pride get the best of him. His heart began to race as he realized what he had to do.

"Steve! Liam! Oh, thank God you haven't left yet."

They both looked toward the sound of a woman's voice. It was Jane. Steve stood as she approached. "What's going on?" Steve asked her.

"Since the last time we talked, I've gone to the hotel twice in hopes of finding you, but you're never there. There's been so much going on since you arrived on the island, I haven't had time to tell you everything that needs to be said."

"Liam and I have been busy," he assured her.

"Isabella would kill me if she knew I was here, but the clerk at the hotel told me you just checked out and were leaving the island. There are a few things I think you should know before you go."

He kept his hand on Liam's shoulder. "We're kind of in a hurry," he said.

"After Liam was born," Jane said, talking fast, "Isabella knew she needed to find you and tell you about him. She knew she'd made a horrible mistake, so she waited until the doctor said it was okay to take Liam on an airplane. She flew to San Francisco and spent months looking for you. She said it was as if you had disappeared from the face of the earth."

"You don't need to explain," Steve told her, but she ignored him.

"She did find three Steve Brennans who fit your description and she called each one. Although they all assured Isabella they were not the Steve Brennan she was looking for, she wasn't convinced, so she flew to Idaho, Missouri, and New Jersey."

Jane sighed. "She did all of this because she was desperate to find you. She didn't stop there, either. Every few years, she and Liam would return to San Francisco to look for you. Isn't that right, Liam?"

Liam nodded.

"I know you need to do what you feel is best for you, but I just couldn't let you leave without knowing the whole story. Isabella did everything in her power to find you, and more important, she always told Liam the truth about you."

Jane's gaze fell on Liam. "What's wrong, Liam? Are you okay?"

"He's going to be fine," Steve assured her. "Everything is going to be just fine."

***

Isabella used a wet cloth to wipe the sink and the counters for the hundredth time. The sun was just beginning to peek over the horizon.

She looked at the clock, and then tapped her foot against the floor, and then looked at the clock again. If she hurried, she could see Steve and Liam one more time before they left.

She wiped her eyes.

Yes, if she could just see them both one more time, she would be able to get through this. She just needed to wave to them as they boarded the ferry.

With her hand on the doorknob, she glanced down at her clothes. Still dressed in her pajama pants, a T-shirt, and big floppy slippers, she didn't care. If she left this very minute, she might make it in time to see them off. There was no time to grab her purse or lock the door. She ran outside and jumped over the three stairs leading to the porch before climbing on her bike and pedaling as fast as she could.

Out of breath and sweaty, she made it to the docks in record time.

She dropped the bike and ran to the pier, her hands gripping the cold railing overlooking the water. She could see the ferry, but it was too far away to make out any familiar faces.

They were gone.

Chills washed over her. She was too late.

A tall bearded man stood alongside her, his gaze set on the ferry. He had an iPod in his shirt pocket and earphones plugged into his ears. She could hear the song "I Will Wait" by Mumford and Sons—a fitting song given the circumstances. The man looked at her, smiled, and then headed back for town.

Although the people on the ferry were now tiny specks, Isabella waved both hands over her head as tears dripped down her cheeks and over her chin. "I will wait…I will wait for you."

Twenty minutes later, Isabella parked her bike at the side of her small house, the house Nana had left her after she passed away two years ago. She missed Nana. If Nana were here now, she would tell Isabella to pull herself together. Nana would remind her of how strong she was and then tell her she would get through this.

The sound of a door closing inside the house alerted her to the fact she'd left without locking the door. Slowly, she made her way up the stairs to the porch. There were voices coming from inside. She reached for the handle and pushed the door wide open.

"Mom!" Liam jumped into her arms.

Isabella held her son tightly. His body was shaking. Her heart swelled with love. She cupped his face and kissed his beautiful cheeks. "What happened? What are you doing here?"

"He didn't want to leave you," Steve said from the other side of the room.

Her head jerked up. It was impossible to read the expression on Steve's face.

"I didn't want to leave you either," he added.

Goosebumps traveled up her spine. "You didn't?"

Steve shook his head, his gaze piercing hers as he moved toward her. "Jane came to see us off. She wanted me to know that you never stopped looking for me. Then Liam reminded me that we all make mistakes."

She couldn't stop the tears from coming.

"I've been a fool, Isabella. I let my stubborn pride get the best of me, but the truth is I have loved you since the time I watched you make your first crème brûlée."

"I burnt it," she said, her voice breaking, her heart swelling, ready to burst.

"I remember." He stepped closer still. "It was the worst crème brûlée I ever tasted."

She smiled, blubbering like a fool as she reached an arm toward him.

The three of them were huddled together, everyone holding tightly as if they were all afraid to let go. After a moment, they all looked at one another with red-rimmed eyes, so happy to be together again after too many years apart.

And then, exactly as it happened in the stories Nana used to tell her when she was small, a gentle wind pushed through the open windows, sounding like a whisper, seeking, searching, its warm airy fingers curling around them, making sure they had all found their heart's desire before leaving in search of another broken heart that might need mending.

Caught In The Surf

Jasinda Wilder

CHAPTER ONE

Kailani Kekoa groaned into the pillow of her sweat-slick arms and wished she could pass out again. Unfortunately, now that consciousness seemed to have gotten a hold on her, it was refusing to let go. The problem with being awake, especially at that particular moment, was that it included not just the ever-present heartache, but also a whole new kind of awfulness that Lani hadn't experienced in quite some time.

She was hung over. Or, actually, if the persistent wavering and blurring of the world past her squinting eyelids was any indication, she was still drunk. Still really, really drunk.

The first order of business was to sit up. She could do this. Seriously. If she could ride the barrel of a thirty-foot swell with one arm in a bag-wrapped cast and win a national championship in the process, then surely she could manage to lever herself upright.

Oh, god. That hurt. Movement, even twisting her head slightly, sent lances of pain shooting through her skull. Once she was upright, the next order of business was to figure out where she was and where she was going.

Maybe finding out *when* she was would be an even better place to start. Lani peered blearily around her. Rows of cracked plastic chairs bolted to threadbare carpeting, an abandoned podium bearing the logo of an airline she'd never even heard of, dirty floor-to-ceiling windows. Darkness hung thick and impenetrable beyond those windows.

Something niggled in the back of Lani's brain. The darkness boded ill, somehow. It shouldn't be dark out. But why not?

Digging in the purse at her feet, Lani withdrew her cell phone and pressed the home button to bring up the screensaver and the clock. 9:40 p.m.

9:40.

Awareness filtered into her throbbing head and then struck like lightning, and was accompanied by a blistering bolt of actual lightning from outside, followed by a crack of thunder so loud and so close it rattled the windows.

Her connecting flight was at 6:15, and that flight had been the last line out of this godforsaken postage stamp of an airport until the following day. And by godforsaken, she meant totally remote. Miles and miles from anything, anywhere — that kind of remote. No hotels, no bars, nothing. Just a single-strip runway a stone's throw from the Pacific Ocean, a glass-walled hut containing a ticket counter, a single row of chairs that were already ancient in the seventies, and a four-foot-long slab of sticky laminate counter in the farthest corner of the lounge area, behind which had been a ragged, silent, well-used sort of woman with pale dishwater-blonde hair and lonely, exhausted brown eyes. The woman hadn't said a word, but she'd served Lani enough Mai Tais to render her unconscious. And, considering Lani's diminutive size, it had taken a shocking amount of rum to do so.

Shit.

Now she was stuck here in this hellhole of an airport until morning. And she appeared to be completely alone. As in, most of the lights had been turned off. As in, the *runway* lights had been turned off.

Shit.

Lani stuffed the cell phone back into her purse, stuffed the purse in turn into her backpack, and stood up. Which might have been a mistake, since she swayed like a hurricane-blown palm tree and then fell back onto the chair. Which hurt, a lot. All this, of course, made her head throb even worse.

Lani let a pained "fuck me" slip out of her mouth and then stood up again, this time more slowly, and stayed standing. Her backpack made it onto her shoulders without mishap, and she even managed a dozen steps in a straight line toward the bar before she stumbled. The bar was empty, of course, but there was a stack of rocks glasses on a web of black rubber behind the counter and a soda gun. Lani reached over the bar, snagged a rocks glass and poured water into it, drank, and then filled it again. She repeated this procedure about six more times, at which point her mouth no longer contained balls of cotton, but her stomach was rebelling the treatment and sloshing noisily.

"Probably wishing you had a Tylenol about now, I'd think," came a rough male voice from somewhere off to her left.

Lani squeaked and jumped. "Holy shit!" She spun in a circle, looking for the source of the voice.

There, in the shadows near a window and a cracked-open door—the faint orange glow of a cigarette being dragged on.

"How long have you been there?" Lani demanded, striding closer to the voice.

"Long enough. Too long."

The voice was odd, Lani decided. There was a definite Southern twang, but there was also a kind of burr, almost Irish. It was a deep, slow voice, and something about it seemed to hit Lani between the shoulder blades and stroke down her spine.

"That's not an answer," Lani retorted. "And yeah, I would kill for a Tylenol. Or some codeine. Or morphine. Or a shovel between the eyes."

"Ain't got none of that, sorry to say." The voice seemed to be rising upward, and the orange glow followed.

Up, up, up. The cigarette tip stopped about a foot and a half above Lani's head, and then glowed brighter, crackling. A stream of smoke was visible for a moment, then was sucked out into the sky beyond the airport.

Now that Lani was conscious, she smelled the rain and, layered beneath it, the ocean.

"If you didn't have any Tylenol, why'd you bring it up?"

The man grunted. "Icebreaker, guess you could call it. There's probably some kinda painkiller in the first aid box under the counter, though."

Lani circled around behind the bar and squatted. There was a battered white metal box with a red cross painted on it. Rusty metal clasps held it closed, sort of, and Lani flipped these open. Sure enough, there were several packets of generic pain reliever. Lani took several packets and replaced the box.

"Thanks," Lani said, ripping one open and shaking the pills into her hand.

"Yup."

Lightning flashed just then, and the man was cast into silhouette. He was gargantuan. Well over six feet tall, maybe even closer to seven. Shoulders and arms so thick, he might as well have been carved from a koa tree.

"Why are you here?" Lani asked, chasing the pills with more water.

"Waiting for the storm to pass," the man said, and reached out to crush his cigarette into an ashtray on the bar. "You?"

Lani hesitated. "Passing through."

The man laughed, a short rumbling chuckle. "Think you missed the 'through' part of that, don't you?"

"Just a little," Lani said, ruefully.

"Got a plan?"

Again, Lani hesitated. She didn't. Not at all. Not even remotely. "No," she admitted. "I have absolutely no clue what I'm going to do."

"Well, your options are limited. Stay here in the airport, or walk to town."

"How far is town?" Lani asked.

"Ten, maybe fifteen miles."

"I don't suppose a cab would come out here, would they?" Lani figured she might as well ask.

"A cab?" He seemed amused by the idea. "Not sure the town, if you can even call it that, has one."

"So, basically, my only option is to stay here."

"Seems so."

"Alone, in a dark, closed airport. In the rain."

"Yep." A stool creaked as the man sat down.

Lani filled her rocks glass with Coke and sipped it. "When you said you were waiting for the storm to pass, what did that mean?"

A long silence. "Well, just that I'm hoping the rain will let up on the sooner side of eventually."

"No shit, Sherlock. I meant why. *Why* are you waiting?"

Another silence. Lani got the idea he was avoiding answering. "Probably 'cause I'd like to get home before it's tomorrow."

Lani cursed mentally. Getting a straight answer from this man was like pulling teeth. "And where's home?"

"Seeker's Island, I guess. At least as close to home as I'd call anything."

"Seeker's Island? What's that? And how are you getting there?" Lani's head was throbbing violently still, and she had to work to contain her temper.

"Seeker's Island. It's…an island. A tiny little place a few miles out thataway." He pointed to the west, toward the ocean. "And I'm gonna fly there."

There was a brief metallic scraping-grinding noise, and flame spurted into life, revealing a striking face made of sharp features, hard lines and angles and planes, deep-set eyes.

"In what?"

He blew smoke out. "An airplane. A seaplane, to be exact."

Lani's heart leapt. Or, well, it shuffled excitedly. No part of Lani would be doing any leaping until the world stopped wavering and her brain stopped trying to gouge a hole in her head through her eyeballs.

"Could you take me with you?"

A pause, tobacco crackling, a long exhale. "Could. For eighty bucks, one way."

Lani just gaped. "You're going anyway. How you gonna charge me?"

"If I wasn't the one flying, I'd charge myself. Gas is expensive. Plus, it ain't gonna be a pretty flight."

"Nothing you just said made any sense." Lani pinched the bridge of her nose. "Like I said, you're going to this island anyway. I don't understand why you can't just take me with you. I won't be any trouble. I won't even talk. I don't take up much space. I've only got the backpack."

"I ain't concerned about the space you'd take up. Shit, you're so small I could probably stow you under my seat." He stood up and slid down a few seats until he was next to her. Suddenly, he seemed to fill the entire airport. "I'm concerned about the fact that I'm flat broke, darlin', and I'm on the end of my gas tank. An economics lesson for you: I'm the supply, you're the demand. I'm your only way to get anywhere, and that's my price. Take it or leave it."

Lani just stared at him. "That's…screwed up in so many ways I don't even know where to begin."

"How about eighty bucks or 'no, thank you.'"

"How about, 'you're an asshole'?" Lani slammed the last of her Coke like it was a shot.

"Fair enough. It's not personal, though. I need the money, and you need the ride."

Lani considered. She had a pair of hundred-dollar bills in her wallet, and that was it. That was all she had to her name. But she really didn't relish the idea of sitting here alone in the dark all night.

"Fine," she said, sighing, "but you're still an asshole." She dug through her backpack and purse to get at her wallet, then handed him one of the crisp bills.

"All day long. Got no change on me," he said, exhaling smoke. "But I'll get it for you once we hit the island."

Lani shrugged as if she didn't care. "What's your name?"

The orange glow brightened, and he blew out a long spume of smoke. "Casey. You?"

"Kailani."

He nodded, peering at her through the dim gloom and the pall of his smoke. "Kailani, hmm? From Hawaii?"

Lani nodded. "All my life, brah."

"Spent a good bit of time on the islands, myself. Had a run to and from the Big Island for about two years. Made good cash, too."

"I lived town side Oahu," Lani said.

Casey just nodded again. "Old army buddy lives town side. Right near Diamond Head, I think. Haven't seen him in a while, though. Might've moved." Casey stood and poked his head out of the cracked-open door. "Looks like the storm's mostly over. We should go now."

Lani stood and slipped her backpack on her shoulders. "I'm ready."

Casey pushed through the door, held it for Lani, and then kicked the wedge of wood away so the door latched. Lani dragged in a deep breath of the tropical air and the rain-thick humidity. After a month of couch-hopping with friends on the mainland, Lani was glad to be somewhere that even remotely resembled home. Even if she was nearly broke, alone, with no plan.

It wasn't raining anymore, although the air did hold dampness like a thick mist. Casey's long-legged strides took him across the tarmac swiftly, and Lani had to run to catch up to him. Even after she caught up, she had to trot two steps for each of his.

"Slow down, would you?" Lani snapped. "Not all of us are a thousand feet tall."

Casey didn't answer, but he did slow his stride so Lani could keep up without having to run. She suspected he was smirking, but it was too dark to tell. He led them across the tarmac to a path leading toward the beach and a long pier, to which was tied a single-engine seaplane, bobbing in the post-storm surf.

Lani stood on the pier, staring skeptically at the bucking airplane. "You sure it's safe to fly like this?" She said the last phrase "la'dis."

"Like what?" Casey untied the plane and stepped easily from the dock to the float of the pitching aircraft.

She gestured to the choppy water. "I wouldn't take a boat out in this. Too rough."

"It's now or wait till morning. The storm's broke, but it may not stay that way. Do I like it? No. Am I worried? Not much." He yelled the last phrase from the cockpit.

"'Not much'? Is that supposed to comfort me?" Lani timed her step from the dock to the plane, but hadn't banked on a swell knocking the plane upward.

She found herself balanced with one foot on the float of the seaplane, fighting for stability. Her lifetime of surfing was all that kept her from ending up in the black brine, and as another wave sent the plane bobbing even further, she knew she wouldn't last much longer. She was too far back to be able to grab the sides of the plane, and her foot was slipping on the slick edge of the float.

A hot, hard, huge hand grabbed her wrist and tugged her forward. Before she had time to react, she was crushed against a massive, rock-solid chest, the scent of sweat and cigarettes and engine oil and sea salt filling her nose. His hand was spread across her back, spanning from between her shoulder blades down nearly to the small of her back.

It was only a split-second, but Lani felt in that instant as if she had been caught by a riptide of sensation, pulled out and sucked under and tumbled until disoriented by his scent and his miles and miles of muscle and his heat.

Reality hit her like a rogue wave.

"Get off me." She pushed away, harder than necessary.

Casey didn't respond, but she felt his eyes and the unspoken questions. She'd nearly succumbed to his embrace. A random stranger in an airplane. A freaking giant nearly two feet taller than she was.

She set her backpack down and took the seat next to Casey, who was pushing buttons and flicking switches. She fitted the earphones to her ears and adjusted the mic. After a moment, the engines sputtered, coughed into deafening life, and Lani felt the rumbling buzz in her belly and her bones.

She refused to look at him, the huge man folded into the tiny cockpit, his head brushing the ceiling, knees splayed sideways, bear-paw hands on the wheel. She refused to look, but she couldn't help seeing him, feeling his enormous presence. A stolen glance out of the corner of her eye showed him to have reddish sandy hair cropped short, rough and craggy features that managed to be somehow handsome in a ferociously masculine way. His shoulders were thick and round, straining against the plain gray T-shirt, and his arms were nearly as big around as her waist. Under the dim glow of the cockpit lights, his skin was fair and freckled and weather-beaten.

He caught her looking and grinned. "I'm six-seven."

"What?" Lani flushed and glanced out the window, seeing little but dark water and thick gray-black clouds.

"I'm not a thousand feet tall. I'm six-foot-seven. Just sayin'."

"Oh. Well…you're still a freaking gorilla."

"I'm more of a bear than a gorilla, if you're comparing me to animals." He let his gaze rake over her body. "And you're a—"

"If you call me a midget or a little person, I'll stab you in the throat with your own pen."

Casey lifted his hands briefly in a gesture of innocence. "Not what I was going to say. I'm friends with a little person, as matter of fact, so I wouldn't say nothing like that." He adjusted the throttle, and the engine picked up tone. "I was going to say you're a pixie."

"Excuse me?" Lani twisted in her seat to glare at him. "A what?"

He flashed a grin at her. "A pixie, like an elf or a fairy or something." He eased the plane away from the dock and twisted it into position toward the open water. "Tiny…and magical."

Lani wasn't sure how to answer that. "I'm not *that* tiny. I'm over five feet."

"Barely."

"Shut up. I'm five-one, I'll have you know." Lani hated how that had come out but couldn't take it back.

She crossed her arms over her chest and refused to be embarrassed. Casey just chuckled under his breath and shoved the throttle to full. Speech was impossible after that, the plane jouncing and jarring over the waves. She let herself glance at Casey and noticed that, despite his teasing moments before, his mouth was now set in a hard line and his granite-slab shoulders were tensed forward. The bounces became longer and higher, and Lani's stomach began to rise into her throat as they touched water once more, then lifted off. She couldn't quite stifle a shriek of panic when a white-capped wave sliced beneath them, big enough to have done damage had it hit them. Casey blew out a soft, barely perceptible breath of his own.

"That was close," Lani said.

"Yep."

"Would that have made us crash?"

Casey shrugged. "Wouldn't have been good."

A long silence ensued then, as the seaplane rose into the air. After a while, Lani couldn't take the silence. She'd never been good at silence. "Where'd you learn to fly?"

"Army." Casey didn't even look at her.

"You were a pilot in the army? Where were you stationed?"

He glanced at her finally, as if debating how much to say. "All over. Japan, Germany, Philippines, Guam, Okinawa, Korea, Ireland. Wasn't regular Army."

"What were you then?"

"Army Rangers. I was a Ranger, but I preferred flying to being in the thick of it."

She peered through the windscreen, seeing nothing and wondering how he knew where they were going. "So you can fly a lot of different kinds of things, then, I bet, right?"

He grunted an answer as a gust of wind buffeted them. "Yeah, I can fly everything from C-17s to these little pond-hoppers, choppers, gliders, you name it. If it goes in the air, I can fly it. 'Cept fighter jets, of course. Though I could, and did once, in a pinch. Hated it. Scary as shit."

"Is this scary for you? Flying in this weather?" Lani felt the aircraft jolt and dip, heard rain blatting against it.

"This ain't weather. It's a bit of rain. And no."

Lani couldn't seem to stop the questions, since they kept her own nerves at bay. She hated flying. "So what would scare you?"

"You ask a lot of questions. I flew a C-130 through the edge of a hurricane once. That was some scary shit. We got caught and didn't have enough fuel to go around it. It just hit us out of nowhere. Rain going sideways, wind blowing so hard it sounded like bullets hitting the walls. We'd drop a thousand feet in about ten seconds, just *whoomp*, so fast you didn't have time to get sick. Then we'd pick up altitude again, only to be blown this way and that and tossed around. I nearly shit myself, I think. Did pee a little, if I remember right." He said the last with a grin.

"That sounds horrifying." She couldn't stop her own grin from spreading at the idea of this massive man peeing his pants.

"It wasn't fun. Made it through intact, though. We ran out of fuel as we were taxiing off the runway." He glanced at Lani, clearly seeing her hands white-knuckled on the armrests. "This ain't nothin' to be worried about. We'll be fine."

She didn't want him to think she was a coward, for reasons she didn't care to examine too closely. "My uncle was a pilot. He used to fly me and my sister around all the time in a tiny little plane just like this. Once, it was just me and Uncle Jimmy. We were halfway to the Big Island when a storm hit us. We were out over open water and, like you said, it just hit. No warning. We crashed. Uncle Jimmy died getting me out of the wreckage. Flying has been difficult ever since. Especially in planes like this."

"Shit, Kailani. Sorry 'bout your uncle. I can promise you we won't crash today, though. You'll be all right."

A gust of wind buffeted them sideways, and Lani clutched the armrest with clawed fingers. When they had evened out, Lani glanced at Casey, who was lighting a cigarette and pinching it between his teeth as he slipped the plastic Bic lighter back in his hip pocket.

"You're smoking? Now?" Lani hated how her voice turned into a squeak at the end.

Casey just grinned, spewing smoke from his nose. "Keeps me calm. This ain't even a storm, Kailani. We'll be fine. Trust me."

"Call me Lani." She didn't address his "trust me" comment. Trusting men wasn't possible, not for Lani, not then.

Another gust of wind knocked them, tipping to the side, and Lani heard a whimper scrape past her teeth.

"This is a storm. I don't give a shit what you say, Mr. Army Ranger." Lani was proud of how steady her voice was.

Casey grinned at her again. "Nah. This is just a little squall. Ain't nothin'. But you're entitled to your fear. Not saying you're not." He rummaged in a backpack between their seats and pulled out a flask, handed it to Lani. "A bit of liquid courage might help."

Lani's stomach turned, but she took the metal flask and swallowed a slug of burning whiskey. "Oh, god. I think I might be sick now."

Casey frowned at her. "Not in my plane, please. I hate cleaning up puke."

Lani shook her head. "I won't. Just nauseous."

After a few minutes, Lani felt the plane dipping and lowering gradually, and then there was a soft, wet thump and the liquid scraping of water past the floats, and they were down. Lights gleamed yellow-orange in the distance, and Lani felt a soft flutter of hope.

Hope for what, she wasn't sure.

He shut off the engine, unbuckled his safety belt, and unfolded his enormous frame from the seat. "Welcome to Seeker's Island," he said.

CHAPTER TWO

Lani just sat for a moment, staring at the soft glow of the lights, feeling the plane rock and bob gently. Casey shoved the door open, and Lani was assaulted by the smell of rain and ocean, and underneath that, the scent of greenery and wet sand. She heard the homey sound of waves sloshing against shore, the gentle drift of rain, the chuck of water on the dock pilings.

He stepped out and extended his hand to Lani. Hesitating in the doorway, Lani stared at his proffered palm. Casey narrowed his eyes at her hesitation, then leaned forward and wrapped his arm around her waist, lifting her from the plane with one arm. He pulled her against his body, held her there for a long moment. His heart thudded against her ribcage, and his thick arm coiled around her waist like a serpent, hard, strong, and unmoving. She found herself unable to look away from him, his pale, sky-blue eyes captivating her attention. Suddenly, she was all too aware of this man, of his scent: engine oil, alcohol, cigarettes, faint cologne.

Something tensed in her, her heart clenching, her body becoming wired and attuned and sensitive. Her palms were flat on his chest, her arms barred vertically between them.

She was also aware that her feet were suspended nearly a foot off the ground.

"Put me down...please," she whispered.

His hands were on her hips then, and she was lowered slowly to the ground, sliding down the length of his body. For a reason she didn't want to think about, she didn't step back from him right away. His heat radiated against her and his eyes held her in place, his mammoth frame blocked out the world and her thoughts and her fears and her past and everything except this ridiculous moment of mesmerized captivation.

Then a breeze swept over them, bringing the tang of brine and the sweet musk of fresh rain, and Lani was shaken awake, brought out of her hypnotized state. She forced herself to step past him and stalk down the dock, cursing herself under her breath.

"Lani." His voice stopped her.

She turned to glance over her shoulder. "Yeah?"

He held her backpack in one huge hand. "Might need this."

She crossed the space between them, hating how her heartbeat ratcheted up as she drew nearer to him. She took the backpack from him, careful not to brush his hand with hers.

"Thanks," she mumbled, and turned away once more.

He let her get off the dock before he called out again. "Know where you're going?"

She stopped, hung her head, and cursed out loud. "Toward the lights?" She sounded petulant.

He chuckled, and she heard the seaplane's door close, and the brief rustle of a rope around a piling. Then he was creaking across the dock and in the sand beside her. Sand sloughed away beneath his feet, covering hers.

"Wouldn't make it too far. Jungle gets thick if you miss the path."

"I grew up on Hawaii. I think I'd be okay in the jungle." She still sounded petulant, damn it.

His chuckle was another deep rumble, and then his fingers curled around her elbow. His touch was like sandpaper on her skin. She flinched at his touch, refusing to acknowledge the fact that her breath was caught in her throat.

"You sure are twitchy. I ain't gonna hurt you, darlin'." He pulled her into a walk as he talked, and he seemed to know exactly where he was going, even though she couldn't see her feet in front of her.

She wasn't twitchy — she just didn't like and didn't understand why her body kept reacting so strongly to this bear of a man. He made her feel things she hadn't felt in a long time. Not since leaving Rafael, and even with him, it had been a while since she felt such strong feelings, such powerful physical reactions to simple things like a hand on her elbow.

He guided her in silence through a pitch-black section of jungle. She sensed trees on both sides, heard the palm leaves swaying in the wind, but couldn't see anything whatsoever.

"Path dips a bit up ahead. Watch your step, darlin'." His voice was an intimate growl in her ear.

She still couldn't figure out his accent. "Where are you from, Casey?" The question slipped out before she could stop it.

He laughed. "I ain't from anywhere in particular. I been all over. Told you that."

"You don't like to answer questions, do you?" Lani said, exasperation bleeding into her words.

"Nope."

"I meant your accent. It's strange. I can't place it."

He laughed. "Oh, that. I was born in Texas, lived there till I graduated high school. I also spent a good bit of time in Ireland. I got a bit of a Texas drawl, but I also got some Irish in there, too."

"That makes sense. I just couldn't figure it out. Sometimes you sound like you just finished roping a steer, and other times I expect you to call me 'lassie.'"

He snorted. "I said Ireland, not Scotland. And I never roped a steer in my life."

A few more steps in silence, and then another question slipped out of Lani's mouth unbidden. "How'd you end up in Ireland? The Army?"

"You ask a lot of questions, pixie-girl. I lived in Ireland after I got out of the Army. A buddy from my Ranger unit was from there."

"I'm not a pixie," Lani snapped.

Of course, he just chuckled. Then he dropped the bomb. "So, Kailani. Who are you running from?"

She stumbled at his words, and his strong hand caught her waist to keep her upright. "I'm not—no one. Why would you think I'm running?"

She felt his gaze boring into her, despite the darkness. A tiny, distant orange-ish glow ahead of them grew larger and brighter.

"You got no luggage, for one thing, just one tiny backpack. You were in *that* airport, for another. You only end up there if you're going to Seeker's Island, or inland. Or if you're running. You're here, on this island, with nowhere to stay, dick for money, and you're twitchy. All that equals to running from someone."

"I'm not twitchy. I just don't like being touched."

"Well, I don't believe that for a second, but I ain't gonna argue with you, *lassie*." Amusement laced his voice.

It was then that Lani finally realized his hand had never left her waist. She blushed in the darkness and sped up to get out of his touch.

"I'm not running. I'm just…getting away."

"And the difference would be what?"

"No one is looking for me." Damn the sadness in her voice.

He didn't answer for several steps. "So what are you getting away from, then?"

"Life. Betrayal."

"Your man cheated on you, huh?"

She stumbled again. That wasn't a sob, it was just…a cough. His hand on her waist steadied her and sent her pulse racing and frightened her.

"Yeah." Her whisper was barely audible in the jungle.

"Stupid of him. Oughta be kicked in the balls for being such a dumbass." His hand stayed on her waist, and she let it.

Why she let his hand stay on her waist, she wasn't sure, other than the fact that it comforted her somehow.

"I did kick him in the balls, actually."

He laughed. "Really?"

She nodded. "Caught him in bed with a contest organizer's assistant. He followed me out of the room, and when he tried to tell me it wasn't what I thought, I kicked him in the sack. 'Cause shit, I know what fuckin' look like, and they were fuckin'. You tell me some shit I wouldn'ta believed dat wen in little kid time, you tellin' me I'm stupid. Deserve a good kick in the balls." She'd slipped back into the way she'd spoken as a teen on the streets of town side, the way she'd spoken before the contests and the gold medals and the press, before she'd buried her past.

Casey just grunted his agreement. They'd come to a stop in a clearing in the jungle. There was a little hut, the kind of thing you'd expect to see on a tropical island, no walls, four wood posts holding up a thatch roof. A flickering streetlight hung from a power line suspended across the clearing, providing the orange glow she'd seen. A pair of dirty, thin, white feet were propped up on a table, while the rest of the body was hidden by a golf cart in which he or she was lying down.

A snore rose from the cart, which turned to a snort of surprise when Casey kicked the side. "Who—wha?" A gangly, skinny, redheaded kid of maybe twenty or so sat up in the Jeep, rubbing his eyes. "Oh, Casey, it's you. Sorry I fell asleep. Mrs. Adams told me you were supposed to be back tonight and to wait for you."

Casey frowned. "Shit, Carl. Didn't need to wait for me. Ain't that far of a walk."

Carl frowned. "You ever try to argue with Mrs. Adams?"

Casey laughed. "Good point." He gestured to Lani with the hand that was no longer on Lani's waist. "This here is Lani. Lani, this is Carl."

Lani recognized the expression on Carl's face, the hopeful surprise as he fumbled to his feet and swept his hand through his hopelessly bushy red hair. "Hi, Lani. Nice to meet you." He shook her hand, holding on just a bit too long. "How long will you be here? On the island, I mean. Of course I meant the island, I mean, where else would I mean, right? I'm just asking because I think Mrs. Adams has a nice room she could let you, if that's where you're going, of course. I can take you anywhere else you might need to go, though, so just ask, 'cause I know just about everywhere on the Island—"

"Carl," Casey interrupted.

"Yeah?" He paused midstream and glanced up at Casey.

"Shut up. You're babbling, and she's tired. Just drive us to Sunseekers'."

"Sure—sure thing, Case." He blushed red and stumbled around the front of the Jeep to get in the driver's seat.

Casey took the backpack from Lani and set it on the passenger seat, then lifted Lani by the waist into the back seat. He settled himself in next to her, his weight pushing the golf cart down toward the ground. Lani's skin tingled where his hands had touched her skin between her tank top and her khaki shorts.

"I'm short, Casey. Not helpless." She glared at him as the golf cart sped away through the darkness.

It hadn't escaped Lani that Casey's behavior toward Carl was, in an almost-subtle way, possessive. It had hinted that Lani was with Casey without coming right out and saying so. She wasn't sure whether to be angry at his presumption, or grateful that it had saved her from any more awkward advances by Carl. As tired as she was, as flustered by Casey as she was, the last thing Lani needed was the fumbling flirtation of a cute and well-meaning but hopelessly gangly kid like Carl.

"I know," Casey said, smirking at her. "You're just fun to toss around."

She couldn't think of an answer that wouldn't turn the conversation into innuendo, so she settled for an exasperated huff, crossing her arms under her breasts. Which, of course, only prompted another tympanic chuckle.

Considering it was a bit after eleven at night, the town was surprisingly still well-lit and alive, a couple bars competing for the patronage of the locals and the tourists, old-looking streetlamps illuminating a quaint downtown area. The cart buzzed through the town and swerved down a side street, skidding to a stop in front of a large yellow Victorian house. Carl left the motor running, and didn't get out. Casey hopped out and grabbed Lani's backpack. Before she could even lift her backside off the seat, Casey had his hands around her waist and was lifting her out and settling her on the ground.

Lani made a sound of exasperation in her throat, spinning in place to smack Casey on the shoulder. "Goddammit, Casey. Quit doing that. I can get out of a goddamn car on my own."

Casey laughed outright. "Sure you can. You're cute when you're pissed, y'know that?"

"And you're cute when you're not talking," Lani retorted.

Carl snorted and then paled when Casey shot him a warning glare. "Guess I'll be heading home now," Carl muttered, and shot away in the Jeep, tires flinging bits of gravel.

Casey led Lani into the lobby of the Sunseekers' Inn. The room was darkened, although there was enough ambient light for Lani to see the sort of kitschy island knickknacks one would expect from a place like this.

"Mrs. Adams is asleep by now," Casey said, reaching over the counter to snag a key from a drawer. "I'll get you into your room, and we'll settle up with her in the morning."

Lani frowned. "Shouldn't we wake her up?"

Casey shook his head. "I made the mistake of waking her up by accident once. It wasn't pretty. I don't care to repeat it. There's only one room open right now anyway."

He held Lani's backpack slung from one shoulder, so she was forced to go along with him down the hallway. He wiggled the key into a yellow-painted door and pushed it open, flicking on a light as he entered. The room was tiny, a queen bed taking up most of the space, with a sliding glass door along one side, and a bathroom and a closet forming one corner. A bureau of drawers opposite the foot of the bed with a twenty-year-old TV set on top of it made the rest of the room. The bed had a quilt that looked suspiciously homemade…and warm.

Suddenly, Lani was exhausted. Passed-out drunk sleep just wasn't very refreshing.

"You look like you're about to fall over where you stand, darlin'." Casey set her backpack on the bed and stood facing her.

"I am," she admitted. "I'm coming from Maine. I took a train from Portland to New York, and a bus from New York to St. Louis, and then a little charter plane from there to the airport where you met me. I've been traveling nonstop, without sleep, for over seventy-two hours."

"Except for that part where you passed out," Casey said.

She tilted her head from side to side. "That doesn't count as sleep. Ever passed out like that? It's not at all like a good night's sleep. Or even a nap."

Casey laughed. "I have, all too frequently. And you're right." He moved past her to crack open the sliding glass door, sliding the screen door in place.

A light, salty breeze and the shushing of the ocean washed over Lani. For the first time in the six months since she'd left Hawaii, she didn't feel quite as homesick. Casey's presence behind her was both nerve-wracking and comforting.

She turned in place and found herself staring up, up, and up into his pale blue eyes. "Thanks for…you know…getting me out of that airport."

"It was my pleasure," he said, then, absurdly, reached down with a forefinger to brush a wayward strand of her black hair out of her mouth. "Mrs. Adams serves breakfast until ten or so, usually. If you're still asleep after that, there's places in town to get a good breakfast."

Lani was frozen solid by his finger's touch on her cheek, and it wasn't until his broad frame was filling the doorway three feet away that she remembered to breathe. He was gone, and she felt the strength flood out of her. After he was gone, she noticed he'd set her one hundred-dollar bill on the bed next to her backpack.

She barely made it onto the bed before sleep overtook her.

***

She woke with sunlight bathing her, warming her. She was still in the same clothes she'd left Portland in, and she was lying diagonally across the bed. She rolled off the bed, stretching as she stared out the patio door. The ocean glinted blue-white not far away, and the familiar scents and sounds of the Pacific Ocean made her feel as if things might, somehow, someday, be okay.

She'd spent the last six months refusing to think about Rafael or his betrayal. She'd gone through the stages of a breakup, of course, getting mad and then sad, crying and drinking herself stupid with friends across the country. Now, while she wasn't exactly home, she was somewhere like it, and reality was crashing back down around her.

She had nothing. The car she drove on Oahu and the house she'd lived in was in Rafael's name. Her clothes, her trophies, her favorite surfboard, which she'd carved herself from a koa tree, everything was back on Oahu. And she just couldn't stomach the thought of seeing him again, seeing him with that stupid slut Allison.

Lani put those thoughts aside once more and took a long, hot shower, washing the grime of travel away. She stepped out of the narrow shower stall and was drying off when a short, heavy knock resounded on her door.

She knew who it was. Only two people even knew she was here, possibly three if Casey had spoken to the innkeeper, Mrs. Adams. Lani debated. She was soaking wet, and this towel was barely big enough to fit around her torso. She could ignore Casey's knock until she was dressed. She should. She didn't want him to see her like this.

It was…dangerous.

But there he was, pounding on the door as if he'd like to break it down. "It's past noon, Lani. I heard the water running, so I know you're up."

She wasn't aware of having made the decision, but the towel was wrapped beneath her armpits and she was swinging the door open. Her mouth went dry. Casey was wearing a pair of navy blue board shorts and nothing else. His body…holy hell. Mile after mile of muscle. Not cut muscle, not toned bodybuilder muscle, but the heavy and hard bulk of a naturally powerful man used to hard labor. She'd stepped back when she opened the door, and he'd followed her in. He was mere inches from her, and suddenly, she felt tinier than ever before. She was used to being the shortest girl in any room, used to looking up at people, reaching up to cabinets. She'd always made up for it with a dominant personality, fiery and fierce and funny. But Casey, he was…so huge. His chest and stomach were coated in fine, curly reddish hairs, his forearms, too. He had the Army Ranger insignia tattooed on his left pectoral.

She barely came to his breastbone, and his eyes were blazing on hers, taking in the rivulets of water streaking down her face and neck. His gaze followed a bead of water as it slid down between her breasts underneath the towel.

She had to crane her neck and stare nearly vertical to meet his eyes. "You're too fucking tall."

He grinned. "And you're too fuckin' short." His smile took the insult out of his words. Her breath stuck in her throat then, because his thumb was brushing across her clavicle, wiping beads of water away. "And wet."

"I just—just took a shower." She hated how that came out, nervous, breathy. She hated that she didn't like it when his hand dropped back to his side.

"Get dressed, pixie. There's some nice swells out there. But you need breakfast first." He turned away and let himself out. "Meet me out front."

Some nice swells. Lani hadn't surfed in six months, the longest she'd ever gone in her whole life. Surfing reminded her of Rafael, of course. She'd met him at a contest in Australia. They'd surfed together every day for five years.

She dug a yellow bikini out of her backpack, wrapped a purple flower-print sarong around her waist, brushed her hair, and left it loose to dry. Black Nike sports sandals, her favorite footwear, and her purse. No, scratch the purse. She dug her wallet from the purse and slipped the loop over her wrist, and stuck her sunglasses on her face. No makeup, because

Casey could take her or leave her as she was.

Casey was waiting in the driver's seat of a golf cart, which seemed to be the only means of transportation on the island. He didn't say anything as she climbed into the passenger seat, but his gaze was appreciative. He tapped the pedal and the cart darted away. He took her to a little café just off the beach, drinking coffee while she ate an omelet.

He didn't talk, didn't ply her with questions, didn't check a cell phone. He just stared out at the water, sipping from the chipped white mug. Lani, after the first few minutes of silence, found it peaceful.

Rafael had always needed to fill the silence with his own voice.

When she was done, Casey tossed a twenty on the table and took Lani's hand in his rough paw. "Come on," he said, pulling her toward the water. "Surf's up."

Lani tugged free and stopped beneath a palm swaying in a stiff ocean breeze. "I don't know."

Casey frowned at her, then sank down to sit cross-legged just inside the shade from the palm tree. "I thought you were a surfer."

"I was…I am." She sat beside him, facing the water.

"Then what's the problem? Have an accident?"

She shook her head. "I met Rafael during a competition. Surfing was our thing. We'd surf together at dawn, every single day. I haven't surfed since he—since I left him."

Casey just stared at her for a long moment. "So?"

"So? What do you mean, *so*? It reminds me of him. It's hard."

"You still in love with him?"

"No. I mean, it still hurts that he betrayed me, but I'm as over him as I'm gonna get."

"You surfed before him, you'll surf after him. Don't let him take away the thing you love, just 'cause he's a dumbass who don't know what a prize he had." Casey spoke the stunning words to the ocean, not looking at her as he said them.

Lani turned on the sand to face him. "I'm no prize." She was facing him, but couldn't look at him. She watched a tiny white spider crawl across the sand.

"That what he said?" His voice was quiet, but his gaze was sharp.

"He didn't have to. He was better than me. He was a better surfer. Came from a better life, had a great family. Better grades at UH. So good-looking it was stupid. People wanted him for movies, commercials, endorsements. I never knew why he was with me. Why he married me."

He looked up sharply at her. "You were married?"

"Am married. At least till he signs. He might've already. I haven't had an address since I left, and I had my mail delivered to a post office box back home. I mailed the papers to him. So until I go back to Oahu, I won't know if he signed off."

"Would he draw it out?"

Lani shrugged. "I don't think so. I agreed to everything, just to be done."

"He fucked you over?" Casey was drawing marks in the sand with a finger.

Lani shook her head. "No. I left, so he got the house and the car, but he gave me a good chunk of change as a settlement. I'll have to appear in court for it to be final, of course. But, for the most part, it's over."

"Relieved?"

Lani didn't answer for a long time, and Casey didn't try to fill the silence. "I don't think 'relieved' is the right word. I thought things were great. I loved him. He…he was all I had. I never suspected. I mean…it was just such a shock. He wasn't gone a lot, wasn't texting all the time or doing anything suspicious. Things between us seemed fine, normal or whatever. I mean, it wasn't like he suddenly stopped wanting me." She paused and looked at Casey, gauging his reaction. His gaze was hard, angry. "Then I came home early one day from a photo shoot for a surfing rag, and he was in our bed with Allison Hoffman. I left, filed the divorce papers from the Big Island, and never went back. So no, I'm not relieved. I don't know what to do. Where to go. I met him when I was eighteen. His family was my—my family. Now I'm just…lost."

She wasn't sure why she was telling him all this, except his alert silence seemed to pull it out of her. He was focused on her, listening.

"You're not lost, Lani." His voice was confident, calm. "You're here. On Seeker's Island. You're you. You love to surf, you have options. You can do anything, be anyone, be *with* anyone you want. It's not an end, it's a beginning."

Lani felt something hot on her face. Stupid tears. "I wish it was that easy, Casey."

"It is. I mean, I'm not saying it's that *easy*, but it's that *simple*." He stood up. "The first step is to go surfing with me."

His hand appeared in front of her face. She could see the calluses, the grease embedded in the lines of hand and under his nails, so deeply ingrained in the skin of his hand that she knew it would never come completely clean, however much he scrubbed.

She took his hand and let him lift her to her feet. He smiled at her, then pulled her by the hand across the sand, around a clump of trees to a surf shop. An old man with smooth, swarthy skin and long, thick black hair sat watching a reality show.

He waved lazily to Casey. "'Sup, Case?"

"Hey, Billy. Can we borrow some boards?" Casey slapped palms with the man, who Lani thought might have been stoned.

"Sure thing, man." He seemed to notice Lani for the first time. "Oh, hey. You're new."

She shrugged. "Yeah. Just got here last night."

Billy stared at Lani as if trying to remember something, his eyes squinting almost shut. "I know you."

Lani shook her head. "No, I don't think so. I've never been here before."

"No, I know that. I mean, I know who you are. But I can't remember why." He turned away, searching the surf shop as if trying to find a clue among the brightly colored boards and Billabong tees.

His gaze settled on a magazine, the surfing magazine Lani had been shooting the cover for when Rafe had betrayed her. There she was, wearing a pale pink bikini, lying in the sand on top of her hand-carved board, late afternoon sunlight bathing her dark skin golden, the very same pair of Ray-Bans she wore in the photograph were on her head now. Her gaze in the photo was wistful, almost longing. You could just barely make out the white crest of a crashing wave in the background.

"You're Kailani Kekoa," Billy said. "I know you. I told you I did. I watched you kick everyone's ass at the Quicksilver Pro."

Lani laughed incredulously. "You must be the one single person in the whole world who could recognize me on sight. You're funny."

Billy frowned. "No way, man, I know that's not true. I used to write for *Surfer*. I've followed your career forever."

"Wait, you're Billy Redhawk?"

"Yeah, man. That's me." He grinned and shook her hand.

Billy had done an article on her a few years back, before she'd gotten any kind of real media attention as a surfer. It was Billy's article that had propelled her into the spotlight, or at least as much of a spotlight as pro surfing ever got.

"That article you wrote. It pretty much made my career." She leaned in to hug Billy, and could have sworn she heard Casey growl behind her.

"Hey, man. I was just writing like I saw it. And I saw you surfing just for fun, you know, practicing. On Oahu. You were pulling some sick moves, just all alone out there on some crazy waves. I'd seen you compete a few times, and you were still great and whatever, but that summer, you were on fire."

Lani remembered. It was the year she'd met Rafael. She'd finally been emancipated, and had gotten the payouts from her previous comp wins, which she couldn't touch on her own until she was legally an adult. She'd found a sense of freedom finally. Then she met Rafael in Sydney before the Quicksilver Pro, and she'd found love. All this had translated into the best surfing of her life. She'd taken the circuit by storm, garnering win after win, and even when she didn't win on points, the style in which she placed second or third had people talking.

Billy lifted himself out of the chair and sidled into a back room, disappearing without a word of explanation. Lani glanced askance at Casey.

"He's an odd bird. Moved here a few years ago, opened this shop, and spends his time watching TV and writing a book he won't tell anyone anything about. Smokes a lot of pot, if you couldn't tell."

Lani laughed. "Yeah, I can tell." She wrinkled her nose. "You smoke?"

Casey stuck his tongue out in a grimace of disgust. "Hell, no. You?"

She felt an absurd sense of relief that he didn't smoke anything besides cigarettes. "No way. My hus—my ex…Rafael smoked a lot, and it always bugged me. He'd surf high. Said it made him loose. I always thought it made him sloppy. He could have been so much better if he wasn't high all the time." She turned away and watched the curling waves crash. "He knew how much I hated him smoking. He never cared."

Casey nodded as if he knew what she meant. "Bad history with it, huh?"

She glanced sharply at him. "What do you know?"

"Nothing." He held up his hands in front of him. "Just guessing. Based on your reaction, I mean."

Lani sighed. "Yeah. Not pot necessarily, just drugs in general. My mom was a meth-head. She'd do anything she could get her hands on, but her drug of choice was meth. I can't tell you how many times I cleaned her up after she'd passed out, drunk and high and useless. I was fending for myself by the time I was nine. I was on the streets by thirteen."

Casey's gaze was knowing. "No dad?"

She shook her head. "Nah. He took off before I was born. I tried to find his ass dat wen I was a teenager, but no one even knew him. Could find no record he ever even exist. Just nothin'." She bit her lip in irritation at her slip into vernacular, and moved out of the shop into the sun. "Don't matter anymore. I'm over him, and I'm over Mom. I'm over it all."

Casey let her walk away, then followed her, stood next to her silently for a long time. Billy seemed to have vanished permanently.

"I grew up in the system," Casey said. "Never had no mom or dad. Bounced from foster home to foster home around the Dallas area for my whole life. Soon as I graduated high school, I joined the Army. I was told my ma was a hooker. Nobody knew my dad. So…you know, I get it."

Lani heard him. Heard what he wasn't saying. His voice said he wasn't over it, but he was okay with it, and he knew what she'd been through. After a few minutes of companionable wave-watching, Billy reappeared, redder in the eye and stinking of pot. He had two boards, one under each arm. He handed one to Casey, a huge longboard. The other he held vertically in front of himself, proffering it to Lani.

She whistled. It was a handmade board like her own, carved from koa, polished and waxed to perfection.

"This is gorgeous, Billy. You make it?"

Billy sputtered. "Me? Hell, no. I can't even whittle a stick. I know a guy in Kaneohe who makes boards in the old way, you know, with shells and shit. Like in that movie with the penguins. He made this for me as a thank you for doing a piece on him."

Lani handed it back to Billy. "I can't take it, Billy, but thank you."

Billy seemed confused. "It's just a board, man. I mean, it's a nice board, but it's still just a surfboard. No one's ever used it, and I figure you could do it justice."

Lani shook her head. "You have any clue how much this is worth? I know that guy in Kaneohe. He taught me how to carve my own board. This board is a collector's item, Billy."

Billy nodded. "I know. But you're Kailani Kekoa." His brown eyes seemed lucid, seeing into her. "Something tells me you need this board more than me."

Lani sensed that to refuse would hurt his feelings, so she took it and ran her hands along its sides, then glanced up at Billy. "Well…thanks. I mean, thank you isn't enough. This is amazing. I'll drop it off when we're done."

Billy just waved her off and unmuted his *Real World* rerun.

She and Casey set out toward the water. Casey jogged into the surf, tossed his board down, and lay across it, paddling toward the horizon. Lani stood just above the waterline, board planted in the sand, hesitating. She had a piece of home in her hands, an opportunity to reclaim a part of herself. So why was she hesitating?

Because she knew if she went out there, she'd start falling for Casey. She'd known him for less than twenty-four hours, but she knew. Just like she'd known about Rafael. She'd spent four hours with him, surfing and talking on the beach, and she'd known she would fall in love with him.

Casey was having the same effect on her. Well, no, that wasn't exactly true. Rafael had charmed her. Worked her. Flirted and romanced her. Pulled her into his orbit. Sucked her under as if the force of his personality and determination to have her was a riptide carrying her out to sea. She'd gone willingly, since he was beautiful and an amazing surfer. He had a family, and they'd welcomed her. That right there had been enough.

Casey? So different. He wasn't trying at all. Not overtly. He teased, he flirted, he sympathized, but something told her he wasn't playing a game. She wasn't sure what he wanted, but she knew, in her soul, if she went out into the water and surfed with Casey…she wouldn't come out the same woman.

Casey sat straddling his board, way out on the water, waiting. He didn't rush her, just sat waiting.

Lani had a vision then. If she didn't go out there, she'd go back to Oahu and pretend to forgive Rafael. He'd wanted to reconcile at first. Right up until the last moment, when they were divvying up their life via e-mail, he kept trying to tell her it was a mistake, he loved her, he missed her, blah blah blah. Lani had known better. She'd heard it in his voice the one time she'd returned his phone call. He'd been wheedling, convincing. Playing her. And Lani wasn't having any of it. She'd realized, once she left Hawaii completely, that he'd never loved her. He'd liked, enjoyed her, been attracted to her. But it wasn't love. He'd spent five years with her, married her, but…she still hadn't been enough for him.

If she went out and surfed…it would be a beginning. Maybe nothing would happen. Maybe they'd be friends, and she'd just stay on Seeker's Island and find something to do.

Or maybe she'd let him seduce her. And she'd get her heart broken all over again.

CHAPTER THREE

She untied the sarong and tossed it to the sand, leaving her sandals and wallet on top of it. One foot into the water, then both. Up to her calves, the board floating next to her. Then Casey smiled at her, and something in the carefree curve of his lips settled her nerves. She pushed the board ahead of her, lay down on it, and paddled out to Casey. He didn't say anything, just sat staring at her, letting his gaze rake appreciatively over her body, then back to her eyes.

Then he leaned over and pushed her off her board, laughing as he peeled away to catch the wave rising up behind them. He crouched on the board, arms wide for balance, and then stood up slowly. Lani held on to her board and rode the wave, watching Casey carve lazily just ahead of the crest. He wasn't a showy surfer, or even very good, but he enjoyed it. He rode easily, comfortable in his balance.

Lani settled back astride her board, paddling out a bit farther to watch the water. There. She felt the energy in the sea change, felt the wave before it was visible. She lengthened her strokes, felt the shift upward faster, knelt on the board, found her balance, and settled into the familiar crouch.

Home. Now, she was home.

The wave was huge, curling and still rising. She let herself ride down it, then carved back up, feeling the water spray her face and soak her hair, felt her heart swell. A grin spread across her face, lighting her up from within. She caught a glimpse of Casey sitting on his board near the shore, watching. There was Billy, standing with his hand shading his eyes. A few other people on shore. She knew when she was being watched.

The wave was going to crest soon; time to ride the barrel. She sliced in an S-curve along the bending side of the wave, jerked the tip skyward, and felt the glee and the lifting stomach of going airborne, clutched the side and tasted salt and set the board down in a perfect slip down the side, crouching as the barrel wrapped around her.

She rode it out, and then, when crest met sea all around her, she let the ocean take her and rolled with it, clutching the board and letting it drag her to the surface. And of course, when she came gasping into the air, Casey was sitting on his board next to her.

"That was awesome, Lani! Nice ride."

She slid astride her board and slicked her hair back. "Thanks. It was great to be back out on the water." She met his eyes. "Seriously, thank you. I probably would've been too chicken to go out if you hadn't made me."

"I didn't make you." His eyes were intense, full of a thousand things she knew he'd never say.

She felt the next wave growing, and turned to meet it.

They surfed for hours, until Lani was sore and exhausted and exhilarated. They finally left the water when Casey's stomach growled loud enough that Lani heard it over the crash of the waves.

A handwritten note was weighted onto the fabric of her sarong by a colored glass stone, the kind of thing tourists used to string onto necklaces.

Kailani,

Keep the board. I always knew I was just holding on to it until it was time to give it away. Watching you surf is payment enough. Maybe that sounds creepy. I hope it doesn't, because I'm not a creeper. I just like watching good surfing.

All the best,

Billy

P.S. Casey is a good man.

Lani read the note through several times, her eyes tearing up. She'd grown up never owning a damn thing except the clothes on her back. Then she'd met Makani on a beach, watched him carving a hunk of tree with primitive tools. She'd watched, rapt, as he slowly and painstakingly turned a tree into a surfboard. He'd ignored her completely, but when she finally stood up to leave, knees sore from sitting in one place from sunset to moonrise, he'd met her eyes, nodded at her.

"You come back tomorrow," he'd said. "I show you this."

So she'd gone back, day after day. She'd never asked, but he always endeavored to feed her. He showed her how to carve boards, using age-old techniques, and he did so without ever having said a word. He kept her busy, and she was thankful, because if she was busy cleaning up shavings and straightening tools and carving, she wasn't on the streets with the drug dealers and pimps. Makani had been the one to pay her fees to enter her first competition.

When she stormed out of the house, Rafael in her wake, she'd gone straight to Makani, and he'd turned Rafael away too, crossing his broad forearms over his thick chest and shaking his head imperturbably. Rafael hadn't been fool enough to argue.

Even now, Makani was the only person in all of Hawaii she missed.

She'd left everything she owned behind except a phone, a charger, some clothes, and her purse; everything else had belonged to Rafael. Even the settlement money was his money. She hadn't been in a competition for over a year, and she'd used the money from the *Surfer* shoot to live on for the last six months. Now she was back to nothing.

And something about being given this board was wreaking havoc on her emotions.

Casey's hands descended to rest on her shoulders, a comforting weight. "He's a nice guy, Billy Redhawk."

"And what he says about you? Is that true?" Lani twisted in place to look up at Casey.

Casey shrugged uncomfortably. "I'd guess that's something you have to decide."

"You gave me my money back," Lani said.

Casey frowned. "Well, I shouldn't have taken it in the first place. You were a person in need, and it was wrong of me to try to profit from it."

Lani's hands had ended up flat on his chest. This was entirely too familiar. Too pleasant. Too right. But yet she wasn't pulling away. If anything, she was being drawn closer by the heat of his body, the strength in his arms, the confident compassion in his eyes. She was being lured in by the way he'd surfed with her for hours and never made it a competition, never pushed the boundaries between them. Every time she and Rafael surfed together, he had turned it into a contest. Who could pull off the best trick, who could get the most air, who could ride the barrel longest. It kept her sharp for contests. But it had strained her. They were close in skill, and if she beat him, he would get pissy. But she liked to win; it was hammered into her psyche. She had to be the best. To survive as she had, she couldn't show weakness.

Casey dragged in a deep breath, as if summoning courage, and then let her go, stepping back. "Go to dinner with me?"

"Like…a date?"

Casey grinned. "It could be, if you want it to be."

Lani shook her head. "I honestly don't know what I want."

Casey closed the space between them, and Lani forgot to breathe. "Liar." His voice was pitched low, so she had to strain to hear. "You do too know what you want. You're just afraid of it."

"I'm not afraid of you."

"I didn't say—" Casey cut himself off with a slow smile as he realized the implications of what Lani had just said. "Then what are you afraid of?"

Lani swallowed hard, and then let the truth out. "Getting hurt. I don't know you. This feels like insta-love and it scares me."

Casey laughed. "Insta-love?"

Lani rolled her eyes. "In romance novels, the characters meet and fall hopelessly in love within the first fifty pages, even though they just met."

"And you're falling in insta-love with me?"

Lani sighed. "No. Just...god. Forget I said anything." She turned away before any more embarrassing truths escaped. "I'm gonna shower. Dinner sounds good."

She'd taken about three steps before she found herself tugged backward by Casey's finger hooked in the back string of her bikini top. "I don't think so. You're not getting off that easy."

Lani twisted, trying to get away. "Let go! You're gonna make my top come off."

She couldn't see his face, but she knew he was grinning. "And that would just be *tragic*." He pulled her backward, and she forced herself to take backward steps toward him. Finally, her back was to his front, and she felt herself tense. "How about I make this easier on you? I'll give you a choice."

She held her breath, wanting to turn and look up at him, but refusing to let herself.

"I'll be waiting outside your door in one hour. If you come out of your room, dressed for a nice dinner, then I'll know you're letting yourself have what you want, fears be damned. If you don't, I'll make sure we're friends. Just friends. It's your choice."

***

Lani swept the last lock of hair into a bobby pin at the back of her head, leaving most of her thick black hair free, just the bangs on top pulled away. She adjusted her dress, which she'd just bought at the thrift store in town. She'd used most of the hour finding the dress, since she had nothing nice of her own, which had only left about twenty minutes for her to shower and get ready. It felt worth it, though. The burnt umber–colored dress was a simple no-name thing, but it fit perfectly, hugging her generous curves and falling just above her knees, and cut low enough to be sexy but high enough not to be slutty. Plus, it had only cost her twenty bucks.

She'd shaved, put on makeup, and all-around made herself feel like a woman again, after six months of slumming it on couches and feeling barely human, let alone like a sultry, sexy woman. She wasn't sure where this was going with Casey, but it never hurt to be prepared.

Casey was wearing a pair of faded blue jeans and a white button-down shirt, sleeves rolled up to his elbows, and a worn brown leather belt. The shirt was tight enough to show his incredibly, gloriously, absurdly muscled physique. His hair was damp and left messy, and as she drew near to him, she caught a whiff of cologne, soap, and cigarettes. Strangely, that last scent didn't bother her like she'd thought it would. It was starting to become a familiar part of Casey-ness.

Just before she left, Lani had changed from the flats she'd originally chosen into a pair of wedge sandals that added four inches to her height. The wedges were a ridiculous use of space in her backpack, but as a short woman, she just couldn't fathom being without height-adding shoes.

Now, with an extra four inches, the top of Lani's head came almost to his breastbone.

"You showed up," Casey noted.

"Despite being eight thousand feet tall, you're kind of a nice guy." Lani gave him a playful shove, and failed to make him even sway in place. She shoved him again, harder this time, frowning; he still didn't budge. "Geez! Huge much?"

Casey laughed. "It's not my fault you're a pixie." He put an index finger to her shoulder and gave her a nudge, forcing her to take a step backward.

Lani growled, feeling her fierce competitive nature take over. She set her legs, placed both palms on his chest and pushed as hard as she could, putting her whole body into the shove. Casey, to her credit, actually had to step back, albeit laughing. He then wrapped his hands around her waist and lifted her into the air, pulling her flush against him.

Suddenly, the game wasn't so funny to Lani anymore. She was forced to wrap her legs around his waist and hold on to his neck as he held her in place, his hands now on the swell of her ass. She was breathless then, feeling the blood rush to her head, between her thighs. With her legs around his waist, she could just barely hook her feet together, and now her eyes were level with his, and his lips were inches away, and her heart was hammering, and his mammoth size was intoxicating.

Powerful didn't begin to describe him, she realized. She was short, but she was stacked and not feather-light. He'd lifted her easily, and the way his hands were sliding across her backside…she squeezed with her legs, and his hands explored her ass more thoroughly.

He hadn't shaved, so his jaw was stubbled with golden-red fuzz. Before she knew what was happening, her palm was smoothing along his cheek, across his jawline and back up to his cheek. His face was getting closer, closer, and her heart was stuttering, hammering one moment and stopping the other. His eyes, palest blue and mesmerizing, held hers, waiting for her to demur.

Stop this? So not happening.

She'd never felt so alive, so safe. She'd always had to be strong, had to survive, had to protect herself. Even with Rafael she hadn't felt safe. Cared for, yes. Not alone, yes. Protected? Safe? Able to be vulnerable? No.

She barely knew Casey. She knew this. She didn't even know his last name. But she instinctively trusted him, and that was enough. Maybe this would be momentary, maybe it would be a one- or two-night thing. That wasn't how Lani normally did things, but then, for her, it had been Rafael her entire adult life, so there was no "normally" for her. This was uncharted territory for her. Was it moving too fast? Should she feel the kind of overwhelming desire for Casey that she did?

The desire was overwhelming, too. She was lost in it, drowning in it, subsumed by it. If he carried her back into the inn, she wouldn't stop him, despite her growling stomach.

On cue, however, her stomach gurgled so loud Casey laughed and set her down, somewhat reluctantly, Lani thought. She forced her own disappointment away and let him lead her on foot across the island to a beachside café.

After they'd ordered, Casey leaned back in his chair and dug his lighter out of his pocket, spinning the wheel idly with his thumb. "So, Lani. You feel better about the future?"

She gave a half-laugh, a sighing huff. "I feel better, but not about the future. Unfortunately, surfing doesn't actually solve problems. I still have no idea where I'm going to live or how, but I'm more hopeful that something will work out."

"You want to know what I think you should do?" Casey flicked the wheel so a spurt of flame pierced the early evening golden glow.

"Sure," Lani said, expecting a smart-ass answer. "Enlighten me."

He pocketed the lighter and leaned forward, covering her hands with his. "I think you should stay on Seeker's Island and give surfing lessons. Locals and tourists alike would pay good money to be taught how to surf by a world champion." His thumb rubbed circles around her knuckles. "I'd be your first customer."

"I thought you were broke."

He smirked. "I am. But I've got a shipment of supplies to ferry tomorrow, and that'll put me in a pretty good spot for a while. Plus, I've got some sky tours set up for the weekend."

"Sky tours?"

"Yeah, nothing crazy, just some flyovers of the island, things like that. Gonna take one guy out and let him fish off the floats for a bit."

At that moment, a parcel deliveryman, decked out in too-short shorts and a too-tight shirt, emerged from the main dining room, glancing around the outdoor patio with a stack of letters in his hand.

"Kelly Connelly?" The deliveryman's voice was loud and brash. "Lookin' for Kelly Connelly. She here?"

Casey shifted in his seat and scratched his forehead with his index finger. If Lani didn't know better, she'd think he was flushing either from embarrassment or from anger, perhaps a bit of both.

"Goddamn Henry Sykes," Casey muttered.

"What?" Lani asked, not sure if she'd heard him right.

Casey just shook his head and waved at the deliveryman, who came over and handed the stack of letters to Lani. "Here you go, Miss Connelly. I just need a signature here—"

Lani frowned in confusion. "I'm not Kelly Connelly. I don't know her."

Casey growled. "I'm Kelly Connelly," he rumbled, snatching the letters and the signature pad and scrawling his name. "Now fuck off, Jack."

Jack frowned at Casey. "Wait a sec, Casey. *You're* Kelly Connelly? I've had these damn letters for a week, thinking Kelly was a girl and she'd come in for them. I been looking over the whole damn island for—for you, I guess."

Casey shot Jack a glare that had the short, overweight, older man stumbling backward. "Yeah, Kelly Connelly, KC…Casey. Now fuck off. Please."

"No problem—"

"If you call me Kelly, you'll be shitting teeth for a week."

Lani stifled a snicker behind her hand, and then had to cover her laughter with a sip of ice water.

Casey glared at her. "What the hell is so funny?"

Lani let her laughter out. "Nothing. You. You're funny. You're threatening that poor man for no reason."

Jack had taken the interruption to scurry away, so now Casey's ire was directed at her. "I hate my name. It's why I go by Casey."

Lani laughed again. "There's nothing wrong with your name. I like it. I think I'll call you Kelly from now on."

His nostrils flared. "You'd better not. I'm serious. I *hate* that name. I ain't a bloody fuckin' girl."

"Come on, Kelly. It's just a name. I think it's cute."

Casey let out a stream of curse words under his breath. "Fuckin' Henry Goddamn Sykes."

Lani cocked an eyebrow at him. "Why do you keep saying that?"

"Henry Sykes is my buddy in Ireland. He thinks, like you, apparently, that I should just own my name, so he makes a point of sending me letters addressed to my real, full name wherever I go. People always seem to find out one way or another, usually because of fuckin' Henry's stupid-ass letters." Casey slugged back his ice water as if wishing it was something stronger, crunching ice and glaring out at the ocean.

Lani reached out and took one of his hands in both of hers. "I'm kidding, Casey. I won't call you Kelly if you really don't like it. Especially if you agree to stop referring to me as a pixie."

Casey relented, grinning at her. "I don't know. I might be willing to let you call me Kelly if that's the deal."

Lani just huffed in irritation. "You're incorrigible."

He winked at her. "You have no idea."

Their food came then, and they enjoyed a relaxed dinner together, their conversation wandering from their histories to life on an island, to some of Casey's stories as a Ranger.

Eventually, long after the sun had set, Casey paid the bill, and they strolled through the lowering twilight gloom. Somehow she found herself leaning into Casey's side as they walked, his hand draped down her side to rest easily on her hip. She let her arm snake around his waist, let her hands slip up under the trailing hem of his shirt. Her fingers skated up and down the hot skin of his side, around the waist of his jeans.

Then they were standing in the hallway between their rooms, an awkward silence descending between them.

"Look, Lani. I'd invite you into my room, but…" Casey shifted his weight from foot to foot, staring at Lani's hand cradled in one of his. "I just don't want you to think I'm pressuring you to move on before you're ready, or…something like that."

Lani frowned up at him. "Did I act like I thought you were

pressuring me earlier?"

He shrugged. "No, I just want you to be…sure."

Lani stepped closer to him, close enough that her breasts brushed his chest. "Sure about what, Casey?"

"This. You and me."

"Why wouldn't I be sure about it?"

Casey sighed. "You're probably gonna take this the wrong way, but try not to. From what you've told me, you've only ever been with that Rafael guy. You just met me. I don't want you to do this with me as a rebound and then regret it. I'm not saying you would, I'm just…I guess I'm trying to protect you from maybe making a decision you're not sure about."

"Is this what you want?" Lani asked. "Is this usual for you?"

Casey looked away, then back. "How about you come in and have a drink with me, and we'll talk about this." He opened his door, and Lani followed him in.

He poured them each a tumbler of whiskey from a square bottle and added a few ice cubes, handing Lani her glass and leaning back against the refrigerator.

Lani took a sip, then set it down, moving toward Casey. "I don't think I need to talk about it. I know I just asked you a question, but the answer doesn't really matter, honestly. I know you want this, and I don't care if this is a normal thing for you. I don't know where this is going for us, but I'm willing to take this one day at a time. I know I want this with you. I really do. It's not a rebound. If this had been a few months ago, maybe it would have been. Now? It's me moving on."

Casey took a long drink from his glass, then set it down on top of the fridge and wrapped his arms around Lani. "Just to be clear, what is the 'this' we're talking about, here?"

She grinned up at him. "Kiss me and find out."

Casey hesitated for a heartbeat, his pale eyes searching hers, then slid his hands down her back to cup her backside, lifted her up slowly, easily. His lips touched hers, gently at first. Just lips, initially, just his mouth on hers, tasting her lips, discovering. She wrapped her arms around his neck, exploring his nape and shoulders, holding him against her mouth, her legs tight around his waist.

She'd never liked being held like this before, but now…she couldn't imagine it any other way.

It was a long, delving first kiss. His tongue slipped between her lips and touched her teeth, found her tongue and tasted it. His hands roamed her backside, spurring the trembling heat in her belly into waves of need.

When the kiss broke, she leaned back and let him support her weight as she unbuttoned his shirt, pulled the sleeves off. She smiled greedily at the sight of his body, of the hard slabs and furrowed ridges of muscle. She smoothed her palms over his shoulders, down his chest to his stomach, turning her hands to face fingertips down.

They were moving, suddenly, as Casey strode toward the bed with Lani still wrapped around him. He twisted in place, sat down on the edge of the bed with Lani now sitting on his knees. His fingers brushed up her knees to her thighs, sliding the hem of her dress up as he went. She lifted slightly so the hem slid from beneath her, and then he was lifting the fabric over her head and tossing it to the floor.

He leaned back, propping his hands on the bed, and stared at her. His chest was rising and falling as he sucked in deep breaths, his eyes going hooded as he gazed at her.

Lani blushed under his scrutiny. "I didn't have any sexy lingerie, so I went with a bikini. Best I could do under short notice."

Casey sat forward, running his hands from knees to hips to ribs, and then his hands paused there, hesitating. "Lani, you're the sexiest woman I've ever seen. You don't need lingerie to turn me on. You do that just by being, just by breathing and being who you are."

His hands slid around her back, down her spine, then back up her sides, pausing at her ribs again. Lani reached up to the middle of her back where the skimpy bikini top was tied. She tugged on the knot, felt the weight of her breasts do the work of untying the top the rest of the way. The triangular bits of fabric fell away, and Lani had to fight her nerves, her instinct to cover herself with her arms. She kept her hands on her thighs, waiting. Casey wasn't breathing, and his hands tensed on her ribs. Lani reached up once more, this time to pull the bobby pins out of her hair, then arched her back and shook her hair out.

This time, Casey reacted. He growled in his chest, and as Lani was running her fingers through her hair, she felt a hot wet touch on the side of her breast. She moaned high in her throat, and her hand shot out to cup the back of Casey's head as he laved kisses around the circumference of her breast, then finally, finally, ran his tongue over her nipple. His fingers found her other breast, and then she was the one barely breathing, gasping as he pinched and kissed, thumbed and licked.

Lani scooted back on his knees, seeking access to his belt. She unbuckled it slowly, peeled it out of the loops, and set it aside. Her fingers found the snap of his jeans, then the zipper, and then she was rising in the air as he lifted up to slide the pants off, kicking them free, and he was naked beneath her.

Her breath hitched in her throat as her fingers closed around his erection. The unreal size of the man was consistent, that was for damn sure. She forced her eyes open and looked down. The sight of him, pink and rigid and veined and huge, made her whimper. Her eyes were locked wide open, and her fingers were skimming over him, up and down his unbelievable length, around his incredible thickness.

Then she met his eyes, and her hand froze on him as she saw the worry in his eyes.

"What is it, Casey?" she asked.

"You're just so tiny, Pixie. I don't want to hurt you." His voice was thick, rough.

Lani smiled at him and resumed her stroking of his erection. "I know I'm short, Casey, but I'm all woman, and I'm not fragile."

"I know, and believe me, I'm well aware that you're all woman. You just looked scared there for a second."

Lani laughed. "Should I be scared, Kelly?"

She was playing coy and sultry, but if she admitted the truth to herself, she was a bit nervous. Not scared, just...nervous. It had been a long time, and he was enormous, not just down there, but in every way.

He didn't answer right away, tracing a finger up her thigh once again, this time stopping at her hip, tugging the end of the string keeping one side of her bottom on. The side fell free, and his fingers slid into the crease where her bent leg met her hipbone. Lani unconsciously flexed her leg, wanting his fingers closer to her core.

So long. It had been so long, and now she couldn't think of anything but more, more, more.

He left the bikini bottom tied on one side, now teasing her with his finger, dipping in between her thighs, close, close, close, but not there, not where she wanted it.

His mouth touched her breastbone, and his middle finger teased nearer her core, touching the smooth skin just beside her labia. "You should be a little scared," he whispered.

"So should you," Lani whispered back, "especially if you don't touch me already."

He laughed, a hot huff between her breasts, and freed the other side of her bikini bottom. She lifted up, and he tossed the negligible bit of fabric aside. Lani felt her heart stutter into a pounding crescendo as Casey pulled her up his thighs. His thickness was nestled now between the damp folds of her core, and Lani shivered all over. Casey's eyes were on her, intent, searching, piercing.

"Not yet," he murmured.

And then she was moving up and forward, and he was lying back on the bed, pulling Lani toward his face. She wasn't sure what he had in mind until he'd tugged her onto her hands and knees with her core positioned over his mouth.

"Oh, God, Casey, I don't know if—oh shit." Lani's breath left her in a rush as his tongue lapped up her crease, tracing fire up her opening, dipping in, pressing against the sensitive, turgid nub that was her clit.

His hands smoothed down her spine, nails scratching here and there, palms now cupping her backside, fingers trailing downward and inward. She found her breath, only to have it stolen once more when his long, thick middle finger slid inside her, curling to rub her just right, sending spasms of intensity pulsating through her body.

Lani had always been a hair trigger. An orgasm had never been a problem for her. Reaching more than one was the problem. Always before, she'd come, and then that was it. No matter what else Rafael did, she was stuck, aroused but unable to cross over the edge again.

So now it didn't surprise her when Casey's tongue and fingers brought her spiraling over the edge almost immediately. She exploded above him, rocking her hips slightly as he tongued and fingered her. What surprised her was when he kept going, despite her obvious orgasm.

"Ride me, Lani. Ride my face, ride my fingers."

He added a finger inside her, carefully, gently, and began to withdraw them and slide them back in. Lani whimpered as the tingling prickling flickers of fire began to wash over her, and she did what he'd suggested, rocking back and down onto him, feeling herself swell and tense and moisten.

She was also not a vocal person in bed. A few whimpers, some quiet moans, but that was about it. Now? Casey was drawing wanton groans from her, loud gasps, and even once, something approaching an actual shriek as he teased her toward the edge for a second time. He brought her close, speeding up his tongue until she was on the burning edge of orgasm, only to slow down and shift his attention and bring her down. Then he'd bring her close like that, and then away. Again and again he did this, until she was crazed with need.

Finally, she could take no more. "Damn it, Kelly. Let me come! Please!"

He growled, and she remembered too late that he didn't like his name, and she'd only meant it as a joke, but his fingers were gone and his tongue was gone and he seemed to be waiting.

She whimpered and rocked on her hips back against him. "I'm sorry, Casey. I'm sorry. I was teasing."

"Say it again, but this time get it right." His voice was low, threatening.

She trembled at the heat in his voice. "Please, *Casey*, make me come."

Two fingers slid inside her and his tongue dipped in against her clit, and then she was there, falling, crying out louder than she'd ever done in her life, coming harder than she thought was possible. She collapsed forward and rolled to her side, limp, shaking, quivering with aftershocks.

She felt Casey leave the bed, cracked an eye open to watch him cross the room in a single stride, crouch and dig through a battered Army rucksack with his last name stitched on a patch. He pulled out a string of condoms from the bottom and ripped one free, set the rest on the nightstand.

Lani shivered again, this time in anticipation. Casey didn't crawl over her, though. He lay on his side next to her, ran his palm over her belly and down her thighs, back up across her pubis. She rolled to her side, grasped his erection, and stroked him in a gentle rhythm.

Casey flinched at her touch, then closed his eyes in pleasure. Just as his hips started to gyrate, he pulled her wrist away from him and reached for her hip, tugging her toward him. Lani didn't hesitate. She slid one leg over his thighs and straddled him, palms flat against his chest. His tip probed her entrance, and Lani trembled. For the space of two heartbeats she paused, staring down into his eyes, asking herself if she had any reservations.

She found none.

He held her hips loosely, his breath coming in long gasps. He was absolutely still except for his breathing, waiting, waiting for her.

She reached between them, took him in her hand, and guided him slowly into her tight wet folds. She felt the pinch of stretching muscles, and she stilled. Casey was frozen, jaw clenched, fingers tight around her hips.

"God, Lani. You're fucking tight."

"It's...oh, god..." She slid him deeper inch by tantalizing inch, "...it's been a while. And you're hung like a fucking rhinoceros."

He laughed, hard and sudden, which twitched him deeper, drawing a sharp gasp from Lani as he drove in. "Sorry, sorry. You okay?"

Lani held still once more, allowing herself to acclimate to his size. The burning of stretching muscle was exquisite, just enough pain to be blissful. And then she felt his hands slide up her ribs to cup her breasts and his fingers brushed her nipples, and a gush of dampness had him sliding deeper and she was unable to hold still any longer.

God, he filled her. She couldn't keep her eyes open, could barely force her body to move from the deliciously intense pleasure of his presence inside her, his huge hard body beneath her. She felt the edge approaching yet again, and he wasn't even moving yet.

"Move, Casey," she gasped.

"Oh, thank fuck," he grunted.

Suddenly she was moving, airborne. He was standing up with her, pinning her spine against the wall. She clenched her legs around his hips, squeezing with all her strength as he lifted her up by her buttocks and lowered her slowly.

A single stroke, and she was flying apart. His hands left her ass and his fingers twined with hers, lifting her arms above her head. The lack of support had him driving so deep, so crazy deep she couldn't breathe, could only rasp a whimper.

His mouth covered hers, crashing in to taste her lips briefly before descending to her breasts and nibbling on her nipples. She was lost in a storm of sensation now, the notion of a single orgasm erased as he owned her body with his.

He drove up, lifting her with the power of his hips, and she came. He wrapped both of her wrists in his and caressed her ass with his free hand, lifting her up and drawing out, sliding slowly until she moaned, mourning his absence.

Then he released her hands and her ass, impaling her on his shaft, and she came.

She heard a sound, a loud, high, cry, and realized it was her voice raised so loud. His breathing was ragged, his eyes hooded and heavy on hers as he fluttered slow, shallow thrusts, buried deep.

Then they were moving again, and he was setting her gently on the kitchen counter. The angle that this position had him inside her was…beyond exquisite. He was tilted slightly away from his body, and as he slid in slowly, she felt him hit every single nerve ending she had, sending bolts of lighting striking her from head to toe.

Her head thunked back against the cabinet, and her breath erupted from her in a loud groan. Her heels scrabbled at his back, her hands on his shoulders pulling him toward her.

"Watch us," he commanded.

Lani opened her eyes and tilted her head forward to watch as he slid in, drew out, slow at first but faster with every stroke. Lani found the sight of his erection stretching her folds and sliding in and pulling out, wet with their mingled essences, unexplainably erotic. Her forehead touched his as they watched their lovemaking together, watched him fill her and draw out, moving faster and faster now, growing confident in his strokes.

The unending firecracker-string of climaxes worked into a crescendo, each one more powerful than the last, each stroke of his body into hers sending her higher and higher, until she realized it wasn't orgasms breaking over her at all, but pre-detonations, quivers of buildup.

Casey was moving frantically now, and she was taking all of him, deep and deep and deeper, and she was panting, whimpering nonstop, chanting "yes" in time to his thrusts.

And then he slowed, pulled out nearly all the way, thrust home hard and tensed, groaning her name. Again he pulled out and powered in, and this time she felt herself come completely undone, fly apart and shatter as he released inside her.

He clutched her against him as they shook together. After a moment, he carried her, still joined to him, and lay back with her straddling him one more.

She collapsed onto him, limp and more sated, more exhausted than ever in her life.

"God, Casey." She could only gasp those two words.

"You got *both* my names right, darlin'."

She laughed, and felt him slip out of her. "I won't deny that."

"Good. You shouldn't."

"I'm not." She traced a pattern on his shoulder with her finger, then lifted her head to meet his eyes. "Thank you, Casey."

He wrinkled his brow. "It was beyond incredible for me, too, babe."

She shook her head. "Not just for that, but yes, thank you for that. I've never come so many times or so hard in my life. I meant thank you for…everything. Bringing me here. Taking me surfing. Helping me let go."

He grinned at her. "So you'll stay and give surfing lessons?"

She sighed. "It just makes sense, I guess, doesn't it?"

"Yeah, it does." He got up, discarded the condom, and settled beside her on the bed, cigarettes and lighter in hand. He lit up, puffed out the first lungful, and then turned to her. "Besides, if you stay, we can do that again. Except maybe on the beach. Or in my plane. Or…anywhere."

Lani rested her head on his shoulder and smiled. "Sounds good to me."

***

"NO! Carl, damn it, you're too far forward on the board!" Lani covered her eyes as Carl wiped out for the fiftieth time in less than an hour.

Casey chuckled behind her. "He'll never learn. He just ain't coordinated enough."

She shook her head, knowing he was right, but also knowing she had to keep trying, since he'd paid for a week's worth of lessons up front. She turned to look over her shoulder. Casey was sitting on a blanket, filling out LLC papers for SkyTours Incorporated. She'd been living on Seeker's Island for over six months by that point, in a little beach house with Casey for two of those months. The sun shifted from behind a cloud and glinted off the half-carat diamond on her ring finger. He'd proposed a month ago, and she realized she really was ready to go forward with it. She'd agreed at the time because she'd been happy and excited, but later had had some reservations, wondering if it was too soon.

Now, watching him scribble with his tongue tip sticking out of the corner of his lips, she realized how much she did want to be his, legally and otherwise. There was only one thing that would make life on Seeker's Island complete, but she didn't think there was a chance of that.

Just then, a seaplane roared past, twisting out over the ocean and returning in a landing descent. Casey had lured his friend Henry Sykes out to fly tours with him, except Henry had left a week ago and hadn't returned yet.

"Henry's back?" she asked.

Casey just grunted, but she could tell by the set of his shoulders that he was feigning disinterest. The seaplane floated to a stop, and the door opened. A flip-flop-clad foot extended, touched the float, and then the whole body appeared, leaping from the cabin directly into the water.

Lani squealed, "Makani!"

Her friend and mentor smiled, shading his eyes with his hand as he slogged through the hip-deep water. He was a short, thick, middle-aged, deeply tanned Hawaiian man with a long black ponytail, shirtless and wearing board shorts. Lani ran across the sand and threw herself into Makani's embrace.

"You're here! How—why are you here?" She was breathless with joy.

He grinned and hugged her tightly, then let go. "I think Hawaii has enough surfboards now, yeah? I think this Seeker's Island needs a few now. Plus, I also hear my favorite surfer girl found the right man for her. I never liked that Rafael *lolo*. Glad you shut of him. This the guy?"

Casey shook Makani's hand, and soon Carl was forgotten as the three wandered across the beach, catching up. Lani hung back as Makani and Casey got to know each other, and she realized that now, finally, she had a family.

She left Makani and Casey sitting under a palm tree drinking Corona, grabbed her board from the sand, and trotted to the water. The sea lapped around her ankles, licked her calves, and then embraced her entirely. She tasted brine, felt the sun hot on her skin, and knew she was home.

ABOUT THE AUTHORS

Eight writers met, many for the first time, on a windy day at an all-inclusive hotel in Cancun, Mexico on February 22, 2013 in a big ass hot tub. What began as a mere spark of an idea to join together to promote and market literally exploded into plans for yearly meetings in faraway lands, including a castle in Ireland. The possibilities were almost as limitless as the Mimosas consumed by Jane Graves.

Every writer in attendance, successful in their own right, had an opinion. Ideas were flowing and excitement building even before Denise Grover Swank talked Theresa Ragan into doing endless shots of tequila. Bonds were made and notes recorded while Colleen Gleason dropped to the floor and performed backbends, inversions, and restorative poses, in hopes that she could get this passionate group of writers to connect with their deeper selves.

Debra Holland was the only one who had her shit together, focusing on both body and mind and doing her best to help others attempt to glimpse the glass half full at any given moment. Liliana Hart, wearing colorful sundress, big sunglasses and giant hats, was the hostess with the mostess, inviting us all to her massive suite with its sprawling bathtub and endless food and drink. Poor sick Dorien Kelly coughed out legal advice over our five days of tropical bliss while Jana DeLeon became the leader in note taking, accountability, and snarky remarks.

Just as the Declaration of Independence was conceived in liberty and justice for all, so was The Indie Voice created in a group effort formed without ego and with unparalleled team spirit.

Discussions about swag and anthologies abounded, and what could have easily become pandemonium amongst a sea of estrogen became instead a perfect blend of wit and intellectual genius. Our mission statement began as "a seamless, effective marketing group that adapts rapidly to change" and by the end of the week became a statement of principles that made much more sense: "Reaching Readers, Travel and Drinks."

Needless to say, bonds were made, friendships were forged, and the moment everyone got home, big ideas did not disappear within hectic work schedules, but instead became reality amongst a deluge of Facebook comments and emails. In hopes of realizing widespread results, two more writers, Jasinda Wilder and Tina Folsom, were suckered into joining The Indie Voice, completing this unique partnership.

Crazy does not begin to describe this wild group of clever and passionate women, but it's a great start.

20439031R00184

Made in the USA
Charleston, SC
10 July 2013